RAVENSONG

TJ KLUNE

RAVENSONG

GREEN CREEK BOOK TWO

TOR PUBLISHING GROUP
NEW YORK

RAVENSONG

Copyright © 2018 by Travis Klune

A Tor Book
Published by Tom Doherty Associates / Tor Publishing Group
120 Broadway
New York, NY 10271

www.tor-forge.com

Tor® is a registered trademark of Macmillan Publishing Group, LLC.

The Library of Congress Cataloging-in-Publication Data
is available upon request.

ISBN 978-1-250-89034-4 (hardcover)
ISBN 978-1-250-29241-4 (international, sold outside
the U.S., subject to rights availability)
ISBN 978-1-250-89035-1 (ebook)

Our books may be purchased in bulk for promotional,
educational, or business use. Please contact your local bookseller
or the Macmillan Corporate and Premium Sales Department
at 1-800-221-7945, extension 5442, or by email at
MacmillanSpecialMarkets@macmillan.com.

First Tor Hardcover Edition: 2023

Printed in the United States of America

0 9 8 7 6 5 4 3 2 1

For those who hear the songs of wolves, listen well:
your pack is howling you home.

"Prophet!" said I, "thing of evil!—prophet still, if bird or devil!—
Whether Tempter sent, or whether tempest tossed thee here ashore,
Desolate yet all undaunted, on this desert land enchanted—
On this home by Horror haunted—tell me truly, I implore—
Is there—is there balm in Gilead?—tell me—tell me, I implore!"
*   Quoth the Raven "Nevermore."*

Edgar Allan Poe,
"The Raven"

RAVENSONG

PROMISES

The Alpha said, "We're leaving."

Ox stood near the doorway, smaller than I'd ever seen him. The skin under his eyes looked bruised.

This wasn't going to go well. Ambushes never did.

"What?" Ox asked, eyes narrowing slightly. "When?"

"Tomorrow."

He said, "You know I can't leave yet," and I touched the raven on my forearm, feeling the flutter of wings, the pulse of magic. It burned. "I have to meet with Mom's lawyer in two weeks to go over her will. There's the house and—"

"Not you, Ox," Joe Bennett said, sitting behind his father's desk. Thomas Bennett was nothing but ash.

I saw the moment the words sank in. It was savage and brutal, the betrayal of a heart already broken.

"And not Mom. Or Mark."

Carter and Kelly Bennett shifted uncomfortably, standing side by side near Joe. I wasn't pack and hadn't been for a long, long time, but even I could feel the low thrum of anger coursing through them. But not at Joe. Or Ox. Or anyone in this room. They had revenge in their blood, the need to rend with claw and fang. They were already lost to the idea of it.

But so was I. Ox just didn't know it yet.

"So it's you," Ox said. "And Carter. Kelly."

"And Gordo."

And now he did. Ox didn't look at me. It might as well have been just the two of them in the room. "And Gordo. Where are you going?"

"To do what's right."

"Nothing about this is right," Ox retorted. "Why didn't you tell me about this?"

"I'm telling you now," he said, and oh, Joe. He had to know this wasn't—

"Because *that's* the right— Where are you going?"

"After Richard."

Once, when Ox was a boy, his piece-of-shit father had left for parts unknown without so much as a glance over his shoulder. It took weeks for Ox to pick up the phone and call me, but he did. He'd spoken slowly, but I'd heard the hurt in every word as he told me *We're not doing okay,* that he was seeing letters from the bank talking about taking away the house he and his mom lived in down that old familiar dirt road.

Could I have a job? It's just we need the money and I can't let her lose the house. It's all we have left. I'd do good, Gordo. I would do good work and I'd work for you forever. It was going to happen anyway and can we just do it now? Can we just do it now? I'm sorry. I just need to do it now because I have to be the man now.

That was the sound of a boy lost.

And here in front of me, the lost boy had returned. Oh sure, he was bigger now, but his mother was in the ground, his Alpha nothing but smoke in the stars, his *mate*, of all fucking things, digging his claws into his chest and twisting, twisting, twisting.

I did nothing to stop it. It was already too late. For all of us.

"Why?" Ox asked, voice cracking right down the middle.

Why, why, why.

Because Thomas was dead.

Because they'd taken from us.

Because they'd come to Green Creek, Richard Collins and his Omegas, their eyes violet in the dark, snarling as they came to face the fallen king.

I had done what I could.

It wasn't enough.

There was a boy, this little boy not even eighteen years of age, bearing the weight of his father's legacy, the monster from his childhood made flesh. His eyes burned red, and he knew only vengeance. It pulsed through his brothers in a circle that never ended, feeding each other's anger. He was the boy prince turned furious king, and he'd needed my help.

Elizabeth Bennett was quiet, letting it happen in front of her. Ever the muted queen, an afghan around her shoulders, watching this goddamn tragedy play out. I couldn't even be sure she was all there.

And Mark, he—

No. Not him. Not now.

The past was past was past.

They argued, baring their teeth and growling at each other. Back and forth, each cutting until the other bled out before us. I understood Ox. The fear of losing those you loved. Of a responsibility you never asked for. Of being told something you never wanted to hear.

I understood Joe. I didn't want to, but I did.

We think it was your father, Gordo, Osmond whispered. *We think Robert Livingstone found a path back to magic and broke the wards that held Richard Collins.*

Yes. I thought I understood Joe most of all.

"You can't divide the pack," Ox said, and oh Jesus, he was *begging.* "Not now. Joe, you are the goddamn *Alpha.* They need you here. All of them. *Together.* Do you really think they'd agree to—"

"I already told them days ago," Joe said. And then he flinched. "Shit."

I closed my eyes.

There was this:

"That's shit, Gordo."

"Yeah."

"And you're going along with it."

"Someone has to make sure he doesn't kill himself."

"And that someone is you. Because you're pack."

"Looks like."

"By choice?"

"I think so."

But of course it wasn't that easy. It never was.

And:

"You mean to kill. You're okay with that?"

"Nothing about this is okay, Ox. But Joe's right. We can't let this happen to anyone else. Richard wanted Thomas, but how long before he goes after another pack just to become an Alpha? How long before he amasses another following, bigger than the one before? The trail is already growing cold. We have to finish this while we still can. This is revenge, pure and simple, but it's coming from the right place."

I wondered if I believed my own lies.

In the end:

"You should talk to him. Before you go."

"Joe?"

"Mark."

"Ox—"

"What if you don't come back? Do you really want him to think you don't care? Because that's fucked-up, man. You know me. But sometimes, I think you forget that I know you just as well. Maybe even more."

Goddamn him.

. . .

She stood in the kitchen of the Bennett house, staring out the window. Her hands were curled against the counter. Her shoulders were tense, and she wore her grief like a shroud. Even though I hadn't wanted anything to do with wolves for years, I still knew the respect she commanded. She was royalty, whether she wanted to be or not.

"Gordo," Elizabeth said without turning around. I wondered if she was listening for wolves singing songs I hadn't been able to hear for a long time. "How is he?"

"Angry."

"That's to be expected."

"Is it?"

"I suppose," she said quietly. "But you and I are older. Maybe not wiser, but older. Everything we've been through, all that we've seen, this is just . . . another thing. Ox is a boy. We've sheltered him as much as we could. We—"

"You brought this upon him," I said before I could stop myself. The words were flung like a grenade, and they exploded as they landed at her feet. "If you'd stayed away, if you hadn't brought him into this, he could still—"

"I'm sorry for what we did to you," she said, and I choked. "What your father did. He was—it wasn't fair. Or right. No child should ever go through what you did."

"And yet you did nothing to stop it," I said bitterly. "You and Thomas and Abel. My mother. None of you. You only cared about what I could be to you, not what it would mean for me. What my father did to me meant *nothing* to you. And then you went and left—"

"You broke the bonds with the pack."

"Easiest decision I ever made."

"I can hear when you lie, Gordo. Your magic can't cover your heartbeat. Not always. Not when it matters most."

"Fucking werewolves." Then, "I was *twelve* when I was made the witch to the Bennett pack. My mother was dead. My father was gone. But still, Abel held out his hand to me, and the only reason I said yes was because I didn't know any better. Because I didn't want to be left alone. I was scared, and—"

"You didn't do it for Abel."

I narrowed my eyes at her. "What the hell are you talking about?"

She finally turned and looked at me. She still had the afghan around her shoulders. At some point she'd pulled her blond hair back into a ponytail, locks of which were loose and hung about her face. Her eyes were blue, then orange, then blue again, flickering dully. Most anyone who looked at her would have thought Elizabeth Bennett weak and frail in that moment, but I knew better. She was backed into a corner, the most dangerous place for a predator to be. "It wasn't for Abel."

Ah. So that was the game she wanted to play. "It was my duty."

"Your father—"

"My *father* lost control when his tether was taken from him. My *father* has aligned himself with—"

"We all had a part to play," Elizabeth said. "Every single one of us. We made mistakes. We were young and foolish and filled with a great and terrible rage at everything that had been taken from us. Abel did what he thought was right back then. So did Thomas. I'm doing what I think is right now."

"And yet you did nothing to fight your sons. To not let them make the same mistakes we did. You rolled over like a *dog* in that room."

She didn't rise to the bait. Instead she said, "And you didn't?"

Fuck. "Why?"

"Why what, Gordo? You have to be more specific."

"Why are you letting them go?"

"Because we were young and foolish once, filled with a great and terrible rage. And that has now passed to them." She sighed. "You've been there before. You've been through this. It happened once. And it's happening again. I'm trusting you to help them avoid the mistakes we made."

"I'm not pack."

"No," she said, and that shouldn't have stung like it did. "But that's a choice you made. Much like we are here now because of the choices we made. Maybe you're right. Maybe if we hadn't come here, Ox would be...."

"Human?"

Her eyes flashed again. "Thomas—"

I snorted. "He didn't tell me shit. But it's not hard to see. What is it about him?"

"I don't know," she admitted. "I don't know that Thomas knew either. Not exactly. But Ox is...special. Different. He doesn't see it yet. And it may be a long time before he does. I don't know if it's magic or something more. He's not like us. He's not like you. But he's not human. Not completely. He's more, I think. Than all of us."

"You need to keep him safe. I've strengthened the wards as best I can, but you need—"

"He's pack, Gordo. There is nothing I wouldn't do for pack. Surely you remember that."

"I did it for Abel. And then for Thomas."

"Lie," she said, cocking her head. "But you almost believe it."

I took a step back. "I need to—"

"Why can't you say it?"

"There's nothing to say."

"He loved you," she said, and I'd never hated her more. "With everything he had. Such is the way of wolves. We sing and sing and sing until someone hears our song. And you did. You heard. You didn't do it for Abel or Thomas, Gordo. Even then. You were twelve years old, but you knew. You were pack."

"Goddamn you," I said hoarsely.

"I know," she said, not unkindly. "Sometimes the things we need to hear the most are the things we want to hear the least. I loved my husband, Gordo. I will love him forever. And he knew that. Even in the end, even when Richard—" Her breath caught in her throat. She shook her head. "Even then. He knew. And I will miss him every day until I can stand at his side again, until I can look upon his face, his beautiful face, and tell him how angry I am. How stupid he is. How lovely it is to see him again, and would he please just say my name." There were tears in her eyes, but they didn't fall. "I hurt, Gordo. I don't know if this ache will ever leave me. But he *knew*."

"It's not the same."

"Only because you won't let it be. He loved you. He gave you his wolf. And then you gave it back."

"He made his choice. And I made mine. I didn't want it. I didn't want anything to do with you. With *him*."

"You. *Lie*."

"What do you want from me?" I asked, anger filling my voice. "What the hell could you possibly want?"

"Thomas knew," she said again. "Even at the brink of death. Because I told him. Because I showed him time and time again. I regret many things in my life. But I will never regret Thomas Bennett."

She moved toward me, her steps slow but sure. I stood my ground, even when she placed a hand on my shoulder, squeezing tightly. "You leave in the morning. Don't regret this, Gordo. Because if words are left unsaid, they will haunt you for the rest of your days."

She brushed past me. But before she left the kitchen, she said, "Please take care of my sons. I'm trusting you with them, Gordo. If I find out you have betrayed that trust, or if you stood idly by as they faced that monster, there will be nowhere you could hide that I wouldn't find you. I will tear you to pieces, and the regret I feel will be minimal."

Then she was gone.

.   .   .

He stood out on the porch, staring off into nothing, hands clasped behind his back. Once he'd been a boy with pretty blue eyes like ice, the brother to a future king. Now he was a man, hardened by the rough edges of the world. His brother was gone. His Alpha was leaving. There was blood in the air, death on the wind.

Mark Bennett said, "Is she all right?"

Because of course he knew I was there. Wolves always did. Especially when it came to their— "No."

"Are you?"

"No."

He didn't turn. The porch light gleamed dully off his shaved head. He took in a deep breath, broad shoulders rising and falling. The skin of my palms itched. "It's strange, don't you think?"

Always the enigmatic asshole. "What is?"

"You left once. And here you are, leaving again."

I bristled at that. "You left me first."

"And I came back as often as I could."

"It wasn't enough." But that wasn't quite right, was it? Not even close. Even though my mother was long gone, her poison had still dripped into my ears: *the wolves did this, the wolves took everything, they always will because it is in their nature to do so.* They lied, she told me. They always lied.

He let it slide. "I know."

"This isn't—I'm not trying to start anything here."

I could hear the smile in his voice. "You never are."

"Mark."

"Gordo."

"Fuck you."

He *finally* turned, still as handsome as he was the day I'd met him, though I'd been a child and hadn't known what it meant. He was big and strong, and his eyes were that icy blue they'd always been, clever and all-knowing. I had no doubt he could feel the anger and despair that swirled within me, no matter how hard I tried to block them. The bonds between us were broken and had been for a long time, but there was still something *there*, no matter how much I'd tried to bury it.

He scrubbed a hand over his face, his fingers disappearing into that full beard. I remembered when he'd first started growing it at seventeen, a patchy thing I'd given him endless shit over. I felt a pang in my chest, but I was used to it by now. It didn't mean anything. Not anymore.

I was almost convinced.

He dropped his hand and said, "Take care of yourself, okay?" He smiled a brittle smile and then moved toward the door to the Bennett house.

And I was going to let him go. I was going to let him pass right on by. That would be it. I wouldn't see him again until . . . until. He would stay here, and I would leave, a reversal of the way it'd once been.

I was going to let him go because it would be easier that way. For all the days ahead.

But I'd always been stupid when it came to Mark Bennett.

I reached out and grabbed his arm before he could leave me.

He stopped.

We stood shoulder to shoulder. I faced the road ahead. He faced all that we would leave behind.

He waited.

We breathed.

"This isn't—I can't. . . ."

"No," he whispered. "I don't suppose you can."

"Mark," I choked out, struggling for something, *anything* that I could say. "I'm coming— *We're* coming back. Okay? We're—"

"Is that a promise?"

"*Yes.*"

"I don't believe your promises anymore," he said. "I haven't for a very long time. Watch yourself, Gordo. Take care of my nephews."

And then he was in the house, the door closing behind him.

I stepped off the porch and didn't look back.

.   .   .

I sat in the garage that bore my name, a piece of paper on the desk before me.

They wouldn't understand. I loved them, but they could be idiots. I had to say *something*.

I picked up an old Bic pen and began to write.

I have to be gone for a while. Tanner, you're in charge of the shop. Make sure you send the earnings to the accountant. He'll handle the taxes. Ox has access to all the bank stuff, personal and shop-related. Anything you need, you go through him. If you need to hire someone to pick up the slack, do it, but don't hire some fuckup. We've worked too hard to get where we are. Chris and Rico, handle the day-to-day ops. I don't how long this is going to take, but just in case, you need to watch each other's back. Ox is going to need you.

.   .   .

It wasn't enough.

It would never be enough.

I hoped they could forgive me. One day.

My fingers were stained with ink, leaving smudges on the paper.

*   *   *

I turned off the lights in the garage.

I stood in the dark for a long time.

I breathed in the smell of sweat and metal and oil.

*   *   *

It wasn't quite dawn when we met on the dirt road that led to the houses at the end of the lane. Carter and Kelly sat in the SUV, watching me through the windshield as I walked up, a pack slung over my shoulder.

Joe stood in the middle of the road. His head was tilted back, eyes closed as his nostrils flared. Thomas had told me once that being an Alpha meant he was in tune with everything in his territory. The people. The trees. The deer in the forest, the plants that swayed in the wind. It was everything to an Alpha, a deep-seated sense of *home* that one could find nowhere else.

I wasn't an Alpha. I wasn't even a wolf. I never wanted to be.

But I understood what he'd meant. My magic was as ingrained in this place as he was. It was different, but not so much that it mattered. He felt *everything*. I felt the heartbeat, the pulse of the territory that stretched around us.

Green Creek had been tied to his senses.

And it was etched into my skin.

It hurt to leave, and not just because of those we were leaving behind. There was a physical *pull* an Alpha and a witch felt. It called to us, saying *here here here you are here here here you stay because this is home this is home this is—*

"Was it always like this?" Joe asked. "For my dad?"

I glanced at the SUV. Carter and Kelly were watching us intently. I knew they were listening. I looked back at Joe, at his upturned face. "I think so."

"We were gone, though. For so long."

"He was the Alpha. Not just for you. Not just for your pack. But for all. And then Richard . . ."

"Took me."

"Yes."

Joe opened his eyes. They were not alight. "I am not my father."

"I know. But you're not supposed to be."

"Are you with me?"

I hesitated. I knew what he was asking. It wasn't formal, not by a long shot, but he was an Alpha, and I was a witch without a pack.

Take care of my nephews.

I said the only thing I could.

"Yes."

His shift came over him quickly, his face elongating, skin covered in white hair, claws stretching out from the tips of his fingers. And as his eyes burst into flames, he tilted his head back and sang the song of the wolf.

THREE YEARS

ONE MONTH

TWENTY-SIX DAYS

TORN APART /
DIRT AND LEAVES AND RAIN

I was six when I first looked upon an older boy shifting into a wolf, and my father whispered, "That's Abel's son. His name is Thomas, and one day he will be the Alpha of the Bennett pack. You will belong to him."

Thomas.

Thomas.

Thomas.

I was in awe of him.

. . .

I was eight, and my father took a needle and burned ink and magic into my skin. "It's going to hurt," he told me, a grim look on his face. "I won't lie to you about that. It's going to hurt like nothing you've ever felt before. You'll think I'm tearing you apart, and in a sense, you're right. You have magic in you, child, but it hasn't yet manifested. These marks will center you and give you the tools to begin to control it. I will hurt you, but it's necessary for who you're supposed to become. Pain is a lesson. It teaches you the ways of the world. We must hurt the ones we love in order to make them stronger. To make them better. One day you'll understand. One day you'll be like me."

"Please, Father," I begged, struggling against the restraints that held me down. "Please don't do this. Please don't hurt me."

My mother looked to speak, but my father shook his head.

She choked on a sob as she was led from the room. She didn't look back.

Abel Bennett sat beside me. He was a large man. A kind man. He was strong and powerful, with dark hair and dark eyes. He had hands that looked as if they could split me in two. I'd seen them grow claws to tear into the flesh of those who dared to try to take from him.

But they could be soft too, and warm. He took my face in them, thumbs brushing the tears away from my cheeks. I looked up at him, and he smiled quietly.

He said, "You are going to be something special, Gordo. I just know it."

And as his eyes started bleeding red, I breathed and breathed and breathed.

Then the needle pressed against my skin and I was torn apart.

I screamed.

.   .   .

He came to me as a wolf. He was large and white, with splashes of black on his chest and legs and back. He was larger than I would ever be, and I had to tilt my head back to see the entirety of him.

The stars were out above, the moon fat and bright, and I felt something thrumming through my blood. It was a song that I couldn't quite make out. My arms itched something fierce. Sometimes I thought the marks on my skin were starting to glow, but it could have been a trick of the moonlight.

I said, "I'm nervous," because this was the first time I was allowed to be out on the full moon with the pack. It had been too dangerous before. Not because of what the wolves could do to me, but because of what I could have done to them.

He cocked his head at me, eyes burning orange with flecks of red. He was so much more than I ever thought someone could be. I told myself I wasn't frightened of him, that I could be brave, just like my father was.

I thought I was a liar.

Other wolves ran behind him in a clearing in the middle of the woods. They yipped and howled, and my father was laughing, tugging on my mother's hand as he pulled her along. She glanced back at me, smiling quietly, but then she was distracted.

But that was okay, because so was I.

Thomas Bennett stood before me, the man-wolf who would be king.

He whuffed at me, tail wagging slightly, asking a question I didn't have an answer to.

"I'm nervous," I told him again. "But I'm not scared." It was important to me that he understood that.

He lowered himself to the ground, lying on his stomach, paws out in front of him as he regarded me. Like he was trying to make himself smaller. Less intimidating. Someone of his position lowering

himself to the ground was something I wouldn't understand until it
was too late.

He made a low whining sound from deep in his throat. He waited,
then did it again.

I said, "My father told me that you're going to be the Alpha."

He pulled himself forward, belly dragging along the grass.

I said, "And that I'm going to be your witch."

He came a little closer.

I said, "I promise that I'll try my best. I'll learn all that I can, and
I'll do a good job for you. You'll see. I'm going to be the best there
ever was." My eyes widened. "But don't tell my father I said that."

The white wolf sneezed.

I laughed.

Eventually I reached out and pressed my hand against Thomas's
snout, and for a moment I thought I heard a whisper in my head.
packpackpack.

.   .   .

"Is this what you want?" my mother asked me when it was just the
two of us. She'd taken me away from the wolves, from my father, telling them she wanted to spend time with her son. We were sitting in a
diner in town, and it smelled of grease and smoke and coffee.

I was confused, and I tried to speak through a mouthful of ham-
burger.

My mother frowned.

I grimaced and swallowed thickly.

"Manners," she scolded.

"I know. What do you mean?"

She looked out the window onto the street. The wind was sharp,
rattling the trees so they sounded like ancient bones. The air was
cold, people pulling their coats tightly around them as they walked
by on the sidewalk. I thought I saw Marty, fingers stained with oil,
walking back to his auto garage, the only one in Green Creek. I
wondered what it felt like to have marks on my skin that could wash
away.

"This," she said again, looking back at me. Her voice was soft.
"Everything."

I glanced around us to make sure no one was listening in, because
my father said our world was a secret. I didn't think Mom understood

that, because she hadn't known such things existed until she met him. "The witch stuff?"

She didn't sound happy when she replied. "The witch stuff."

"But it's what I'm supposed to do. It's who I'm supposed to be. One day I'll be very important and do great things. Father said—"

"I know what he said," and it was sharp. She winced before looking down at the table, her hands folded in front of her. "Gordo, I—you need to listen to me, okay? Life is . . . it's about the choices we make. Not the choices made *for* us. You have the right to set your own path. To be who you want yourself to be. No one should decide that for you."

I didn't understand. "But I'm supposed to be the witch to the Alpha."

"You're not *supposed* to be *anything*. You are just a child. This can't be placed upon your shoulders. Not now. Now when you can't decide for yourself. You shouldn't be—"

"I'm brave," I told her, and suddenly I needed her to believe me more than anything in the world. This felt important. *She* was important. "And I'm going to do good. I'm going to help many people. Father says so."

Her eyes were wet when she said, "I know, baby. I know you are. And I'm very proud of you. But you don't *have* to. I need you to listen to me, okay? I need you to hear me. It's not—this isn't what I wanted for you. I didn't think it would ever be like this."

"Be like what?"

She shook her head. "We can—we can go wherever you want. You and me. We can leave Green Creek, okay? Go anywhere in the world. Away from this. Away from magic and wolves and packs. Away from all of *this*. It doesn't need to be this way. It could be us, Gordo. It could be just us. Okay?"

I felt cold. "Why are you—"

Her hand shot out and gripped my own across the table. But she was careful, as she always was, not to push back the sleeves of my coat. We were in public. My father said people wouldn't understand the tattoos on someone so young. They would have questions they didn't deserve the answers to. They were human, and humans were weak. Mom was human, but I didn't think she was weak. I had told him as much, and he hadn't responded. "All I ever wanted was to keep you safe."

"You do," I told her, trying my best not to pull my hand away. She was almost hurting me. "You and Father and the pack."

"The pack." She laughed, but it didn't sound like she found anything funny. "You are a *child*. They shouldn't be asking this of you. They shouldn't be doing *any* of this—"

"Catherine," a voice said, and she closed her eyes.

My father stood next to the table.

His hand came down upon her shoulder.

We didn't talk about it after that.

.   .   .

I heard them fighting a lot, late into the night.

I pulled my blankets up around me and tried to block them out.

She said, "Do you even *care* about him? Or is it just your legacy? Is it just your goddamn *pack*?"

He said, "You knew it would come to this. Even from the beginning, you knew. You knew what he was supposed to be."

She said, "He is your *son*. How *dare* you use him this way. How dare you try and—"

He said, "He is important. To me. To the pack. He will do things that you can't even begin to imagine. You're human, Catherine. You could never understand the way we do. It's not your fault. It's just who you are. You can't be blamed for things beyond your control."

She said, "I saw you. With her. The way you smiled. The way you laughed. The way you touched her hand when you thought no one was watching. I saw, Robert. I *saw*. She's human too. What makes her so goddamn different?"

My father never answered.

.   .   .

We lived in town in a small house that felt like home. It was on a street with Douglas fir trees all around it. I didn't understand why the wolves thought the forest was a magical place, but sometimes, when it was summer and the window was open as I tried to sleep, I swore I heard voices coming from the trees, whispering things that weren't quite words.

The house was made of brick. My mother laughed once, wondering if a wolf would come and blow it down. She laughed, but then it faded and she looked sad. I asked her why her eyes were wet. She told me that she needed to go make dinner and left me in the front yard, wondering what I'd done wrong.

．　　　．　　　．

I had a room with all my things. There were books on a shelf. A leaf I'd found in the shape of a dragon, the edges curled with age. A drawing of myself and Thomas as a wolf given to me by a child in the pack. I asked him why he'd drawn it for me. He said it was because I was important. Then he'd smiled at me, his two front teeth missing.

When the human hunters came, he was one of the first to die.

．　　　．　　　．

I saw her too.

I shouldn't have. Rico was yelling at me to hurry up, papi, why are you such a slowpoke? Tanner and Chris were looking back at me, slowly pedaling their bikes in circles around him, waiting for me.

But I couldn't move.

Because my father was in a car I didn't recognize, parked on the side of the street in a neighborhood that wasn't ours. There was a dark-haired woman in the driver's seat, and she was smiling at him like he was the only thing in the world.

I'd never seen her before.

I watched as my father leaned forward and—

"Dude," Tanner said, startling me as he pedaled back to me. "What're you looking at?"

"Nothing," I said. "It's nothing. Let's go."

We left, the playing cards clothespinned to our bike spokes rattling loudly as we pretended we were on motorcycles.

．　　　．　　　．

I loved them because of what they were not.

They weren't pack. They weren't wolves. They weren't witches.

They were normal and plain and boring and wonderful.

They made fun of me for wearing long-sleeved shirts, even in the middle of summer. I took it because I knew they weren't being mean. It's just how we were.

Rico said, "You get beat or somethin'?"

Tanner said, "If you do, you can come live with me. You can sleep in my room. You'll just need to hide under my bed so my mom doesn't see you."

Chris said, "We'll protect you. Or we can all just run away and live in the woods."

Rico said, "Like, in the trees and shit."

We all laughed because we were kids, and cursing was the funniest thing.

I couldn't tell them that the woods wouldn't be the safest place for them. That things with glowing eyes and razor-sharp teeth lived in the forest. So instead I told a version of the truth. "I don't get beat. It's not like that."

"You got weird white-boy arms?" Rico asked. "My dad says that you must have weird white-boy arms. That's why you wear sweatshirts all the time."

Tanner frowned. "What're weird white-boy arms?"

"Dunno," Rico said. "But my dad said it, and he knows everything."

"Do I have weird white-boy arms?" Chris asked, holding his arms out in front of him. He squinted at them and shook them up and down. They were thin and pale and didn't look weird to me. I was envious of them, of their wispy, downy hairs and freckles, unmarked by ink.

"Probably," Rico said. "But that's my fault for being friends with a bunch of gringos."

Tanner and Chris shouted after him as he pedaled away, cackling like a loon.

I loved them more than I could say. They tethered me in ways the wolves could not.

.   .   .

"Magic comes from the earth," my father told me. "From the ground. From the trees. The flowers and the soil. This place, it's . . . old. Far older than you could possibly imagine. It's like . . . a beacon. It calls to us. It thrums through our blood. The wolves hear it too, but not like us. It sings to them. They are . . . animals. We aren't like them. We are *more*. They bond with the earth. The Alpha more so than anyone else. But we *use* it. We bend it to our whim. They are enslaved by it, by the moon overhead when it rises full and white. We control it. Don't ever forget that."

.   .   .

Thomas had a younger brother.

His name was Mark.

He was older than me by three years.

He was nine and I was six when he spoke to me for the first time. He said, "You smell weird."

I scowled at him. "I do *not*."

He grimaced and looked down at the ground. "A little. It's like . . . the earth. Like dirt and leaves and rain—"

I hated him more than anything in the world.

.   *   .

"He's following us again," Rico said, sounding amused. We were walking to the video store. Rico said he knew the guy working behind the counter and that he'd rent us an R-rated movie and not tell anyone. If we found the right movie, Rico told us that we could see some tits. I didn't know how I felt about that.

I sighed as I glanced over my shoulder. I was eleven, and I was supposed to be a witch, but I didn't have *time* for wolves right then. I needed to see if tits were something I liked.

Mark was there on the other side of the street, standing near Marty's auto shop. He was pretending he wasn't looking at us, but he wasn't doing a very good job.

"Why does he do that?" Chris asked. "Doesn't he know it's weird?"

"Gordo's weird," Tanner reminded him. "His whole family is weird."

"Screw you," I muttered. "Just—just wait here. I'll deal with this."

I heard them laughing at me as I stalked away, Rico making kissing noises. I hated all of them, but they weren't wrong. My family was weird to everyone who didn't know about us. We weren't Bennetts, but we might as well have been. We were lumped in with them when people whispered about us. The Bennetts were rich, though no one knew how. They lived in a pair of houses in the middle of the woods that many outsiders came to from all around. Some people said they were a cult. Others said they were the mafia. No one knew about the wolves that crawled just underneath their skin.

Mark's eyes widened as he saw me approaching. He looked around like he was plotting his escape. "You stay *right* there," I growled at him.

And he did. He was bigger than me, and the impossible age of fourteen. He didn't look like his brother or father. They were muscled and larger than life, with short black hair and dark eyes. Mark had light brown hair and big eyebrows. He was tall and thin and seemed nervous whenever I was around. His eyes were ice, and I thought about them sometimes when I couldn't fall asleep. I didn't know why.

"I can stand here if I want to," he said with a scowl. His eyes shifted to the left, then back to me. The corners of his mouth went down even farther. "I'm not doing anything wrong."

"You're following me," I told him. "*Again*. My friends think you're weird."

"I *am* weird. I'm a werewolf."

I frowned. "Well. Yeah. But—that's not—ugh. Look, what do you want?"

"Where are you going?"

"Why?"

"Because."

"To the video store. We're going to see some tits."

He blushed furiously. I felt a strange satisfaction at that.

"You can't tell anyone."

"I'm not going to. But why do you want to—never mind. I'm not following you."

I waited, because my father said wolves weren't as smart as us and sometimes needed a little time to work things out.

He sighed. "Okay. Maybe I was, but only a little bit."

"How can you follow someone only a little—"

"I'm making sure you're safe."

I took a step back. "From *what*?"

He shrugged, looking more awkward than I'd ever seen him. "From . . . like. You know. Bad guys. And stuff."

"Bad guys," I repeated.

"And stuff."

"Oh my god, you are so *weird*."

"Yeah, I know. I just said that."

"There are no bad guys here."

"You don't know that. There could be murderers. Or whatever. Burglars."

I would never understand werewolves. "You don't need to protect me."

"Yes, I do," he said quietly, looking down at his feet as he shuffled his sneakers.

But before I could ask him what the hell *that* meant, I heard the most creative curse ever uttered burst from the auto shop's open garage door.

"Goddamn motherfucking son of a bitch *whore*. Bastard cunt, aren't you? That's all you are, you bastard *cunt*."

My grandpap would let me hand him tools as he worked on his 1942 Pontiac Streamliner. He'd have oil under his fingernails and a handkerchief hanging out of the back pocket of his overalls. He muttered a lot while he worked, saying things I probably wasn't supposed to hear. The Pontiac was a dumb broad who sometimes wouldn't put out, no matter how much he lubed her up. Or so he said.

I didn't know what any of that meant.

I thought he was wonderful.

"Torque wrench," he would say.

"Torque wrench," I would reply, handing it over. I was moving stiffly, the latest session under my father's needles only a few days past.

Grandpap knew. He wasn't magic, but he knew. Father had gotten it from his mother, a woman I'd never met. She'd died before I was born.

There'd be more cursing. And then, "Dead blow mallet."

"Dead blow mallet," I said, slapping the hammer into his hand.

More often than not, the Pontiac would be purring again before the day was over. Grandpap would be standing next to me, a blackened hand on my shoulder. "Listen to her," he would say. "You hear that? That, my boy, is the sound of a happy woman. You gotta listen to 'em, okay? That's how you know what's wrong. You just listen, and they'll tell you." He snorted and shook his head. "Probably something you should know, too, about the fairer sex. Listen, and they'll tell you."

I adored him.

He died before he could see me become the witch of what remained of the Bennett pack.

She killed him, in the end. His lady.

He swerved to miss something on a darkened road. Went into a tree. Father said it was an accident. Probably a deer.

He didn't know I'd heard Grandpap and Mother whispering about taking me away just days before.

Abel Bennett said, "The moon gave birth to wolves. Did you know that?"

We walked through the trees. Thomas was at my side, my father next to Abel. "No," I said. People were scared of Abel. They would stand in front of him and sputter nervously. He'd flash his eyes and they'd calm almost immediately, like the red brought them peace.

I'd never been scared of him. Not even when he held me down for my father.

Thomas's hand brushed against my shoulder. Father said wolves were territorial, that they needed their scent on their pack, which was why they always touched us. He hadn't been happy when he'd said it. I didn't know why.

"It's an old story," Abel said. "The moon was lonely. The one she loved, the sun, was always at the other end of the sky, and they could never meet, no matter how hard she tried. She would sink, and he would rise. She was dark and he was day. The world slept while she shone. She waxed and waned and sometimes disappeared entirely."

"The new moon," Thomas whispered in my ear. "It's dumb, if you think about it hard enough."

I laughed until Abel cleared his throat pointedly.

Maybe I was a little scared of him.

"She was lonely," the Alpha said again. "And because of it, she made the wolves, creatures who would sing to her every time she appeared. And when she was at her fullest, they would worship her with four paws upon the ground, heads tilted back toward the night sky. The wolves were equal and without hierarchy."

Thomas winked at me, then rolled his eyes.

I liked him very much.

Abel said, "It wasn't the sun, but it was enough for her. She would shine down upon the wolves, and they would call to her. But the sun could hear their songs while he tried to sleep, and became jealous. He sought to burn the wolves from the world. But before he could, she rose in front of him, covering him completely, leaving only a ring of red fire. The wolves changed because of it. They became Alphas and Betas and Omegas. And with this change came magic, scorched into the earth. The wolves became men with eyes red and orange and violet. As the moon weakened, she saw the horror they had become, beasts with bloodlust that could not be sated. With the last of her strength, she shaped the magic and pushed it into a human. He became a witch, and the wolves were calmed."

I was enchanted. "Witches have always been with wolves?"

"Always," Abel said, fingers brushing against the bark of an old tree. "They are important to a pack. Like a tether. A witch helps keep the beast at bay."

My father hadn't spoken a word since we'd left the Bennett house. He looked distant. Lost. I wondered if he even heard what Abel was saying. Or if he'd heard it countless times before.

"You hear that, runt?" Thomas said, running a hand through my hair. "You keep me from eating everyone in town. No pressure." And then he flashed his orange eyes and snapped his teeth at me. I laughed and ran ahead, hearing him chasing after me. I was like the sun and he was the moon, always chasing.

Later my father would say, "We don't need the wolves. They need us, yes, but we have never needed them. They use our magic. As a tether. It binds a pack together. Yes, there are packs without witches. More than have them. But the ones that *do* have witches are the ones in power. There's a reason for that. You need to remember that, Gordo. They will always need you more than you could ever need them."

I didn't question him.

How could I?

He was my father.

I said, "I promise that I'll try my best. I'll learn all that I can, and I'll do a good job for you. You'll see. I'm going to be the best there ever was." My eyes widened. "But don't tell my father I said that."

The white wolf sneezed.

I laughed.

Eventually I reached out and pressed my hand against Thomas's snout, and for a moment I thought I heard a whisper in my head.

packpackpack

And then he ran with the moon.

My father came to me after. I didn't ask where my mother was. It didn't seem important. Not then.

"Who is that?" I asked him. I pointed at a brown wolf prowling near

Thomas. His paws were large and his eyes narrowed. But Thomas didn't see him, instead focusing only on his mate, snuffling in her ear. The brown wolf pounced, teeth bared. But Thomas was an Alpha-in-waiting. He had the other wolf by the throat even before he hit the ground. He twisted his head to the right and the brown wolf was knocked to the side, hitting the ground with a jarring crash.

I wondered if Thomas would hurt him.

He didn't, though. He went and pressed his snout against the brown wolf's head. He yipped, and the brown wolf pushed himself up. They chased each other. Thomas's mate sat and watched them with knowing eyes.

"Ah," my father said. "He will be Thomas's second when Thomas becomes the Alpha. He is Thomas's brother in all but blood. His name is Richard Collins, and I expect great things from him."

THE FIRST YEAR /
KNOW THE WORDS

The first year, we headed north. The trail was cold, but it wasn't frozen.

There were days when I wanted to strangle the three Bennett wolves, listening to Carter and Kelly snap at each other in their grief. They were callous and mean, and on more than one occasion their claws popped out and blood was shed.

Sometimes we slept in the SUV, parked in a field, rusted farm equipment buried in overgrown vines sitting off in the distance like hulking monoliths.

The wolves would shift on those nights, and they'd run, burning off the almost manic energy from having been trapped in a car all day.

I would sit in the field, legs crossed, eyes closed, and breathe in and out and in and out.

If we were far enough away from a town, they would howl. It wasn't like it'd been in Green Creek. These were the songs of sorrow and heartache, of anger and rage.

Sometimes they were blue.

But most times, they burned.

Other times we'd be in a shoddy hotel off the beaten path, sharing too-small beds. Carter snored. Kelly kicked in his sleep.

Joe often sat with his back against the headboard, staring down at his phone.

One night a couple weeks after we'd left, I couldn't sleep. It was the middle of the night and I was exhausted, but my mind was racing, my head pounding. I sighed and turned over on my back. Kelly was next to me in the bed, curled and facing away, hugging a pillow.

"I didn't think it'd be like this."

I turned my head. On the other bed, Carter huffed in his sleep. Joe's eyes glittered in the dark as he looked at me.

I sighed as I looked back at the ceiling. "What?"

"This," Joe said. "Here. Like we are. I didn't think it'd be like this."

"I don't know what you're talking about."

"Do you think . . ."

"Spit it out, Joe."

Christ, he was so fucking young. "I did this because it's the right thing to do."

"Sure, kid."

"I'm the Alpha."

"Yeah."

"He needs to pay."

"Who are you trying to convince here? You or me?"

"I did what I had to. They—they don't understand."

"Do you?"

He didn't like that very much. There was a low growl in his voice when he said, "He killed my father."

I pitied him. This shouldn't have happened. Thomas and I weren't exactly the best of friends—we couldn't be, not after everything— but that didn't mean I wished for any of this. These boys should never have had to witness their Alpha fall under the weight of feral Omegas. It wasn't fair. "I know."

"Ox, he . . . he doesn't understand."

"You don't know that."

"He's angry with me."

Jesus. "Joe, his mother is dead. His Alpha is dead. His ma—*you* dropped a bomb on him and then left. You're goddamn right he's angry. And if it's at you, it's because he doesn't know where else to direct it."

Joe didn't say anything.

"He text you back?"

"How did you—"

"You stare at that phone enough."

"Oh. Um. Yeah. He did."

"Everything all right?"

He laughed. It was a hollow sound. "No, Gordo. Everything is not all right. But nothing has come back to Green Creek."

If I were a better man, I would have said something comforting. Instead I said, "That's what the wards are for."

"Gordo?"

"What."

"Why did you—why are you here?"

"You told me."

"I *asked* you."

For fuck's sake. "Go to sleep, Joe. We have an early start."

He sniffled quietly.

I closed my eyes.

      · · ·

I didn't know them. Not as well as I should have. For the longest time I didn't care. I wanted nothing to do with packs and wolves and Alphas or magic. When Ox had let spill that the Bennetts were back in Green Creek, my first thought was *Mark* and *Mark* and *Mark,* but I pushed it away because that was the past and I wouldn't have any of it.

The second thought was that I needed to keep Oxnard Matheson far away from the wolves.

It didn't work.

Before I could stop it, he was already too far gone.

I kept them at arm's length. Even when Thomas came to me because of Joe. Even when he stood in front of me and begged, even when his eyes flashed red and he *threatened,* I didn't allow myself to know them, not as they were now. Thomas still had the same aura of power around him he always had, but it was more intense. More focused. It hadn't been this strong, even when he'd first become the Alpha. I wondered if he'd had another witch at some point. I was shocked at the burn of jealousy at the thought, and hated myself for feeling that way.

I agreed to help him, to help Joe, only because I wouldn't let Ox get hurt. If Joe hadn't been able to control his shift after everything he'd been through, if he'd been slowly turning feral, it'd mean Ox was in danger.

That was the only reason.

It had nothing to do with a sense of responsibility. I owed them nothing.

It had nothing to do with Mark. He had made his choice. I'd made mine.

He'd chosen his pack over me. I'd chosen to wash my hands of them all.

But none of that mattered. Not anymore.

I was forced to know them, whether I wanted to or not. I'd lost my mind when I'd agreed to follow Joe and his brothers.

Kelly was the quiet one, always watching. He wasn't as big as Carter and probably never would be. Not like Joe, who I thought was going to grow and grow and grow. It was rare, but when Kelly smiled, it was small and quiet with a bare hint of teeth. He was smarter than the rest of us combined, always calculating, taking things in and processing them before the rest of us could. His wolf was gray, with splotches of black and white on his face and shoulders.

Carter was all brute force, less talk, more action. He snapped and snarked, bitching about anything and everything. When he wasn't driving, he'd kick up his boots on the dash, sinking down low in his seat, the collar of his jacket flipped up around his neck and brushing against his ears. He weaponized his words, using them to inflict as much pain as possible. But he also used them as a distraction, deflecting as best he could. He wanted to be seen as cool and aloof, but he was too young and inexperienced to make it work. His wolf resembled his brother's, dark gray, but with black and white on his hind legs.

Joe was . . . a seventeen-year-old Alpha. It didn't make for the best combination. That much power after that much trauma and being so young wasn't something I wished on anyone. I understood him more than the others, only because I knew what he was going through. Maybe not the same—magic and lycanthropy weren't even in the same ballpark—but there was a kinship that I tried desperately to ignore. His wolf was white as snow.

They moved together, Carter and Kelly circling around Joe whether or not they realized it. They deferred to him, mostly, even as they gave him shit. He was their Alpha, and they needed him.

They were all so different, these lost boys.

But they did have one thing in common.

All three were assholes who didn't know when to shut the fuck up. And I was stuck with them.

"—and I don't know *why* you think we should keep doing this," Carter said one night a few weeks after we'd left. We were in Cut Bank, Montana, a little town in the middle of nowhere, not far from the Canadian border. There was a small pack near Glacier National Park that we were heading toward. A wolf we'd stumbled upon in Lewiston told us they'd recently dealt with Omegas. The wolf had trembled under Joe's Alpha eyes, fear and reverence battling all over his face. We'd stopped for the night, and Carter had immediately started in.

"Give it a rest," Kelly said tiredly, frowning as he tried to find a TV channel that wasn't hard-core porn from the eighties.

Carter snarled at him wordlessly.

Joe stared at the wall.

I flexed my hands and waited.

Carter said, "What happens when we get to this pack? Have any of you thought this through? They'll tell us Omegas were there, but what the fuck else?" He glared at Joe. "You think they'll know where that bastard Richard is? They *won't*. No one does. He's a ghost and he's haunting us. We're—"

"He's the Alpha," Kelly said, eyes flashing. "If he thinks this is what we're supposed to do, then we're going to do it."

Carter laughed bitterly as he started pacing the length of the shitty hotel room. "Good little soldier. Always falling in line. You did it with Dad, and now you're doing it with Joe. What the fuck do either of you know? Dad is *dead* and Joe's a *kid*. Just because he was a goddamn little prince doesn't give him the right to take us away from—"

"That's not fair," Kelly said. "Just because you're jealous that *you* weren't going to be the Alpha doesn't mean you get to take it out on the rest of us."

"*Jealous?* You think I'm *jealous?* Fuck you, Kelly. What the hell do you know? I was the firstborn. Joe was Daddy's little boy. And who the fuck were you? What do you have to offer?"

Carter knew where to cut. He knew what would make Kelly bleed. What would get a reaction. Before I could move, Kelly launched himself at his brother, claws extended, eyes orange and bright.

Carter met his brother with fangs and fire, teeth sharpened and hair sprouting along his face as he melted into his half shift. Kelly was fast and scrappy, landing crouched on his feet after his brother backhanded him across the face. I stood, feeling the flutter of a raven's wings, needing to do *something* before the goddamn cops were called and—

"*Enough.*"

A burst of red hit me in the chest. It said *stop* and *now* and *alpha i am the alpha,* and I stumbled at the force of it. Carter and Kelly went stock-still, eyes wide, little whimpers crawling from their throats, wounded and raw.

Joe stood near the bed. His eyes were as furious red as Thomas's had ever been. He hadn't shifted, but it looked like it was a close thing. His mouth was twisted, hands in fists at his sides. I saw a trickle of blood dripping onto the dirty carpet. He must have popped claws and was digging them into his palm.

And the sheer *power* emanating from him was devastating. It was wild and all-encompassing, threatening to overwhelm us all. Carter and Kelly began to tremble, eyes wide and wet.

"Joe," I said quietly.

He ignored me, chest heaving.

"*Joe.*"

He turned to look at me, teeth bared.

I said, "Stop. You have to pull it back."

For a moment I thought he was going to ignore me. That he'd turn back to his brothers and strip away *everything* from them, leaving them as docile, empty husks. Being an Alpha was an extraordinary responsibility, and if he'd wanted to, he could have forced his brothers to follow his every whim. They would be mindless drones, their free will hanging in tatters.

I would stop him. If it came to that.

It didn't.

The red in his eyes leeched away, and all that remained was a scared seventeen-year-old boy in front of me, face wet as he shook.

"I'm," he croaked out. "I don't—Oh god, oh—"

Kelly moved first. He pushed past Carter and pressed himself against Joe, rubbing his nose near Joe's ear and into his hair. Joe's fists were still clenched at his sides as Kelly wrapped his arms around him. He was stiff and unyielding, eyes wide and on me.

Carter came then too. He took both his brothers in his arms, whispering quietly to them words I couldn't make out.

Joe never looked away from me.

They slept that night on the floor, the floral-print comforter and pillows pulled from the bed and made into a little nest. Joe was in the middle, a brother on either side. Kelly's head rested on his chest. Carter's leg was thrown over the both of them.

They slept first, exhausted from the assault on their minds.

I sat on the bed above, watching over them.

It was late into the night when Joe said, "Why is this happening to me?"

I sighed. "It had to be you. It was—" I shook my head. "You're the Alpha. It was always going to be you."

His eyes glittered in the dark. "He came for me. When I was little. To get at my dad."

"I know."

"You weren't there."

"No."

"You're here now."

"I am."

"You could have said no. And I wouldn't have been able to force you. Not like them."

I didn't know what to say.

"Dad wouldn't have done that. He wouldn't have—"

"You aren't your father," I said, voice rougher than I expected.

"I know."

"You are your own person."

"Am I?"

"Yes."

"You could have said no. But you didn't."

"You need to keep them safe," I told him quietly. "This is your pack. You are their Alpha. Without them, there is no you."

"And what did you become? When there was no us?"

I closed my eyes.

He didn't speak for a long time after that. The night stretched on around us. I thought he was asleep when he said, "I want to go home."

He turned his head, face against Carter's throat.

I watched them until the sun rose.

*   *   *

He dreamed, sometimes, dreamed these furious nightmares that caused him to wake up screaming for his dad, his mom, for Ox and Ox and Ox. Kelly would take his face in his hands. Carter would look helplessly at me.

I didn't do much of anything. We all had monsters in our dreams. Some of us had just lived with them longer.

The Glacier wolves pointed us north. Their pack was small, living in a couple of cabins in the middle of the forest. The Alpha was an asshole, posturing and threatening until Joe said, "My father was Thomas Bennett. He's gone now, and I won't stop until those who took him from me are nothing but blood and bone."

Things were calmer after that.

Omegas had come to their territory. The Alpha pointed at a pile of dirt with a wooden cross surrounded by flowers. One of her Betas, she said. The Omegas swarmed like hornets, violet eyes and slobbering maws. They'd died, most of them. The ones who had escaped had done so barely. But not before they'd taken one of her own.

Richard hadn't been among them.

But there were whispers farther into Canada.

"I knew Thomas," the Alpha said to me before we left. Her mate fawned over the boys, plying them with bowls of soup and thick slices of bread. "He was a good man."

"Yeah," I said.

"I knew you too. Not that we've ever met."

I didn't look at her.

"He knew," she said. "What you'd gone through. What price you paid. He thought you'd come back to him one day. That you needed time and space and—"

"I'll wait outside," I said abruptly. Carter looked at me, cheeks bulging, broth dripping down his chin, but I waved him away.

The air was cool and the stars were bright.

Fuck you, I thought as I stared up at the expanse. *Fuck you.*

We didn't find Richard Collins in Calgary.

We found feral wolves.

They came at us, lost to their madness.

I pitied them.

At least until they outnumbered us and went for Joe.

He cried out as they cut into his skin, his brothers screaming his name.

The raven spread its wings.

I was exhausted by the time it was over, covered in Omega blood, bodies littering the ground around me.

Joe was propped up between Carter and Kelly, head bowed as his skin slowly knit back together. His breath rattled heavily in his chest. He said, "You saved me. You saved *us*."

I looked away.

As he slept, I picked up the burner phone I carried. I highlighted Mark's name and thought how easy it would be. I could press a button and his voice would be in my ear. I would say I was sorry, that I never should have let it go as far as it did. That I understood the choice he'd made so long ago.

I texted Ox instead.

Joe's fine. Ran into some trouble. He's sleeping it off. He didn't want you to worry.

That night I dreamed of a brown wolf with its nose pressed against my chin.

A phone rang while we were in Alaska.

We stared down at it, unsure of what do to. It'd been four months since we left Green Creek behind, and we were no closer to Richard than we'd been before.

Joe swallowed thickly as he picked up the burner phone off the desk of yet another nameless motel in the middle of nowhere.

I thought he was going to ignore it.

Instead he connected the call.

We all heard it. Every word.

"You fucking asshole," Ox said, and I wanted nothing more than to see his face. "You *don't* get to do that to me! You hear me? You *don't*. Do you even fucking *care* about us? Do you? If you do, if even a part of you cares about me—about *us*—then you need to ask yourself if this is worth it. If what you're doing is *worth* it. Your family needs you. I fucking need you."

None of us spoke.

"You asshole. You bastard."

Joe put the phone on the edge of the bed and sank to his knees. He put his chin on the bed, staring at the phone as Ox breathed.

Kelly eventually sat next to him.

Carter did too, all of them staring at the phone, listening to the sounds of home.

We drove along a dusty back road, flat green fields stretching out all around us. Kelly was behind the wheel. Carter was in the seat next to him, window rolled down, feet propped up on the dash. Joe was in the back with me, hand hanging out of the SUV, wind blowing between his fingers. Music played low on the radio.

No one had spoken in hours.

We didn't know where we were going.

It didn't matter.

I thought of running my fingers over a shaved head, thumbs tracing eyebrows and the shell of an ear. The low rumble of a predatory growl building in a strong chest. The way a tiny stone statue felt in my hand for the first time, the heft of it surprising.

Carter made a low noise and reached to turn up the radio. He grinned at his brother. Kelly rolled his eyes, but he had a quiet smile on his face.

The road stretched on.

Carter started singing first. He was off-key and brash, loud when he didn't need to be, getting more words wrong than right.

He was alone for the first stanza.

Kelly joined in at the refrain. His voice was sweet and warm, stronger than I would have expected. The song was older than they were. It had to come from their mother. I remembered being young, watching her flip through her record collection. She'd smiled at me peeking around the corner in the pack house. She'd beckoned me over, and when I stood by her side, she touched my shoulder briefly and said, "I love music. Sometimes it can say the things you can't find the words for."

I looked over at Joe.

He was staring at his brothers in awe, looking more alive than I'd seen him in weeks.

Carter glanced back at him. He grinned. "You know the words. Come on. You got this."

I thought Joe would refuse. I thought he'd go back to staring out the window.

Instead he sang with his brothers.

It was quiet at first, a little wobbly. But as the song went on, he got louder and louder. They all did until they were *shouting* at each other, sounding happier than they'd been since the monster from their childhood had reared his head and taken their father from them.

They sang.

They laughed.

They *howled*.

They looked at me.

I thought of a boy with eyes of ice telling me that he loved me, that he didn't want to leave again but he had to, he had to, his Alpha was demanding it, and he would come back for me, Gordo, you have to believe I'll come back for you. You are my mate, I love you, I love you, I love you.

I couldn't do this.

And then Joe put his hand on mine.

He squeezed, just once.

"Come on, Gordo," he said. "You know the words. You got this."

I sighed.

I sang.

We were all hungry like the woooooolf.

We drove on and on and on.

And in the furthest recesses of my mind, I heard it again. For the first time.

It whispered *pack* and *pack* and *pack*.

. . .

I knew it was coming. Every text, every phone call got harder to ignore. It was a pull toward home, a weight on our shoulders. A reminder of all that we'd left behind. I saw how much it hurt Carter and Kelly when they heard their mother had finally shifted back. How much it pulled at Joe when Ox asked questions he couldn't answer.

Mark never said anything.

But then I never said anything to him either.

It was better this way.

Which was why I didn't argue too much when Joe first said, "We have to ditch the phones."

His brothers put up a fight. It was admirable, going against their Alpha. They begged me to tell him no, to tell Joe he was wrong. That there was a better way to go about it. But I couldn't, because I was dreaming of wolves now, of pack. They didn't know what I did.

Hadn't seen the way the hunters had come to Green Creek without warning, come to the house at the end of the lane to deal in death. We had been unaware. Unprepared. I had seen Richard Collins fall to his knees, the blood of his loved ones staining the ground around him. His head had tilted back and he had *screamed* his horror. And when the new Alpha had put his hand on his shoulder, Richard had lashed out. "You did *nothing*," he snarled. "You did *nothing* to stop this. This is your fault. This is on *you*."

So when Joe turned to me, looking for validation, I told him he was being stupid. That Ox wouldn't understand, and did he *really* want to do that to him?

But that was all.

"It's the only way," he said.

"Are you sure?"

Joe sighed. "Yes."

"Your Alpha has spoken," I told Carter and Kelly.

I took their phones.

They slept badly that night.

The moon was just a sliver when I opened the motel door and stepped out into the night.

A dumpster sat at the edge of the parking lot.

Joe's phone went in first. Then Carter's. Kelly's.

I held mine tightly.

The screen was bright in the dark.

I highlighted a name.

Mark

I typed out a text.

I'm sorry.

My thumb hovered over the Send button.

Like the earth. Like dirt and leaves and rain—

I didn't send the message.

I threw the phone in the dumpster and didn't look back.

SPARK PLUG ELECTRODE /
LITTLE SANDWICHES

I was eleven when Marty caught us sneaking into the garage.

I didn't know why I was so drawn to it. It wasn't anything special. The garage was an old building covered in a layer of grime that looked as if it'd never be washed away. Three large doors led to bays with rusty mechanical lifts inside. The men who worked there were rough, dip tucked firmly in their cheeks, tattoos covering their arms and necks.

Marty himself was the worst of them. His clothes were always stained with dirt and oil, and he had scowled constantly. His hair was thin and wispy, sticking up around his ears. Pock scars marred his face, and his rattling cough sounded wet and painful.

I thought him fascinating, even from a distance. He wasn't a wolf. He wasn't imbued with magic. He was terribly, painfully human, gruff and volatile.

And the shop itself was like a beacon in a world that didn't always make sense to me. Grandpap was a couple of years in the ground, and my fingers itched to touch a torque wrench and a dead blow mallet. I wanted to listen to the purr of an engine to see if I could hear what was wrong with it.

I waited until a Saturday when no one else was around. Thomas was with Abel, doing whatever Alphas and future Alphas did in the woods. My mother was getting her nails done in the next town over. My father said he had a meeting, which meant he was with the dark-haired woman I wasn't supposed to know about. Rico was sick, Chris grounded, Tanner on a day trip to Eugene that he had bitched about for weeks.

With no one to tell me no, I went to town.

I stood for a long time across the street from the garage, just watching. My arms itched. My fingers twitched. There was magic in my skin that had no outlet. Grandpap's tools had mysteriously disappeared after his old lady killed him, my father saying they weren't important.

And just when I'd gathered up enough courage to cross the street, I felt a little tug at the back of my mind, a simple awareness that was getting more and more familiar.

I sighed. "I know you're there."

Silence.

"You might as well come out now."

Mark stepped out from the alley next to the diner. He looked embarrassed but defiant. He wore jeans and a Ghostbusters shirt. The sequel had just come out. Rico and Tanner and Chris and I were going to go see it. I thought about inviting Mark too for reasons I couldn't quite understand. He still got on my nerves, but he wasn't so bad. I liked the way he smiled sometimes.

"What are you doing?" he asked.

"Why?"

"You've been standing there for a long time."

"Stalker," I muttered. "If you must know, I'm going to go to Marty's."

He glanced across the street, a frown on his face. "Why?"

"Because I want to see inside."

"Why?"

I shrugged. "It's—you wouldn't understand."

He looked back at me. "Maybe I can if you just tell me."

"You bother me."

He cocked his head like a dog. "That was a lie."

I scowled at him. "Stop it. You don't get to do that. Stop listening to my heartbeat."

"I *can't*. It's so loud."

I didn't know why I had a loud heart. I hoped nothing was wrong with me. "Well, try anyway."

He was smiling a little now. "I don't bother you."

"You do. You really do."

"Let's go, then."

"What? Go where? What are you—*hey*. What are you doing?"

He was already marching across the street. He didn't look back even when I hissed his name.

I ran after him.

His stride was longer than mine. For every step he took, I needed to take two. I told myself that I would be bigger than him one day. It didn't matter that he was a wolf. I would be bigger and stronger and I'd follow *him* around, see how he liked it.

"We're going to get in trouble," I whispered furiously.

"Maybe," he said.

"Your dad is going to be so mad."

"So is yours."

I thought hard. "I won't tell them if you won't."

"Like a secret?"

"Yeah. Sure. Like a secret."

He looked strangely pleased. "I've never had a secret with you before."

"Uh, *yeah*. You have. You're a *werewolf*. I'm a *witch*. That's like, so secret."

"That doesn't count. Other people know that. This is just a secret for you and me."

"You're dumb."

We made it across the street. The garage doors were open. An old boom box blasted Judas Priest. I could see two cars inside, and an old pickup. One of the guys was under the truck. Marty was bent over a 1985 Chevy Camaro IROC-Z with an older man in a suit. The car was sleek and red, and I wanted nothing more than to put my hands on it. The hood was up and Marty was fiddling with something. The man in the suit looked irritated. He glanced at his watch and tapped his foot.

I leaned against the side of the garage, Mark at my side. His fingers brushed against mine, and I felt something like a pulse of magic along my arm. I ignored it.

"—and when did the engine light come on?" Marty was saying.

"I told you," the man in the suit said. "Last week. There's no stalling, no hesitation. It doesn't shake, it doesn't—"

"Yeah, yeah," Marty said. "I heard you. May be a faulty wire somewhere. These sports cars, they look nice, but they're built for shit. You get all the pussy you want for a chunk of change, but they fall apart and you're stuck with it."

"Can you fix it or not?" The man in the suit didn't sound very happy. I wondered if he didn't get enough pussy. I wondered what pussy was.

"Grab the owner's manual," Marty said. "It better be in English or it ain't gonna be for shit if the repair book I got doesn't tell us anything. Let's go into my office and take a look."

The man in the suit let out a huff but did as Marty said. He leaned into the IROC-Z and grabbed the manual from the glove compartment before he followed Marty toward the back office.

Now was my chance. The pretty girl was just sitting there, wide open. Waiting for me. I was going to lube her up and put my fingers inside, just like Grandpap had taught me.

"I'm going in," I whispered to Mark.

"Okay," he whispered back. "I'm right behind you."

Judas Priest gave way to Black Sabbath as we stepped inside. It smelled of man and metal, and I breathed it all in. The guy under the truck shifted slightly but otherwise didn't move. Marty and the man in the suit were back in the office, blocked by a car on a lift.

The IROC-Z was there, waiting for me. She was gorgeous, a candy-apple red with black trim and silver rims. The man in the suit didn't deserve her.

I bent over her engine, searching for something, *anything*.

"Light," I muttered to Mark.

"What?"

"I need a *light*. When I ask for something, you hand it over. It's how you work on cars."

"How am I supposed to find a light?"

"With your *eyes*."

He mumbled something, but I ignored him, taking her all in.

"Light," he eventually said. I stuck out my hand. It was a small flashlight. It wasn't much, but it'd do.

"Come on, you little bitch," I said.

"What? You don't need to call me names. I got the—"

"Not *you*," I said. "It's something you do when you work on cars. You curse at them while you figure out what's wrong. My grandpap taught me that."

"Oh. It helps?"

"Yeah. When you curse at it enough, you finally figure it out."

"That doesn't make sense."

"It works. Trust me."

"I trust you," Mark said quietly, and I felt another little curl of magic crawl along my skin. He pressed along my side, bending over the engine with me. His shoulder brushed against mine. "So we just call it names."

"Yeah," I said, feeling slightly flushed. "I mean, that's . . . yeah."

"Okay. Um. You . . . asshole?"

I laughed. "You're so bad at this."

"I've never done it before!"

"So bad."

"Whatever. I'd like to see *you* do better."

I tried to think what Grandpap had said. "Come on, you insignificant bastard. What the hell."

"Whoa," Mark breathed. "That . . . your *grandpa* taught you that? *My* grandpa had hair sticking out of his ears and always forgot who I was."

"He taught me a lot," I said. "Everything, really. Try it again."

"Okay. Let me think. Uh—how about, what's wrong with you, you strange whore?"

I choked. "Oh my god."

"Why won't you tell me your secrets, you fucking shithead."

"I don't know why I even let you come with me."

"Asshole motherfucking dick—"

He was good. I could give him that. But before I could even think of telling him so, I saw it.

"There," I said, pointing the flashlight. "See? Right there? That's what's wrong."

"I don't see anything," Mark said.

"It's—ugh, just give me your hand."

He didn't hesitate.

Later, much, much later, I would think about this moment. The first time we'd held hands. The first time we touched of our own choice. His hand was bigger than mine, his fingers thick and blunt. His skin was darker and warm. The bones felt brittle, and I knew of the blood that thrummed just underneath. My father had made sure of it. I belonged to it, to the Bennetts, because of what was in my own blood.

But I was only eleven years old. I didn't understand then what it meant.

He did, though.

Which was why he inhaled sharply when I took his hand in mine, why out of the corner of my eye I saw the flash of orange in the dark underneath the hood of the car. He growled a little, deep in his chest, and I *swore* in that moment the raven took flight. I—

"What the hell do you think you're doing?"

I dropped his hand, startled at the angry voice coming from behind us.

Before I could completely turn around, Mark was in front of me, pushing me behind him. I stood on my tiptoes, peering over his shoulder.

Marty stood there, looking flushed and pissed off. The man in the suit was confused, his tie loose around his neck.

Marty's eyes narrowed when he saw me. "You. I know you. I've seen you before. You belonged to Donald."

Donald Livingstone. My grandpap. "Yes, sir," I said, because I'd learned early on that if you were polite to adults, maybe you could get out of trouble.

"And *you*," Marty said to Mark. "I've seen *you* following this one around."

"I keep him safe," Mark said. "He's mine to protect."

My hand tightened on his shoulder. I didn't understand what he meant. We were pack, yeah, and—

"Boy, I don't give two fucks *what* you do just as long as you don't do it here. Get the hell out of here. This is no place for—"

"Spark plug electrode!" I blurted out.

Marty blinked at me. "What?"

I pushed Mark out of the way. He squawked angrily but crowded back into me, not letting any space between us. I didn't have time for his werewolf idiocy. I had a point to make. "The check engine light. It's because of the spark plug electrode. There's motor oil built up around it."

"What is he talking about?" the man in the suit asked. "Who is this kid?"

"Spark plug electrode," Marty said slowly. "Is that right."

I nodded furiously. "Yeah, yes. Yes, sir. It is."

Marty took a step toward me, and for a moment I was sure Mark was going to wolf out. But before he could, Marty brushed by me and bent over the IROC-Z. "Flashlight," he muttered, hand extended.

"Flashlight," I said promptly, handing it over.

It took him a moment, but then, "Huh. Would you look at that. Must have missed it. Eyes aren't what they used to be. Getting too old for this shit. Kid, come here."

I went immediately. Mark did too.

"Excess oil," Marty said.

"Yes, sir."

"Could be an oil consumption problem."

"Or something with the emissions system."

"Or the ignition system."

"Fuel injection. The hose, maybe."

He shook his head. "Fuel isn't leaking. No deterioration."

"What are they talking about?" the man in the suit asked.

"I don't know," Mark said. "But Gordo knows a lot. More than anyone I know. He's good and smart and smells like dirt and leaves and—"

I banged my head on the hood of the car. I yelped at the bright flash of pain. Mark was there in an instant, hands on my shoulders. "Would you *stop* telling him what I smell like?" I hissed at him through gritted teeth. "You sound so *weird*."

Mark ignored me, putting his hands on my face and tilting my head down as he inspected what I assumed was probably going to be a gushing wound that would require stitches and would leave a horrific scar that—

"A little bump," he murmured quietly. "You need to be more careful."

I pulled away. "Well, *you* need to—"

"Easy fix," Marty said. "Should only take a couple of hours, barring the need to order any parts. Go have a cup of coffee at the diner. A slice of pie."

The man in the suit looked like he was going to argue, but nodded instead. He glanced curiously at Mark and me before he turned and walked out of the garage and into the sunshine.

Marty turned back to me. "Gordo, right?"

I nodded slowly.

He rubbed a hand through the gray stubble on his jaw. "Donald was a good man. Stubborn son of a bitch. Cheated at cards." He shook his head. "Denied it, but we all knew. He talked about you."

I didn't know what to say to that, so I kept my mouth shut.

"He taught you?"

"Yeah. Yes. Everything I know."

"How old are you?"

"Fifteen."

Mark coughed.

Marty snorted. "Want to try that one again?"

I rolled my eyes. "Eleven."

"Your pa do cars?"

"No."

He looked at Mark. "Bennett, ain't ya?"

"Yes," Mark said.

He nodded slowly. "Strange bunch."

We said nothing because there was nothing *to* say.

Marty sighed. "You've got an eye, kid. Tell you what."

.   .   .

"You can't tell my father," I told Mark as we walked away from the garage. "He won't let me go back. You know he won't."

Mark glanced at me. "This is what you want?"

Yes. It was. It was what I *needed*. I didn't know much else outside of pack life. Nothing I had aside from Chris and Tanner and Rico was *mine* and mine alone. Father didn't like them and went so far as to try to forbid me from seeing them outside of school. But my mother had stepped in, one of the few times she'd ever stood up to him. I needed normal, she said. I needed something more, she said. He hadn't been happy about it, but he'd relented. I'd hugged her for a long time after that. "Yeah," I said. "This is what I want." Then, "It's another secret. Just between you and me."

His lips twitched at that, and I knew I'd won. "I like having secrets with you."

There was a strange twist in the pit of my stomach.

.   .   .

"Tethers," Abel said as he sat behind the large desk in his office. My father stood at the window, looking out to the trees. Thomas sat next to me, quiet and serene as he always was. I was nervous because this was the first time I'd been allowed into Abel's office. My arms were sore from days under my father's needles. "Can you tell me what you know about them?"

"They help to remind a wolf they're human," I said slowly, wanting to get it right. I needed Abel to see he could believe in me. "They keep a wolf from getting lost in the animal."

"That's true," Abel said. He spread his hands out on the desktop. "But it's more than that. Much more."

I glanced at my father, but he was lost to whatever he was seeing.

"A tether is the strength behind the wolf," Abel said. "A feeling or a person or an *idea* that keeps us in touch with our human sides. It's a song that calls us home when we're shifted. It reminds us of where we come from. My tether is my pack. The people who count on me to keep them safe. To protect them from those who would do us harm. Do you understand?"

I nodded, though I didn't really. I looked at Thomas. "What's yours?"

"Pack."

That surprised me. "Not Elizabeth?"

"Elizabeth," Thomas said with a sigh, sounding dreamy like he always did when he mentioned her. Or saw her. Or stood next to her. Or thought about her existence. "She's . . . no. She's more to me."

"Who would have guessed," Abel said dryly. Then, "Tethers aren't just for wolves, Gordo. We're called by the moon, and there is magic in that. Like there is magic in you."

"From the earth."

"Yes. From the earth."

It hit me then, what he was trying to say. "I need a tether too?" It was an immensely terrible thought.

"Not yet," Abel said, sitting forward. "And not for a long time. You're young and just beginning. Your marks haven't been completed. Until they are, you won't require one. But one day you will."

"I don't want it to be just one person," I said.

My father turned. He had a strange look on his face. "And why is that?"

"Because people leave," I said honestly. "They move or they get sick or they die. If a wolf had a tether and it was a person and they died, what would happen to the wolf?"

The only response was the ticking of the clock on the wall.

Then Abel chuckled, eyes crinkling kindly. "You are a fascinating creature. I'm so very happy to know you."

"I didn't know about tethers," I told my father as we left the Bennett house. "For witches."

"I know. There is a time and place for everything."

"Is there other stuff you haven't told me?"

He wouldn't look at me. Some kids ran by us, laughing as they growled at each other. He sidestepped them deftly. "Yes. But you will learn, one day."

I didn't think that was fair, but I couldn't say so to my father. Instead I said, "Who's your tether? Is it Mom?"

He closed his eyes and turned his face toward the sun.

"How could you?" I heard her say, voice tight and harsh. "Why would you do this to me? To us?"

"I didn't ask for this," my father said. "I never asked for any of this. I didn't know she would get—"

"I could tell her. I could tell everyone. What you are. What *they* are."

"No one would believe you. And how would that look for you? They would think you're crazy. And it would be used against you. You would never see Gordo again. I'd make sure of it."

"I know you've done something to me," my mother said. "I know you've messed with my mind. I know you've altered my memories. Maybe this isn't real. Maybe none of this is real. It's a dream, an awful dream from which I can't awake. Please. Please, Robert. Please let me wake up."

"Catherine, you're—this is unnecessary. All of this is. She'll leave. I promise. Until it's done. You can't go on like this. You just can't. It's killing you. It's killing *me*."

"Like you care," she said harshly. "Like you give a *damn* about anything that isn't *her*—"

"Lower your voice."

"I won't. I won't be—"

"Catherine."

The voices fell away as I pulled the comforter over my head.

"Your mother isn't feeling well," Father said. "She's resting."

I stared at their closed bedroom door for a long time.

She smiled at me. "I'm fine. Honey, of course I'm fine. How could anything be wrong when the sun is shining and the sky is blue? Let's have a picnic. Doesn't that sound lovely? Just you and me, Gordo. I'll make little sandwiches with the crusts cut off. There's potato salad and oatmeal cookies. We'll take a blanket and watch the clouds. Gordo, it'll be just you and me and I'll be the happiest I've ever been."

I thought she was lying.

"Get your ass in gear!" Marty hollered at me from across the garage. "I don't pay you nothing to have you just *standing* there with your dick hanging out. Move, Gordo. *Move.*"

"How did you know?" I asked Thomas when I was twelve. It was a Sunday, and as was tradition, the pack had gathered for dinner. Tables had been set up behind the Bennett house. Lacy white cloths had been spread out over them. There were vases filled with wild-flowers, green and blue and purple and orange. Abel was at the grill, smiling at the noise and bustle that rose around him. Children laughed. The adults smiled. Music played from a record player.

And Elizabeth was dancing. She looked beautiful. She wore a pretty summer dress, her fingertips streaked with paint. Most of the day she'd been in her studio, a place where only Thomas was allowed, and only when she invited him in. I didn't understand her art, the slashes of color on canvas, but it was wild and vital and reminded me of running with wolves underneath a full moon.

But here she was now, swaying with the music, her dress flaring around her knees as she spun in a slow circle. Her arms were outstretched, her head tilted back and eyes closed. She looked peaceful and happy, and it caused a bittersweet pang in my chest.

"I knew from the moment I saw her," Thomas said, eyes never leaving Elizabeth. "I knew because no one I'd ever met before had made me feel the way I did then. She's the loveliest person I've ever seen, and even back then, I knew I was going to love her. I knew I was going to give her anything she could ever ask for."

"Wow," I breathed.

Thomas laughed. "Do you know what the first thing she said to me was?"

I shook my head.

"She told me to stop sniffing her."

I gaped at him.

He shrugged easily. "I wasn't very subtle."

"You were *smelling* her?" I asked, aghast.

"I couldn't help it. It was . . . do you know that moment right before a thunderstorm hits? The sky is black and gray, and everything feels electric? Your skin is humming and your hairs are standing on end?"

I nodded.

"That's what she smelled like to me. Like an approaching storm."

"Yeah," I said, still unsure. "But—like, you were *sniffing* her."

"You'll learn," Thomas told me. "One day. Maybe sooner than you might think. Oh, would you look at that. My brother approaches. What auspicious timing that is, given our discussion."

I turned my head. Mark Bennett was walking toward us, a determined expression on his face. Ever since the day he'd followed me into Marty's, things had been . . . less weird. He was still a little creepy, and I told him over and over again that I didn't *need* him to protect me, but he wasn't as bad as I thought he'd been. He was . . . nice. And he seemed to like me a whole hell of a lot for reasons I didn't quite understand.

"Thomas," Mark said, sounding slightly strangled.

"Mark," Thomas replied, sounding amused. "Nice tie. Isn't it a little warm for that?"

He blushed, the red crawling up his neck to his cheeks. "It's not—I'm trying—god, would you just—"

"I think I'll go dance with Elizabeth," Thomas said, patting me on the shoulder. "It'd be a shame to let a moment go to waste. Don't you think, brother?"

"Why are you dressed like that?" I asked him. He was wearing a red tie over a white dress shirt and slacks. He was barefoot, and I couldn't remember if I'd ever seen his toes before. They curled into the grass, the green bright against his skin.

"I'm not, it's just—" He shook his head. "I wanted to, okay?"

I frowned. "O-kay. But aren't you hot?"

"No."

"You're sweating."

"It's not because I'm hot."

"Oh. Are you nervous?"

"What? No. *No.* I'm not nervous. Why would I be nervous?"

I squinted at him. "Are you sick?"

He growled at me.

I grinned at him.

"Look," he said gruffly. "I wanted to. Okay. Can I . . ."

"Can you . . ."

He looked like he was about to explode. "Do you know how to dance?" he blurted out.

I stared at him.

"Because if you did, and if you wanted to, we could—I mean, it's fine, right? It's fine. We can just stand here. Or whatever. That's fine too." He fidgeted, tugging at the end of his tie. He looked at me, then away, then back at me.

"I don't have any idea what you're talking about," I admitted.

He sighed. "I know. I'm just . . ."

"Sweating."

"Would you *stop* saying that?"

"But. You are."

"God, you're such a dick."

I laughed at him. "Hey, I'm just pointing out—"

"Gordo!"

I turned.

My mother. She beckoned me toward her. Father had said she'd been sick again, that she wouldn't be coming. He'd dropped me off, saying he'd return later, that he had business to attend to before he would return. I didn't ask what that business was.

And now she was here, and she had a frail smile on her face. Her hair looked unkempt, and she was wringing her hands.

"Is she okay?" Mark asked. "She's—"

"I don't know," I said. "She wasn't feeling well earlier and—I'll go see what she wants. Hold on, okay? I'll be right back. And maybe you can tell me why you're in a tie."

Before I could walk away, he grabbed my hand. I looked back at him. "Be careful, okay?"

"It's just my mom."

He let me go.

"Hi," she said when I reached her. "Hi, sweetheart. Hi, baby. Come here. Can I talk to you? Come here."

I went, because she was my mother, and I would do anything for her.

She took me by the hand and pulled me around the house. "Where are we—"

"Quiet," she said. "Hold on. They'll hear."

The wolves. "But—"

"Gordo. Please. Trust me."

She'd never said that to me before.

I did as she asked.

We went around the house to the driveway. I saw her car parked behind all the others. She led me to it and opened the passenger door, motioning for me to get in. I hesitated, glancing back over my shoulder. Mark was there, standing next to the house, watching us. He took a step toward me, but my mother pushed me into the car.

She was around the front and inside before I could turn myself over in the seat.

There were two suitcases in the back seat.

I said, "What's happening?"

She said, "It's time."

Dirt flew up as she reversed in the driveway, nearly hitting another car.

I said, "Why are you—"

She put the car in drive and we flew down the lane. I looked in the side mirror at the houses behind us. Mark was gone.

On my twelfth birthday, there was a party.

Many people came.

Most were wolves.

Some were not.

Tanner and Chris and Rico got dropped off by their parents. It was the first time they'd been to the houses at the end of the lane, and their eyes were wide.

"Dios mío," Rico breathed. "You didn't say you were rich, papi."

"This isn't my house," I reminded him. "You've *been* to my house."

"It's pretty much the same thing," Rico said.

"Oh man," Chris said, looking down at the badly wrapped gift in his hand. "I got you a gift at the dollar store."

"I didn't even get you a gift," Tanner said, staring at the streamers and balloons and the tables filled with food.

"You can go in on mine," Chris told him. "It was only a dollar."

"How many bathrooms does that house have?" Rico demanded. "Three? Four?"

"Six," I muttered.

"Whoa," Chris and Tanner and Rico whispered.

"It's not my house!"

"We only have one," Rico said. "And everyone has to share."

I loved them, but they were a pain in my ass. "I only have one at my house—"

"You don't even have to wait to shit," Tanner said.

"I hate when I have to wait to shit," Chris said.

They looked at me expectantly.

I sighed. "I don't even know why I invited you."

"Are there three *cakes?*" Rico said, voice high-pitched.

"It's a pop gun," Chris said, shoving the present into my hands.

"It's from the both of us," Tanner said.

"You owe me fifty cents," Chris told him.

"You have burgers and hot dogs *and* lasagna?" Rico asked. "*Mierda.* What kind of white nonsense *is* this?"

The Bennetts had gone overboard. They always did. They were powerful and rich, and people respected them. Green Creek survived because of them. They donated money and time, and even though townies still sometimes whispered *cult*, they were an oddity beloved.

And I was part of their pack. I heard their songs in my head, the voices connecting me to the wolves. I had ink driven into my skin, binding me to them. I was them and they were me.

So of course they did this for me.

Yes, there were three cakes. And burgers and hot dogs and lasagna. There was also a pile of presents almost as tall as I was, and the

wolves would touch my shoulder and hair and cheeks, covering me
in their scent. I was ingrained in them, in the earth around us. The
sky above was blue, but I could feel the hidden moon calling for the
sun. There was a clearing far off in the woods where I had run with
beasts as large as horses.

Happy birthday, they sang to me, a chorus washing over me.

My mother didn't sing.

My father didn't either.

They watched.

Thomas said, "You're almost a man now."

Elizabeth said, "He loves you, you know. Thomas. He can't wait
for you to be his witch."

Abel said, "This is your family. These are your people. You are one
of us."

Mark said, "Can I talk to you for a moment?"

I looked up, mouth full of white cake with raspberry filling.

Mark stood next to the table, shuffling his feet. He was fifteen, and
gangly. His wolf was a deep chestnut brown that I liked to run my
fingers over. Sometimes he would nip at my hand. Other times he
would growl deep in his throat, his head near my feet. And one day,
weeks from this moment, he'd stand before me, sweating in a tie.

He still insisted I smelled like dirt and leaves and rain.

It didn't bother me much anymore.

He had nice shoulders. He had a nice face. His eyebrows were
bushy, and when he laughed, it was rusty and sounded like he was
gargling gravel. I liked the way it crawled deep from his belly.

"You should probably keep chewing," Rico whispered to me.
"Because you have cake in your mouth."

Chris squinted at me. "It's also on his chin."

Tanner laughed. "You have frosting on your nose."

I choked the cake down, glaring at them.

They smiled at me.

I used a napkin to wipe my face. "Yeah," I said. "You can talk to me."

He nodded. He was sweating. It made me nervous.

He took me into the trees. Birds called. The leaves twisted on the
branches. Pinecones littered the ground around us.

He didn't speak for a long time.

Then, "I have a present for you."

"Okay."

He turned to look at me. His eyes went from ice to orange, then back again. "It's not the one I want to give you."

I waited.

"Do you understand?"

I shook my head slowly.

He looked frustrated. "Dad says I have to wait before—I just want you to be my—argh. One day I'm going to give you another present, okay? It's going to be the best thing I could ever give you. And I hope you'll like it. More than anything."

"Why can't you give it to me now?"

He scowled. "Because apparently it's not the right time. Thomas could do it, and he—" Mark shook his head. "It doesn't matter. One day. I promise."

I wondered at them sometimes. Thomas and Mark. If Mark was jealous. If he ever wanted what Thomas would become. If he had wanted to be Thomas's second instead of Richard Collins. Mark's mother had died giving birth to him. One moment everything was fine, and the next she was just . . . gone. Only he remained.

Sometimes I thought it was a fair trade. I wanted him here. I had never known her.

I never told anyone that. It felt wrong to say the words out loud.

Mark said, "I brought this for you instead."

In his hand was a little piece of wood. It had been carved by a clumsy hand. It took a moment for me to see what it had been shaped into.

The left wing was smaller than the one on the right. The beak was squarer than anything else. The bird had talons, but they were blocky.

A raven.

He'd carved me a raven.

It looked nothing like the one on my arm. My father had been meticulous, his magic being forced into my skin, burning its way underneath and into my blood. It had been the last thing and had hurt the worst. I had screamed until my voice broke, Abel holding my shoulders down, his eyes on fire.

Somehow, I thought this meant more.

I reached out and traced a finger along a wing. "You made this."

"Do you like it?" he asked quietly.

I said "yes" and "how" and "why, why, why would you do this for me?"

He said, "Because I couldn't give you what I wanted. Not yet. So I want you to have this in its place."

I picked it up, and how Mark *smiled*.

. . .

"Where are we going?" I asked Mom again as we passed a sign that said YOU'RE LEAVING GREEN CREEK PLEASE COME BACK SOON! "I have to—"

"Away," my mother said. "Away, we're going away. While there's still time."

"But it's Sunday. It's *tradition*. They're going to wonder where—"

"*Gordo*."

She never yelled. Not really. Not at me. I flinched.

She gripped the steering wheel. Her knuckles were white. The sun was in our faces. It was bright, and I blinked against it.

I could feel the territory *pulling* at me, the earth around us pulsing along the tattoos. The raven was agitated. Sometimes I thought it would one day just fly from my skin into the sky and never return. I never wanted it to leave.

I pushed my hips up so I could reach into my pocket.

I pulled out a little wooden statue and clutched it in my hands.

Up ahead, a covered bridge led out of Green Creek and into the world beyond. I didn't like to go out into the world very much. It was too big. Abel told me that one day I would have to, because of what I was to Thomas, but that was far away.

We didn't make it to the bridge.

"No," my mother said. "No, no, no, not like this, not like this—"

The car fishtailed slightly to the right as she slammed on the brakes. Dirt kicked up around us, the seat belt pulling at my chest. My neck snapped forward, and I clutched at the wooden raven in my hand. I stared at her with wide eyes. "What happened—"

I looked out the windshield.

Wolves stood on the road. Abel. Thomas. Richard Collins.

My father was there too. He looked furious.

"Listen to me," my mother said, voice low and quick. "They are going to tell you things. Things you shouldn't believe. Things that are *lies*. You can't trust them, Gordo. You can never trust a wolf. They don't love you. They *need* you. They *use* you. The magic in you is a *lie*, and you can't—"

My door jerked open. Thomas reached in and unbuckled my seat belt, then pulled me out of the car as neat as you please. I was shaking as he held me, my legs wrapped around his waist. His big hand was on my back, and he was murmuring in my ear that I was safe, you're safe, Gordo, I've got you, I've got you and no one can take you away again, I promise.

"All right?" Richard asked me. He smiled, but it didn't reach his eyes. It never did.

I nodded against Thomas's shoulder.

"Good," he said. "Mark, he was worried about you. But I suppose that's what happens when someone takes your ma—"

"Richard," Thomas growled.

Richard raised his hands. "Yeah, yeah."

My mother was shouting. My father was talking to her quietly, jabbing a finger pointedly but never touching her.

Abel didn't say a word, just watching. And waiting.

"She's sick," my father told me later. "She has been for a long time. She thinks—she gets these thoughts in her head. It's not her fault. Okay? Gordo, I need you to understand that. It's not her fault. And it's not yours. She would never hurt you. She's just . . . she's sick. And it makes her do things she doesn't want to do. Makes her say things she doesn't want to say. I've tried to help her, but . . ."

My voice was small when I said, "She told me not to trust them. The wolves."

"It's the sickness, Gordo. It's not her."

"Why?"

"Why what?"

"Why is she sick?"

Father sighed. "It happens sometimes."

"Will she get better?"

My father never answered me.

"*Mi abuelo* went crazy," Rico said. "All looney tunes. He gave me candy and money and farted a lot."

Tanner elbowed him in the side.

"She's not crazy," Chris said. "Just sick. Like, the flu or something."

"Yeah," Rico muttered. "The *crazy* flu."

The sounds of the cafeteria echoed around us. I hadn't touched my lunch. I wasn't very hungry.

"It'll be okay," Tanner said. "You'll see."

"Yeah," Chris said. "What's the worst thing that could happen?"

⬩ ⬩ ⬩

There came a scratching at my window in the middle of the night. I should have been scared, but I wasn't.

I got up from my bed and walked to the window. Mark stared at me from the other side.

I pushed the window up. "What are you—"

He jumped inside.

He took me by the hand.

He led me to the bed.

I slept that night, Mark curled around my back.

⬩ ⬩ ⬩

Her name was Wendy.

She worked at the library in the next town over. She had a dog named Milo. She lived in a house near the park. She smiled a lot and laughed very loud. She didn't know about wolves and witches. One time, she went away for months. No one told me why. But she came back. Eventually.

She was young and pretty, and when my mother killed her for being my father's tether, everything changed.

⬩ ⬩ ⬩

"What happens when you lose your tether?" I asked Abel one day when it was just him and me. Sometimes he would put his hand on my shoulder when we walked in the woods, and I felt at peace. "If it's a single person?"

He didn't speak for a long time. I thought he wasn't going to answer.

Then, "If it's illness or disease, a wolf or a witch can prepare themselves. They can rein in their wolf or shore up their magic. They can look to another person. Or a concept. Or an emotion."

"But what if it's not like that? What if you can't prepare?"

He smiled down at me. "That's life, Gordo. You can't always prepare for everything. Sometimes you'll never see it coming. You have to hold on with all of your might and believe that one day, everything will be okay again."

. . . .

"Gordo."

I was still caught in a dream.

"Gordo, come on, you need to wake up. Please, please, please wake *up*."

I opened my eyes.

There was a flare of orange above me in the dark.

"Thomas?"

"You need to listen to me, Gordo. Can you do that?"

I nodded, unsure if I was awake.

"I need you to be strong. And brave. Can you be brave for me?"

I could, because he would one day be my Alpha. I would do anything he asked me. "Yes."

He held out his hand.

I reached out and took what was offered.

He helped me dress before he led me down the hall of the Bennett house. The wood floors creaked underneath our feet. My father had left me here earlier. He'd told me he'd come back for me. I didn't know when I'd fallen asleep.

There were men in the Bennett house. Men I'd never seen before. They wore black suits. They were wolves. Betas. Richard Collins was speaking to them quietly. Elizabeth stood near Mark. He saw me and started toward me, but she put a hand on his shoulder, holding him back.

Abel Bennett stood near the fireplace. His head was bowed.

The strange men grew quiet as Thomas took me to Abel. I could feel their eyes on me, and I did my best not to squirm. This felt important. Bigger than anything that had come before.

The fire popped and crackled.

"I have asked much of you," Abel finally said, "for one so young. I had hoped we would have more time. That the need would never arise, not until Thomas was—" He shook his head before looking down at me. Thomas never left my side. "Do you know who I am, Gordo?"

"My Alpha."

"Yes. Your Alpha. But I am also the Alpha of all the wolves. I have . . . responsibilities. To every pack there is. One day Thomas will have the same responsibilities. Do you understand?"

"Yes."

"It's his calling, much like it's been mine."

Thomas squeezed my shoulder.

"And you, too, have a calling, Gordo," Abel said. "And I am afraid I must ask you to take your place at my side until the day Thomas assumes his rightful place as the Alpha of all."

My skin grew cold. "But my father is—"

Abel looked far older than I'd ever seen. "I have a story to tell you, Gordo. One that you never should have heard in your young life. Will you listen?"

And because I couldn't refuse him anything, I said, "Yes, Alpha."

He told me then.

About a sickness in the mind.

How it could make people do things they didn't want to.

It made them lose control.

It made them angry.

It made them want to hurt other people.

Mom had been kept away. Until she could get better. Until her mind could be cleared. But she'd escaped.

She'd gone to the next town over.

She had gone to the house of a woman named Wendy, a librarian who lived near the park.

A woman who was my father's tether.

Because sometimes, the heart wanted something it should not have.

There was a fight.

Wendy died.

I was drowning.

The eyes of the strange men burned orange.

My father had felt his tether break.

His magic burst. It had made him do a terrible thing.

Later, I would see the footage on the news, even though Abel told me to leave the TV off. Of a neighborhood in a little town in the Cascades leveled to its foundations. People died. Families. Children. My mother.

My father did not.

"Where is he?" I asked numbly.

Abel nodded to one of the strange wolves. He stepped forward. He was tall and moved with grace. His eyes were hard. The very sight of him caused my head to spin. "He will be taken," the strange man said. "Far away from here. His magic will be stripped so he can't hurt anyone again."

"Where?"

The man hesitated. "I'm afraid I can't tell you that. It's for your own safety."

"But—"

"Thank you, Osmond," Abel said.

The man—Osmond—nodded and stepped back with the others. Richard leaned over and whispered in his ear.

You can't trust them, Gordo, she whispered in my ear.

"I will give you time," Abel told me, not unkindly. "To process. To grieve. And I will answer all your questions I can. But we are vulnerable now, Gordo. Your father has taken your mother from you, but he has also taken himself from *us*. We need you now more than ever. I promise that you'll never be alone. That you will always be cared for. But I need you now. To accept your place."

Thomas said, "Dad, maybe we should—"

Abel flashed his eyes. Thomas fell silent. He looked back at me. "Do you understand?"

I felt sick. Nothing made sense. The raven was screaming somewhere in my head.

I said, "No."

"Gordo," Abel said. "You must rise. For your pack. For us. I must ask you to become the witch to the wolves."

•   •   •

Mark held me as my grief exploded.

He whispered promises in my ear that I desperately wanted to believe.

But all I could hear was my mother's voice.

You can't trust a wolf.
They don't love you.
They need you.
They use you.
The magic in you is a lie.

THE SECOND YEAR / IT WAS MIDNIGHT

Joe started speaking less and less as the second year dragged on. It didn't matter, though. We all heard his voice in our heads.

· · · ·

We told ourselves the trail wasn't gone. That Richard Collins was still out there, moving. Planning. We kept our ears to the ground in case anything came up.

One night outside Ottawa, Carter disappeared for hours. He came back smelling of thick perfume, lipstick on the hinge of his jaw.

Kelly was angry at him, asking him how he could be so selfish. How he could even think of fucking some woman when they were all so far from home.

Joe didn't say anything. At least out loud.

I lit a cigarette near the ice machine. The smoke curled up around my head in a blue fog.

"You gonna say something too?" Carter asked me after he'd slammed the motel door behind him.

I snorted. "Not my business."

"Are you sure about that?"

I shrugged.

He leaned against the siding of the motel, eyes closed. "It was something I needed to do."

"I didn't ask."

"You're an asshole, you know that?"

I blew smoke out my nose. "What do you want me to say? That you're right and Kelly's wrong? You're your own man and can do what you want? Or that Kelly has a point and that you should be thinking with your head and not your dick? Tell me, please. Tell me what you want me to say."

He opened his eyes. They reminded me so much of his mother's that I had to look away. "I want you to say *something*. Jesus Christ. Joe's barely talking. Kelly is in one of his goddamn moods. And you're just standing there like you don't give two shits about any of us."

All I wanted to do was have a fucking cigarette in silence. That's all I asked for. "I'm not your father."

That didn't sit well with him. A low rumble rolled from his chest. "No. You're not. He actually cared about us."

"Well, he's not here. I am."

"By choice? Or because you feel guilty?"

I narrowed my eyes at him. "And what the fuck would I have to feel guilty about?"

He pushed himself off the wall. "I don't remember, you know? What happened when the hunters came. I was too little. But my father told me. Because it was my history. He told me what you did. How you tried to save—"

"Don't," I said coldly. "Don't you say another word."

He shook his head. "It's my history, Gordo. But it's yours too. You ran from it. From your *mate*. Mark didn't—"

I was up in his face even before I knew I was moving. My chest bumped against his, but he stood his ground. His eyes were orange, but his teeth were blunt. "You don't know the first goddamn thing about me. If you did, you would know that *I* was the one who stayed behind. *I* was the one who was left in Green Creek while your *father* took off with the pack. I kept the fire burning, but did any of you ever stop to think of what it did to me? You're nothing but a subservient child who doesn't know what the fuck he's doing."

He snarled in my face.

I didn't flinch.

"That's enough." Joe stood in the open doorway to the motel room. It was the first time we'd heard his voice in days.

"We're just—"

"Carter."

He rolled his eyes and pushed past me, stalking back out into the dark.

We listened as his footsteps faded.

"You shouldn't have interrupted us," I told Joe coolly. "It's better to have it out now than to let it fester. It'll hurt more if you don't."

"He's wrong, you know."

"About?"

Joe looked exhausted. "You do care about us."

He closed the door behind him.

I smoked another cigarette. It burned on the way down.

Another full moon. We were in the Salmon-Challis Forest in the middle of Idaho, miles and miles from any signs of civilization. The wolves were hunting. I sat next to a tree, feeling the moon against my skin. My tattoos were brighter than they'd been in a long time.

If I stood then and went to the SUV, it'd take less than two days to get back home.

Green Creek had never felt so far away.

A wolf appeared. Kelly.

He held a rabbit in his mouth, neck broken, hair matted with blood.

He dropped it at my feet.

"I don't know what the hell you want me to do with this," I told him irritably, pushing it away with my foot.

He yipped at me and turned back toward the forest.

Joe came next. Another rabbit.

"For all you know, this kind of rabbit is endangered," I told him. "And you're contributing to its demise."

I felt a burst of color in my head, sunshine bright and warm. Joe was amused. He was laughing. He didn't do that when he was human.

He dropped it at my feet.

"For fuck's sake," I muttered.

He sat next to his brother, facing the trees.

I waited.

Carter came, eventually. He was dragging his feet. He carried a fat gopher in his jaws.

He wouldn't look me in the eye as he dropped it next to the rabbits.

I sighed. "You're an idiot."

He nosed the gopher toward me.

"But so am I."

He looked up slowly.

"Stupid fucking mutts," I said, and there was *sunshine* and *pack* and a tentative question of *??friendfriendfriend??*

I reached out my hand.

He pressed his nose against my palm.

Then his tongue came out and he drooled all over me.

I glared at him as I pulled my hand back.

He cocked his head.

I cooked the rabbits.

The wolves were pleased.

I told them I wasn't going to touch the gopher.

They were less pleased.

Their songs that night were still full of grief and rage, but they had a thread of yellow running through them.

Like the sun.

.   .   .   .

"What are you doing?" Kelly asked me. Another night, another random hotel room somewhere in rural Washington. Carter and Joe were out getting food. We'd spent the past few nights sleeping in the SUV, and I was looking forward to a bed.

But first I needed to get rid of all the excess.

I stood shirtless in the bathroom, staring at the mirror, not recognizing the man who stared back at me. The dark beard on my face was quickly growing out of control. Black hair fell past my ears and curled at my neck. I was bigger too, somehow harder than I'd been before. The full tattooed sleeves on my arms looked stretched far wider than they'd ever been. Roses surrounded the raven, thorns wrapping around its talons. Runes and archaic symbols stretched along my forearms: Romanian, Sumerian, Gaelic. An amalgamation of all those who had come before me. Marks of alchemy, of fire and water, of silver and wind. They had been carved into me by my father over a period of years, the raven being the last.

All except for the one on my chest above my heart. That'd been mine. My choice. It wasn't magic, but it'd been for me.

Kelly saw it. His eyes widened, but he knew better.

A wolf's head, tilted back and baying at the moon.

Buried in the design of his neck was a raven, wings spread and taking flight.

My choice.

Mine alone.

Mine.

I'd kept it covered for so long that I hadn't even thought about it when I'd come in here and stripped off my shirt, wanting to do *something* to keep my skin from crawling.

"You just gonna stare?" I said to Kelly, challenging him.

He shook his head. "I'm just—it doesn't matter. I'll leave you alone."

Goddammit. "I'm thinking."

He looked startled.

"About?"

"I could use a haircut."

He said "yeah" and "me too." He pushed a hand through the thick mop on the top of his head, blond fading darker. He had the beginnings of his own beard, like he hadn't shaved in a week, but it was scraggly and thin. He was just a fucking kid.

I looked down at the cheap set of clippers I'd picked up at our last stop. "Tell you what," I said slowly, thinking of a rabbit left at my feet. "You help me, and I'll help you."

He shouldn't have looked so excited over something so meaningless. "Yeah?"

I shrugged. "Might as well."

He frowned. "But I don't—I've never cut anyone's hair before."

I snorted. "Not cutting. Buzzing. Buzz it all off."

He looked horrified. I almost laughed at him. Almost.

I said, "I'll go first. And then you can tell me if you want me to do it for you."

His hands shook a little as I sat on the toilet. His knees bumped against mine. He looked down at me like he couldn't figure out where to start. "Front to back. Top, and then the sides. We'll save the back for last."

He was still unsure.

I remembered his father standing next to me, hand on my shoulder, and I said, "Hey. You don't have to—"

"I can do this."

"Then do it."

His touch was soft at first, tentative. It felt good and safe, almost like it'd been before Kelly was even alive. When *pack* had meaning, when witches and wolves and hunters hadn't done all they could to take everything from me. I hated how it felt. I leaned into his touch.

It wasn't sexual, not that I wanted it to be. And I sure as shit wasn't Thomas Bennett.

But it was something.

He turned the clippers on.

They buzzed near my ear.

Hair fell onto my shoulders, my lap. To the towel on the floor.

He tilted my head forward and backward. To the side. On and on it went.

He saved the back for last, just as I said.

Eventually he turned the clippers off.

I felt lighter.

I brushed a hand over my head, fingers scraping against the barest of stubble.

He took a step back.

I stood.

The man who stared back in the mirror was harder still. The breadth of his chest. The strength in his arms. A thin layer of dark growth across his skull.

He was a stranger. I wondered if even he knew who he was anymore.

He looked like a wolf.

"Is it okay?" Kelly asked. "I didn't—"

"It's fine," I said, voice rough. "It's . . . fine."

"My turn. I want the same."

I blinked. My reflection blinked back. The tattoos seemed a little brighter then. "Are you sure? I could probably take some scissors and—"

"I want the same," he repeated.

Carter and Joe came back when I was halfway done. Kelly's nostrils flared, and the raven shifted lightly on my arm even before they opened the door.

We ignored them as they called out for us.

"Keep going," Kelly said. "All of it."

"What the fuck," I heard Carter say faintly from the bathroom doorway.

Joe didn't speak.

When I finished, I set the clippers on the counter and reached down to brush off Kelly's shoulders. He stood in front of me until we were eye level. I took him by the chin and turned his head slowly from side to side.

I nodded and took a step back.

He watched himself in the mirror for a long time.

He looked older. I wondered what Thomas would think of the man he'd become. I thought he'd be devastated.

"Do me," Carter demanded. "I want to look like a badass mother-fucker too."

Goddammit.

Joe was last. We stood in that tiny bathroom, his brothers crowding around me, watching him. He reached up slowly and tugged on his hair before looking at his hands. I wondered if he saw the wolf underneath.

"Okay," he said. "Okay."

From then on, every few weeks, we'd do it all over again. And again. And again.

.   .   .

There was a secret pocket in my duffel bag.

I hadn't opened it since we left, no matter how intense the urge.

.   .   .

"When did you know?" Joe asked me in a whisper, his brothers asleep in the back seat, the hum of the tires on pavement the only other sound. We had crossed from Indiana into Michigan an hour before.

"Know what?"

"That Ox was your tether."

My hands tightened on the steering wheel. "Does it matter?"

"I don't know. I think so."

"He was . . . a kid. His father wasn't a good man. I gave him a job because he knew cars, but he wasn't a good man. He took more than he gave. And he didn't—Ox and his mom deserved more. Better than him. He hurt her. With words and with his hands."

A car passed us going in the opposite direction. It was the first one we'd seen in over an hour. Its headlights were bright. I blinked away the afterimage.

"Ox came to me. Needed help, but he didn't know how to ask for it. But I knew. He wasn't mine, but I knew."

"Even back then?"

I shook my head. "No. It was . . . it took longer. Because I didn't know how else to . . . I didn't know how to *be* who I was anymore. I hated wolves, and I hated magic. I had a pack, but it wasn't like it was before."

"The guys from the garage."

I nodded. "They didn't know. They *don't* know, and I hope they never find out. They don't belong here in this world."

"Not like we do. Not like Ox does."

I hated that. "Does he? Don't you ever think what his life would be like if you hadn't found him?"

Joe laughed bitterly. "All the time. Every day. With everything I have. But it was—it was candy canes and pinecones. It was epic and awesome."

Dirt and leaves and rain—

"Is that how you justify it?"

"It's what forces me out of bed when I want nothing more than to fade away."

The yellow lines on the road blurred.

"I gave him a shirt with his name on it. For work. For his birthday. It was wrapped in paper with snowmen on it because it was all I could find." I sighed. "He was fifteen years old. And it was . . . it shouldn't have happened. Not like that. Not without him knowing. But I couldn't stop it. No matter how hard I tried. It just—snapped into place. In a way that it couldn't with Rico. Chris. Tanner. They're my pack. My family. Ox is too, but he's . . ."

"More."

I was helpless in the face of it. "Yeah. More. I guess he is. More than people expect. More than *I* expected. He became my tether after that. Because of a shirt. Because of snowman wrapping paper."

"What was it? Before? Your tether."

"I don't know. Nothing. I didn't—aside from wards, I didn't do magic. I didn't want it. I didn't want any of it."

"Was it Mark, once?"

"Joe," I said, the warning clear in my voice.

Joe stared out at the dark road ahead. "When you don't speak, when you lose your voice, it causes you to focus on everything else. You spend less time worrying about what to say. You hear things you might not have heard before. You see things that would have stayed hidden."

"It's not—"

"They found me. My dad. Mom. After . . . he took me. They found me, and I wanted nothing more than to tell them thank you. Thank you for coming for me just like you said. Thank you for letting me still be your son even though I was cracked right down the middle. But I just . . . couldn't. I couldn't find any words to say, so I said nothing at all. I saw things. That I might not have seen."

"I don't understand."

Joe said, "Carter. He puts up a front. He's big and strong and brave, but when I came home, he cried longer than anyone else. For a long time, he wouldn't let anyone else touch me. He'd carry me everywhere, and if Mom or Dad tried to take me from him, he'd snarl at them until they backed away.

"And Kelly. I had . . . bad dreams. I still do, but not like they used to be. I would close my eyes and Richard Collins would be standing above me again in that dirty cabin in the woods, and he'd be telling me that he was only doing this because of what my father had done, how he'd killed their entire pack, that my father had taken everything away from him. And then he'd break my fingers one by one. Or he'd hit my knee with a hammer. You can't go through what I did and not dream. He was there every time. And when I would wake up, Kelly would be there in the bed next to me, kissing my hair and whispering that I was home, home, home."

A splatter of rain against the windshield. Just a few drops, really.

"Mom and Dad would . . . well. They would treat me as if I was fragile. Like something precious and broken. And maybe I was. To them. But it didn't last, because Dad knew what I was capable of. What I could become. I was home for two months before he carried me on his back out into the trees and told me what it meant to be an Alpha."

He was smiling. I could hear it. God, how it fucking ached.

I knew where he was going. Who was left.

Joe said, "Mark."

"Don't."

"I couldn't figure out what it was. Why he seemed to be with us, but not. There's a signal. It's chemical. It's the scent of what you're feeling. It's like you're . . . sweating your emotions. And he was happy, and he laughed. He could be angry. He was quiet and gruff. But there was always something blue about him. Just . . . blue. It was like when my mother went through her phases. Sometimes she was vibrant. Sometimes she raged. She was fierce and proud and overcome. But then everything would be blue, and I didn't understand. It was azure and indigo and sapphire. It was Prussian and royal and sky. And then it was midnight, and I understood. Mark was midnight. Mark was sad. Mark was *blue*. And it was part of him for as long as I could remember. Maybe it was always there and I just hadn't seen it. But since I couldn't speak for fear of screaming, I watched. And I saw it. It's with us now. On our skin. I can see it in you, but it's buried under all the anger. All the rage."

"You don't know what the fuck you're talking about," I said through gritted teeth.

"I know," he said. "After all, I'm just a kid who has had everything taken from him. What could I possibly understand about loss?"

We didn't speak for a long time after that.

.   .   .

In the border town of Portal, we came across a wolf. He whimpered at the sight of us, leather jackets, the dust of the road on our boots. We were tired and lost, and Joe's nostrils had flared when he pressed the wolf against the side of a building in a back alley. The rain hadn't let up for days.

But the wolf's eyes were violet in the dark.

He said, "Please, let me go. Please don't hurt me. I'm not like them. I'm not like him. I didn't mean to hurt anyone. I should have never gone to Green Creek—"

Carter and Kelly growled, teeth lengthening.

"Why were you in Green Creek?" Joe said, voice soft and dangerous.

The wolf was shaking. "They thought—you were *gone*. There was no Alpha. It was unprotected territory. We—*he*—thought we could get in. That if we took it for our own, Richard Collins would reward us. He would give us anything we wanted, anything we—"

Blood spilled over Joe's hand around his neck.

"Did you hurt them?" he asked.

The Omega shook his head furiously, choking as Joe's grip tightened. "There was only a few of them, but they—oh god, they were a *pack*. They were stronger than we were, and that goddamn human, he said his name was *Ox*—"

"Don't you fucking say his name," Joe snarled in his face. "You don't *get* to say his name."

The Omega whimpered. "There were a few of us that didn't want to be there. I just wanted—all I wanted was to find a pack again, to not— he showed us mercy. He let us crawl out of town. And I ran. I ran as fast as I could, and I promise you I won't go back. Please don't hurt me. Just let me go and you'll never see me again, I swear. I can feel it pulling me down. In my head. I'm losing my mind, but I *swear* you'll never see me again. You'll never—"

For a moment I thought Joe wouldn't listen.

For a moment I thought Joe would tear out the Omega's throat.

I said, "Joe."

He snapped his head toward me. His eyes were red.

"Don't. It's not worth it."

White hair sprouted along his face as he began to shift.

"Is he telling the truth?"

Joe nodded slowly.

"Then Ox let him live. Don't take that away. Not here. Not now. He wouldn't want you to."

The red faded from the Alpha's eyes.

The Omega slumped against the wall, sliding down as he sobbed.

Carter and Kelly led their brother from the alley.

I crouched in front of the Omega. His neck was healing slowly. The blood dripped down onto the collar of his jacket.

The rain poured down.

I said, "There were wolves. With the human."

The Omega nodded slowly.

"A brown wolf. Big."

"Yes," he said. "Yes, yes."

"Was he hurt?"

"I don't—no. I don't think so. Everything happened so fast, it was—"

"Richard Collins. Where is he?"

"I can't—"

"You can," I said, rolling up the right sleeve of my jacket. The rain was cold against my skin. "And you will."

"Tioga," he gasped. "He's been in Tioga. Omegas came to him, and he told them to wait. That the time would come."

I said, "Okay. Hey. Hey. Calm down. I need you to listen to me, okay?"

His eyes were bulging.

"Do you still hear him? Does he still call for you? In your head. Like an Alpha."

"Yeah, yes, I can't, it's so *loud,* it's like there's something more, and he's calling me to him, he's calling for all of us to—"

"Good. Thank you. That's what I needed to hear. Do you know there are mines underneath this town?"

His chest heaved. "Please, please, I won't go to him no matter how hard he calls, no matter what he does, I won't—"

"You're an Omega. It won't matter. Live long enough and you'll lose your mind. You said it yourself."

"No, no, nonono*no*—"

I snapped my fingers in his face. "Focus. I asked you a question. Did you know there are mines under this town?"

His head snapped side to side. It looked painful.

"Just gravel and sand, mostly. But if you dig deep enough, if you go into the earth, you will find things that were missed."

"What the hell are you—"

I pressed my hand flat against the ground. The raven's wings twitched. Two wavy lines on my arm lit up. I breathed in. I breathed out. It was there. I just had to find it. It wasn't the same as it was back home. It was harder here. Green Creek was different. I hadn't realized how much.

"Witch," the Omega hissed.

"Yes," I agreed quietly. "And you just had an Alpha's claws around your throat and lived to tell the tale. You went to my home and were shown mercy. But I am not a wolf. And I'm not exactly human. Veins underneath the earth. Sometimes so deep they will never be found. Until someone like me comes along. And I'm the one you should be scared of. Because I'm the worst of them all."

His eyes turned violet.

He began to shift, face elongated, claws scraping along the brick of the alleyway.

But I'd found the silver in the earth, buried far beneath the surface.

I pulled it up and up and up until a little ball of silver struck my palm, molten and hot. The raven's talons dug into the roses, and I slammed my hand against the side of the Omega's head as he reached for me. The silver entered one side of his head and exited the other.

His shift pulled back.

The violet faded.

He slumped against the brick.

His eyes were wet and unseeing. A drop trickled down his cheek. I told myself it was the rain.

I stood, knees popping. I was getting too old for this shit.

I turned and left the Omega behind, rolling down the sleeve of my jacket.

I felt the beginnings of a headache coming on.

The others were waiting for me at the SUV. "What did he say?" Carter demanded. "Did he know—"

"Tioga. I saw it on the map earlier. It's an hour away. Richard was there. Might still be."

"What did you do with the Omega?" Kelly asked, sounding nervous. "He's okay, right? He's—"

"He's fine," I told them. I'd learned a long time ago how to lie to wolves. And the rain would have muffled the sound of his heartbeat. "He won't be bothering us again. Probably across the border already."

Joe stared at me.

I didn't blink.

He said, "Kelly, it's your turn to drive."

And that was it.

. . .

It was in Tioga that Joe lost control.

Because Richard *had* been there. His scent was all over a motel outside of town, and while it was faded, it was *there*, buried under all the Omega stink. We had been so close. So goddamn close.

Joe howled until his voice broke.

His claws tore into walls.

His teeth shredded the bed.

Kelly huddled at my side.

Carter's face was in his hands as his shoulders shook.

Joe only pushed back the wolf when sirens sounded in the distance.

We left Tioga behind.

After that day, Joe spoke less and less.

. . .

Toward the end of that second year, on a day when I thought I couldn't take another step, I opened the secret pocket in my duffel bag.

Inside was a wooden raven.

I stared at it.

I stroked one of its wings. Just once.

The wolves slept, dreaming their dreams of moons and blood.

And when I finally closed my eyes, all I saw was blue.

ABOMINATIONS

Six months after I turned thirteen, I kissed Mark Bennett for the first time.

Seven months after I turned thirteen, hunters came and killed everyone.

But before then:

"She's pregnant," Thomas whispered to me.

I stared at him in shock.

His smile was blinding.

"*What?*"

He nodded. "I wanted you to know before anyone else."

"Why?"

"Because you're my witch, Gordo. And my friend."

"But—Richard, and—"

"Oh, I'll tell him. But it's you, okay? It'll be you and me forever. We are going to be our own pack. I will be your Alpha, and you will be my witch. You're my family, and I hope my child will be yours too."

Somehow, my heart was mending.

I worried, briefly, when I breached the surface of my grief, what would happen to me. I was only twelve, and my mother was dead, my father was imprisoned in a place where he could never escape, and I was alone.

It'd been all over the news for weeks. This poor little town where a major gas leak had taken place, leveling an entire neighborhood. Sixteen people had lost their lives, forty-seven more injured. A freak accident, investigators said. It was a one-in-a-million thing. It never should have happened. We will rebuild, the governor said. We will not abandon you. We will mourn those lost, but we will come back from this.

My mother and father were counted among those deceased. My mother had been identified by her teeth. No trace of my father had ever been found, but the fire had burned so hotly that that was expected. We're sorry, I was told. We wish we could tell you more.

I nodded but didn't speak. Abel's hand was a heavy weight on my shoulder.

And under the next full moon, I became the witch of the most powerful pack in North America.

There was pushback, of course. I was so young. I had just been through a significant trauma. I needed time to heal.

Elizabeth was the loudest of all of them.

Abel listened. He was the Alpha. It was his job to listen.

But he sided against those who would shield me.

"He has his pack," Abel said. "We will help him heal. All of us. Isn't that right, Gordo?"

I didn't say a word.

.   .   .

It didn't hurt. I thought it would. I didn't know why. Maybe it was because the tattoos had hurt, or maybe because all I knew was pain when I opened my eyes every morning, but I still expected more.

But underneath the moon, with a dozen wolves standing before me, eyes glowing, I became their witch.

And it was *more*.

I could *hear* them, louder than I ever had before.

They said, *ChildBrotherPack*.

They said, *LoveOursWitchOurs*.

They said, *We will keep you safe we will keep you with us you are ours you are pack you are Son LoveBrotherHome*.

They said, *Mine*.

.   .   .

"Dude," Rico said, standing in an ill-fitting suit and hand-me-down tie, "this sucks."

I stared down at my hands.

"Like, really sucks."

I lifted my head to glare at him.

"Qué chingados."

Whatever that meant.

Tanner and Chris came back over to us, arms laden with food. We were at the Bennett house. We'd buried my mother. Had an empty casket for my father. Elizabeth told me a wake was another tradition. People brought food and ate until they could eat no more.

I wanted to go to bed.

Tanner's mouth was full. "Dude, they have these little sandwiches that have *eggs* in them."

"So I can smell," Rico said.

Chris handed me some kind of bread. "I don't know what this is. But it has nuts in it. And my mom says nuts don't let you be sad."

"That's not a thing," Rico said.

"That sounds nuts," Tanner said. "Get it? Because of the—yeah. You get it."

We all gaped at him. He shrugged and ate more egg sandwich.

"Where's mine?" Rico asked.

"I brought you a taquito," Chris said.

"That's racist."

"But you like taquitos!"

"Maybe I wanted the crazy nut bread! I'm sad too!"

"You're all so stupid."

They grinned down at me. "Oh look," Rico said. "It speaks."

I cried then. For the first time that day. With a hand full of nut bread and surrounded by my best friends, I cried.

. . .

Abel and Thomas handled everything. No social worker came to try to take me away. School wasn't disrupted. Our house was sold, and all the money was put away in a savings account I never touched. There was life insurance too, for the both of them. I didn't care about the money. Not then. I barely understood what was going on.

I moved into the Bennett house. I had my own room. I had all my own things.

It wasn't the same.

But I had no other choice.

The wolves sheltered me from the rest of the world even as they hid things from me.

But I found out. Eventually.

. . .

Mark refused to leave my side.

On the nights when I couldn't stand the sight of another person, he would stay outside my door.

Sometimes I would let him in.

He would motion for me to turn around, facing away from him. I did.

On those nights, the hard ones, I would hear the rustle of clothes being discarded. The snap and groan of muscle and bone.

He would nuzzle my hand when I could turn back around.

I would climb into bed, and he would jump up beside me, the bed-frame groaning under the combined weight. He would curl around me, my head under his chin, his tail covering my legs.

Those were the nights I slept the best.

Marty was smoking a cigarette in the back of the shop when I came back for the first time.

He arched an eyebrow at me as he ashed the cig onto the ground.

I shuffled my feet.

"Couldn't go to the funeral," he said. "Wanted to, but a couple of the guys called in sick. Flu or some shit." He coughed wetly before spitting something green on the asphalt.

"Yeah," I said. "It's okay."

"Thought about you."

It was nice of him to say. "Thanks."

He blew out a thick plume of rank smoke. He always rolled his own cigarettes, and the pungent tobacco made my eyes water. "My dad died when I was a baby. Mom hung herself when I was fourteen. Took to the road after that. Didn't take any handouts."

"I don't want anything."

He scratched his scruffy jaw. "No, I don't expect you do. Can't pay you much."

"I don't need much."

"Yeah, you got those Bennetts in your pocket, don't ya."

I shrugged because no matter what I said, he wouldn't understand.

He stubbed out the cigarette on the bottom of his boot before dropping it into a metal coffee can already filled to the brim with discarded butts. He coughed again before leaning forward in his lawn chair, the white and green and blue nylon fraying. "I'll work your ass off. Especially if I'm paying you."

I nodded.

"And if that Abel Bennett tries to give me hell, I'll drop you fast. We clear?"

"Yeah. Yes."

"All right. Let's get your hands dirty."

I knew then what the wolves meant when they said that a tether didn't have to be a person.

"Look at her," Rico said, sounding awed.

We looked.

Misty Osborn. Her hair was crimped, and she had big front teeth. She laughed loudly and was one of the popular girls in the eighth grade.

"I like older women," Rico decided.

"She's thirteen," Chris said.

"You're twelve," Tanner said.

I said nothing. It was warm, and my sleeves were long.

"I'm going to ask her to the dance," Rico said, looking as if he was steeling himself.

"Are you *insane?*" Chris hissed at him. "She would *never* go with you. She likes jocks."

"And you're really not a jock," Tanner pointed out.

"Just gotta change her mind," Rico said. "Not that hard. Make her see behind my skinny nonjock body. Just you watch."

We watched as he stood from the lunch table.

He marched over to her.

The girls around her giggled.

We couldn't hear what he was saying, but from the look on Misty's face, it wasn't anything good.

He nodded a lot. Waved his arms around like a lunatic.

Misty frowned.

He pointed at her, then back at himself.

Misty frowned even more.

She said something.

Rico came back to the table and sat down. "She said my English was very good for someone born in another country. I've decided she's a jerk and not deserving of my love and devotion."

Tanner and Chris glared at her from across the lunchroom.

When she stood to leave, tossing her hair, my fingers twitched. Her metal lunch table jerked to the left, knocking her in the leg. She tripped and fell, her face in Tuesday's lumpy mashed potatoes.

Rico laughed. That was important to me.

They talked about girls sometimes, Rico more than the others. He loved the way they smelled and their tits, and sometimes he said they gave him a boner.

"I'm going to get so many girlfriends," he said.

"Me too," Chris said. "Like, four of them."

"That sounds like so much work," Tanner said. "Can't you just have one and be happy with it?"

I didn't talk about girls. Not even then.

We were out behind the house, Mark and me.

He was saying, ". . . and when I shifted for the first time, I scared myself so badly, I shit myself. Surrounded by everyone, I just shit. I squatted down like a dog and everything. That's when I think Thomas decided he wanted Richard to be his second instead of me."

I laughed. It felt strange, but I did it anyway.

Mark was watching me.

"What?" I asked, still chuckling.

He shook his head slowly. "Uh—nothing. I just—it's nice. Hearing you. Like this. I like it. When you laugh."

Then he blushed furiously and looked away.

I carried the wooden raven wherever I went. Whenever I couldn't breathe, I would squeeze it until it pressed into my flesh. There would be an imprint in my palm for hours.

One time the wing cut me, and I bled on it.

I hoped it would leave a scar.

It didn't.

Osmond came back to Green Creek. Men in suits followed him. He wanted to speak to Abel and Thomas. He didn't want me there.

Abel ignored him. "Gordo, if you please."

I followed them into Abel's office.

The door shut behind us.

"He's a child," Osmond said as if I wasn't in the room.

"He's the witch to the Bennett pack," Abel said evenly. "And he belongs here as much as anyone. And even if I didn't insist upon it, my son would."

Thomas nodded without speaking.

"Now that that's out of the way," Abel said, settling in behind his desk, "what brings you to my home that a phone call wouldn't have sufficed?"

"Elijah."

"I don't know any Elijah."

"No, you wouldn't. But you would know her by her true name."

"And I wait with bated breath."

"Meredith King."

And for the very first time, I saw something akin to fear on Abel Bennett's face. "Now that is something I did not expect. She's . . . she'd be Thomas's age, wouldn't she?"

Osmond looked unfazed. "She has picked up the mantle of her father."

"Dad?" Thomas asked. "What is he talking about? Who is—"

Abel smiled thinly. "You would have been too young to remember. The Kings were . . . well. They were a rather aggressive clan of hunters. They believed all wolves were an affront to God and it was their duty to rid them from the earth. They came for my pack. And we made sure very few walked away." His eyes flashed red. "The patriarch, Damian King, was gravely injured. He lived, but barely. As did his son, Daniel. The rest of his clan did not. Meredith was his other child, but she would've only been around twelve at the time. But it seems as if she's decided to resume her father's work." He looked back at Osmond. "Elijah. How curious."

"A prophet of Yahweh," Osmond said. "A god from the Iron Age in the Kingdom of Israel. Yahweh performed miracles through Elijah. Raising the dead. Raining fire down from the sky. At Jesus's side during his Transfiguration on the mountaintop."

"A little on the nose," Abel said. "Even for the Kings. Wasn't there another brother as well?"

"David," Osmond said. "Though he was shunned because he no longer had the will to hunt."

Abel nodded slowly. "How surprising. And this Elijah?"

"She is killing wolves."

Abel sighed. "How many so far?"

"Two packs. One in Kentucky. Another in North Carolina. Fifteen in total. Three of them children."

"And why has she not been contained?"

Osmond wasn't pleased. "She remains underground. We've dispatched teams after her, but her clan is elusive. They are small in number, but they move quickly."

"And what do you ask of me?"

"You're our leader," Osmond said. "I'm asking you to *lead*."

.   .   .

Osmond left unfulfilled. But before he did, I stopped him on the porch.

He looked down at me with barely disguised disdain.

I dropped my hand. "Can I—"

"Your father."

I nodded.

Osmond stepped away from me. I thought his teeth were longer than they'd been just a moment before. "He won't bother anyone ever again. His magic has been stripped. Robert Livingstone was strong, but we tore it from his skin. He is nothing but a shell."

Osmond left me standing on the porch.

Standing next to his car was Richard Collins.

He was smiling.

.   .   .

I turned thirteen, and Mark put his arm around my shoulders.

It caused my stomach to twist.

I wondered if that was why I didn't stare at girls like Rico.

His nose was in my hair, and he was smiling.

I never wanted it to stop.

.   .   .

My mother was buried near a red alder tree. Her stone was small and white.

It said,

CATHERINE LIVINGSTONE
SHE WAS LOVED

I sat with my back against the tree and felt the earth beneath my fingertips.

"I'm sorry," I told her once. "I'm sorry that I couldn't do more."

Sometimes I pretended she answered me.

She said, "I love you, Gordo. I love you."

She said, "I am so proud of you."

She said, "Why didn't you believe me?"

She said, "Why didn't you save me?"

She said, "You can't trust them, Gordo. You can never trust a wolf. They don't love you. They *need* you. The magic in you is a lie—"

My fingers dug into the earth.

Carter was wrinkled and pink and screamed a tiny scream.

I touched his forehead and he opened his eyes, quieting down almost immediately.

Elizabeth said, "Would you look at that. He likes you, Gordo." She smiled at me, skin pale, tired as I'd ever seen her. But still she *smiled*.

I leaned down and whispered in his little ear, "You will be safe. I promise. I'll help keep you safe."

A tiny fist pulled on my hair.

When I kissed Mark Bennett for the first time, it wasn't planned. It wasn't something I set out to do. I was awkward. My voice broke more often than not. I was moody and had a small hair on my chest that didn't seem to know if it was coming or going. I had zits and unnecessary erections. I accidentally blew up a lamp in the living room when I was angry for no apparent reason.

And Mark Bennett was everything I was not. He was sixteen and ethereal. He moved with grace and purpose. He was smart and funny and still had a tendency to follow me wherever I went. He brought me food while I was at the shop, and the guys gave me shit. Marty would holler that my *boy* was here, and I had fifteen minutes or he was going to fire me. Mark's nostrils would flare as I approached, and he would watch me as I rubbed grease from my fingertips with an old cloth I kept in my back pocket. He would say hey, and I'd say hey back, and we'd sit outside the garage, our backs against brick, our legs crossed. He'd hand me a sandwich he'd made. He always watched me eat it.

It wasn't planned. How could it be when I didn't know what it would mean?

It was a Wednesday in the summer. Carter was crawling and babbling. No other wolves had been hurt by the woman known as Elijah. The pack was happy and healthy and whole. Abel was a proud Alpha, doting on his grandson. Thomas preened. Elizabeth rolled her eyes. The wolves ran under the light of the moon and smiled in the sun.

The world was a bright and brilliant place.

My heart still hurt, but the sharp ache was fading. My mother was gone. My father was gone. My mother had said the wolves would lie, but I trusted them. I had to. Aside from Chris and Tanner and Rico and Marty, they were all I had left.

But then there was Mark, Mark, Mark.

Always Mark.

My shadow.

I found him in the woods behind the pack house.

He said, "Hey, Gordo."

And I said, "I want to try something."

He blinked. "Okay."

"Okay?"

He shrugged. "Okay."

There were bees in the flowers and birds in the trees.

He was sitting with his back to a big-leaf maple. His bare feet were in the grass. He wore a loose tank top, his tan skin almost the color of his wolf. His fingernails were bitten, a habit he had yet to break. He brushed a lock of hair from his forehead. He looked happy and carefree, an apex predator who feared little. He watched me, curious what I was on about but not pushing it.

"Close your eyes," I said, unsure of what I was doing. What I was capable of.

He did, because I was his friend.

I got to my knees and shuffled toward him.

My heart thundered in my chest.

My skin was sweaty.

The raven fluttered.

I leaned forward and pressed my lips to his.

It was warm and dry and catastrophic.

His lips were slightly chapped. I would never forget that.

I didn't move. Neither did he.

Just the slightest of kisses on a warm summer day.

I pulled away.

His chest heaved.

His opened his eyes. They were orange.

He said, "Gordo, I—"

His breath was harsh against my face.

I said, "I'm sorry, I'm sorry, I didn't mean—"

He put his hand over my mouth. My eyes felt like they were bulging.

"You have to mean it," he said quietly. "You have to be sure."

I didn't understand. Mark was my friend, and I—

"Gordo," he said, eyes still alight. "There's—I can't—"

He stood before I could blink. I fell back on my ass.

Then he was gone.

⁎　⁎　⁎

Thomas found me later. The sky above was streaked orange and pink and red.

He sat beside me.

He said, "I was seventeen when I met a girl who took my breath away." He was smiling, staring off into the trees.

I waited.

He said, "There was . . . there wasn't anything like her. She . . ." He chuckled as he shook his head. "I knew then. Elizabeth disliked me on sight, and Dad said I needed to respect that. Because women needed to be respected. Always. Regardless of what I thought, I could never force her into anything she didn't want. And I *knew* that, of course. Because to even think otherwise was terrible. So I became her friend. Until one day, she smiled at me and I—it was everything. I'd never seen anyone smile at me like that before. She was my . . ."

"Mate," I said.

Thomas shrugged. "I never really liked that word. It doesn't encompass all that she is. She is the best part of me, Gordo. She loves me for who I am. She's fierce and sharp and doesn't let me get away with anything. She holds me up. She points out my faults. And honestly, if the world was fair, she would be the next Alpha and not me. She'd be better at it. Better than my father. Better than anyone. I'm very lucky to have her. The day I gave her my stone wolf was the most nerve-racking day of my life."

"Because you thought she'd say no?"

"Because I thought she'd say yes," he corrected gently. "And if she did, it would mean that I was going to have someone at my side for the rest of my days. I didn't know if I deserved that. And Mark feels the same way. He's been waiting for this moment for a long time. He's . . . scared."

I blinked. "Of what? What does that have to do with you and Elizabeth—"

It hit hard.

I said, "Wait."

I said, "Hold up."

I said, "Are you saying what I think you're—"

I said, *"What."*

. . .

I ignored Mark for three days.

Dead animals appeared on the front porch.

Elizabeth laughed at me, swaying with Carter in her arms.

. . .

"Why didn't you tell me?" I shouted at him.

"You're *thirteen,*" he growled at me. "I'm three years older than you. It's *illegal.*"

"That's—okay, that's actually a pretty good argument."

He looked smug.

I narrowed my eyes at him.

He looked less smug.

"I'm not a child."

"That's probably not the best rebuttal since *yes, you are.*"

"Fine," I said. "Then maybe I'll just go kiss someone else."

He growled.

. . .

"I need to find someone to kiss," I demanded.

Rico and Tanner and Chris stared at me with wide eyes.

"Not it," Tanner said.

"Not it," Carter said.

"Not—goddammit." Rico sighed. "I never say it fast enough. Fine. You know what? I don't even care. Pucker up, lover boy."

I stared at Rico in horror as he started walking toward me, arms outstretched.

"Not *you*."

"Wow. Racist much? *Puto*."

"I'm not *racist*—you're my—god, I *hate* this so fucking much!"

"Mark?" Tanner asked sympathetically.

"Mark," Chris agreed.

"If I was white, I bet you would have kissed me," Rico said.

I grabbed him by the face and pressed my lips against his.

Tanner and Chris made matching sounds of extraordinary disgust.

I pulled away from Rico with a wet smack.

He looked dazed.

I felt better.

      .   .   .

I told Mark.

He shifted, clothes tearing as he fled into the woods.

"You're kind of a dick, Gordo," Abel said mildly. "When you're old enough, know that I approve wholeheartedly."

      .   .   .

I was on front-desk duty when a young woman came into the shop.

She smiled at me.

She was pretty. Her hair was black as night and her eyes as green as the forest. She wore jeans and a low-cut blouse. She looked barely older than Mark.

The guys in the garage whistled.

Marty told them to shut the hell up, though his eyes lingered appreciatively too.

"Hello," she said.

"Can I help you?" I asked, nervous for reasons I didn't understand.

"I hope so," she said. "My car's making a funny noise. Just drove it across the country. Trying to get to Portland for school, but I don't know if I'm going to make it."

I nodded. "We can probably get you in quick enough." I clicked on the old computer in front of me and opened the scheduling program.

She looked amused. "Aren't you a little young to be working here?"

I shrugged. "I know what I'm doing."

"Do you. How sweet." Her smile widened. She leaned forward, elbows on the counter. Her nails were painted blue. They were chipped. She tapped them against the counter. A small silver cross hung on a thin chain around her neck. "Gordo, is it?"

I looked up at her sharply. "How did you know that?"

She laughed. It sounded sweet. "Your name's stitched on your shirt."

I flushed. "Oh, right."

"You're cute."

"Thank you? Um, it looks like I have an opening in an hour. I could squeeze you in if you don't mind waiting?"

"I don't mind." Her eyes were bright.

She reminded me of a wolf.

.   .   .

Mark came and brought me lunch.

She was sitting in the waiting room, flipping through an ancient magazine.

The bell rang overhead as he walked in.

"Hi," he said, sounding shy. It was the first time he'd come in since the whole *you-kissed-me-and-then-I-ran-because-of-wolfish-feelings-as-you're-my-mate-and-I-neglected-to-tell-you* fiasco.

"Look who decided to show up," I said.

I barely remembered the woman was there.

"Shut up," Mark mumbled, setting a brown paper bag on the counter.

"It's not a dead rabbit, is it?" I asked him suspiciously. "Because I swear to god, Mark, if it's another dead—"

"It's ham and swiss."

"Oh. Well, that's better."

"Dead rabbit?" the woman said.

Mark flinched. I jerked my head toward her.

She arched an eyebrow at us.

I said, "Inside joke."

She said, "Huh."

Mark's nostrils flared.

I pinched his arm to remind him he was in *public,* for fuck's sake. He couldn't go around sniffing everyone.

He looked at her for a moment longer before turning back to me.

"Thank you," I told him.

He preened just a little.

He was so predictable.

.   .   .

"Take me a couple of days to get the parts in," Marty told her. "Won't take long to get it fixed once in, but your car is German-made. Don't see those around here much. You could drive it, but I can't guarantee you won't make the problem worse and break down in the middle of nowhere. You're in the country, girlie."

"So I noticed," she said slowly. "That's . . . unfortunate. I did see a motel on my way into town."

He nodded. "It's clean. You tell Beth I sent you. She'll give you a discount. Green Creek is small, but we're good people. We'll treat you right."

She laughed, eyes twinkling. She glanced at me again before looking back at Marty. "I suppose we'll see."

.   .   .

That night Abel sat on the porch, waving as members of his pack arrived for the full moon the next night. He looked content.

"Gordo," he said as I came out to tell him dinner was almost ready, "come here for a moment."

I went.

He put his hand on my shoulder.

And for a while, we just . . . were.

.   .   .

The last supper.

We didn't know it.

We gathered and laughed and shouted and stuffed ourselves full.

Mark pressed his foot against mine.

I thought of many things. My father. My mother. The wolves. The pack. Mark and Mark and Mark. It was a choice, I knew. I might have been born into this life, this world, but I had a choice. And no one would take that from me.

I wondered when Mark would offer me his wolf.

I wondered what I would say.

I felt weighted and real and tethered.

Thomas winked at me.

Elizabeth cooed over the child in her arms.

Abel smiled.

Mark leaned over and whispered, "This is us. This is our pack. This is our happiness. I want this. With you. One day, when we've both grown up."

.   .   .

She was in the diner when I went in the next morning, my turn to get coffee for the guys. She was sitting in a booth alone, her head bowed in prayer, hands folded in front of her. She looked up the moment I stepped into the diner.

"Gordo," she said. "Bright and early."

"Hello," I said. "How're you . . ." I blanked on her name.

"Elli," she said.

"Elli. How are you?"

She shrugged. "I'm okay. It's . . . quiet here. It takes some getting used to."

"Yeah," I said, unsure of what else to say. "It's always like that."

"Always? I don't know how you can stand it."

"I've been here all my life."

"Have you? Curious."

A waitress waved at me from behind the lunch counter, moving to get the coffees ready.

I started to walk toward her when a hand closed around my wrist.

I looked down. The nails had been repainted. They were red.

"Gordo," Elli said. "Can you do me a favor?"

I breathed in and out. "Sure."

She smiled. It didn't quite reach her eyes. "Can you pray with me? I have been trying all morning, and for the life of me, I can't quite get it right. I think I need help."

"I'm not the best person to—"

"Please." Her grip on my arm loosened.

"Uh, sure."

"Thank you," she said. "Sit down, if you don't mind."

"I don't have long. I gotta get to work."

"Oh," she said, "it won't take long. I promise."

I slid into the booth across from her. The diner was empty aside from the two of us. The breakfast rush had already passed, and lunch wouldn't start for a few hours. Jimmy was behind the grill, and the waitress—Donna—was standing in front of the coffee machine.

Elli smiled. She brought her hands in front of her, folding them together. She looked down at mine as if encouraging me to do the same.

I slowly lifted my hands in front of me. The cuffs of my work shirt slid down my wrists a little.

"Dearest Father," she said, eyes on me, "I am but your humble servant, and I seek your guidance. I have found myself in a moment of crisis. You see, Father, there are things in this world, things that take away from your natural order. Abominations that go against everything you stand for. I have been tasked under your will to strike these abominations down where they stand.

"By the power of your Holy Spirit, reveal to me, Father, any people I need to forgive and any areas of unconfessed sin. Reveal aspects of my life that are not pleasing to you, Father, ways that have given or could give Satan a foothold in my life. Father, I give to you any unforgiveness, I give to you my sins, and I give to you all ways that Satan has a hold of my life. Thank you for your forgiveness and your love.

"My Father, in your Holy Name, I bind all evil spirits of the air, water, ground, underground, and netherworld. I further bind, in Jesus's name, any and all emissaries of the satanic headquarters and claim the precious blood of Jesus on the air, atmosphere, water, ground, and their fruits around us, the underground and the netherworld below."

I moved to stand.

Her hand snatched out and grabbed my wrist again.

"Don't," she said. "You would do well, Gordo Livingstone, to *stay where you are.*"

"Okay, Gordo?" Donna asked as she brought a tray of coffees over to me.

I nodded slowly. "Just a prayer."

The woman across from me smiled.

Donna looked unsure, but she set the tray down. "It's already on the tab. You tell Marty he needs to square up by the end of the month, okay?"

"Yeah," I said. "I'll tell him."

Donna turned and walked away.

"Elijah," I said quietly.

"Good," she said. "That's real good, Gordo. You're so *young*." She took my hand and pressed her lips against it. I felt the quick flick of her tongue against my skin. "You know only the ways of the beast. They have indoctrinated you early. It's a shame, really. I don't know if you can yet be saved. I suppose only time will tell if there can be a cleansing. A baptism in the waters of salvation."

"He'll know," I said quietly. "That you're here. In his territory."

"You see, that's where you're *wrong*," she said. "I am not an Alpha. Or a Beta. Or an Omega." She cocked her head at me. "I am not you."

"You know what I am."

"Yes."

"Then you should know what I'm capable of."

She chuckled. "You are nothing but a child. What could you possibly—"

I reached up with my free hand and pulled back my sleeve.

She stared down at the raven surrounded by roses with something akin to awe. "I had heard, but—" She shook her head. "I am sorry for what has happened to you. That you didn't have a choice in the matter."

"I could scream," I told her. "I could scream right now. A woman grabbing a boy like you are. You wouldn't get far."

"Aren't you a feisty one. Tell me, Gordo, do you really think you can outsmart me?"

"I know what you are."

She leaned forward. "And what am I?"

"A hunter."

"Of? Say it, Gordo."

"Wolves."

She stroked my arm. "Good. That's good, Gordo. Scream if you want. Scream as loud as you can. In the end, it won't matter. Not this close to the full moon. Because even now, a pack of wolves has gathered in the woods to revel in their bloodlust. Monsters, Gordo. They are nothing but monsters who have sunk their teeth and claws deep into you. I will free you from them."

My head felt stuffed, my skin hot. "You won't get close."

She grinned. She looked like a shark. She let go of my arm and reached down into her lap. She pulled up a small walkie-talkie and set it on the table between us. She pressed the button. It beeped once. "Carrow," she said.

She let the button go.

There was a crackle of static.

Then, "Carrow here, over."

She said, "Are you in position? Over."

"Yes, ma'am. Ready. Over."

"And the wolves? Over."

"Here. Gathered in the clearing. Over."

"And you have them surrounded? Over."

"Yes. Ah—there's, ah. Children. Over."

She nodded slowly. "All of age," she said. "They have been lost to their wolves."

"Don't do this," I said. "Please don't do this."

Meredith King said, "It is my duty. By the grace of God, I shall wipe them from this earth. Tell me, Gordo. Do you love him?"

"Who?" There were tears in my eyes.

"That boy. The one who came to see you yesterday. The wolf. I thought he would smell it on me. The blood of the others. But you distracted him quite nicely. Do you love him?"

"Fuck you."

She shook her head. "The other packs. They didn't have a witch. They were . . . easy. But I have been building toward this moment. This day. Here. Now. Because if you cut off the head, the body dies. The king. The prince. You will thank me. In the end."

I placed my hands on the table, palms up.

She shifted in her seat and—

A sharp pain in my wrist, like a bee sting in the middle of summer.

I looked down.

She withdrew her hand, the syringe already hidden away.

I said, "No, you can't do this, you canna do thissss pleassse it's not—"

The colors of the world around me began to bleed.

Everything slowed down.

I heard words of concern coming from somewhere far, far away.

"Oh now," the hunter Elijah said in response. "He was jusssst feeling a little sssssick. I'll help him. I'll get himmmmmmmm—"

It was dark, after.

.   .   .

I dreamed I was with the wolves.

We ran, and the trees were tall and the moon was bright, and I belonged to them and with them, and I tilted my head back and *sang*.

But the wolves didn't sing with me.

No.

They screamed.

.   .   .

I woke slowly.

My tongue felt thick in my mouth.

I opened my eyes.

I was lying in the forest.

The canopy above me gave way to the stars in the sky. The moon was fat and full.

I pushed myself up.

My head ached. I could barely think through it.

A whimper off to my left.

I turned.

A large brown wolf was crawling toward me. Its back legs had been broken. Its coat was matted with blood. It was in obvious pain, but still it dragged itself toward me in the dirt and the grass.

I said, "Mark."

The wolf whined.

I reached for him.

He licked the tips of my fingers before he collapsed, eyes closed.

The fog cleared.

I felt it then. The broken shards within me. As if I'd been shattered into pieces. It wasn't like when my mother had died. When my father had killed her.

It was more.

It was so much more.

"No," I whispered.

Later, when Mark had healed enough to stand on his own, we moved through the woods.

He led the way, limping awkwardly.

Everything hurt.

Everything.

The forest wept around us.

I could feel it in the trees. In the ground beneath my feet. In the wind. The birds were crying, and the forest shook.

My tattoos were dull and faded.

A human man lay next to a tree. He wore body armor. There was a rifle at his feet. His throat had been ripped out. He stared sightlessly into nothing.

Mark growled.

We moved on.

I reached through the bonds of *packpackpack*, but they were broken.

I said, "Oh god, Mark, oh god."

He rumbled deep in his chest.

We found the clearing. Somehow.

The air smelled of silver and blood.

Humans lay on the ground, mangled and gored.

And wolves. So many wolves. All shifted.

All dead.

The bigger ones.

The smaller ones.

I cried out at the anguish of it all, trying to find someone, anyone who—

Movement off to the right.

A woman stood there, pale in the moonlight. She held a baby.

Elizabeth Bennett said, "Gordo."

Two wolves were at her side.

Richard Collins.

And—

Thomas Bennett moved toward me. His wolf was bigger than I'd ever seen it before. His eyes never left me. Every step he took was slow and deliberate. When he stood in front of me, I understood all that we had lost.

And what he had gained.
His eyes flared red in the deep, dark night.
Through my horror, I said the only thing I could.
Alpha.

THE THIRD YEAR / NOT YET

Some nights I dreamed of the moon and blood and Mark dragging his broken body toward me.

Other nights I dreamed of kissing him on a warm summer afternoon.

"You say his name, sometimes," Carter told me once.

"Who?"

"Mark."

"I have no idea what you're talking about."

He rolled his eyes. "Yeah, okay, Gordo. Sure you don't."

"I will fucking turn your tongue to silver if you don't shut up, Carter. I swear to god."

He grinned at me, waggling his eyebrows. "Is it *those* kind of dreams? You know, the ones where you and Mark are all rubbing on each—you know what, I just realized that's my uncle and I'm going to stop talking now."

Kelly gagged.

Joe stared out the window.

Goddamn Thomas for leaving me with these assholes.

.   .   .

There were stretches of days and weeks when we'd be spinning our wheels.

We ate shitty diner food in Bonners Ferry, Idaho.

We slept in a ramshackle motel on the outskirts of Bow Island, Alberta.

The wolves left massive paw prints in the dunes of the Great Sandhills.

We drove along lonely stretches of road in Nowhere, Montana.

Some days we didn't speak for hours and hours.

Then there were the other days.

.   .   .

"What do you think they're doing right now?" Kelly asked, feet up on the dash. His head was against the headrest, face turned toward his brother.

Carter was silent for a long time. Then, "It's Sunday."

"I know."

"There's tradition."

"Yeah. Yeah, Carter."

He said, "Mom's probably in the kitchen. There's music playing in the background. A record on her old record player. She's dancing. Slow. And she's singing along."

"What song?"

"I don't—maybe Peggy Lee. That . . . sounds right."

"Yeah. It does. Peggy Lee singing 'Johnny Guitar.'"

I didn't move as Kelly's voice broke. His brother did. He reached across the console and took Kelly by the hand. The tires rolled against the cracked pavement. I didn't look away. I was enraptured by the sight in front of me. Somewhere to my right, Joe breathed but didn't speak.

"'Johnny Guitar,'" Carter agreed. "I always liked that song. And Peggy Lee."

"Me too," Kelly said, sniffling quietly. "She's real pretty. Song is sad, though."

"You know how Mom is. She likes—she likes that kind of music."

"What else?"

"She's in the kitchen with Peggy Lee asking Johnny to play it again. And she's getting dinner ready because it's tradition. There's roast and mashed potatoes, the kind with sour cream and potato skins."

"And probably some pie too, huh?" Kelly asked. "Because she knows how much you like pie."

"Yeah," Carter said. "Apple pie. There's probably some ice cream in the freezer. Vanilla bean. You get warm pie topped with melted ice cream and I swear, Kelly, there's nothing better."

"And she's not alone, right? Because the others are there with her."

Carter opened his mouth once, twice, but no sound came out. He coughed and cleared his throat. Then, "Yeah." His voice was hoarse. "Ox is there. And he's smiling, okay? He's smiling in that way he does. A little goofy with the side of his mouth. And he's watching her dance and sing and cook. She's handing him a basket filled with rolls fresh from the oven, covered in that green dish towel. He'll take it outside and put it on the table. And when he comes back inside, she'll ask him if he remembered to put the cloth napkins out, because we aren't uncivilized here, Ox, we may be wolves, but we have *some* decorum."

Kelly was crying quietly, head bowed. His brother squeezed his hand tight. These men, these large, intimidating men, were clinging to each other, and almost desperately so.

I opened my mouth to say something, *anything*, when Carter said, "And Mark's there too," and I nearly bit my tongue clean through. Carter looked straight at me in the rearview mirror. "Mark's there too. He's watching over them both. He's humming along with Mom and Peggy Lee. And he's thinking about us. Wondering where we are. What we're doing. If we're okay. He's hoping that we're coming home. Because he knows we belong with him. With them. Because it's Sunday. It's tradition. And he's—"

Joe growled angrily. It sent a chill down my spine.

Carter fell silent.

Kelly wiped his face with the back of his hand.

I looked over in time to see a single tear fall from the Alpha's cheek.

No one spoke for a long time after that.

* * *

Birch Bay, Washington.

There lived an old witch, someone I didn't want to even think about, much less see. But none of the wolves argued with me when I told them to point the SUV west. They were out of ideas. We hadn't had a lead in months. Richard Collins was playing with us, and we all knew it.

The witch didn't seem surprised when we rolled up to his tiny house on a cove. "I see things," he said from his chair on the porch, even though I hadn't said a word. "You know this, Gordo Living-stone."

His eyes were milky white. He'd been blind since he was a child, early in the last century.

He stood, back hunched. He shuffled slowly through the door.

"You know," Carter said, "this is the point in horror movies where I usually shout at the screen for the people to *not* go inside the house."

"You're a werewolf," I muttered. "You're the one that's usually waiting for the people inside the house."

He looked offended.

I ignored him.

Gravel crunched under my feet as I followed the witch inside. The porch steps creaked before I walked through the darkened doorway.

Seagulls called just outside an open window. Farther on, there was the low rush of the tide washing against a rocky beach. The air was cool, and the house smelled of salt and fish and mint. Overhead, hung on strings from the ceiling, were the skulls of cats and small rodents. He was old-school magic, the type that always had a caldron bubbling as he rolled bones from a cup made from an ancient tree.

He was also completely out of his mind, which is why he was a last resort.

"What in the fuck," Carter muttered after walking into the rather large skull of an animal I didn't think I'd ever seen before.

"It's certainly not the interior design choice *I* would have gone for," Kelly whispered to him.

"You think? Nothing says 'welcome to my murder shack' like skeletons hanging from the ceiling."

"Is that a jar of eyeballs on the shelf?"

"What? No, don't be stup—that's a jar of eyeballs on the shelf. Well, now I'm officially that person that shouldn't have gone inside the house."

Joe came in last. He crossed the threshold and his eyes briefly flared red.

The old witch stood near a cast-iron stove. He was stoking the fire inside. Embers sparked out, landing on his skin. He didn't flinch. He closed the stove and put the charred poker next to it before settling down in an old recliner. He stared in my direction, head cocked.

"Don't touch the jar of eyeballs," Kelly hissed at his brother.

"I just want to *see* it—"

"What are they prattling on about?" the witch asked.

"Eyeballs," I said mildly.

"Ah," he said. "Yes. Those. Eyes of my enemies, those are! Scooped them out myself with a dull and rusty spoon. The wolves I took them from kicked and screamed, but to no avail. They were of the curious sort, much like yourselves, touching things that didn't belong to them."

"Eep," Carter said.

Kelly covered his eyes with a hand.

I snorted, shaking my head.

Joe said nothing.

The old witch cackled. "Ah, youth. Such a waste."

"We don't mean to intrude," I started, but stopped when he waved me off with a gnarled hand.

"Yes," he said, "you did. You meant that specifically. It's the reason you're here. I may be old, Gordo Livingstone, but I can still smell the bullshit you always seem to sling. And don't give me that look. You are nearly forty years old. Keep making that face and it'll freeze like that. You'll end up looking like me."

I stopped scowling at him.

"That's better," he said. "You would think with your mate being back in Green Creek, you'd have learned happiness again. Though I suppose the events of the past few years took much of that away."

The fire snapped and popped. The seagulls called. I began to wish we'd never set foot inside Birch Bay as I felt the eyes of my pack slide over to me.

He put a hand next to his ear. "What's that? Nothing else to add? Then maybe we shall just sit here and wait until someone has the balls to say what they're thinking. Lord knows I don't. Lost those a few years back. Cancer, if you can believe it."

Carter made a choking sound.

The old witch grinned. He still had a few teeth left. "Wolves. Bennetts, I believe. I've always liked the Bennetts. Foolish bunch, but their hearts were usually in the right place. Who do we have here?"

Kelly opened his mouth to speak but closed it when I gave a sharp shake of my head. I nodded toward Joe. He watched me for a moment, mouth in a thin line. Then he nodded and stepped forward.

The floorboards creaked, and the old witch turned toward him.

"My name is Joseph Bennett," he said quietly, voice rusty with disuse. It'd been months since he'd spoken in more than a grunt.

"Alpha," the witch said with a deferential tilt to his head.

Joe's eyes widened slightly. "And these are my brothers. My second, Carter. My other brother, Kelly."

Carter waved.

Kelly elbowed him in the stomach.

I sighed.

The witch nodded. "I knew your great-grandfather. William Bennett. He begat Abel. Abel begat Thomas. Thomas begat you. Tell me, Alpha Bennett, who are you?"

Joe balked.

"Because," the witch continued, "I'm not sure if you know. Are you an Alpha? A brother? A son? One half of a mated pair? Are you a leader, or do you seek nothing but vengeance? You can't have both. You cannot have it all. There isn't enough room in your heart, though it beats as a wolf. There is strength within you, child, but even one such as you cannot live on rage alone."

"My father—"

"I know of your father," the witch snapped. "I know he fell much like his father did. One would think the Bennett name is cursed with how much you suffer. Cursed almost as much as the Livingstones. You have so much in common, it's a wonder you can even find where one of you ends and the other begins. Your families have always been intertwined, even if the bonds were broken."

Carter and Kelly turned slowly to stare at me.

"I'm doing what I have to," Joe said, a quiet growl in his voice.

"Are you?" the witch asked. "Or are you doing what your anger has demanded of you? When you give in to it, when you let your wolf become mired in fury, you no longer have control."

"Richard Collins—"

"Is a monster who has lost himself to his wolf. He has forsaken a tether, and his eyes have become clouded in violet because of it. He is an Omega, a monster hell-bent on taking something that never belonged to him. But you, Joseph. You are not him. You will never be him, no matter how much you have to be in order to justify your actions."

"Didn't I tell Joe that exact same thing?" Carter whispered to Kelly.

"No," Kelly whispered back. "You told him he was a fucking idiot and you wanted to go home because you hated how motels smelled like spunk and regret."

"So . . . almost the same thing, then."

"They understand," Joe said, sounding angrier.

"They?" the witch asked, though we all knew full well who Joe meant.

"They," Joe said. "Them. My pack."

"Ah. Those you left behind. Tell me, Joseph. You face the monster from your youth. You lose your father. You become an Alpha. And your *first* response is to tear your pack apart?" He shook his head.

"Ox—"

"Oxnard Matheson will play his part," the old witch said, causing all of us to freeze. "He will become who he is supposed to be. The question that remains is whether you will do the same."

Joe bared his teeth. "What do you know about Ox?"

The witch remained undaunted. "Enough to know the path you have set yourself on has diverged from his. Is this what you want? Is this what you set out to do? Because if so, then you have succeeded."

Joe's eyes started to bleed red. Before I could move, he launched himself at the old man.

He barely made it a few feet. The witch raised a hand and the air *rippled* around his fingers. Joe was knocked across the room into his brothers. They all fell to the floor with arms and legs flailing.

I shook my head.

The old witch smiled at me. "Children these days."

"You're baiting them."

He shrugged. "Have to get my kicks somewhere. Not every day I'm visited by royalty."

I snorted. "Royalty."

"The Bennett line is as royal as it gets."

"I suppose."

"Do you?" He tapped his fingers on the table. "I was also speaking about *you*."

I sighed as the wolves squawked, trying to pick themselves up by shoving each other. "It's not like that. Not anymore."

"Isn't it?" the witch asked me, not fooled. He nodded toward the wolves. "Theirs is a story of fathers and sons. Oxnard's is the same, or so the bones tell me. And then there's you."

I touched the roses underneath the raven on my arm. "It's not the same."

"It is, Gordo, and the sooner you realize it, the sooner you'll realize your full potential. You have already set yourself upon the right path. You have found yourself a pack again."

"Get off me, Carter!" Kelly snarled. "Jesus *Christ*, you're heavy."

"Are you saying I'm *fat?*" Carter yelped. "I'll have you know that women *like* it when I lay on top of them."

"We're not your *floozies*," Joe growled.

"I should hope not. We're *related*. That's disgusting. Besides, you only *wish* you could get someone as hot as me. And who the fuck says floozies? What are you, ninety-four and reliving the glory of your youth?"

"Did you just *fart?*" Kelly screeched, sounding horrified.

"Yeah," Carter said, and I could hear the smile in his voice. "Gas station microwave burritos are not so good on my intestines, apparently."

"Get off! Get off!"

I groaned, my face in my hands.

"Yes," the old man said as he chuckled, "you have definitely found yourself a pack."

I dropped my hands and looked at him. He was smiling quietly, eyes staring off into nothing. "We need—"

"I know what you need," he said. "And I will help you as best I can. But you cannot go on like this forever, Gordo. None of you can. If, in the end, this endeavor proves futile, you must return to Green Creek. For too long it was without its Alpha and wolves, and only a witch to guide it. And now the witch is gone, along with the Alpha. I fear what will become of it if this persists. There are only a few places of such power left in this world. The balance must be kept. You know this better than anyone."

"You hear that?" Carter said. "He's going to tell us how to kill the bad guy!"

"That's not what he said," Kelly muttered.

Joe didn't speak.

I turned to look at them. They were still on the floor, bodies tangled together. But they looked . . . content. More so than I'd seen them in a long time. Even Joe. I wondered if they'd forgotten how much a pack needed to touch, needed to feel each other's warmth.

It was time they started remembering that.

Maybe it was time I did too.

In the end, I knew the wolves—at least Carter and Kelly—were disappointed with how it all played out. The old witch muttered under his breath and then turned the wooden cup over. The bones spilled across the tabletop, landing scattered almost pointlessly. I never learned to read bones because it was an archaic magic, more tied to sight than the earth like I was. There were times I didn't even believe in it, but the old witch was one of the few left who practiced, and I had run out of ideas. Maybe it would turn out to be nothing but mindless hocus pocus, but . . .

Carter and Kelly leaned eagerly over the table, staring down at the bones as if they would reveal all the mysteries of the world. They looked like idiots.

Joe stood quietly next to me.

The old witch squinted at the table.

"This is so exciting," Carter whispered to Kelly.

"I'm not sure what we're supposed to be looking at."

"I know. That's what makes this so exciting."

"Huh. Okay. Now I'm excited too."

The old witch sat up in his chair and said, "Fairbanks."

We stared at him.

He stared sightlessly back at us.

"Fairbanks," I said slowly.

"The answers you seek are in Fairbanks."

"Like," Kelly said, "as in Alaska?" He squinted at the table, trying to see what the witch had seen.

"I really fucking hate Alaska," Carter muttered, eyeing the bones as if they'd betrayed him.

"Richard Collins is in Fairbanks?" Joe asked.

The old witch looked up at him sharply. "I didn't say that. I said the answers you seek are there. This will set you on the proper path. It will begin to lead you home."

"Home," Kelly breathed.

"Home," the witch repeated.

Carter stepped back from the table. "Great! Wonderful. Awesome. What the hell are you all doing still standing around? We gotta get moving. Alaska, here we come!" He was already halfway out the door before he turned and stuck his head back in. "Thank you. Your help is appreciated. But also, maybe consider not hanging the skeletons of someone's pet from your ceiling. It's very *I shouldn't be trusted to babysit your children.* Just a suggestion."

And then he was out the door.

Kelly stood to follow. He paused, looking at Joe and me before he turned to the old witch. "Thank you," he said quietly and then went after his brother.

"How are we supposed to know you're telling the truth?" Joe asked.

"Joe," I snapped at him. "Don't insult—"

"It's fine," the old witch said. "He doesn't know me. It's a fair question to ask."

"But—"

"Gordo."

I crossed my arms over my chest and glared at both of them.

The witch said, "You don't have to trust me, Alpha. I am not your pack. I live here, in this place, and I know how it looks. How I appear. But I have a certain . . . fondness for wolves. I always have." He stood slowly and moved toward a bookshelf on the far wall. He took a large volume from the middle shelf. He turned and came back to the table, sliding the book toward Joe.

Joe glanced at me. I jerked my head toward the witch.

He took the book.

The cover was made of leather, red and cracked. There was a faded gold leaf carved into it.

Joe opened it slowly.

It'd been hollowed out.

Inside, resting atop a deep blue cloth, was a small, ornate stone wolf.

"His name was Arthur," the old witch said quietly. "He gave that to me when we were young. And we lived and loved until one day, he and our entire pack were taken from me by the rage of men. I begged and pleaded with them, but my words fell on deaf ears. They . . . well. They saved Arthur for last. I managed to escape. And after, I knew nothing but revenge. It consumed me. When finally the last man had fallen, I no longer recognized myself." He reached up and dragged a finger across his face. "I was old. And I still hadn't allowed myself to grieve. I felt hollow, Alpha. And there was nothing left to fill my empty heart. I had taken the lives of those who had harmed me and mine, but I was alone." He took the book back from Joe, placing his hand atop the wolf. "I sit here, day after day, waiting for release.

Waiting for death. Because I know when my heart no longer beats, my beloved will be waiting for me, and we will howl together in the stars." He chuckled wetly, shaking his head. "You cannot become me. You cannot let yourself become consumed. If you do, you run the risk of never finding your way home. Trust an old witch when he says he understands more than most. I have loved a wolf with my whole heart. I know, Alpha. I *know*."

Joe nodded slowly. He turned to leave but stopped himself. Instead, he went to the old witch and knelt by his chair. He brought both hands up and cupped the ancient face before him. He allowed his half shift to come over him, his eyes burning in the dark room. His claws scraped against the man's face, little pinpricks denting in the skin. A low rumble emanated from his throat.

"Oh," the old witch said, sighing happily as his eyes closed. "Oh, oh, how wonderful it is to hear a wolf again. These old bones are singing. Thank you, Alpha. Thank you." He turned his head and kissed a sharp claw.

Joe stood abruptly and left the little house in the cove.

The fire was almost out.

"Thank you," I said quietly.

The old witch wiped his eyes. "Bah. I have done my part. Now you must do yours. I fear your journey is far from over. There is Richard Collins, yes, and he can never be brought back. But there is far worse than the likes of him. Do not let yourself be distracted."

"My father."

"Yes," he whispered. "Richard Collins is nothing but a weapon, blunt and focused. But even one such as him can be manipulated. Monsters always can. Your story will not end with Richard Collins. I fear there is more ahead for you, Gordo."

I nodded slowly. I was almost to the door when I heard my name said again.

I didn't look back.

"What I said to Joe, it was meant for you too."

My hands trembled.

"A wolf needs his tether, yes. But so does a witch. You have had three in your lifetime. Oxnard. Your pack here. But before them, there was another."

I turned angrily. "It can't be like that again. Not after—"

"Only because you won't let it. You carry so much anger in your heart, Gordo. Just like your father. It's all you've known for too long. Those boys, they . . . they look to you. Would you have them become the man you are now? Or the man you were supposed to be?"

"It's better this way."

"For who?" He laughed bitterly. He scooped the bones back in the cup. "For you? Or for Mark Bennett? Because I have never seen a wolf love another as much as he loved you. Not even Thomas and his mate. He loved you. He *loved* you. And you forsook him. Do you know what I would give? For just one more day with—" He cut off with a choking sound. His hands shook as he spilled the bones once more. They clattered on the table. They looked like nothing to me. "It's happening," he whispered.

"What do you see?"

He looked away. "It's . . . hidden. Most of it. The bones aren't everything. You know that as well as I do. They can't be everything."

"Tell me."

The old witch sighed. "You will be tested, Gordo Livingstone. In ways that you haven't yet imagined. One day, and one day soon, you will have to make a choice. And I fear the future of all that you hold dear will depend on it."

A chill ran down my spine. "What choice?"

He shook his head. "I cannot see that far."

"That's not fair."

He looked up at me with sightless eyes. "For those called upon, it never is."

I turned and walked out of the house.

The wolves watched me through the windshield.

I flexed my hands.

And then walked down the porch and into the gravel.

We were halfway down the driveway when the wolves sighed as one.

"What is it?" I asked.

Joe Bennett said, "His heart. It just . . . stopped. He's . . ."

We headed north.

Joe wouldn't speak again until we were face-to-face with the hunter David King.

We crossed the border into Canada again.

It felt . . . different, this time. Like we were finally headed in the right direction.

I wondered how often hope felt like a lie.

I stared down at the wooden raven.

I zipped the pocket closed before I could pick it up.

I needed to focus.

Outside of Fairbanks, Alaska, it was the middle of an oddly mild winter. Patches of green grass peeked through snow, and the stench of blood surrounded a cabin in the middle of the woods.

"He was here," Carter said, eyes blazing. "He was *here*."

"Is he gone?" I asked.

Kelly nodded. "There's a heartbeat inside, but it's human. It's beating really fast. Like it's scared."

"It could be a trap," I said, eyeing the cabin. "We need to move— goddammit."

Carter had already taken off toward the cabin.

His brothers followed.

"Fucking idiots," I muttered, but ran after them.

Carter had already burst through the cabin door, causing it to splinter and break off its hinges. He was half-shifted, hair sprouting along his face as his fangs grew. Kelly was right behind him, more in control but eyes bright orange. A large bird screeched overhead as Joe hit the porch, shoes having split as his feet sprouted claws.

I was inside the house only seconds later.

There was blood. A lot of it. It splattered the floor and walls. The cabin was one large room, a kitchen off to the right and a living room/ bedroom to the left. The small table in the kitchen had been over- turned. The chairs had been tipped over. An old futon lay in pieces, the mattress torn to shreds and streaked with red.

And there, slumped against the wall, was a naked man.

His chest and torso and legs had been slashed. He had ragged, gaping wounds that I knew had been made by claws. His breath was stuttering in his chest, and the skin that wasn't covered in blood was slick with sweat. His eyes were closed.

Richard Collins was gone.

Carter and Joe prowled around the cabin, nostrils flaring.

Kelly knelt before the injured man, hand shaking as he reached out to—

The man's eyes snapped open, his hand up before we could move and wrapping around Kelly's wrist. Kelly fell back on his ass, startled at the sudden movement. His brothers were snarling, and I—

"Wolves," the man whispered. "It's always the wolves."

And then he passed out.

. . .

I cleaned and bandaged his wounds as best I could with what I could find in the debris of the cabin. Kelly helped me right the futon while Joe and Carter disappeared into the forest surrounding the cabin, seeing if they could pick up the scent.

Kelly was crouched next to me, grimacing as I wrung out a cloth over a basin of water, now more red than clear. "He was here."

"Yeah," I muttered, dropping the cloth to the floor.

"Why?"

"Why what?"

"Why was he here? Who is this guy? Why would Richard want him?"

I pointed to a mark on the man's chest, near his right shoulder. It'd been split right down the middle, but I could still see the shape of it. The design. The ink in his skin.

Kelly squinted at it. "Is that . . . a . . . crown?"

"It's a sigil. The mark of a clan."

Kelly took in a sharp breath. "Of *hunters?*"

"Yes."

"Why are we *helping* him? He wants to kill us!"

"I doubt he can do much of anything right now. Turn off the eyes, kid."

Kelly ground his teeth together, but the orange faded to its natural blue. They weren't as frozen as his uncle's, but it was close.

I looked away.

"Do you know it?"

I sighed. "I do."

"And?"

"It's not important. They're all gone now. He's nothing but an outlier. Probably got out when he was your age." Because I didn't recognize him. He hadn't been one of the bodies lying on the ground while I'd walked through the forest, Mark weak and broken at my side. If he had been, if I'd come across him still breathing, I would have put my hands over his mouth and nose and—

"Gordo?"

Kelly was staring at me, a strange look on his face. I realized just how tense I was. I couldn't let him see me like this. Not now. Not when—

"Go check on your brothers. See if they need your help."

"But—"

"Kelly."

He growled at me but stood and did as he was told. He pushed against the useless door, the hinges creaking, wood splintering further. I heard him howl as he left the house, and there was a burst of *BrotherPack where* before Carter sang back *hereherehere* from somewhere in the woods.

I scrubbed a hand over my face and looked back at the man.

His eyes were open.

"Wolves," he whispered. "Wolves, wolves, *wolves*—"

"Hey," I said sharply before he could get more agitated. "*Hey.* Look at me. King, *look at me.*"

That got him. His eyes widened briefly as he turned his head toward me. "Who are—" He coughed weakly. "Who are you? How do you know my name?"

"The tattoo on your chest. The mark of your clan."

"An old life."

"I figured as much."

He blinked slowly. "You're not a wolf."

"No."

"Your arms are glowing."

"They tend to do that."

"You're a witch."

"Astute, for a hunter."

His teeth were bloody when he grinned. "I *told* you. That was an old life."

"Was he here?"

King closed his eyes. "The beast. Yes. Yes. He was here."

Fuck. We must have missed him by an hour. Maybe less. For all I knew, he could still be somewhere nearby. I needed more. I remembered the words of my father and muttered under my breath, a hand outstretched over King's body. A mark on my left wrist flared to life, and I *pulled* some of the pain, the agony, the *hurt* from the hunter and into me. I grimaced against the sharpness of it, the way it rolled up my arm and into my chest and gut, moving like molten lava. If he lived, it'd be slow going for a while.

"Ahhh," he said, relaxing into the shredded mattress. "That's . . . that's nice."

"It isn't much," I warned him. "And it's not permanent."

"That's okay. Pain means I'm alive. Probably won't win any beauty contests, but if I hurt, it means I'm still here."

"Richard Collins."

His eyes opened again. They were clearer than they'd been before. "He came for me. I thought—I grew lazy. I didn't look over my shoulder as much. It'd been years since—" He shook his head. "I didn't even hear him coming."

"You know why he came."

"Yes."

"Because of what your clan did."

"*Yes.*"

"The wolves outside. Do you know who they are?"

"Does it matter?"

"Bennetts. All of them. And I am Gordo Livingstone."

He was up and moving even before I said my name. He moved quickly for a man so injured. I didn't know where the knife came from, but it flashed toward me. But I had been running with wolves for going on three years, and I wasn't the man I used to be.

He brought the knife down toward me as I brought my forearm up under his wrist. It knocked the trajectory of the knife up and over my shoulder. I backhanded him across the face and then reached back, grabbing his wrist and twisting it *just* before the point of breaking. He grunted as the knife clattered to the floor behind me. I shoved him back onto the bed.

His chest was heaving as he stared at me with wide eyes.

"That was rude," I told him mildly.

"I had *no* part in what happened to you," he said, sounding panicked. "I had already been shunned by my clan beforehand."

"Why were you shunned?"

"Because I couldn't do it. I wasn't—I couldn't kill." He squeezed his eyes shut. "A hunter who can't kill is useless. My father couldn't stand the sight of me. He turned to my brother Daniel instead. And then there was always my sister. She . . ."

"Who is your sister?" Then, "Oh, Jesus—"

"Meredith King. Elijah."

I wrapped my hand under his chin, fingers and thumb digging into his cheeks. Blood and sweat made my grip slick, but I held on tight. My teeth were bared as I bent so close to his face that our noses brushed. "I could kill you right now and no one would stop me. Your *family* killed mine. Give me one good reason why I shouldn't break your neck right here."

"I don't *have* a family," he said, voice breaking. "And it doesn't matter. Not anymore. If he found me once, he could find me again. If it's not you, then it will be him. Or those kids out there. I haven't had a thing to do with my family in *decades,* but I am still a King. I can never escape that."

I squeezed tighter. It would be *so easy.* All I would have to do was twist my hand to the right, and his neck would *pop* and—

"Gordo."

I closed my eyes.

"Gordo, let him go."

"You don't know who he is. What his family has done."

There was a hand on my shoulder. "I don't. But this isn't who you are."

I laughed bitterly. "You don't know the first thing about me."

The grip on my shoulder tightened. "I am your Alpha. I know you better than you think."

"Goddamn you," I breathed, letting King's face slip from my grasp. He gasped, shoulders shaking as I fell back on my ass.

Joe Bennett stood above me. His brothers were at the door behind him, watching. Waiting.

The Alpha bent over the hunter.

King's eyes were wide.

Joe's were red.

"Do you know who I am?" Joe asked quietly.

King didn't speak. He only nodded.

"Good. My witch has helped you. I will do you the favor of letting you live. But only because I ask for a favor in return."

"What?"

"Oxnard Matheson. Green Creek. You go there. And you tell him I said 'not yet.'"

The wolves sighed at the door.

"Do you understand, hunter?"

"Y-yes. Yes."

"Repeat it back to me."

"Oxnard M-Matheson. Green Creek. Not yet. Not yet. Not yet."

"Good." Joe stood upright, eyes fading. "Stay here until you can move again. Richard won't return."

"How do you know?"

Joe grinned wildly. "Because he knows I'm right behind him."

And then he turned and walked away, pushing through his brothers and leaving the cabin behind. Carter and Kelly followed him a moment later.

I pushed myself up, dusting off my jeans.

King said, "I heard—I heard Thomas Bennett was gone."

I contemplated picking up his knife from the floor and driving it into his chest. "And?"

"I've never met an Alpha before. He's . . . strong. Stronger than I've ever seen a wolf be."

"He's just a kid," I muttered.

"Maybe. But that's what this is all about, isn't it? Power. It always has been."

I was done here. I turned and headed for the door.

Then, "Livingstone."

I sighed. "What?"

"They didn't all die."

A chill ran down my spine. I turned slowly to look back at him. His skin was pale, and I wondered if he'd ever make it to Green Creek to give Ox the Alpha's message. "Who didn't all die?"

He coughed. It sounded wet. "When they came for Abel Bennett. The pack. Green Creek. They didn't all die. Some crawled away. Some ran. But others . . . they watched from the trees."

"Elijah."

He smiled weakly. "She'll come. When you least expect it. And if you think the beast is the worst thing in this world, you haven't seen anything yet."

"Gordo!" Carter shouted from the road. "We gotta move!"

"Don't die," I told King. "You have work to do."

And then I turned and followed my pack.

.   .   .

He did die.

Months later, after we realized the deaths were circling back toward home. Toward Green Creek and those we'd left behind.

He did die.

What was left of him was in pieces. In the end, Richard Collins found him in a motel in Idaho. His severed head was found on the bed. A contact had sent me the photos.

Words were written in blood on the wall.

YET ANOTHER FALLEN KING

Joe howled for hours that night.

.   .   .

When the sun rose the next morning, we all heard his voice whispering in our heads.

It said *home* and *home* and *home*.

FOUR THINGS / ALWAYS FOR YOU

I was thirteen when I kissed Mark Bennett for the first time.
A month later, hunters came and killed most of our pack.
Things weren't the same after that.

. . .

It baffled many people.
How a group of men could be killed by a pack of wild animals.
The men couldn't be identified.
Bears, they said. Maybe it was bears.
But no animals—bears or otherwise—were ever found.
It became legend more than anything.
Within a year, people spoke about it less and less.

. . .

I kissed Mark Bennett for the second time when I was fifteen years old.
Elizabeth was pregnant with another child.
Carter was walking and talking.
Thomas Bennett still had a haunted look about his red eyes, but he accepted his responsibilities as the Alpha of all.
Many men came to Green Creek. Wolves. From back East.
They followed Osmond, who bowed reverently every time Thomas stood before him.
"He's an odd man," Thomas told me once.
"He's a kiss-ass," I sneered.
Thomas's lips twitched. "That too."
"I don't like him."
"You don't say."
And that was that.

. . .

Richard was gone.
He left shortly after the hunters came.
That hurt Thomas almost as much as the loss of his pack, though he didn't say it out loud.
I knew, though. He was my Alpha, and I knew.

Mark was eighteen. I kissed him because I wanted to and because I needed it.

He kissed me back briefly. I tried to deepen it, but he wouldn't let me.

"You're young," he said, eyes flickering orange as if he was trying to retain control. "I can't do this. Not yet."

I shoved him away and stalked into the woods.

He didn't follow me.

"Oye," Rico said as the clamor of the lunchroom rose around us. "Look. Gordo. We've been talking."

I looked up to see them all staring at me, Rico and Tanner and Chris. I almost got up and left. Instead I said, "I don't even want to know."

"Yeah," Chris said. "We figured you were going to say that."

"So this is an intervention," Tanner said. "But with friends." He frowned. "A friend-tervention."

"Stop," I told him. "Please."

He looked relieved.

"We've been talking," Rico repeated. "And now we need to talk to you."

"About?"

Chris leaned toward me from across the table. He didn't seem to notice his elbow was in his macaroni and cheese. "Love."

I hated them so much. "Love."

Rico nodded. "Love, papi."

"Love," Tanner added, completely necessarily.

"What *about* love?" I asked, even then realizing how ridiculous that sounded.

"Your love for boners."

I wondered then if I could get away with causing the ground to open up beneath them and swallow them all whole. I would need to act distraught, of course, and maybe even cry a little at the loss of my friends. But it would be worth it. "Rico. What. The *fuck*. Are you talking about?"

"You like penis," Rico said sagely. "Like I love the titties."

Chris nodded.

Tanner said, "I've got macaroni on my elbow."

"I hate all of you," I told them. "You have no idea."

"Chris," Rico said.

Chris pulled out a notepad. He flipped it open and waved it in my face. "I've written down seventeen instances in which you were staring at Mark with a gross look on your face. I have dates and times and everything."

"I was supposed to be the one writing it," Tanner said, "but my handwriting is terrible."

"The worst," Rico said. "It looks like ancient Greek."

"What the hell are you talking about?" I growled at them.

"You love Mark," Chris said, squinting down at his notepad. "Last week. Saturday. Three thirty-seven in the afternoon. Main Street. Mark walked by the diner window with a friend, and Gordo sighed dreamily before asking who the girl was and why she was standing so close to Mark."

"I didn't do *any* of that."

"You said you thought she was probably a bitch who wanted to get her claws in him," Tanner said, wiping off his elbow. "Claws, Gordo."

"We could go on," Rico said, arching an eyebrow at me.

"For fuck's sake," I muttered.

"Chris!"

"Two weeks ago. Tuesday. Five forty-six in the evening. At Marty's. Mark brought Gordo dinner, and Gordo made SMF at him."

"SMF?"

"Suck My Face," Rico said. "It's a look you get when Mark stands near you like you want to tell him to suck your face."

We got detention for three days after I started a food fight when I threw my milk carton at Rico's head. If it exploded before it hit him and drenched all three of them with far more liquid than should have been in that tiny carton, well. No one needed to know that but me.

. . .

"I don't want to suck your face," I told Mark later.

He blinked. "What?"

I scowled at him. "Nothing. Fine. Whatever. How's *Bethany*."

He smiled, slow and sure. "Good. She's . . . good. Sweet girl."

"Great," I said, throwing my hands up in the air as I stalked away. "Fine. That's just *swell*."

He laughed and laughed and laughed.

• • •

Things were happening. Things that I wasn't privy to. I wasn't always invited into meetings with Thomas and Osmond and the wolves from back East. Hell, I wasn't even sure where *back East* was, exactly. But even though I still heard my mother's voice in my head sometimes, I trusted Thomas. I trusted him to know the right thing to do. What it meant to be an Alpha, to have a pack.

I shouldn't have.

• • •

Marty said, "Oh man. That's . . . that doesn't feel right."

And then he collapsed in the middle of the garage.

I reached him first.

His skin was slick with sweat.

His breathing was erratic.

He ended up in the hospital for a couple of weeks after they put a stent in his artery.

"A balloon," he told me, looking grumpy as a nurse flitted around him. He scowled at her and tried to get her to leave him alone, but she told him she'd dealt with far worse than the likes of him. "They stuck a goddamn balloon in me, blew it up, then put in a stent. Helps the ticker keep chugging along." He grimaced. "Apparently have to make some *dietary changes*." He didn't look very happy about that.

"No more diner food," I told him seriously.

"No more diner food," he said morosely.

• • •

Four things happened during my fifteenth year.

Four things that would forever change the way I saw the world.

• • •

The first thing.

Thomas called me into his office. Elizabeth was sleeping upstairs. Mark was . . . I didn't know where Mark was. Probably with *Bethany*. Osmond and the wolves from back East had been gone for days. The house was quiet, just the way I liked it.

So when Thomas called me into his office, I wasn't expecting anything serious.

He motioned for me to close the door behind me. I did, and took a seat across from where he sat at his father's desk.

"Gordo," he said warmly. "How are you?"

"Fine," I said. "But maybe cut the bullshit."

He arched an eyebrow at me.

I shrugged.

"Remember when you were scared of me?" He flashed his eyes and snapped his teeth.

I laughed. "I was just a kid."

"You're still a kid."

"I'm fifteen," I said, puffing out my chest just a little.

"You are. And a pain in my ass."

"You love me."

"I do," he said, and even though I wouldn't say it, his words filled me with such a sense of pride that it almost took my breath away. He smiled, though, because he knew. He always knew. "Which is why I've brought you here. We need to talk. Man-to-man."

That sounded good to me. I nodded. "I agree. Time to talk man-to-man."

"I'm glad to hear that. What are your intentions with my brother?"

The sound I made would haunt me for years to come. Added to the fact that I started sputtering and that spittle shot out onto his desk, I was surprised he didn't kick me out of his pack right then and there.

He didn't, though. He just sat there, letting me drown, looking amused.

"What are you *talking* about?" I managed to say.

"My brother," he said slowly, as if I was an idiot. Which, to be fair, I was offering no evidence to the contrary. "What are your intentions?"

"My *intentions*? What are you—oh my god, you can't just— *Thomas*."

"How curious your reactions are at the mere mention of Mark."

"Not *mentioning*. Asking my *intentions*."

"Right," he said easily. "My apologies."

"Damn right I get your apologies! What were you thinking?"

"That you're his mate. And that you've kissed him. Twice."

"That *asshole!*" I bellowed. "Where does he get off telling you—"

"He brought you gifts."

"Dead *animals*."

"Rather dated, but he's got an old soul. Always has. And you know the traditions of wolves, Gordo. You've been in the pack since you were a child."

"I am going to murder him," I promised Thomas. "I'm sorry if you love your brother, but I am going to drop-kick him with silver-toed boots."

"Should he not have told me?"

I sputtered more. It went on for a good, long minute.

"I am here as your Alpha," Thomas said, finally putting me out of my misery. "And I have received a formal request from one of my Betas."

I groaned and slumped farther in my chair.

Thomas put his hand on my hair. It felt good. Like home. "Don't ever change, Gordo," he said quietly. "No matter what happens, stay as you are. You are a wonderful creature, and I am very happy to know you."

I sighed. When I spoke, my voice was slightly muffled. "I like him."

"I should hope so."

"But he says we have to wait."

"There is that, yes. You are fifteen years old. He is three years older than you. Nothing . . . untoward should occur until you're of legal age."

I lifted my head and glared at him. "You were *seventeen* when you met Elizabeth. She was *fifteen*."

"And I only made my intentions known," he said. "Nothing more. Because to claim one as mate is a request. There is always a choice. I was very lucky that she chose me, in the end."

"Didn't she tell you this morning that if you were to come near her again with your penis, she was going to claw your face off?"

He grinned. It was a dazzling thing to see. "She's nine months pregnant. She's allowed to say whatever she wishes. And if she wanted to claw my face off, I would let her."

I sighed. "I like your face where it is."

"Thank you, Gordo."

"Mark, huh?"

Thomas shrugged. "If it makes you feel any better, he was very nervous when he came to see me."

"Nervous? Why?"

Thomas spread his fingers out over the desk, tracing scars in the wood. "Mark is—he cares. Deeply. For his pack. For his Alpha. For you. And now that he is to be my second—"

"What about—"

"Richard made his choice," Thomas said, an edge to his voice. "He . . . he didn't understand. Doesn't understand. And I can't find fault with that. It . . . he needs to find his own way. And I hope that one day, our paths shall cross again. I will welcome him home with open arms and embrace him as my brother. If that doesn't happen, I cannot find fault in him for it. He lost much that day. As did all of us. Grief . . . it tends to change people, Gordo. As you are well aware."

I nodded, not trusting myself to speak.

"But Mark will make a fine second. He is brave and strong. A very good wolf, if I do say so myself. Why, I doubt there is a better wolf in any other pack out there—"

So I said, "Are you trying to pimp your brother out to me?"

The Alpha of all sighed. "I wish you wouldn't say it like that."

"Because it sounds like you're trying to pimp your brother out to me."

"Is it working?"

I slumped down in my seat. "No. Maybe."

"You do not have to accept," Thomas said. "Mark would never force you. I wouldn't allow it. You are young yet. There is a whole wide world out there for you to explore. I only ask that you not . . . string Mark along, whatever your decision. If you need time, tell him. If you don't feel the same way, say so. You are your own person, Gordo. You will never be defined solely as the mate of a wolf."

"But what happens to Mark if I say no?"

Thomas smiled. "He will be upset, but he'll learn to live with it. And one day, there may be another that catches his eye and speaks to his wolf as you do."

"It's probably going to be Bethany," I muttered.

"Possibly."

I glared at him. "She's awful."

"Oh? She seemed rather nice to me."

"*What*? You met her? When? *Why*? Did Mark bring her to—and now you're laughing at me. You never met her, did you."

"Nope."

"I hate you."

His smile widened. "Oh, how your heart just showed that was a lie. That makes me happy, Gordo. My little witch."

I loved Thomas Bennett.

. . . .

I said, "Here's the thing. If I say yes, you don't own me. You don't control me. You don't get to tell me what to do. I am a witch to the Alpha Thomas Bennett. I am my own man. I can fry the hair off every part of your body with a single *thought*. You don't get to treat me like I'm weak or fragile. If we have to fight one day, then we'll do it side by side. And I reserve the right to change my mind. Especially if you are going to be friends with *Bethany*, because she is the absolute worst." I took a breath and let it out slow. "Okay, how was that?"

Elizabeth stared at me with wide eyes, her hand on her distended stomach.

Carter sat at her feet, gnawing on wooden blocks. He waved at me with a chubby hand.

Elizabeth said, "I think . . . huh. I think that was much better than what I said to Thomas. And—oh. *Oh*." She grimaced, bottom lip sucked up between her teeth.

"Are you okay?" I asked, panicked. Thomas and Mark were in town, and I'd been asked to watch over Elizabeth.

"Yeah," Carter said, voice high and sweet. "Okay?"

"Okay," she said. "More than. This one is . . . active. Here, Gordo. Feel."

I moved slowly and carefully, making sure to avoid little fingers and toes below me. Carter latched on to my leg, gnawing on my pants and growling in a low voice.

Elizabeth took my hand and placed it against her belly.

At first, there was nothing.

Then—

A push back against my palm and fingers. A pulse of something low and happy. My tattoos flared along my arms.

"Is that . . . ?" I asked in awe.

"He knows you," she said, a quiet smile on her face. "He knows his pack is waiting for him."

. . .

In the end, it wasn't as I planned.

I didn't say everything I'd practiced with Elizabeth.

Mark came through the door, followed by his brother, and I said, "The baby touched me and made my magic glow, and it was weird because I know it's supposed to be a wonderful thing, but I think it was my fault because all I was doing was practicing telling you that if you gave me your wolf, I'd take it, but I am a witch, so I could neuter you where you stood, you understand me? And—"

Mark Bennett gathered me in his arms, and there I stayed for the longest time.

.   .   .

The second thing.

"She wants to see you now," Thomas said. He looked tired, and his hair stuck out every which way, but his eyes were bright.

He held open the door for me.

Light filtered in from the large wall of windows that opened out to the forest behind the Bennett house. The sky above was gray. Little drops of rain splattered against the glass, trickling down. The scent of blood was thick in the air. Below us, wolves moved throughout the house. Osmond and others from back East, here to help Elizabeth through the birth of her second child.

She sat propped up against pillows in the bed. She was pale, and her hair was pulled back loosely. She wore no makeup, and there were dark circles under her eyes, but I didn't think she'd ever looked more beautiful.

"Hello," she said. "Would you like to meet the newest member of our pack?"

He lay cradled in her arms, tucked tightly in a deep blue blanket. He wore a cap over his head. His skin was pink and wrinkled. His eyes were shut, and he squirmed slightly. His mouth opened, then closed, opened, then closed.

Elizabeth said, "His name is Kelly."

"Kelly," I whispered in awe.

I leaned down and kissed him on the cheek. I told him quietly that I was very happy to meet him. That he was very lucky to have the parents he did. That I would always keep him safe, no matter what.

Thomas watched us from the doorway, ever the proud Alpha.

.   .   .

The third thing was . . . I should have seen it. I should have seen it coming.

I should have known.

Because nothing lasts forever.

My mother.

My father.

My pack taken from me by the hands of hunters.

I should have known that everything else would be taken from me too.

But I didn't expect it to be because of Thomas Bennett.

.   .   .

Kelly was four months old when Osmond came to the house again on a blustery afternoon.

He disappeared with Thomas into the office, Mark closing the door behind them. The dark-suited Betas stood outside the house next to nondescript SUVs.

Elizabeth had a frown on her face as she nursed Kelly.

Carter was sleeping in his bedroom, the door propped open.

Elizabeth said, "Gordo, please. A word."

The air felt charged. Something was happening.

I stood before her, a cloth over Kelly and her breast.

She said, "I need you to listen to me. Can you do that?"

"Yes."

"Whatever happens, whatever is decided, you must remember. You will always be our pack. You will always belong to us, just as much as we belong to you. No matter what. That will never change."

My skin itched. The hairs on my neck stood on end. "I don't understand."

"I know you don't. But I love you. Thomas loves you. *Mark* loves you. You are the witch to the Bennetts, and you always will be."

"What are you—"

"Gordo."

I turned my head.

Mark stood in the open doorway of Thomas's office. He looked furious. His eyes flickered between fire and ice. The ends of his fingers were pointed and sharp.

He said, "Thomas needs to speak with you."

.   .   .

In the end, it was simple.

Thomas Bennett was the Alpha of all, just as his father had been before him.

Green Creek had been a safe haven tucked away from the rest of the world.

He had been given time to heal. To pick up the pieces of his shattered pack. To make himself whole once again so that he could do what he must. He was a leader, and it was time for him to lead.

Which meant leaving Green Creek.

And heading East.

"But what about school?" I demanded, feeling slightly hysterical. "And my friends. And the garage! I can't just *leave* everything—"

Thomas said, "You won't be."

Silence fell.

Thomas watched me from across his desk.

Mark paced angrily behind us.

Osmond stared blandly at me from near the window.

But I only had eyes for my Alpha. "I won't be *what*."

Thomas said, "Green Creek needs to be protected. And I will be entrusting that protection to you. Which is why, Gordo, you will be staying. Here. In Green Creek."

I blinked. "What do you mean? I thought you said the pack was leaving."

He sat forward in his chair. "We are. Elizabeth. My sons." His eyes flickered over my shoulder. "Mark. All of us. But you will remain."

"You're leaving me."

He reached for me across the desk.

I pushed my chair back quickly so I was just out of reach.

That hurt him. I could see it clear on his face.

Good. I hoped it hurt badly.

"Gordo," he said, and he'd *never* sounded like that when speaking my name, like he was *pleading* with me. "This was not a decision made lightly. In fact, it is one of the hardest choices I've had to make in my life. And you have every right to be angry with me, but I need you to listen. Can you do that for me?"

"Why?" I asked, my lip curling into a sneer. "Why the fuck should I listen to *anything* you have to say? You told me the pack was leaving but that I'm *not*. Obviously that means I'm not your—wait. Wait a goddamn minute." I closed my eyes, my hands curling into fists at my sides. "How long have you known?"

"I don't—"

"Elizabeth. Just now, she told me—she knew. What was happening. She didn't just overhear." I opened my eyes. Thomas's head was bowed. I glanced over my shoulder at Mark. He wouldn't look at me. "You all knew. Every single one of you." I nodded toward Osmond. "It's why he's been coming here. You've been . . . what. Planning this? How long?"

"A while now," Osmond said. "We were waiting for Kelly to be born before—"

"Osmond," Thomas warned.

"He has a right to know," Osmond said, furiously calm.

"You're damn fucking right I do," I snarled at them. "How could you even *think* about leaving me behind? What have I ever done to make you—"

"You're human," Osmond said.

Mark growled at him angrily. "You don't get to—"

"Mark," Thomas said sharply. "That's enough."

Mark fell silent.

"And Osmond, if you speak again without prompting, I will ask you to leave my territory. Are we clear?"

Osmond didn't looked pleased at that. "Yes, Alpha."

Thomas looked at me again. I didn't know what he saw. I was fifteen years old and being betrayed by the one person I never thought capable of such a thing.

He said, "I need you to hear me. Can you do that, Gordo?"

I thought about hurting him. Making him feel like I felt. Flayed open and bleeding.

But I wasn't my father.

I nodded tightly.

He said, "You are human, and wonderfully so. I hope that will never change. But there is . . . distrust. Amongst the wolves. Because of the hunters. Because of what they have done. We aren't the only ones who have lost those we loved."

I was horrified. "I would *never* hurt—"

"I know," Thomas said. "You have my trust. You always have. I have faith in you, maybe more than anyone else in this world."

"But?"

"But others are not so easily persuaded. There is . . . fear. Hunters and. . . ."

"And?"

"Tell him," Mark spat from behind me. "He deserves to know. Since you've made this decision, you tell him."

Thomas's eyes filled with fire, but it was brief. It faded away, and he was left looking far older than I'd ever seen him. He looked down at his hands. "Livingstone," he eventually said.

"What? I don't—" It hit me then. "My father. They think I'm going to be like my father. I'm human, as were the hunters. I'm a witch, just like my father. And you're letting them use that against me. They don't trust me. And since they don't trust me, you are leaving me here. You chose them over me."

"No, Gordo. Never that. I would never—"

"Then stay here."

"He can't," Osmond interrupted. "He has a responsibility to—"

"I don't give a *fuck* about responsibility," I snapped. "I don't *care* about who he is to you, to everyone else. He's *my* Alpha, and I am asking him to choose me."

My mother's heart had been broken long before I knew what to look for.

My father's heart had been broken by the death of his tether, but I never saw it before he exploded in a furious burst of rage and magic.

This was the first time I'd ever witnessed a heart breaking up close.

And the fact that it was my Alpha's heart made it that much worse. I could see it, the moment it happened.

His hands shook and his mouth tightened into a thin line. His breath stuttered in his throat, and he blinked rapidly. In my head, I heard whispers of *pack* and *brother* and *love*, but there was also a song of mourning, and it ached so bitterly that I thought I would fall apart at the midnight-blue weight of it.

I knew then that nothing I could say would change anything.

Mark must have too, because there was the telltale sound of clothes tearing as muscles and bones popped and shifted. I turned in time to see a flash of brown as he fled, lost to his wolf.

The raven fluttered on my arm, its talons digging into the thorns of the roses. It hurt, but I welcomed the pain.

"Leave us," Thomas said, never looking away from me.

"But—"

"Osmond. Leave us before you'll have no choice but to *crawl* from this house."

For a moment I thought Osmond was going to defy him. But in the end, he nodded and left, closing the door behind him.

Somewhere in the house, I could hear Kelly crying.

Thomas said, "I love you. Always. You must remember that."

I said, "I don't believe you."

"You will be taken care of. I've asked Marty to—"

"Marty," I said with a hollow laugh. "Of course."

"I'm *trying*," Thomas said, voice breaking. "Gordo, I will do everything in my power to return to you, or to have you with us. But I cannot ignore what my position asks of me. I must do what I have to. There are people depending on me to—"

"And what about me?" I asked, wiping my eyes. "Don't I matter at all?"

He stood swiftly. He moved around his desk, but I took a step back. He said, "Gordo, you—" and I said, "Don't touch me, please don't touch me, I want to hurt you and I don't know if I can control it, so please don't touch me."

He didn't.

"You'll see," he begged. "I promise it won't be long. Soon we'll come home to you, or you'll come with us. You will always be our witch, Gordo. You will always be my pack."

He reached for me again.

I let him.

He hugged me close, his nose buried in my hair.

My arms stayed at my sides.

*   *   *   *

It took two weeks.

Two weeks to pack up the house at the end of the lane.

Two weeks for me to move into Marty's little house with sunflowers that grew wild and unkempt in the back.

Two weeks for a FOR RENT sign to go up at the empty blue house that we hadn't used since our pack had been taken from us.

Elizabeth kissed me on the morning they left, telling me she'd call me every day.

Carter cried, unsure of what was happening.

I pressed my cheek against Kelly's and he blinked at me, hand in my hair.

Thomas stood before me, hands on my shoulders, asking me if I could just say something, *anything* to him. But I hadn't spoken to him since that day in his office, so I said nothing.

Mark was the last. Because of course he was.

He hugged me.

He made promises I didn't believe he could keep.

He had made his choice.

He said, "Gordo."

He said, "Please."

He said, "I love you, I need you, I can't do this without you."

He said, "I left something for you. Okay? And I know we said we were going to wait, but I need you to see it. I need you to know I will keep my promises. For you. Always for you. Because nothing will stop me from coming back for you. I promise, okay? I promise you, Gordo."

He kissed my forehead.

And then he was gone.

I watched as they drove away.

Marty came, eventually. He put his hand on my shoulder, fingers digging in. "I don't expect to understand what's going on. But you always have a home with me, kid."

So I said, "I'm a witch. The Bennetts are werewolves. And they chose others over me."

.   .   .

Later, after Marty had drunk himself into a hysterical stupor and finally passed out, I went to my new room in his house. Mark and Thomas had unpacked the boxes, trying to set it up just the way I'd had it in the Bennett house.

It wasn't the same.

A small box had been left on the pillow, wrapped with a red ribbon.

Inside was a stone wolf.

I wanted to shatter it into pieces.

Instead I touched it with the tip of my finger and began to wait for my heart to finish breaking.

.   .   .

The fourth thing that happened during my fifteenth year barely registered because it seemed so inconsequential.

"The house," Marty said, sitting back in a ratty lawn chair in the back of the garage, cigarette smoke curling up around his head, bad heart be damned. "The one for rent. Next to where you used to live."

"What about it?" I asked, head tilted back toward the sun.

"Someone rented it out, so I hear."

It didn't matter. I was still buried under waves of anger. "Yeah?" I said, because that was what normal people did.

"A family. Mom. Dad. They've got a little kid too. Saw them out and about. Seem like the nice enough sort. Kid's quiet. Got these big eyes. Always staring. The guy asked about work. Said I didn't have any openings right now, but we'd see."

"Bill's getting on. Might be time for him to retire."

Marty snorted. "Yeah. You tell him that and let me know what happens."

I opened my eyes, blinking against the sunlight.

"Just thought you should know," Marty said, blowing out smoke. "In case you need to—I don't know." He glanced over his shoulder back into the garage. Loud music was playing. The guys were laughing. Marty leaned forward, dropping his voice. "In case you need to check them out. In case they're . . . werewolves. Or whatever."

"They're not."

"How do you know?"

"I'd know."

He stared at me for a beat before shaking his head. "I'm never gonna understand how that shit works. Just . . . I don't know. They didn't give me any weird vibes. So I don't think they're anything but down on their luck. Cute kid, though. Little slow, I think. But cute. Name's Ox, if you can believe that. Poor bastard won't stand a chance."

Whatever. It didn't matter. "Yeah, Marty. Sure."

He sighed as he stubbed his cigarette out on the bottom of his boot before dropping it into the half-filled coffee can. He stood, knees popping. He ran a hand over my head. "Couple more minutes. Then get back to work." He went back inside the garage.

He left his pack of smokes out.

I snagged one, struck a match, and held the fire to the tip.

I inhaled.
It burned.
But it was enough.
I barely even coughed.

GREEN CREEK / PLEASE JUST WAIT

J oe spoke for the first time in weeks.
He said, "It's time to go home."

. . .

Mark came back for the first time six months after they left.
He said, "Hey, Gordo. Hi. Hello."
I slammed the door in his face.
He waited outside my window until I finally let him in.

. . .

We pointed the SUV toward Green Creek.
Kelly said, "What if they don't want us to come back?"
Carter hugged him close.

. . .

Rico said, "We're going out and getting drunk. I'm tired of being six-teen years old and never having gotten intoxicated. It's like I'm doing *nothing* with my life. There's a party, and we're going."
Tanner said, "My dad will kill me if we get caught."
Chris said, "I gotta watch Jessie. Mom's gotta work late."
I said, "Yeah, sure. Okay."
We got drunk. I had the third kiss of my life with a boy from a school two towns over. He tasted of cherries and beer, and I didn't regret a single thing until I opened my eyes the next morning and promptly threw up over the side of the bed.

. . .

We took our time. What should have taken two days of straight driv-ing, we stretched out and out and out.
On the fifth day, when we slept out under the stars because we couldn't find a motel, Kelly asked me if I was nervous.
"About?" I asked, taking a deep drag off my cigarette. The tip flared brightly in the dark. It reminded me of wolf eyes.
He wasn't fooled. He nudged his boot against mine.
"No," I said.
"How did you do that?"
"What?"

"You just lied. But your heart didn't give you away."

"Then how do you know I lied?"

"Because I know you, Gordo."

"It doesn't matter," I said, and that was that.

.   .   .

I waited for Thomas to call me and tell me he needed me, that the pack needed me with them and that he was sorry he'd ever left me behind.

The call never came.

.   .   .

I dreamed sometimes. Of him. His broken body crawling toward me, his brown paws digging into the dirt, a low whine coming from his throat. I'd wake up gasping, and I'd reach for the wooden raven as if it meant something, as if it would help in any way.

It didn't.

And then there were the nights I dreamed of Thomas Bennett, his son Joe crouched above him, begging him to get up, to just get up, my magic the only thing holding the beast back from taking what he so desperately wanted. I dreamed of that impulse I'd had, that tiny, miniscule impulse where I'd thought about dropping the barrier and letting Richard descend upon Thomas because he deserved it. He'd taken everything from me, and in that moment, when Joe lowered his claws to his father's chest and the beast *howled* in anger, I'd understood Richard Collins.

I never told anyone about that.

.   .   .

I turned seventeen and lost my virginity. His name was Rick, and he was rough and unkind, his lips latching on to the back of my neck as he thrust into me, and I *relished* the pain because it meant I was alive, that I wasn't numb to the way the world really worked. He came and slipped from me, the condom sliding from his dick and landing wetly on the pavement in the alleyway. He said thanks, I needed that, and I said, yeah, sure, my pants around my ankles. He walked away, and I laid my head against the cool brick, trying to breathe.

.   .   .

I said, "He's circling."

Joe looked at me, head cocked. He wasn't the boy who'd left Green Creek three years before. He was harder now, and bigger. His head was shaved, his beard in need of a trim. He had filled out and was as big as his brothers. He wore the mantle of the Alpha well, and I thought if the boy that he'd once been wasn't lost for good, he would do great things.

"Richard. He's circling. Whatever he's after. His endgame. You. Green Creek. I don't know. But it's coming, Joe. And you need to be ready."

There was a song in my head, and it sang, *PackBrotherWitch what makes you think i'm not* and *let him come let him come let him come.*

I thought then the boy I'd known was gone.

. . .

I was seventeen when I graduated early. I wanted it done and over with.

Mark was there.

I looked for the others.

He was alone.

"They wanted to be here," Mark said.

I nodded stiffly.

"But Thomas didn't think it was safe."

I laughed bitterly. "Doesn't seem to have a problem with me being here."

He said, "It's not that. It's—Elizabeth's pregnant."

I closed my eyes.

. . .

We crossed into Oregon on a back road in the middle of nowhere.

There were no signs.

But I knew.

So did the wolves.

Carter's and Kelly's eyes were orange.

Joe's were red.

They were singing. I tilted my head back and sang along with them.

. . .

Marty died.

One moment he was there and laughing and yelling at me to get my ass in gear, and the next he was on his knees, his hands clutched to his chest.

I said, "No, please, no."

He looked at me with wide eyes.

He was gone before I even heard the sirens of the ambulance.

That night I called my pack, needing to hear their voices. I got an answering machine.

I didn't leave a message.

.   .   .

"Oh man," Carter said. "Do you think Mom will make her roast for us? Like, roast and carrots and mashed potatoes."

"Yeah," Kelly said. "And there will be so much gravy. I'm going to put gravy on *everything*."

That sounded good to me too.

.   .   .

He left me the garage.

I blinked in disbelief at the lawyer standing in Marty's old office. "Excuse me?"

"It's yours," he said. He wore a frumpy suit and seemed to be perpetually sweating. He reached up with a handkerchief and wiped his brow. The collar of his shirt was soaked. "The garage. The house. The bank accounts. All of it. He amended his will two years ago. I advised against it, but you know how he is. Was." He wiped his forehead again. "No offense."

"Son of a bitch," I breathed.

.   .   .

Green Creek was two hours away when Joe pulled over to the side of the road.

His hands tightened on the steering wheel.

We didn't speak.

We just breathed.

Finally I put my hand on his shoulder and said, "Okay, Joe. Okay."

He nodded, and after a beat, we drove on.

Eventually, we passed a sign on the side of the road. It was in need of a paint job, the wood splintered and worn.

It said WELCOME TO GREEN CREEK.

.   .   .

"His name is Joe," Mark whispered to me over the phone. "And he's perfect."

I blinked away the burn.

Later, I would hear from Curtis Matheson that they'd bought the blue house they'd been renting. Got it for real cheap too, or so he said.

We ditched the SUV northwest of town. The summer air was sticky and warm.

Joe walked into the woods, hands outstretched, fingers brushing along tree trunks.

His brothers followed as they always did.

I brought up the rear.

The earth pulsed beneath my feet with every step I took.

My tattoos ached.

The raven's wings fluttered wildly.

Eventually we found ourselves in a clearing.

Joe fell to his knees and bent forward, putting his forehead into the grass, hands on either side of his head.

We stood above him. Watching. Waiting.

There was a knock at the door.

I groaned, the early morning light filtering in through the window. It was my day off, and I could tell the hangover was going to be a bitch. My mouth felt rank, my tongue thick. I blinked up at the ceiling.

It was about that time I realized I didn't know the name of the man snoring in the bed next to me.

I remembered bits and pieces. He'd been at the roadhouse the night before. I wasn't legal to drink, but no one cared. I'd been four beers in, and I'd seen him eyeing me from the other end of the bar. He looked like a trucker, worn ball cap pulled low on his head, eyes hidden in shadow. He was the type that had a wife and two point five kids back home in Enid, Oklahoma, or Kearney, Nebraska. He'd smile at them and love them, and when he was on the road, he'd look for any willing thing with a warm hole. He needed to work his way up to it, though, and I waited for him to down his whiskey, making sure he was watching as I tilted my head back, exposing my neck as I took a long drink from the wet bottle. His eyes tracked the slow movement of my throat as I swallowed down the beer.

I left a few bills on the bar, rapping my knuckles against the wood before pushing my way up from the stool. Things were hot and hazy. A trickle of sweat dripped down my hairline to my ear.

I was out the door, cigarette lit. I took maybe three steps before the door opened again.

He wanted to take me in the alley.

I told him I had a bed a few blocks away.

He gripped my hips as he mouthed at my neck, scraping his lips up until his tongue was in my ear.

He told me his name, and I told him mine, but it was lost.

He fucked like a man used to furtive gasps in back rooms or rest stops. I choked on his cock, his grip tight in my hair. He told me my mouth was pretty, that I looked so good on my knees. He wouldn't kiss me, but I didn't mind. He pressed me facedown against the mattress, grunting as he fucked me.

When he finished, he slumped onto the bed next to me, mumbling how he just wanted to close his eyes for a while.

I got up and picked up the condom he'd let fall to the floor. I flushed it and then stared at myself in the mirror for a long time. There were teeth marks on my neck, a bruise sucked into my chest.

I turned off the light and collapsed next to him.

And now a knock, knock, knock at my door.

The nameless man snored. He looked rougher in the morning light. Tired, and older. He hadn't even taken off his wedding ring.

"Yeah," I said, voice like gravel. "Yeah, yeah, yeah."

I pushed myself off the bed, finding yesterday's jeans on the floor. I pulled them up, not bothering to button them. They hung low on my hips. I shuffled to the door, wondering how much coffee I had left. I hadn't been shopping in days.

I opened the door.

Mark's nostrils flared.

His gaze skittered over the marks on my neck and chest.

I leaned against the doorway.

"Who?" he asked in a barely contained growl.

"You don't call, you don't write," I said, rubbing a hand over my face. "What's it been? Five months? Six?" Six months. Fifteen days. Depending upon what time it was, eight or nine hours.

"Who is he?"

I grinned lazily at him as I scratched my bare hip. "Don't know. Got his name, but you know how it goes."

His eyes flashed orange. "Who the *fuck* is he?" He took a step toward me.

You can't trust them, Gordo. You can never trust a wolf. They don't love you. They need you. They use you.

I stood up straight. The raven shifted. Roses bloomed. The thorns tightened. "Whoever the fuck he is is no goddamn concern of yours. You think you can show up here? After *months* of radio silence? Fuck off, Mark."

His jaw tightened. "I didn't have a choice. Thomas—"

I laughed. It wasn't a very nice sound. "Yeah. Thomas. Tell me, Mark. Just how is our dear Alpha? Because I haven't heard from him in *years*. Tell me. How's the family? Good? Got the kiddos, right? Building a pack all over again."

"It's not like that."

"The fuck it isn't."

"Things have changed. He's—"

"I don't care."

"You can shit all over me all you want. But you don't get to talk about him like that." He was pissed. Good. "Regardless of how angry you are, he's still your Alpha."

I shook my head slowly. "No. No, he's not."

Mark took a step back, startled.

I gave him a mean smile. "Think about it, Mark. You're here. You can *smell* me. Underneath the spunk and sweat, I'm still dirt and leaves and rain. But that's it. Maybe you're too close, maybe you're overwhelmed by the very sight of me, but I haven't been pack for a long time. Those bonds are broken. I was left here. Because I was human. Because I was a *liability*—"

He said, "It's not like that" and "Gordo" and "I promise you, okay? I would never—"

"A little late, Bennett."

He reached for me.

I knocked his hand away.

"You don't understand."

I snorted. "There's a world of things I don't understand, I'm sure.

But I'm a witch without a pack, and you don't get to tell me shit. Not anymore."

He was getting angry. "So—what. Poor you, huh? Poor Gordo, having to stay behind for the good of his pack. Doing what his Alpha told him. Protecting the territory and fucking anything that moves."

I felt dirty. Nasty. "You wouldn't touch me," I said flatly. "Remember? I kissed you. I touched you. I *begged* for it. I would have let you fuck me, Mark. I would have let you put your mouth on me, but you told me no. You told me I had to *wait*. That things weren't right, that the timing wasn't right. That you couldn't be distracted. You had *responsibilities*. And then you disappeared. For months on end. No calls. No check-ins. No *how you doin', Gordo? How you been? Remember me? Your mate?*" I rubbed a couple of fingers against the mark on my neck. It burned so good. "I would have let you do so much to me."

His eyes burned. His teeth were sharper. "Gordo," he growled, sounding more wolf than man.

I took a step toward him.

He tracked every movement, ever the predator.

"You can, you know," I told him quietly. "You can have me. Right now. Here. Choose me. Mark. Choose me. Stay here. Or don't. We can go anywhere you want. We can leave right now. You and me. Fuck everything else. No packs, no Alphas. No *wolves*. Just . . . us."

"You would have me be an Omega?"

"No. Because I can be your tether. You can still be mine. And we can be together. Mark, I'm asking you, for once in your life, to choose me."

And he said, "No."

I expected it. I really did.

It still hurt more than I thought it would.

For a moment my magic felt wild. Like it couldn't be controlled. Like it would burst from me and destroy everything in sight.

I was my father's son, after all.

But the moment passed, and left in its wake was nothing but a smoking crater.

He said, "Gordo. I can't—you can't expect me to—it's not *like* that—"

I took a step back.

His anger was gone. Only fear remained.

"Of course you can't," I said, voice hoarse. "What was I thinking?"

I turned and went back into the house, leaving the door wide open.

He didn't follow.

The unknown man was blinking blearily as I went back into my bedroom. "What's going on?"

I didn't answer. I went to the nightstand and opened the drawer. Inside was a box, and in this box was a stone wolf I'd taken out time and time again, a promise broken over and over. I turned on my heels and was back down the hall, my mother's voice in my head, telling me wolves *lie*, they *lie*, Gordo, they *use* you, and you may think they love you, they might even *tell* you they do, but they *lie*.

They always do.

I was a human.

I had no place with wolves.

He was still standing on the porch.

His eyes widened when he saw the box in my hand.

He said, "No."

He said, "Gordo."

He said, "Just wait. Please just wait."

I held it out to him.

He didn't take it.

I said, "You take it. You take it now."

Mark Bennett said, "Please."

I thrust it against his chest. He flinched. "Take it," I snapped.

He did. His fingers trailed against mine. Gooseflesh prickled along my bare shoulders. The air was cool, and I thought I was drowning.

"It doesn't have to be this way."

"You tell Thomas," I said, struggling to get the words out while I still could. "You tell him I don't want anything to do with him. That I don't want to see him again. You tell him to stay out of Green Creek."

Mark looked shocked. "Or what?"

"Or he won't like what I'll do."

I let myself have one last look at him. This man. This wolf. It was a second that lasted ages.

And I turned and went inside, slamming the door shut behind me.

He stood on my porch for a long minute. I could hear him breathing.

Then he left.

I allowed myself one last tear over Mark Bennett.

But that was it.

I would see him again, though I didn't know it then. Years would go by, but one day he would return. They all would. Thomas. Elizabeth. Carter. Kelly. Joe. Mark. They would come back to Green Creek, and behind them, a beast that would mean the death of Thomas Bennett.

We surrounded Joe as we stood in front of the Bennett house for the first time in three years, one month, and twenty-six days.

In front of us stood a pack that we didn't belong to.

Elizabeth.

Rico.

Chris.

Tanner.

Jessie.

A wolf in glasses who I didn't recognize.

Mark.

A man whose father had told him once that people would give him shit for the rest of his life. That he wouldn't amount to anything.

And somehow, he had become an Alpha.

ONE

YEAR

LATER

FUCKING IDIOT /
SONG OF THE ALPHA

Oxnard Matheson said, "You're being a fucking idiot."

I didn't look up from the computer. I was trying to figure out how to work the expense reports on the new program a certain bespectacled wolf had downloaded, but technology was an enemy I had yet to destroy. I was giving very real consideration to putting my fist through the monitor. It had been a long day.

So I did what I did best. I ignored him in hopes that he would go away.

It never worked.

"Gordo."

"I'm busy." I hit a button on the keyboard and the computer chimed an error message at me. I hated everything.

"I can see that. But you're still a fucking idiot."

"Great. Wonderful. Fantastic."

"I don't—"

"Whoa," another voice said. "It's, like, super intense in here right now."

I barely resisted the urge to bang my head against the desk.

Robbie Fontaine stood next to Ox, glancing curiously back and forth between us. He wore a work shirt with his name stitched into it, a gift from Ox that I'd rolled my eyes at, given that no one had asked *me* about it. He wore thick hipster glasses that he absolutely did not need. His eyes were so dark they were almost black, and he was grinning that knowing smile that I couldn't stand. He winked at me when he caught me watching him. He was insufferable.

"You guys fighting again?" he asked.

"I didn't hire you," I told him.

"Oh, I know," he said easily. "Ox did, though. So." He shrugged. "Kind of the same."

"The last time you tried to work on a car, you set it on fire."

"Right? Weird. Still don't know how that happened. I mean, one moment everything was fine, and the next there were these *flames*—"

"You were supposed to be rotating the tires."

"And they somehow spontaneously combusted," he said, speaking slowly as if *I* was the asshole. "But that's why we have insurance, right? Besides, I only work the front office now. I have it on good authority that people like having a little eye candy to look at when they drop off their cars. I suppose that's to be expected when the rest of you look so . . . you know. Brutish."

"I didn't hire him," I told Ox.

"Don't you have things to do?" Ox asked him.

"Probably," Robbie said. "But I think I'd rather be standing right where I am. What's Gordo being a fucking idiot over? Is it the whole Mark thing?"

"I'm trying to work here," I reminded them. It was useless, but it still needed to be said. Ox had a bug up his ass, which meant he was going to say his piece. Ever since he'd become an actual Alpha, he'd been insufferable that way.

"Why are we staring at Gordo?" another voice said, and I groaned. "*Lobito*, are you giving the boss man shit again?"

"Rico, I *know* you're supposed to be doing the oil change on that Ford and the Toyota."

My friend grinned at me as he squeezed into the office. "Probably," he said. "But! The good news is that I will get to them eventually. What's happening in here seems to be far more interesting. In fact, hold on a second." He leaned out the doorway toward the interior of the garage. "*Oye*! Get your asses in here. We're having an intervention."

"Oh my god," I mumbled, wondering how my life had become this way. I was forty years old, and I belonged to a pack of meddlesome bitches.

"Finally," I heard Tanner mutter. "It was starting to get sad."

"Even *I* was getting worried," Chris said. "And you know how I don't like getting worried."

The office was small, and I was sitting behind the same old chipped desk that Marty had bought secondhand years before. A moment later five grown men squeezed inside the doorway and were staring at me, waiting for me to do *something*.

I hated them so goddamn much.

I ignored them and went back to working on the expense invoice.

Trying to work on the expense invoice.

I'd told Ox there was no need to update the software. It was working just fine.

But *he* said that *Robbie* said he couldn't handle a program that had been made in the late nineties. I'd responded diplomatically, saying that Robbie probably hadn't even had pubes in the late nineties. Ox had stared at me. I had stared back.

The software was updated the next day, much to Robbie's glee.

I spent the next four days trying to figure out ways to send him back where he'd come from.

The computer chimed another error message as I hit F11.

Rico, Chris, and Tanner all snickered at me.

Maybe if I threw the computer at their heads, it would start working like it was supposed to.

I would certainly feel better.

But chances were they'd come back with their stitched-up, broken faces, and then I would feel bad and maybe actually start to *listen* to their bullshit—

"He's pouting," Rico whispered to Chris and Tanner.

"Aw," they said.

That was the problem with having your oldest friends as your employees and members of your pack. You had to see them every day and could never escape them, no matter how hard you tried. This was, of course, all Ox's fault for telling them about werewolves and witches to begin with, a mistake I had yet to forgive him for.

"You realize I could kill you with nothing but the power of my mind," I reminded them.

"I thought you said you couldn't do that?" Tanner asked, sounding a little worried.

"That's because he can't," Ox said. "It doesn't work like that."

"This is your fault," I told him.

He shrugged.

"Zen Alpha bullshit."

"Isn't it weird?" Rico asked. "I mean, ever since that day when he and Joe had mystical moon magic sex and became mates or whatever—"

"Would you stop calling it that?" Ox growled, eyes flashing red.

"Well, that's what it was," Chris said.

"He bit you and everything," Tanner pointed out.

"And then you came out smelling like a whorehouse with a weird smile on your face," Rico said. "And bam! Zen Alpha by way of mystical moon magic sex. That must have been one hell of an orgasm."

That . . . wasn't far from the truth. As disturbing as it felt, there'd been a singular moment when we'd *all* been hit with a wave of *something* while Ox, the kid I'd watched grow up right before my eyes, and another Alpha wolf fucked and—

"Oh, Jesus," I groaned, wishing I was anywhere else.

"Yeah," Rico said. "I'm thinking about it now too. I mean, butt sex and whatever, but no homo, right?" He frowned as he looked at Ox. "I mean, that's not a prerequisite for being in a pack, right? Because I don't know if I've told you this, but I'm pretty freaking hetero. Even if I've seen more naked men in the past few years than I've seen my entire life. Because werewolves."

"Well," Chris said. "There was that one time that you—"

"Oh, that's *right*," Tanner said. "That time that you—"

"Tequila," Rico said with a shudder.

"What time where you did what with who?" Robbie asked.

Rico frowned at him. "Why do you sound so surprised? I could get any guy I wanted!"

"I mean, you guys are attractive, I guess. For old people."

We all glared at him except for Zen Alpha, who stood with his arms crossed, exuding serene.

"Old?" Rico said slowly. "Little wolf, I might not like you right now."

"Maybe get you some tequila and see if you change your mind," Robbie said, waggling his eyebrows. "Is this shop talk? Am I doing shop talk right now? Beers and boobs!"

"Your fault," I told Ox again. "All of this. Every single person in this room aside from myself is your fault."

Ox smiled calmly. It was infuriating. "You're being a fucking idiot."

Dammit. I thought they'd been distracted enough. "I'm actually working right now, in case you couldn't tell. Which is something you should consider doing."

No one moved.

"You're all fired," I tried instead.

They just stood there.

I tried a different route. "Fuck you all very much."

"Just tell him you love him," Robbie said. "Even old people like you deserve to get your head out of your ass."

"How's Kelly? And take off those glasses. You don't need them and they make you look stupid."

He immediately turned red and began to sputter.

Ox put his hand on Robbie's shoulder, and there was *hush* and *calm* and *packpackpack*, and Robbie started breathing evenly. Even my anger at their intrusion faded slightly, which was unfair. In less than a year, Ox had become as strong an Alpha as I'd ever seen. Maybe even more so than Thomas or Abel Bennett. We thought it had to do with him having been a human Alpha before Joe had been forced to bite him.

Whatever the reason, Ox was unlike any werewolf I'd known. And since he and Joe had officially mated, their reach extended over all of us, the packs combining, though not without difficulties. Carter and Kelly still tended to defer to Joe and the others to Ox, but they were both our Alphas when it came down to it. I'd never heard of a pack headed by two Alphas before, but I was used to witnessing the impossible in Green Creek.

Ox was careful, though, because there came a point where the question of free will arose. If Ox or Joe wanted to, they could force their own will upon their Betas or their humans and make them act as they saw fit. It was a thin line to walk, being an Alpha versus exerting their control. If they wanted to, both of them combined could make us mindless drones.

But the look of horror on Ox's face the first time he'd accidentally done that was enough to show it would never happen. Not that I thought he would ever do it to begin with. It wasn't the type of person he was, no matter what he'd become.

But there were moments, like this one with Robbie, where he'd *push* and we'd all feel it. It wasn't about control. It was about being pack, about being connected in ways I'd never felt before. Even when it'd been a handful of us on the road circling around Joe, it hadn't been like this. Those years were born of desperation and surviving in the big wide world. We were home now, and complete.

For the most part.

Which was why they all stood in this small office, ready to dig into me again.

But before they could, a sharp twinge rolled over my arm. I looked down to see two lines begin to ripple quickly, glowing a deep forest green.

Ox and Robbie stiffened.

Even the humans felt it, if the looks on their faces were any indication.

Ox's eyes were on fire and his voice deep when he said, "The wards. They've been breached."

.   .   .

Ox, Robbie, and I were in Ox's old truck. I was behind the wheel, Robbie between us as Ox radiated anger near the window. The others were following behind in Rico's car. It was the middle of October, and the leaves in the trees around Green Creek were bursting in orange and red. Halloween decorations lined the shops on Main Street. Styrofoam pumpkins sat in the diner windows. The sky was already beginning to fade toward night, and the sidewalks were full as people left work.

We were barely out of town when Ox's phone rang. He put it on speaker and set it on the dash.

"Ox," a low voice said. "You felt it."

Joe Bennett, sounding as if he were growling through a mouthful of fangs.

Ox said, "Yes. From the woods."

"The others."

"With me. Jessie is still at the school. You?"

"Mom. Carter. Kelly. All at home."

Out of the corner of my eye, I saw Ox glance at me. Then, "Mark?"

A brief hesitation. "He's on his way."

"We'll be there soon."

The phone beeped as Ox shoved it in the glove compartment. I counted down from three in my head, and as soon as I hit *one*, he said, "Gordo. He's going to—"

"Drop it, Ox. It doesn't matter."

"This isn't over."

"I said *drop it.*"

"I'm really uncomfortable right now," Robbie mumbled between us.

We drove the rest of the way in silence.

.   .   .

We hit the dirt road that led down to the Bennett houses. Rocks and dust kicked up around us as the steering wheel tried to jerk in my hands. The others were close behind us.

"Brakes need work," I said mildly.

"I know."

"Maybe bring it in. Could get you a deal."

"You know the owner or something?"

"Or something."

He was still tense, but he rolled his eyes, showing many teeth when he smiled. Robbie sighed between us, hand on his Alpha's arm.

The houses came into view. The blue one where Ox had once lived with his mother. The much larger Bennett house, set farther back in the trees. The pack SUVs were parked in front next to Jessie's little Honda.

"I thought she was staying at the school?" Robbie asked.

Ox growled low in his throat. "She was supposed to. She never listens."

She was waiting on the porch with the others. Her long hair was pulled back into a tight ponytail, a grim look on her face. She was harder than that little girl Chris had brought into the shop all those years ago after their mother died, and stronger. In fact, out of all the humans in the group, she was probably the deadliest. She carried only a staff inlaid with silver, but she had knocked almost everyone in the pack on their back at one point or another.

Elizabeth stood next to her. She was as graceful as always, looking as regal as the queen she was. She didn't move as much as she seemed to float. She was older now, the lines on her face more pronounced. She had survived the loss of her pack before building another one, only to lose her mate and Alpha to the claws of the beast and her sons to the road. She had scars, but they were buried underneath her skin. Her grief had lessened over the years, and she no longer looked as haunted as she once was. Ox had told me that she had started painting again, and though it was blue, he thought the green relief would come soon.

Carter and Kelly stood on either side of their mother. Their time on the road had changed them, and in the year since they'd returned, they still sometimes struggled to reconcile who they were now with who they once had been. Carter was still big, a muscular wolf who was quicker to anger than he'd been before. His head was still shaved as if he was a soldier.

Kelly had lost some of his mass since he'd come back. He was the softer of the two, and though he still looked like his brothers—all that blond hair and those sky-blue eyes—he'd let himself settle better back home than Carter had. Carter sometimes still looked as if he wasn't sure he'd finally made it home. Kelly had found his place again, and it was almost as if he'd never left.

But they all bore the past few years of monsters and separations like badges of pride. They weren't the kids they once had been. They had witnessed things most would never see. They had fought for their lives and their packs against a beast who had taken much from them. They'd won, but we were not without our losses.

Joe stood a little ways away from them. His arms were folded behind his back, head tilted slightly up. His eyes were closed, and I knew he was breathing in his territory and whatever had breached the wards I'd placed. I had a good idea of what it was, but it was better to be safe than sorry.

Ox was out the door even before I'd turned off the truck. He pointed at Jessie as he walked by them, saying, "I told you to stay at the school."

"Remember last week when I knocked you against the tree?" she asked sweetly, tapping her staff against her shoulder.

He snapped his teeth at her, but she just laughed. He made his way to Joe, put his hand to the back of his neck, and squeezed. They stood side by side without speaking. Watching, waiting.

"Okay," I said. "Okay."

"Okay?" Robbie asked, and I flinched. I'd forgotten he was sitting right next to me.

"Get out. And take off those damn glasses."

He winked at me, sliding over the bench seat and through the door Ox had left open. Kelly stiffened slightly at the sight of him as Robbie walked toward the house. I didn't know what the hell was going on between the two of them, and I didn't want to. I had other things to worry about.

The guys had pulled up behind me and were chattering nervously as I opened the driver's door. Rico was popping the clip out of one of his .40 S&W semiautomatics. Tanner was doing the same. Chris looked as if he were about to stab himself in the eye with one of his knives. They worried me greatly.

I tried not to notice who wasn't there.

It didn't work out too well.

"Elizabeth," I said, nodding as I approached the porch.

She smiled softly at me. "Gordo. Never a dull moment."

"No, ma'am."

"He's on his way."

"I didn't ask."

"You were thinking it."

Jessie coughed, but it sounded like she was covering up a laugh.

"It doesn't matter."

"I'm sure," Elizabeth said evenly. She reached out and rubbed a hand along my arm, leaving a trail of light as my tattoos lit up under her touch. It'd taken a long time to get used to being touched by wolves again, and I tended to avoid lying in the piles they sometimes did, but I didn't shove them away anymore. Ox was pleased at it, as was Joe. I put up a good front.

"Ox talk to you?" Carter asked.

"He tried."

"Stubborn, huh." He eyed me up and down. "Should probably work on that."

I narrowed my eyes at him. "Did you put him up to it this time?"

He said, "No," and at the same time, Kelly said, "Sure did."

Jessie coughed harshly again.

"Assholes," I muttered. "Mind your own damn business."

"Grumpy old man," Kelly teased.

"That's what I called him," Robbie said. "But then he got the murder eyebrows he sometimes does. Like right now."

They all laughed at me.

I left them on the porch.

Ox and Joe still weren't speaking when I approached, though Ox's hand was still on Joe's neck. Joe glanced at me as I came to stand at his side. His eyes flashed at me, and I felt the pull of *pack* as my arm brushed his.

It'd been . . . difficult, trying to reconcile the difference between my Alpha and my tether. There'd never been two Alphas in charge of a single pack before, and for a while, I wasn't sure it was going to work. I was drawn to Joe because he was all I'd known for three years. I was tied to Ox because he kept me sane.

It hadn't been fair to him. To Ox. Making him my tether as I had, all over a work shirt with his name stitched in the front. He didn't know about the monsters in the dark. But the roar in my head lessened, the anger quieting anytime he was near. By the time I realized what was happening, it was too late. And then the Bennetts returned to Green Creek, bringing with them a lifetime of memories I'd forced myself to forget.

It'd been made more difficult the first time Thomas had come to me asking for help with Joe, who couldn't seem to hold his shift. Or when I'd seen Mark for the first time in years, standing on the sidewalk in Green Creek like he'd never left.

Nothing about this had been easy. But I thought it was getting better.

"Ox talk to you?" Joe asked.

Okay, it wasn't getting better at all. Fuck every single one of them.

"Murder eyebrows," Ox murmured.

"We have other things to worry about," I reminded them.

"Sure, Gordo," Joe said easily. He'd found peace since returning to Green Creek, especially after the death of Richard Collins. He was his father's son, much to my dismay. He was calm and strong and not above a little manipulation if the situation called for it. I told myself it wasn't malicious, but I still struggled with the idea of Thomas Bennett, though he was nothing but ash and dust spread throughout the woods around the Bennett house. "Other things. But I'm pretty good at multitasking, in case you didn't know."

"Omega?"

Joe bumped his shoulder against mine. "Yes."

"Like the others?"

"Probably. Your wards give us plenty of warning. I trust them. Like I trust you."

It shouldn't have made me feel as warm as it did. "You're just trying to get on my good side."

He squinted at me. "Is it working?"

"No."

"Kelly's right, you know."

"About?"

"Grumpy old man."

"I will light you on fire right here. Right now."

Joe laughed quietly before he looked back out toward the forest. Whatever it was, Omega or something else, it was getting closer. Overhead, the sky was fading and the first stars were coming out.

"Mark's coming," Ox murmured.

I popped my knuckles.

Joe snorted, shaking his head.

I heard him before I saw him. I would recognize the sound of those large paws upon the earth anywhere. I told myself to stay where I was, to keep looking straight ahead, but there was *brother* in my head, and *love* and *pack* and *markmarkmark* as the other wolves picked up on the thread from their Alphas.

Even the humans heard it, faint though it was. I was tied to the pack because of my magic, which is why I could hear the songs in my head.

My mother's voice whispered to me, reminding me that wolves *used* and they *lied*, but I pushed it away. Whatever Thomas knew—or didn't know—no longer mattered. He was gone, and Ox had been turned.

Carter said, "Must have left his car at—"

"Shut *up*, Carter," Kelly hissed.

"Oh. Shit. Right. That of which we do not speak so as to not hurt Gordo's feelings."

"He can hear you!"

"We can all hear you," Elizabeth told her son.

"Someone needs to say it," Rico muttered. "He's stupid."

"How's that nice girl of yours?" Elizabeth asked him.

"Which one?"

"Melanie, was it?"

"Oh. Fine. I think? I mean, I haven't spoken to her in a few months."

"He's on to Bambi now," Tanner said.

"Bambi," Robbie said. "That's . . . I don't know what that is."

"She's hot," Chris said. "She's got a huge set of—"

"You're not at the garage," Jessie reminded him.

"—of feelings. That. Are nice."

"Good save," Tanner muttered.

"She's got the biggest feelings," Rico said. "Like, sometimes, she puts her feelings all over me—"

"We need more women in the pack," Jessie said with a sigh.

"I think we hold our own," Elizabeth said lightly.

I turned and looked over my shoulder.

A large brown wolf was weaving through the cars. His shoulders were as tall as the hood of Ox's truck, ears twitching on top of his massive head. His paws left prints in the dirt that were bigger than my hand. His gaze darted around the pack gathered before him before it landed on me. It stuttered and stuck before it fell away.

I turned back toward the woods.

There came the shift of bone and muscle behind me.

"You think I'd be used to seeing werewolves who turn into naked people by now," Rico said. "But that doesn't seem to be the case."

"You can be one of those naked people," Robbie said. "Just let Ox or Joe turn you and you can show your junk outside like everyone else."

"Please don't give him any ideas," Chris said, sounding horrified. "There are certain things that no one should see."

"Don't be racist. And besides, we grew up together. You've seen me naked hundreds of times. We all jerked off together when we were twelve!"

Joe and Ox turned slowly to look at me.

I glared back at them. "I had nothing to do with that. If anything, it's Ox's fault for bringing them into the fold to begin with."

"Why did you have to tell everyone?" Chris demanded.

"Oh, please," Rico said. "We're in a pack of werewolves who we can sometimes hear in our heads. We don't have boundaries anymore."

"Why does he still think we're mind readers?" Kelly whispered.

"I don't know," Carter said. "But don't remind him we're not. I like learning things that will scar me for life."

"I've never jerked off with them," Tanner said.

"You were sick that day," Rico told him. "Otherwise we would have asked you too."

Ox and Joe had offered to turn the humans in the pack. Jessie had refused outright, saying she didn't want it. Chris had followed her shortly after, and whether or not it had to do with his sister, I

RAVENSONG   161

didn't know. Tanner was more reticent, and out of all the humans, I thought he'd be the one most likely to agree to be turned. But he never did anything without knowing everything he could about it, and I thought it was only a matter of time before he asked Ox to bite him.

Rico, on the other hand, didn't seem to give two shits one way or another. He'd made Ox and Joe promise to turn him if it was a life-or-death situation, but he seemed to be okay being who he was.

I was relieved. The idea of any of them being able to pop claws gave me anxiety.

"Got here as quick as I could," a low voice said. "We know what it is yet?"

"Appears to be an Omega," Elizabeth said.

"Another one? That's the third this month."

"Curious, isn't it? I left you a pair of pants just inside. Kelly, could you grab them?"

I heard the screen door open, and I tried desperately to focus on the approaching Omega. There was no need for me to glance over my shoulder to get an eyeful of—

Joe bumped my shoulder again.

I turned to look at him.

He grinned.

"Shut up," I muttered.

Before he could respond, Mark Bennett came to stand beside me.

His hair was shaved close to the scalp, the barest hint of stubble. His beard was as full as it'd ever been, finely trimmed and lighter than the deep, dark brown of his wolf. His eyes were that ice blue they'd always been, cold and searching. He wore a pair of loose jeans hanging dangerously off his hips but thankfully zipped up and buttoned. He was shirtless, hair covering his bulky chest and flat stomach. His skin was hot as his arm brushed against mine—an aftereffect of a recent shift.

"Gordo," he said, sounding faintly amused as he always did when he said my name.

"Mark," I said in return, resolutely staring straight ahead.

Ox and Joe sighed in unison, the insufferable Alphas that they were.

"Good day?"

"Fine. Yours?"

"Fine."

"Good."

"Great."

"Idiots," Joe muttered.

Before I could even begin to acknowledge *that*, an Omega burst through the tree line.

It was a woman, and she looked as if she'd seen better days. Her clothes were in tatters, her feet bare and caked with dirt. Her hair was wild around her face, and she *hesitated* at the sight before her, the rest of the pack spreading out behind us at the ready. We'd been back in Green Creek for just over a year and in that time had become a finely oiled machine. We knew our strengths. We were aware of our weaknesses. But there'd never been a pack quite like this one, and we had clawed our way into who we were now.

The Alphas stood side by side.

I popped my neck.

Carter, Joe's second—his enforcer—growled.

Ox's second, Mark, came to stand behind him and to the left.

Kelly stood with his brother.

The humans were next.

Elizabeth and Robbie brought up the rear.

There were twelve of us. The Bennett pack.

And one Omega.

Which is why I was surprised when her eyes flashed violet and she charged at us, half-shifted and snarling.

No one behind us made a sound.

I pressed two fingers against an earth rune on my arm, digging my fingernails in deep enough to draw blood.

The ground rolled beneath the Omega's feet, causing her to stumble forward, her hands shifting into paws as they hit the dirt. Dirty gray hair sprouted along her arms as she struggled to maintain her balance. It was a battle she lost, and she went down hard on her shoulder, fangs bared, eyes alight as they fell on me. Her growl was a feral thing as she snapped her jaws in my direction.

Mark stepped forward, the muscles in his back shifting as he tried to step in front of me, like he was *protecting* me. His hand came back behind him, as if he was getting ready to shove me away. This mother-fucker thought he could—

She was up and moving, hurtling toward us.

Mark tensed.

But it was over before it really began.

Ox moved quicker than a man his size should have been able. One moment he stood with Joe, and the next his hand was around the Omega's neck, stopping her forward momentum. She made a painful choking sound, her legs and arms jerking forward. He lifted her off the ground, her feet kicking out as she tried to impale him with her claws. She didn't get the chance before he slammed her back down into the ground with a bone-jarring crunch, crouched over her, his face in hers, eyes ablaze.

And then he roared.

It bowled over us, a blast that rolled through the forest. The Beta wolves whimpered quietly. The humans covered their ears. Even Joe flinched.

My tattoos burst to life, the colors swirling up and down my arms. The raven's beak opened in a silent scream, the roses blooming underneath, full and bright.

The song of the Alpha was a tremendous thing, and no one sang it like Oxnard Matheson.

The Omega instantly shifted back to human, the violet flickering out of her eyes. She started crying, a low, painful sound as she curled up into herself. She muttered *Alpha* over and over again, shoulders shaking.

"Robbie," Joe said, watching Ox as he removed his hand from the Omega's throat, "call Michelle Hughes. Tell her we have another one."

PINPRICKS OF LIGHT /
BONES AND DUST

Elizabeth and Jessie took the woman away. She continued to tremble, her head hanging low, dirty hair around her face. Elizabeth put an arm around her shoulders and whispered in her ear. Jessie followed behind them, glancing back at Ox before disappearing into the house. If the Omega was anything like the ones before, they would be fine. But if not, Elizabeth would handle it.

"She's not going to be happy," Joe was telling Ox when I turned back to them.

"Michelle isn't happy about anything," Ox said, rubbing his hands on his work pants. "Ever. You know that."

"Still."

"I don't give a shit about her happiness. We warned her this was happening and she did nothing. This is on her as much as it is us, no matter what she says."

Robbie was pacing in front of the house, talking quietly into his cell phone. He looked aggravated before he snapped, "I don't *care* what I'm interrupting. You tell her the Alphas of the Bennett pack need to speak to her. *Now.*" He waited a beat before sighing. "Good help is so hard to find these days. No, I was talking about *you.* Move your ass! Jesus Christ."

"You're bleeding."

Mark was there, standing far too close for someone half-dressed. He frowned at my arm. I looked down. A small trickle of blood leaked from the indentations I'd made with my fingernails. His nostrils flared. I wondered what it smelled like to him, if it was copper laced with lightning.

"It's nothing," I said, stepping back when it looked like he was going to reach for me. "I've had worse."

"You cut yourself."

"I did what I had to."

He scowled at me. "You didn't need to bleed for it to work."

I snorted. "Because you know so much about magic."

"Oh, right, I haven't been around it for my entire life or anything."

"Don't," I warned him.

"Gordo—"

"And what was that, by the way?"

That stopped him. "What?"

"You getting in my way."

His bushy eyebrows did a complicated dance. "She was targeting you."

"I can handle myself."

"I didn't say you couldn't."

"I don't need you to—"

"As if you haven't made *that* abundantly clear. You're pack, Gordo. I would have done the same for anyone else here."

Goddammit. That shouldn't have stung like it did. So I said, "How's Dale?" knowing full well the nasty curl that crawled along my words.

His eyes flashed orange. "Dale's *fine*. I didn't know you cared so much about his well-being."

I grinned at him. "What can I say? I'm a nice guy. Can't wait to meet him. Thinking about telling him about your hairy time of the month?"

His jaw tightened.

I stared back.

"I wish I'd thought to bring popcorn," I heard Chris mutter.

"This is better than those *Real Housewives* shows that I absolutely do not watch or have recorded on my DVR," Rico whispered back.

"I thought you said those were there because of Bambi?" Tanner asked.

"They are. That's exactly why they're there. Not because I watch them by myself ever."

"I need to get a girlfriend," Chris said with a sigh. "I'm tired of seeing naked people I don't want to have sex with."

"That sounds like too much work," Tanner said.

"That's because you're aro. You don't *want* a girlfriend."

"Maybe you should just learn to be happy with yourself. Being aromantic doesn't have anything to do with that."

"Shut the fuck up, Tanner. You're making me feel bad."

"Humans are so weird," Kelly muttered.

"True that," Carter said. "Hey, question. Why are you staring at

Robbie like you can't decide if he's a large bug or if you want to rub against him?"

Kelly growled at his brother and stomped inside, the door slamming shut behind him.

"I'm having such a wonderful time," Carter said to no one in particular.

"Michelle's getting online," Robbie said, shoving his phone back in his pocket. "She's not very happy. Just so you know."

Ox shook his head. "Not my problem. Robbie. Mark. Gordo. With Joe and me. Carter, run these idiots through their drills."

"What!"

"Why!"

"What the hell did *we* do?"

Ox glared at them.

Rico rolled his eyes. "Yeah, yeah, yeah. *Alfa* says jump, we say how high. Got it. I think I liked it more when you weren't all *grr. Bastardo.*"

I followed Ox and Joe into the house as Carter gleefully began to bark orders at the others, who grumbled. I felt Mark watching me before he muttered something under his breath that I couldn't quite make out and made his way inside.

Kelly was in the large kitchen, frowning at the pots and pans on the stove, looking as if he was trying to figure out what his mother had been up to before the Omega had breached the wards. Elizabeth and Jessie were nowhere in sight. The old pipes groaned in the walls. They must have had the Omega in one of the bathrooms, trying to get her cleaned up.

Ox opened the door that led to his and Joe's office. I hesitated at the doorway as I always did before I entered, flashes of a long-ago life punching me in the gut. My father burning his magic into my skin, Abel's eyes bright as they shone down on me. Abel sitting across from me at his desk, telling me my mother was dead and that my father had killed her. Thomas sitting in the same place saying they were leaving and I was staying here because I was *human*. Thomas asking me for help. Joe dividing the pack, breaking Ox's heart even further. This place carried with it an angry history, one that I still hadn't come to terms with.

"Okay?" Mark asked from behind me.

I glanced over my shoulder. He'd thankfully found a sweater hanging on a rack near the door, though it pulled tight against his chest. I didn't let my gaze linger. "Fine."

He nodded but didn't say anything else.

"Are you guys having a moment?" Robbie asked from somewhere behind him. "Maybe you could let me in so I don't have to stand here awkwardly while you work through it."

Mark's lips twitched.

I walked into the office, and he did the same. Robbie followed, closing the door behind us. The room was soundproofed to protect from any prying ears such as those belonging to the Omega upstairs. Joe and Ox stood near the far wall in front of a large mounted screen. Robbie hooked up his phone to a cable that somehow allowed us to video-conference through the TV. I still had my old flip phone from before we left to follow Richard Collins. Robbie sighed every time he saw it.

"Mark," Ox said, "I want you to stay silent. Not out of sight. But just watch."

He nodded slowly. "For?"

"Anything she's not telling us."

I blinked. "You think she knows more than she's saying?"

"She says a lot," Joe said. "For someone who doesn't say anything at all."

"People in power usually do," Robbie muttered, tapping on his phone. "And not that I don't appreciate the invite to the head honcho meeting, but why am I here?"

"Because she knows you," Joe said. "And I think she still trusts you."

He rolled his eyes. "I think that ended the moment I chose Ox over her. And not like that," he added hastily, eyes going wide as he looked at Joe. "I'm so over Ox. Not that I was ever *into* Ox. It was Stockholm syndrome or something. I've got my eye on something different."

"Uh-huh," Joe said dryly. "And by something different, you mean my brother."

Robbie swallowed thickly. "I'm going to shut up now."

Joe grinned, razor-sharp. "Good plan."

Ox reached over and switched the screen on. It lit up a bright blue as Robbie continued to tap his phone. He looked back up at his Alphas and said, "Ready?"

Joe nodded.

The screen went dark and beeped once, twice, three times.

And then Michelle Hughes appeared.

She was beautiful, in a cold, aloof way. She was somewhere around my age, though she looked younger. Her hair was dark and rested artfully on her shoulders, her makeup minimal. She smiled, but it didn't reach her eyes. I don't know if it ever did.

"Alpha Bennett," she said. "Alpha Matheson. How lovely it is to see you again. And so soon after our last meeting."

"Alpha Hughes," Joe said evenly. "Thank you for taking the time to speak to us. I know it's late in Maine."

She waved him away. "I'll always make time for you. You know that."

Robbie coughed. It sounded sarcastic.

Her eyes flickered over to him. "Robbie. You're looking well."

"Yes, ma'am. Thank you, ma'am. Doing just fine."

"That's good. Your pack seems to be treating you well."

Your pack.

"They are," he said, puffing out his chest proudly. "They're good Alphas."

"Are they? Curious." Then, "Livingstone."

"Michelle," I said, sounding bored.

She was good. She gave away nothing at my disrespect. "And Mark Bennett. Why, this is quite the gathering. All for one little Omega."

"The third this month," Ox reminded her, though she already knew.

"Does it live?"

"*She* does," Joe said. "She wasn't a threat. We don't kill indiscriminately."

Mark tensed beside me but said nothing.

"No? Ox might say otherwise. As I'm sure you're aware by now, during your little . . . sojourn to parts unknown, the blood of many Omegas was spilled upon your territory."

"You know why," Ox said, calm as ever.

"Yes," she said. "Because they were acting in service of Richard Collins, the pathetic little things that they were. Or at the very least, they were trying to capture his attention. And now that he's dead, well. They have to go *somewhere*."

"Why here?" I asked.

She barely looked at me, instead choosing to answer to the Alphas. "Somehow Richard was able to gather the Omegas behind him. They listened to him. They followed him. He wasn't an Alpha, not then, but he acted like one."

Joe shook his head. "That shouldn't have been possible."

She arched a perfectly shaped eyebrow. "No? Neither should Alpha Matheson here. Before his change, he was nothing but a human." She had a look of faint disdain on her face. "And yet there was still something about him, wasn't there? Enough that the pack you left behind chose him to lead. Well, the wolves, anyway."

"Ox is nothing like Richard," Joe said, voice clipped. No one talked shit about his pack. I'd seen what Joe was capable of when pushed. Michelle was pushing, though I didn't know why.

"They're more alike than you think," Michelle said. "Ox may not have Richard's penchant for . . . chaos, but they aren't like anyone I've ever seen before. And even though his reign ended rather quickly, from what you've said, Richard got his wish. He was an Alpha, if only for a moment."

She was right. Even as I'd watched, unable to stop him, Richard had thrust his hand into Ox's chest. I'd seen the blood and the wet *pieces* of Ox falling to the ground. And there had been a brief, terrible second when Richard's eyes had bled from violet to red. Ox's pack didn't talk about it much. How they'd felt Richard bursting through them, even the humans. Where once it'd been *love* and *brother* and *sister* and *pack*, what remained was nothing but rage and bloodlust, a furious pull into black tinged with red. Richard Collins had taken the Alpha from Ox. Therefore, he'd become the Alpha to Ox's pack.

Joe had ended that as quickly as it'd started.

But they hadn't forgotten how it'd felt, brief though it was.

"And you took that from him," Michelle continued. "You killed him. Richard was the Alpha to the Omegas. When he died, that passed on to you. And oh, they're fighting it, I'm sure. Resisting the pull. But Green Creek was lit up like a beacon in the dark. Some can't help but seek you out. Coupled with the draw of the Bennett territory, I'm only surprised there haven't been more."

Ox and I exchanged a glance. The rest of the wolves didn't react. Michelle was dangerously close to a truth she didn't even know was within her grasp, something we'd kept from her since the day Oxnard Matheson had been turned into an Alpha wolf.

Because she was right. Somehow, Richard *had* managed to gather Omegas behind him, and though he hadn't been an Alpha—in fact, toward the end, his eyes had been violet and crazed—they had followed him. They had *listened* to him.

Alpha to the Omegas was something of a misnomer. Richard Collins had only been an Alpha for seconds before Joe killed him.

Joe's eyes had burned as bright as I'd ever seen them before he bit Ox, giving the Alpha power *back*.

And with it had come the Omegas who had amassed behind Richard.

It'd been a whisper at first, in Ox's head.

But it soon turned to a roar.

There were a few days following Ox's transition from human to wolf where we thought *he* was turning feral.

And then it began to spread to others. Elizabeth. Mark. Chris. Tanner. Rico. Jessie. Robbie.

They, too, began to feel it, like an itch under their skin that could never be satisfied. They were . . . moodier than they normally were. Quick to anger, especially after Joe and Ox mated.

We should have realized what it was sooner.

Ox was hearing the voices of the Omegas. They had followed Richard.

And now they had latched on to Ox.

Ox had figured it out before everyone else.

Together we shut down the connection. We couldn't sever it. It was as if we closed a door and locked it firmly. They still scratched at it, still threw themselves against it, trying to break it down, but I was strong, and Ox was stronger.

We didn't know what would happen if Ox opened that door. If he didn't fight the bonds anymore. What would happen to him. To his pack, the ones who had stayed behind. Even though we were all one now, there was still a thin division.

Or if the Omegas themselves shattered it and poured through.

We would never find out, not if I had any say in it.

Michelle Hughes didn't know any of this. And we planned to keep it that way.

"How many more do you think there could be?" Joe asked, deflecting before she could continue.

"Oh, I can't even begin to speculate. But they will be dealt with, no matter what. We can't afford to have our world exposed, no matter what the cost."

"But why did she go after Gordo?" Robbie asked.

Michelle leaned forward as I sighed and looked up at the ceiling.

"Um," Robbie said. "Forget I said that. She didn't go after Gordo. Ha ha ha, just joking. Just a really awful joke that I shouldn't have—"

"Robbie," Ox said.

"Yep. Got it, boss. Shutting up now."

"Did she?" Michelle asked. "Fascinating. Gordo?"

"It was nothing," I said, keeping my voice even. "I was in front of everyone else. The closest target. Nothing more."

"Nothing more," she repeated.

I stared back blandly.

She hummed a little under her breath. Then, "Tell me, Gordo, when was the last time you heard from your father?"

Oh, so *that's* how she wanted to play. "Before Osmond took him away," I said coolly as Mark's fingers brushed against mine. "Before he said that his magic would be stripped and he would never escape from where *you* all would be holding him. Much like you were supposed to be holding Richard."

Her eyes narrowed. "That was unfortunate—"

"Unfortunate? People died. I think it's a little more than *unfortunate*."

"I didn't know you cared about Thomas Bennett," Michelle said, losing a bit of her composure. "You made that abundantly clear after he—"

And Joe said, "*Enough.*"

Mark's hand was in mine, holding my fingers tight. I tried to find the strength to pull away but couldn't do it.

"My apologies, Alpha," Michelle said, mask firmly back in place. "That was uncalled for."

"You're damn right it was," Ox snapped. "We don't always see eye to eye. I get that. But you have no place speaking to the Bennett witch that way. Do it again and we're going to have a problem. Do you understand?"

It obviously pained her to say, "Of course," but I couldn't find a fuck left to give. "That being said, I stand by my inquiry."

"Which is?"

"Robert Livingstone."

Mark squeezed my hand. I thought my bones would break.

"We know he was working with Richard," she said, "though the question still remains in what capacity. If he was working *for* Richard, or if—"

"He wouldn't have."

Everyone turned to stare at me.

I hadn't meant to say that out loud.

Michelle was smiling again. "What's that now, witch?"

I cleared my throat. "He wouldn't have been working for Richard. He would have loathed the wolves."

"How do you know that?" Ox asked. "You told me he—"

"My mother. She . . . hated. This life. Pack and wolves and magic." They lied, she said, they used, they didn't *love*. "She wanted to take me away from it. My father wouldn't let her. I think, in the end, he was altering her memories somehow." I shrugged. "And then she found out about . . . his tether. How it was another woman. My mother killed her. My father killed my mother, and more. It was my mother's last act. The only way she could get revenge against him for all that he'd done. He couldn't handle the loss, so he . . . And then to have you all take his magic from him. To have his own brethren strip him of his magic under orders from wolves, well. He would have hated them. You. So, no. He wasn't working for Richard. If anything, Richard was working for him, though he wouldn't have known it. I wouldn't be surprised if my father *let* Richard think he was in charge. But Richard was nothing but a puppet. A weapon my father would have used in order to take out as many of us as he could. He wouldn't have cared about Richard wanting to become an Alpha. My father used Richard."

"And how do you know all this?" Michelle asked, leaning forward on her desk. She had a glint in her eyes that I didn't understand.

I said, "I'm my father's son. And had it been me in his place, I can't say I wouldn't have done the same."

Mark said, "You're wrong."

I blew smoke out my nose. The porch light was off, and I could barely make him out in the dark. The air was cool, and the leaves swayed in the trees. It was cloudy now, and it smelled like rain. He hadn't come from inside the house. After the meeting with Michelle had ended, he'd been one of the first out of the room, not looking back. I didn't blame him. There wasn't much to look back to.

I grunted at him, ashing the butt into my hand. Sparks burned against my palm, the pain like little pinpricks of light that reminded me I was alive.

"You're wrong."

"About?"

"That you would have done the same."

"You don't know that."

"I do."

"What do you want, Mark?"

"I don't know how you can't see it."

"See *what*?"

He said, "That you're nothing like him. You never have been. You came from him, but he didn't shape who you are. We did that. Your pack."

"The pack." I snorted in derision. "Which pack, Mark? The one I have now? Or the one that abandoned me here?"

"I never wanted—"

I was suddenly very tired. "Go away, Mark. I don't want to do this right now."

The bitterness was sharp and pungent. "Like that's a surprise."

I inhaled. It burned. I exhaled. Smoke leaked from my nose and curled up around my face, hanging like a storm cloud.

"I thought . . ." He laughed, but it didn't sound like he found anything funny. "I thought things would be different. After."

After we'd come back.

After Richard was dead.

After the separate packs had come together.

Always after, after, after.

"You thought wrong."

"I guess I did."

I felt him watching me.

The tip of the cigarette flared in the dark. It looked like the color of his eyes as a wolf.

He growled low in his chest. I heard the grinding shift of bone and muscle.

I looked back a moment later.

The clothes he'd been wearing lay on the porch.

He was gone.

Ox was waiting for me when I went back inside. "You told me once it was a wolf who killed your mother."

Shit. "I lied."

"Why?"

"I wanted you to hate them as much as I did. I was wrong."

He nodded slowly. "You don't, though. Hate them. Not anymore."

"It's . . . no. I mean, it's complicated."

"Is it?"

Fucking werewolves.

The girl. The Omega.

She was broken.

"Alpha," she pleaded. "Alpha."

She reached for Ox.

She reached for Joe.

She saw me, and her eyes flashed violet.

She growled, a cornered animal ready to lash out.

Elizabeth whispered in her ear, her hand around the Omega's arm. Little trails of blood dripped from where her claws dug in.

The Omega snapped her jaws at me.

Elizabeth jerked her arm harshly.

"Jessie," Ox said, "move away."

Jessie did, slowly and never taking her eyes off the Omega.

"Mom," Joe said, "maybe you should—"

Elizabeth didn't look at him when she said, "Hush, Joe."

Joe hushed.

She whispered and whispered.

The Omega stared at me with wide eyes.

Eventually violet faded to a muddy brown. Her hair was wet and plastered to her shoulders. She had a towel wrapped around her chest and waist.

Her face was puffy and pale.

"Alpha," she said again, voice breaking. "Please. Alpha."

Her hands were claws as she held them toward Ox. Toward Joe.

Joe said, "She's just like the others."

"She's an Omega," Elizabeth said, her grip ever-tight. Her fingers were slick with blood. "She doesn't know any better. None of them do."

"Alpha," the Omega said through a mouthful of fangs. "Alpha, Alpha, Alpha."

Ox said, "I don't understand."

"I know. You wouldn't. Not now."

"I've seen Omegas. When they came here. Before. With Thomas. And after, when you all were gone. Even with Richard, they had . . . they weren't like this. They still were in control. And after . . . I don't know. I thought we'd closed that door."

Ah, yes. The door. The connection to the Omegas he'd felt after Richard Collins had become an Alpha. We didn't talk about it much. "How is it?"

"The same as always."

I told myself I believed him.

He sat behind the desk in the office. Joe had refused to leave his mother's side while she looked after the Omega. It was late. The humans had gone home. Carter and Kelly were on patrol, running the edges of the territory. Robbie was in his room. Mark was . . . well. I didn't need to think about where Mark was. It was none of my business.

I picked at a long scar in the wood on the surface of the desk. It'd come from one of the kids in the old pack, still not in control of her shift. She'd died when the hunters had come. "They degrade."

Ox scrubbed a hand over his face. He looked tired and oh so young. "What?"

I chose my words carefully. "Omegas. They degrade. The tether, it's . . . a bond. It's metaphysical. An emotion. A person. A spiritual attachment. It holds a wolf to their humanity. Keeps them from getting lost to the animal."

"And a witch."

I looked up at him. He was watching me, head cocked. "I don't—"

"You said it holds a wolf to their humanity. It works the same for witches. You told me that once." He closed his eyes and leaned back in the chair. It creaked under his weight.

"I told you a lot of things."

"I know."

"We're not talking about me."

"Maybe we should."

"Ox."

"You do this, you know. Deflect." He opened his eyes. They were human. "I don't know why."

I scowled at him. "I know what you're doing. This whole Zen Alpha bullshit doesn't work on me. I'm not one of your wolves, Ox, so knock it off."

He smiled quietly. "You got me. But then, I'm your tether. I don't want you to—how did you put it? Degrade."

"Kiddo, I'll kick your wolfy ass into next week, so help me god. Mark my words."

He laughed. It was a good sound. A strong sound. Warmth bloomed in my chest at pleasing my Alpha again, and I ignored it.

He waved me on. "You were saying?"

"Those Omegas. The ones before. They aren't the same. They weren't as far gone. The longer a wolf doesn't have a tether, the more feral they'll be. It's not a quick process, Ox. And it's not easy. Losing your mind never is."

"Do you remember her? The barefooted woman. Marie."

Oh, I did. She'd been beautiful, except for the crazy in her eyes. She'd been before Richard. A precursor. "She was on her way. Not as bad as the others, but she would have gotten there. They all do. In the end."

He watched me close. "You've seen it. Before."

I nodded.

"Who?"

"I didn't know his name. My father wouldn't tell me. He came to stay with us. His pack had been wiped out. Hunters. I was just a kid. Abel tried to help him. Tried to help him find a new tether, something to latch on to. But it didn't work. He was lost in his grief. His Alpha was dead. His mate was dead. His pack had been destroyed.

He had nothing left." I looked down at the scar in the desktop. "Nothing worked. It was—he was slowly losing his mind. Have you ever seen that up close, Ox? It starts in the eyes. They grow . . . vacant. More and more vacant. Like a light is fading. You can see they understand what's happening to them. There's a knowledge there. An understanding. But they can't do anything to stop it. Eventually he lost himself to his wolf. He was completely feral."

"What happened to him?"

"The only thing that could be done."

"He was put down."

I shrugged. "Abel did it. Said it was the least he could do. My father made me watch."

"Jesus."

That didn't even begin to cover it. "It was necessary. To see what needed to be done. It was a mercy, in the end." I thought of the wolf in the alley of a forgotten Montana town, silver through the head.

"You were just a kid."

"So were you with all the shit you went through. And look at you now."

He wasn't amused by that. "The others, then."

The ones who had found their way to Green Creek. "What about them?"

"We gave them to the gruff man."

"Philip Pappas."

"And he took them East. To Maine. To *her*."

"They're better equipped to deal with Omegas." I didn't know how much I actually believed that.

But Ox let it go. "And if they couldn't be saved? If they couldn't find their tether?"

I stared at him, unblinking. "You know what happened then."

He banged his fist on the desk. He was still a man, but barely. Ox was always in control and rarely lost himself to anger. Zen Wolf. "I didn't want to send them to their deaths."

I shook my head. "Sometimes there's no other choice, Ox. A feral wolf is dangerous to everyone. Wolves. Witches. Humans. Can you imagine what would happen if a feral wolf found its way into a town? If that woman upstairs gave in to her wolf and trotted into Green Creek? How many people would die before she could be stopped?

And if you had the chance to do something about it, and then didn't, those deaths would be on you. Could you live with yourself knowing you could have ended it before it began?"

He looked away, jaw tensed. He was angry. I didn't know at who.

"My father told me once that sometimes, for the good of many, you have to sacrifice the few."

"Your father is a bastard."

I laughed. "You're not going to get any argument from me there."

"But then so was mine."

"Cut from a different cloth, but the end result was the same. Yours used fists. Mine used words."

"And mine is nothing but dust and bones," Ox said. "Even then, he still haunted me for a long time, saying I was gonna get shit all my life."

"I'm glad he's dead," I said, uncaring how it sounded. "He didn't deserve you. Or Maggie."

"No. He didn't. And Mom and me didn't deserve what he did to us. But he's gone, and his ghost is fading."

"That's—"

"But what about you?"

I took a step back. "What *about* me?"

He spread his fingers out across the desktop. "Your father. He's bone and flesh. Magic, still. Again. Somehow."

"I haven't heard from him. I don't know where he is." The office felt smaller. Like the walls were closing in.

Ox's eyes widened slightly. "I know that. That's not what I'm saying."

"Then maybe get to your fucking point, Ox."

"How did you manage? Before me."

"Fuck you," I said hoarsely.

"You said I was your tether."

"You *are*."

"And you said that there hadn't been one for a long time before me."

"Ox. Don't."

"How did you keep your mind?" he asked gently. "How did you keep yourself from giving in to your animal?"

A wooden raven, but he didn't fucking need to know that. No one did. It was mine. It was for me. I survived when everyone else had left me behind, and no one could take that from me. Not even Ox. He didn't need to know there'd been days I'd held on to it so tightly, it'd cut into my flesh, blood dripping down my arms. "Do you trust me?" I asked him through gritted teeth.

"Yes," he said in that calm voice that was driving me up the fucking wall. "Almost more than anyone."

"Then you need to trust me when I say to back off. That's not open for discussion."

He watched me.

I struggled not to fidget.

Eventually he nodded. "Okay."

"Okay?"

He shrugged. "Okay. Mark thinks Michelle knows more than what she's saying."

I struggled to keep up with the conversational whiplash. "I don't—I thought that much was obvious. She's playing games. It's political. She still doesn't know what to make of you. She doesn't like what she doesn't understand."

"Does anybody?"

"I don't understand you, but I like you just fine."

"She wants Joe."

And that didn't sit right. "What did she say after you kicked us out of here?"

"Same old, same old. That she's supposed to be temporary. That Joe needs to assume his rightful place. That the wolves are getting restless. They need him, she says. Everyone needs him to be who he's supposed to be."

"And Joe?"

Ox grinned, and I was reminded of the first time I'd met him when his daddy had brought him to the garage and I'd bent down to eye level, asking him if he'd wanted a pop from the machine. The smile he gave then was almost the same as the one now. He was pleased. "Appealed to her ego. Told her he thought she was doing a fine job and that he'd step in when he thought it was time."

"And that *worked*?"

"Alphas need constant validation, apparently. Though she didn't need much convincing."

"Yeah. I can see that. You're all a bunch of needy bitches."

"Fuck off, Gordo."

"You're doing a good job, though."

"Thank you. It's nice of you to— Oh, you asshole."

I laughed at him. It felt good. It usually did when he was near. Joe might have been the Alpha I turned to, but Ox was the tether that kept me whole.

"She's sending him again," Ox said finally.

"Pappas."

"For the girl."

"It's the right thing to do."

He was looking at me, but he wasn't seeing me. "Is it? Because I wonder."

"Ask him, then. When he gets here."

"He'll tell me what he thinks I want to hear. What Michelle will tell him to say."

I smiled. "Then find a way to make him break."

GOOD IDEA / TICK TICK TICK

The girl said "Alpha" and "please" and held out her hands. She grew agitated at the sight of me.

Other times she cried, arms wrapped around herself, rocking back and forth.

Elizabeth looked pained, brushing her hands through the girl's hair. She would whisper little things and sing songs that caused my heart to ache.

Joe told the humans to stay away from her. He didn't want to take the chance of the Omega lashing out.

No one argued. She made them uneasy, the way her empty eyes stared straight ahead, only coming to life when Joe or Ox came in the room.

Ox tried to bring her back. Pull her away from the madness. For a brief moment, I thought it worked.

His eyes bled, a low rumble in his throat.

Her eyes cleared, and she blinked slow and sure like the fog was burning away and she—

Her eyes turned violet. She cowered away from him, backing herself into a corner, even as she reached toward him, claws sliding out from the tips of her fingers, oily and black.

"Alpha," she babbled. "Alpha, Alpha, Alpha."

. . .

I didn't stay at the house most nights. I had my own little home. My own space. It'd once been Marty's, and then Marty and me. Now it was just mine. It wasn't anything grand, but I'd missed it almost as much as I'd missed Ox when we'd been gone. The first time I'd stepped inside after returning to Green Creek, my knees had felt weak and I'd slumped against the door.

It was in a quiet neighborhood at the end of a street, set farther back than the other houses. It was made of brick, so the wolves could huff and puff all they wanted. A maple tree grew in the front yard with as many leaves on the ground as were in its limbs. Bright flowers bloomed in the spring, golds and blues and reds and pinks. A small deck attached to the back, big enough for a chair or two. Some nights I'd sit there, feet propped up on the railing, a cold beer in one hand and a cigarette in the other as the sun set.

There were two bedrooms. One had always been mine. The other was Marty's, now an office. There was a kitchen with old appliances and a bathroom with a medicine cabinet made of wood. The floor was carpeted, and it needed to be replaced soon, some of the edges frayed and worn.

The roof was new. Ox and the guys had helped.

The Bennett house belonged to the pack. But this house was mine.

Sometimes when I came home, I'd put the keys in the bowl on the kitchen counter and I'd stand there, listening as the house creaked and settled around me. I'd remember Marty moving in the kitchen, telling me that all a man needed was a few ingredients and he'd have a feast. More often than not it was a TV dinner nuked in the microwave. He'd been married once, he'd told me, but it hadn't stuck. "We both wanted different things," he'd said.

"Like what?"

"She wanted me to sell the garage. I wanted her to fuck off."

He laughed every time he said it. It would always devolve into a smoker's cough, wet and sticky, his face red as he slapped his knee.

He wasn't magic.

He wasn't a wolf.

He wasn't pack.

He was a human man who smoked too much and cursed with every other word.

His death had hurt.

I thought I'd seen Mark at the funeral, standing at the fringes of the surprisingly sizable crowd. But when I'd pushed my way through the well-wishers, he was gone, if he'd been there at all. I'd told myself I was projecting.

After all, the wolves were gone.

A few days after the Omega came from the trees, I opened the door to my little house. My neck was stiff and my shoulders ached. It'd been a long day, and I wasn't as young as I'd once been. The work took a toll on my body. I had a bottle of old pain pills in the drawer of the nightstand next to my bed, but they always made me feel muddled and slow. They were probably expired anyway.

A TV dinner in the freezer called my name. Spicy enchiladas that gave me heartburn. A can of beer left from the twelve-pack. A cigarette to finish it all off. A meal fit for a king. A perfect way to spend a Friday night.

It would have been, anyway, had there not been a knock at the door even before I could make my way down the hall toward the bedroom.

I thought about ignoring it.

Then, through the door, "Don't even think about it, Gordo."

I groaned.

I knew that voice. I heard that voice every day.

I'd just said good*bye* to that voice a couple of hours before.

I opened the door.

Rico, Chris, and Tanner stood on my front porch.

They'd obviously gone home and cleaned up. Showers and a change of clothes. Rico wore jeans and a shirt that proclaimed him to be a LOVE MACHINE under long-sleeved flannel. Chris had on his old leather jacket that had once belonged to his father. Tanner was wearing a collared button-down shirt untucked over khakis.

And they were all watching me expectantly.

I said, "No, absolutely not," and tried to slam the door in their faces.

Before I could, they pushed their way inside.

I thought about splitting open the floor beneath their feet and burying them underneath my house.

I didn't, because it would make a mess I'd have to clean up later.

And also because there'd be questions.

"We're going out," Rico announced grandly, as if he were the answer to all my problems.

"Good for you," I snapped. "Have fun. Now leave. And where the hell do you think you two are going?"

Chris and Tanner were walking down the hall toward the bedrooms. "Don't worry about us," Chris called over his shoulder. "Just stand there and continue looking angry."

"Robbie was right," Tanner told him. "I never really noticed the murder eyebrows before. Now I can't stop thinking about them."

"You better not touch anything!" I shouted after them.

"Yeah, they're going to touch a lot of things," Rico told me, patting me on the shoulder as he passed me by on the way to the kitchen. I could do nothing but follow him, muttering death threats under my breath. He opened the fridge, frowning down at the contents. Which, admittedly, wasn't much.

"I haven't been to the store in a while," I muttered.

"This is sad," he said. "This makes me sad."

"Well, you could leave. Then you wouldn't be sad anymore."

He reached into the fridge and snagged my last beer. He closed the door and popped the top of the can. "No. Couldn't even do that. Because I'd be thinking about you here and I would still be sad." He took a long sip.

I stared at him.

He belched.

I stared some more.

He grinned.

I absolutely did not have to hold myself back from punching him in the face. "Why are you here, Rico?"

"Oh! That. Right. I'm glad you asked."

"I'm not going to like this, am I."

"No, probably not. Well, at least not at first. But then you will *love* it."

"We're going out," Chris said, coming into the kitchen.

"And you're going with us," Tanner said, right behind him.

"It's been too long since it's been just us," Rico said, and drank more of my beer. "Everything has been all wolves and pack and scary shit coming out of the trees wanting to eat me. And don't even get me started about the Alphas working our asses into the ground."

"Why do we have to run?" Chris asked, head tilted back toward the ceiling. "For *miles*, even. I mean, I get the whole *running away from monsters* thing, but I already know how to do that." He patted his trim stomach. "Do you think I asked for this? Maybe I *wanted* a beer gut."

"And don't forget the other wolves," Tanner said, arms folded across his chest. "They're just as bad. They don't even get sweaty. And they have fangs. And claws. And can jump really high."

"It's completely unfair," Rico agreed. "Which is why we're not inviting any of them, and we're going out to drink too much tonight for our ages, and we'll wake up tomorrow regretting everything."

No. Absolutely not. "The shop—"

"Ox and Robbie are opening tomorrow," Tanner said easily.

"I've got invoices to—"

"Jessie said she'd handle them," Chris said. "I invited her to go along with us, but she said, and I quote, 'I would rather watch my ex-boyfriend and his werewolf mate have sex.'" He frowned. "I think she actually meant that too."

"I don't like any of you enough to—"

"You're full of shit," Rico said. "*Pendejo.*"

I groaned. "Can't I just have one night to myself?"

"No," they all said.

"Tanner and I put clothes out on your bed," Chris said. "Go change."

"Because you can't be trusted to dress yourself," Tanner agreed.

"Fuck you."

"Maybe if Bambi is willing to share," Rico said, grinning lecherously at me. "Get your ass in gear, Livingstone. Time waits for no man."

*   *   *

Green Creek had two bars. The Lighthouse was the one everyone went to on Friday nights. Mack's was the one most people tried to avoid, given that the glasses were dirty and Mack was more than likely to spit in your drink and spout obscenely racist rhetoric while watching the old television mounted on the wall perpetually showing old episodes of *Perry Mason.*

We went to the Lighthouse.

There was no lighthouse in Green Creek. We weren't anywhere near the ocean. It was just one of those things that nobody questioned.

The parking lot was full when we pulled up in Tanner's truck. Loud honky-tonk poured out from the open doorway, along with bright bursts of laughter. People stood outside in groups, smoke curling heavy up toward the night sky.

"Crowded tonight," Chris said.

"We could just go home," I pointed out.

"Nah."

"*I* could just go home."

"Nah."

The guys opened the doors and slid from the truck.

I didn't move.

Rico leaned his head back in. "Get out. Or I'll shoot you. I'm carrying."

"You wouldn't."

His eyes narrowed. "Try me, Gordo."

Rico had gotten scarier since he'd found out about werewolves. I almost believed him.

I got out of the truck.

People waved at us as we headed inside. It was the price of living in a small town. Everyone knew everyone. I was the guy who fixed their cars, who sometimes ate in the diner. I was a townie. The same with the guys. Sure, Chris and Tanner had left for a while, but they'd come back, the world too big for them. Rico had already been working for me. Chris and Tanner had followed shortly. And after that, they never left.

But that's all we were to them. The guys from the garage. Townies. I wondered what they would think if they knew everything.

I nodded in response, not wanting to stop for even a few short words. I hoped we'd find some dark corner, get a couple of pitchers, and get out of here in an hour or two. If I'd really wanted to, I could have begged off, but it'd been a long while since we'd done this, just the four of us. We'd tried it once after the death of Richard Collins. We hadn't spoken much, staring down at our beers, the guys still too pissed at me for leaving.

But then life had happened. We got busy. The pack. The garage. Rico met Bambi. Tanner started taking some business classes online so he could do more with the shop and pack finances. Chris began grilling Elizabeth and Mark on all things wolf related, trying to find out as much as he could about a world that he hadn't known existed for most of his life.

I saw them every day still. But we all had other things going on.

Well, *they* all had other things going on.

I was doing my best to ignore the obvious, working too much and sleeping too little.

"My *baby!*" a woman shrieked.

"Mi corazón," Rico purred as his arms suddenly became full of blonde hair, flowery perfume, and fake tits.

Bambi was . . . Bambi. She was a townie who had worked at the bar since she'd graduated high school, which, unfortunately, wasn't as long ago as I would have liked. She was a small-town girl who slung beers to a mostly male crowd, pretty and a little rough around the edges. Her nails were a bloodred, as were her lips, and she wore a revealing pair of shorts that probably got her more tips. She had a towel over her shoulder as she put her arms around Rico's neck, peppering his face with sticky kisses, leaving lipstick on his cheeks and chin.

Tanner looked horrified.

Chris was amused.

Rico had himself an armful of Bambi.

I rolled my eyes.

A man I didn't recognize was stumbling by behind her. For a moment I thought he'd keep on going.

Instead he pulled his hand back and slapped Bambi on the ass.

She tensed.

I sighed.

Almost quicker than I could follow, she whirled around, grabbed the man by the arm, and twisted it up behind his back. He squawked in pain as she kicked the backs of his knees, forcing him down. His beer bottle shattered on the floor. People in the bar fell silent as she pulled his arm up behind him almost to the point of breaking. "Touch me again without my permission," she said, her voice high and sweet, "and I'll rip off your balls. Understood?"

The man nodded frantically.

"Good," she said, kissing his cheek. "Now get out. And if I catch you in my bar again, I will *end* you."

She let him go and he pulled himself up, only to be met by two large men who worked for Bambi as security. They took him by his arms and led him out of the bar.

The music picked up again.

People began talking loudly.

"I love her so goddamn much," Rico whispered in awe.

"Yeah," Chris said. "Question. Once she comes to her senses and breaks up with you, what's the appropriate amount of time in the bro code to wait before I can ask her out?"

"Six months," Tanner said.

"Make it seven," Rico said. "Just so I have enough time to mend my broken heart. And when you do, always remember that I got there first."

"Gordo," Bambi said, a knowing grin on her face. "Well, aren't you a sight for sore eyes. These degenerates finally dragged you out, huh?"

"I'm wounded," Rico said.

People underestimated Bambi. Her name. Her looks. The fact that she owned a bar when she herself was only a few years past legal drinking age. But she was almost as terrifying as the wolves and smarter than most gave her credit for.

And for whatever reason, she adored Rico. I wouldn't cross her, but I did question her taste in men.

"Against my will," I assured her.

She clapped her hands. "Good. I'm glad it worked. The table in the back is ready for you guys. Sit down and I'll bring a couple of pitchers." She kissed a dazed Rico on the cheek before she pushed her way into the crowd, hollering at people to get the fuck out of her way.

"Don't know what she sees in your ugly mug," Chris said, shoving Rico.

"My Latin flavor," Rico snapped back, a goofy grin on his face. "She got tired of white bread."

Tanner rolled his eyes but started leading the way toward the back of the bar.

Sure enough, there was an empty booth in the back, a folded card on the table saying it was RESERVED (DON'T SIT HERE IF IT'S NOT MEANT FOR YOU, ASSHOLES) in girlish pink script. She confused me greatly.

Rico shoved me onto the bench first, then slid in next to me. Tanner and Chris took the other side. Chris pulled a small notepad from a pocket lining the inside of his jacket. He opened it, putting it on the table before him. He frowned, patting his outside pockets, before pulling out a stubby pencil that looked like it'd been gnawed on repeatedly.

"Okay," he said, opening the notepad to a fresh sheet of paper. "The meeting to get Gordo laid can now commence."

And it had been going so well.

"What," I said flatly.

"What is Gordo looking for in a man?" Tanner asked, sitting back on the bench.

"He needs to be a little mean," Rico said, rubbing his chin thoughtfully. "Can't be sensitive, because Gordo is an asshole and would make sensitive people cry."

"Seriously," I said. "What."

"Uh-huh," Chris said, writing something down on the notepad. "Needs to be mean. Got it. What else?"

"Has to have facial hair," Tanner said. "He has a kink for facial hair. Gotta have that beard burn on his asshole."

"What in the *fuck* are you talking about—"

"Should probably be taller too," Rico mused. "Gordo likes 'em big."

"Hairy and fat," Chris muttered, hunched over the notepad.

"Not *fat*," Rico said. "Well, not that there's anything wrong with being heavier." He squinted at me. "You okay with some meat on the bones? Some cushion for your pushin'? I know you're versatile. Why I know that, I don't care to think about."

"I am going to murder all of you," I promised him darkly.

"He likes them a little wolfish," Tanner said.

"Wolfish," Chris said, pencil scratching along paper.

"Able to hold their own in a fight," Rico said.

"Probably has to know about his *my-arms-glow-in-the-dark* secret too," Tanner said.

"They don't glow in the *dark*—"

"That's true," Rico agreed. "And should be someone he's comfortable around. Someone he knows."

"Right, right," Chris said.

Bambi appeared as if by magic, holding a tray with two pitchers and four frosty mugs in one hand. She set it expertly down on the table without spilling a drop. She smiled at Rico as she set the mugs in front of us and the pitchers in the middle of the table. "What are y'all up to?"

"Trying to get Gordo laid," Rico said cheerfully.

"Ooh," she said. "Man or woman?"

"Man."

"I'm on it," she said before she disappeared from whence she'd come.

I angrily poured myself some beer. It was more foam than liquid.

Rico took the other pitcher and began filling the remaining mugs. "What else?"

"Is anything else necessary?" Chris asked, frowning down at the notepad.

"I think that pretty much narrows it down," Tanner said.

"Okay," Rico said. "Hit me with it."

Chris picked up the notepad and held it close to his face, squinting at the words. "Okay. Based upon our criteria of being hairy and big and wolfish and knowing about how Gordo uses Force lightning because he's pretty much a Jedi—"

I furiously choked down foam.

"—that leaves us with two choices for Gordo to get laid."

"Awesome," Rico said. "That makes our job so much easier. Who are they?"

"Carter or Mark Bennett."

I sprayed foam on the table.

Rico patted me on the back. "Good choices, though I feel one is more obvious than the other. Pros and cons?"

"Carter is young," Tanner said before belching. He wiped his mouth. "Could probably get it up more than one time in a night. He's also probably eager to learn. A real crowd-pleaser, if you know what I mean. Kids are always eager." He grimaced. "I wish I hadn't phrased it like that."

"And he's big," Rico said. "And we know he's hung because of all the times we've seen him naked. Because werewolves. Which does wonders for my self-esteem."

"Big penis," Chris said, writing on the notepad.

"And he's a second to Joe," Tanner said. "Which means he's a real go-getter."

"Good point," Rico said. "Cons?"

"He only sleeps with women," Chris said.

"So far," Tanner said. "But didn't Kelly say wolves were all fluid? Maybe he hasn't yet found a man to rev his engine." He looked at me. "Maybe he shouldn't start with Gordo. He's more of a work-your-way-up-to. Or a last resort."

I pointed my mug at him. "You'll be the first to die."

"And while he's young, he might be *too* young for Gordo," Rico said. "Gordo tends to like them a bit more . . . mature. Actually have some grass on the field, you know?"

"And you'll be second," I growled at him.

"I also haven't detected any sexual chemistry between the two of them," Chris said. He glanced at me. "Did anything happen on the road? One night, maybe, when you two were feeling a little bit lonelier than usual, maybe you gave in and he sucked your—"

"I'll save you for last," I warned him. "While the screams of the others still echo in your ears."

"Let's move on to Mark," Rico said. "Pros and cons?"

"There's a history there," Tanner said before chugging the rest of his beer.

"Is that a pro or con?" Chris asked, filling my empty mug. Less foam this time.

"I don't know," Rico said. "Gordo, is that a pro or con?"

I wiped my mouth, enraged.

"I'll put it in both," Chris decided.

"He's Gordo's type," Tanner said.

"He pretty much *defined* Gordo's type," Rico said.

"Do you know how long it takes for a person to suffocate?" I asked them. "Usually around three minutes. I can make it one and a half."

They ignored me. "And he's big," Tanner said.

"And hairy," Chris added. "Except for the top of his head."

"All that chest hair," Rico said. "Man, being in a werewolf pack with mostly men must be like a buffet for the gay guys." He kicked me underneath the table. "Is it a buffet for you? All that man flesh on display?"

"Too bad Jessie's not a wolf," Tanner sighed.

"That's my *sister*," Chris snarled at him, trying to stab him with the pencil.

"Elizabeth is hot for an older lady," Rico said. Then his eyes widened. "Please don't tell her I said that. I don't want to do an Ox versus Richard Collins impression and see my insides on my outsides."

"Wow," Tanner said. "Too soon, man. Too soon."

Chris shook his head at Rico, obviously disappointed.

"Lo siento," Rico said. "It felt wrong as soon as I said it, but I was already committed. Won't happen again. Where were we?"

"Mark and Gordo," Tanner said.

Chris nodded. "So far we have so many more pros than cons."

"Cons," Rico said. "Cons, cons, cons. Oh! I got one. Like, they broke up and stuff for reasons Gordo has really yet to explain, even though he's Mark's mystical moon magic mate, or whatever. And he hasn't told us why neither of them have pulled their heads out of their asses since Gordo got back, even though they sometimes stare at each other like they want to choke on some dicks."

I glared at him.

He shrugged. "What? You know it's true."

"Choke on some dicks," Chris mumbled, writing exactly that on his notepad.

"I'm not telling you shit," I retorted. "In fact, you're all fired. And you're kicked out of the pack. And I never want to see any of you again. Ever."

Rico nodded sympathetically. "Yeah, I'd probably say the same thing if I was you and surrounded by friends who are much smarter."

"Why can't you just leave this alone?"

"Because we're your buddies," Tanner said. "We've had your back longer than anybody else. We've earned the right to call you out on your shit."

"Jessie told me that you were getting pathetic," Chris admitted. "She said ever since Mark met Dale—ow, who the fuck just *kicked* me?"

"We agreed not to mention his name!" Rico hissed at him. "Que te jodan."

"You didn't have to *kick* me. Your boots have steel toes, you dick!"

"Jessie said you were grumpier than normal," Tanner said, glaring at Chris.

"I'm not grumpier than normal," I said. "I'm *always* like this."

"Eh," Rico said. "More or less. But it's gotten a little worse. The wolves are starting to feel it." He looked over his shoulder before leaning forward. "You know," he whispered, "through their *feelings*." He wiggled his fingers at me.

"You're all fucking stupid," I said. "And the next person that opens their mouth will find out what life is like without testicles."

They all stared at me.

I stared back at each of them in turn to make sure they knew I was serious. Magic didn't work like that, but they didn't know it.

As much as I wanted to smash their faces onto the table, they were only looking out for me as they always had. Tanner had been right. I'd known them longer than almost anyone. They'd been there through the worst of it, even if they hadn't known what was happening. The destruction of my first pack, being left behind by my second. Mark asking his Alpha for permission to court me. Mark giving me his wolf. Me giving him an ultimatum and Mark choosing his pack.

Mark, Mark, Mark.

They'd tried to keep Dale from me. Like I cared. Like I was *fragile*. Like the very idea of Mark with someone else would be so devastating, I wouldn't be able to function.

I'd lived more of my life without him than I ever did with him.

It didn't matter to me. Mark could do what he wanted.

I didn't give a shit. Just because *I* hadn't been with anyone else in years didn't mean a damn thing. It was—

"Oh fuck," Chris said, eyes wide. "This wasn't supposed to happen."

"What?" Tanner asked, looking out into the crowd. "What are you—oh shit. Um. Gordo! Hey, Gordo!" He slapped the top of the table. "Hey, man. Look at me! Look right at me. So, let's talk about something different. Like . . . um. Oh! Are you still thinking of opening another garage? That would be great. Just . . . great."

"What the hell is wrong with the two of you?" Rico asked, eyes narrowed.

Chris jerked his head like he was having a seizure, eyes darting back and forth.

Rico looked over his shoulder. He made a weird noise in his throat and started coughing.

I turned to see what they'd been staring at.

"No!" Tanner said, kicking my shin.

"What's your problem?" I growled at him, reaching down and rubbing my leg.

"Nothing," he said. "My bad. Totally didn't mean to do that. Just . . . hey! Gordo!"

"What?"

"How are you? *Really*. I feel like we haven't talked in long time. You know?"

"We went to lunch today," I reminded him. "Just the two of us. For an hour."

"Right," Tanner said, nodding furiously. "So nice of you. Did I say thanks for that? Because that was just . . . nice. I appreciate—oh my fucking god, why is he coming over here? Is he *insane*?"

Rico twisted in his seat, getting onto his knees on the bench. "Vete," he hissed. "Vete!"

"Who the hell are you—"

"Hey, guys. How's it going?"

Mark Bennett stood next to the table. He looked good. His head was freshly shaved, and his beard had been recently trimmed. He wore a sweater I'd never seen before, a maroon V-neck that clung to his arms and shoulders. His jeans were tight around his thighs, and he towered over me. There was a pulse of *packpackpack* somewhere deep inside my head, and whether it came from him or me, I didn't know. The humans could feel it, but they couldn't broadcast it. So it had to be from one of us. There was something more, something that felt *green* and *blue*, but I couldn't latch on to it, couldn't parse through it before it pulled away as quickly as it'd come. It was a thought—an idea—but he'd taken it back. We'd learned early on how to shield ourselves from members of our pack. No one was privy to everything in our heads. I could push. A question sent out like the ripples on the surface of a lake. And maybe he'd answer. But I didn't think I wanted to know.

Especially when I saw a man standing next to him.

He was thin, with pale skin and dark eyes. His hair was artfully messy. He looked to be a little younger than me. He smiled nervously down at us, lips twitching. He was standing close to Mark, their arms brushing. He looked ordinary next to Mark. Most people did.

"Hey," I said, averting my gaze. "Mark. What a surprise."

"I didn't know you were going to be here."

"Neither did I."

"Yeah," Rico said, sounding like he was trying not to laugh or scream. I didn't know which. "We brought him out tonight. You know. Human night and whatnot."

I stomped on his foot underneath the table.

"I meant *boys'* night," he yelped. "Mierda."

"Dale," Tanner said. "Nice to see you again."

I turned slowly to look at him.

He blanched. "Uh. I mean . . . ignore me. I've had too much to drink."

"Hi, Tanner," Dale said, his voice low and gravelly. It was deeper than I thought it would be. I didn't like it. "Chris. Good to see you too."

Chris just nodded and drank the rest of his beer in one long, slow gulp.

"Hi," Dale said, and I realized he was talking to me. "I don't think we've met."

The guys at the table held their breath.

Fucking idiots.

I grinned up at Dale, turning on the charm. He looked a little dazzled. Mark didn't. He looked like he was regretting his very existence. I didn't blame him. There was blood in the water, and I felt like circling. "Yeah. How about that. Seems you've met everyone else here." Chris slumped. Tanner was stock-still, as if I wouldn't see him sitting right in front of me. "I'm Gordo. Great to meet you." I held out my hand, and he shook it politely.

"Gordo," he said. "I've heard a lot about you."

"Have you?" I said, forcing myself to sound amused. "Well, how about that. You talk about me, Mark?"

"Of course I do," Mark said quietly, those ice eyes on me. "You're important."

I struggled to keep the smile on my face. It was a battle I almost lost. "Right," I said. "Important. Because we go way back."

"A long time."

Dale looked confused, but he said, "Old friends, huh?"

I turned my grin back to him. "Since we were kids. We grew up together. Then he left and I stayed here. We grew apart. You know how it is."

"Oh?" Dale said, looking at Mark. "I didn't know that."

"I had to leave," Mark said, hands in fists at his sides. "Family thing."

"Yeah," I agreed. "Family. Because nothing is more important than family."

"Right," Dale said slowly, glancing between the two of us. "It can be the most important thing."

"Oh, I don't know," I said. "Sometimes a family of choice is better than that of blood. But that's not for everyone." I nodded at the guys at the table. "Ain't related to any of these assholes, but they're still mine. For the moment."

"We're so dead," Rico whispered to Tanner and Chris.

"And *some*times people are put into positions where they have no choice at all," Mark said evenly.

"Oh my god," Tanner breathed. "Do they have to do this *now*?"

Dale laughed uncomfortably. "I think maybe I'm missing something here."

I waved him away. "Nah. You aren't missing a thing. Because *I'm* not missing a thing. Right, Mark?"

"Right," Mark said, eyes narrowing.

Rico cleared his throat. "As fun as this is—and believe me, I've never been more entertained in my life—we don't want to keep you from your . . . night out."

"You could join us," Chris offered. Then the blood left his face as he glanced at me. "Uh, no. Don't do that. Go away." He winced. "I didn't mean that the way it sounded. Just don't . . . be here."

Tanner put his face in his hands.

"It's okay," Dale said. He seemed like such a nice guy. I fucking hated nice guys. "We won't intrude. It's been a while since I've had this one all to myself. Gonna take advantage of that."

"Christ," Rico muttered. "Of all the things to say."

"Sounds fun," I said cheerfully. "Nice to meet you. I'm sure we'll see each other again."

"You too," Dale said before pulling Mark toward the bar.

I watched them disappear into the crowd before I slowly turned back toward the table.

Rico, Tanner, and Chris sank even lower in their seats.

I took a long drink of my beer.

"He's nice," Chris tried.

"Works in a coffee shop," Tanner added. "Over in Abby."

"We only met him once," Rico said. "And while we told him to his face that we thought he was a great guy, obviously we were lying, because why would we even think something like that when you're our friend?"

"When you least expect it," I said. "When it's slipped your mind. When you've forgotten this moment, that's when I'll come for you."

I shouldn't have felt as good as I did at the look of fear in their eyes.

I was drunk.

Not smashed, but beyond tipsy.

I felt good.

The beer was heavy in my stomach.

"Gotta take a leak," I told them over the din of the crowded bar.

They nodded, not looking up from their electronic trivia tablets. The notepad had been put away, and there'd been no further talk of pros and cons.

I pushed myself up from the table. My head was swimming pleasantly. I made my way through the crowd, feeling hands slap my back, hearing my name said in greeting. I smiled. Nodded. But I didn't stop.

There was a line for the women's restroom.

Small-town women, all.

The urinal was in use in the men's room, a hand propped against the wall as the guy pissed. The stall door was shut, and from inside came the sound of retching.

The bathroom felt too warm. It smelled of piss and shit and vomit.

I went back out into the bar.

It was warmer now.

Things were starting to spin a little.

I needed air.

The front of the bar was too crowded.

I went to the side of the bar.

Bambi winked at me as she poured drinks.

I tilted my head toward the back door behind the bar.

"Go for it," she shouted over the noise. "Still looking for you, if you know what I mean?"

I did. I didn't care.

The night air was a shock against my heated skin.

The door shut behind me, the sounds of the bar muffled.

I took a deep breath and let it out slowly.

The alleyway was empty. It had rained while we were inside. Water dripped down from gutters stuffed with dead leaves. A car drove by out on the road, the tires rolling against wet pavement.

"Fuck," I muttered, rubbing my forehead. I was going to feel like shit tomorrow. I was getting too old to spend a night out drinking without paying for it. Once upon a time, I could have pounded back beers until one in the morning and then been up and ready to get into the shop at six. Those days were long past.

I walked down the alley, away from the street. A dumpster sat to the right against the wall of the bar. The hardware store was to the left. I trailed my fingers against the brick, damp and rough.

I stood on the other side of the dumpster and pissed against the wall.

I groaned at the release. It went on for ages.

I shook myself before tucking my dick back into my jeans.

The thought of going back inside was terrible.

I fished my smokes out of my pocket and slid a cigarette out of the crumpled pack. I stuck it between my teeth. I couldn't find my lighter. I must have forgotten it at home. I looked around, making sure I was alone before I snapped my fingers once. A little spark and then a small bloom of fire at my fingertips. My arms were covered, but I felt the warm pulse as a small tattoo near my left elbow flickered to life.

I brought the flame to the tip of the cigarette and inhaled. It burned my lungs. The nicotine washed through me, and I sighed out a stream of smoke.

Water dripped onto my forehead.

I closed my eyes.

A voice off to my right. "Those things will kill you."

Of course. "So it's been said."

Footsteps came closer. "I remember your first one. You thought you were cool. And then you started coughing so hard, I thought you were going to throw up."

"Gotta get used to it. First one always hurts." Oh, the games we played.

"Does it?"

I inhaled.

"I've tasted it, you know. On your tongue."

I grinned lazily. "Yeah. I know. You always complained, though I think you liked it."

"It was like burning leaves. Smoke in the rain."

"How poetic of you."

He snorted. "Yeah. Poetic."

I opened my eyes, looking down at the way the smoke twisted around my fingers. "What do you want, Mark?"

He was covered in shadow, standing more toward the mouth of the alley. People stumbled by behind him on the street, but they took no notice of us. For them, we didn't exist.

I should have known he'd follow me out here.

Or maybe I *had* known.

"Who says I want anything?" he asked.

"You're here."

"So are you."

"Who says I want anything?"

Twin flickers of orange like the end of my cigarette burned in the dark. "I never said you did."

People thought I was tough. A redneck. The rough guy from the garage. They weren't wrong. But they didn't know everything about me. I spat on the ground. "Dale seems nice. Safe and soft. Tell me, Mark. Do you think he's wondering where you are right now? Did you tell him you'd be right back after you saw me leave?"

"He's with a friend of his."

I inhaled. I exhaled. The smoke was blue and gray. "Already meeting the friends. Though I suppose it's fair, since he's apparently met mine."

"You're angry with me."

My smile was full of teeth. "I'm not anything with you."

"You're pack."

And I felt the *push* of it, from him, from the wolf in the alley. It was hot and vibrant, a whisper of *WitchPack* in the back of my mind. "Funny how that worked out, isn't it? Our first one destroyed, our second one leaving me behind. And here we are again. Our third. I wonder if other wolves get as many chances. If other witches have had as many Alphas as I have."

"The first hurt," he said, taking a step farther into the alley. "The second almost killed me."

"Didn't stop you. Thomas whistled and you went *running* like a good dog."

A low growl rolled across the brick. "He was my brother."

"Oh, I know. Get the fuck outta here, Mark."

And for a moment, he hesitated.

I thought he'd turn around. Leave whatever this was that made my head hurt. The beer felt greasy in my stomach, and I wished I'd never come outside.

But he didn't.

One moment he was still ten feet away, and the next he was in front of me, the long, hard line of his body pressed against mine. My back was to the brick, his hand in a loose grip around my throat, thumb and forefinger digging into the hinges of my jaw.

I breathed and breathed and breathed.

"You fight this," he growled near my ear. "You always fight this."

"You're fucking right I do," I said, hating how hoarse my voice sounded. A jolt of electricity was running just underneath my skin, and he knew it. He had to. My neck and underarms were slick with sweat, giving off chemical signals that I wanted to keep secret.

He dug his fingers in tighter, twisting my head to the side. His nose came to my neck, and he inhaled sharply. He dragged his nose up my throat to my cheek. His lips scraped against the underside of my jaw, but that was it.

"There's anger," he said quietly. "It's smoke and ash. But underneath, there is still dirt and leaves and rain. Like there always was. Like the first time. I remember it. I never smelled anything like it before. I wanted to consume it. I wanted it rubbed into my skin so it would never leave me. I wanted to sink my teeth into it until your blood filled my mouth. Because the first one always hurts."

"Yeah?" I asked. I reached up and grabbed the back of his head, holding him to me. "Then get a good sniff. Suck it in, wolf."

I felt the pinprick of claws dimpling my skin as he pressed his hips against mine. He inhaled deeply, and I fought to keep my eyes from rolling back. Instead I dragged my hand from the back of his head down to his neck and over his shoulders until I could press it flat against his chest between us.

There was a beat of nothing, the *tick tick tick* of water dripping, and then the air rippled around us, the raven's wings fluttering. A wall of air slammed into him, knocking him back against the opposite wall. His eyes lit up, fangs lengthening as he growled at me.

"I hope it was worth it," I said, voice cold. "Because if you try and touch me again, I'll fry your ass. You get me?"

He nodded slowly.

I took a last drag of my cigarette before I dropped it and crushed it beneath my boot. The smoke leaked out of my nose. Music throbbed from inside the bar.

And then I walked away, heading toward the street.

But before I could turn the corner, I heard him speak.

Fucker always got the last word.

"This isn't over."

TOO LATE / WILD ANIMAL

P hilip Pappas came the next day.

I didn't trust the people from back East. I never had. They always came with an air of superiority, thinking they knew more than they actually did. They were always watching, taking in everything they could, systematically cataloguing all the tiny details to report back to the powers that be who were too chickenshit to actually come themselves.

Osmond had been the first. He betrayed us to Richard Collins. He had paid for his crimes with his life.

Robbie Fontaine had been the second, though Ox had told me he'd never been anything like Osmond. He was bright-eyed and eager, a pawn in a game he didn't know he was part of. I would have loved to have seen the look on Michelle Hughes's face when she realized that Robbie had defected to Ox's pack. Oh, I was sure she played the part of the understanding Alpha. Everyone knew a wolf—a Beta—had a choice when it came to a pack. Any Alpha who forced a pack member to stay was considered dangerous and dealt with swiftly. Granted, I'd rarely heard of that happening, but the power of the Alpha could be intoxicating. The bigger and stronger the pack, the more powerful the Alpha became. Having Betas leave broke bonds and lessened the strength of a pack.

From what I understood, Robbie hadn't necessarily *belonged* to Michelle. He'd been more of a drifter, forming just enough of a bond to keep from becoming an Omega. It still must have pissed her off to find that the man she'd ostensibly sent to spy on what remained of the Bennett pack had ended up joining it. I hoped it burned.

Philip Pappas was another story. Ox called him the gruff man. He was a no-nonsense Beta I'd met only once before the Omegas had started coming to Green Creek. He'd come as one of Osmond's Betas on a visit to Thomas after Abel had died.

He wore wrinkled suits and skinny ties and looked perpetually exhausted. His hair was thin, and he had black-gray stubble that looked as if it itched. His hands were big and his eyes constantly narrowed. He didn't take shit from anyone, which is why I thought he was perfect as Michelle's second.

I didn't trust him.

I didn't trust anyone outside of the Bennett pack.

"Where is she?" he asked as he sat in the office across from Ox and Joe. Mark was in one corner, Carter in another. I stood near the window, flicking the lid of my silver lighter over and over, watching the ears of the wolves twitch each time the metal snapped together. Two of Pappas's wolves remained outside, not invited inside the Bennett house.

"With my mother," Joe said, leaning forward, elbows on the desk.

Pappas nodded. "Like the others?"

"Yes," Ox said, arms across his chest. "Exactly like the others. It's strange."

Pappas arched an eyebrow. "They're Omegas. Everything about them is strange. It's . . . unnatural. A wolf isn't meant to be an Omega. We're not supposed to be feral."

"Then why are there so many of them?" Ox asked.

Pappas kept a blank face. He was good. "I didn't know a handful was considered many."

I snorted.

He glanced at me. "Something to say, Livingstone?"

"Richard Collins certainly seemed to have more than a handful."

"An aberration."

"Was it?" I asked. "Because it seemed a little more than an aberration."

He didn't like me. That much was obvious. I didn't give a fuck. "What are you trying to say?"

Joe cleared his throat, shooting me a glare before looking back at Pappas. "I think what Gordo means is that there seems to be more Omegas than any of us think."

Pappas nodded slowly. "Do you know how many wolf packs there are in North America?"

Joe looked at Ox, who hadn't taken his eyes off the wolf in front of him. "Thirty-six in twenty-nine states. Twenty-one in three spread out over Canada."

"And on average, how many members are in each pack?"

"Six."

Pappas looked impressed, though he tried to hide it. "Twenty years ago, there were ninety packs. Thirty years ago, close to two hundred."

Ox barely blinked. "What changed?"

Mark cleared his throat. I glanced at him. He was looking down at the floor. "Hunters."

Pappas tapped his fingers in a staccato beat on the desktop. "Clans and clans of hunters whose duty it was, or so they claimed, to take out as many wolves as possible. Humans who came with their guns and their knives in the name of killing the monsters. They cut the wolves down indiscriminately. Men. Women. Children. Those that escaped kept on running. Sometimes they joined together in groups, forming makeshift packs."

"How is that possible?" Carter asked, frowning. "They wouldn't have had an Alpha."

Pappas shrugged. "We don't know. Bonds were formed, frayed and rotten though they were. It slowed down the descent into becoming feral. And then someone like Richard comes along, an abnormally strong Beta in his own descent who could almost be an Alpha, and they gathered behind him. They needed someone to follow. He was a light in the dark, and they swarmed around him. Michelle wasn't wrong when she told you that when he became an Alpha, if only for a moment, they all felt it. And then that was taken away. Of course they would be drawn here."

"We didn't see hunters on the road," Carter said. "Aside from David King, there was no one else."

"That's because, like wolves, their numbers were thinned," Pappas said. "Age or death or fear of reprisal. Revenge, if you will." He glanced at me and then looked back at the Alphas. "It's why David King was on the run, after all."

"They won't come here," Joe said, sounding sure of himself. "The hunters. Whatever's left of them. They know better."

I said, "I don't think that's—"

Ox said, "What happened to the others? The Omegas you took from here. Eight of them over the last six months." He knew. I'd told him already. He was testing Pappas.

"Dead," Pappas said without hesitation. "All of them. We had no choice. They were already too far gone."

"And I assume you did everything you could. That *Michelle* did everything she could."

"She did."

"He's not lying," I said quietly.

Ox looked at me. He was angry. I could feel that, a wave of blue and red washing through the thread that bound me to him. It came as *why* and *gordo* and *i don't know what to do he'll take her kill her she's going to die.*

"She could hurt someone," I told him, trying to ignore his anguish. I needed him to keep a level head. "Maybe she won't want to, but by the time it happens, what she wants won't matter. She'll be gone. Nothing will be left but claws and fangs and a desire to hunt. You've tried. Joe has too. You can't keep her here. She could hurt someone. What if it's Jessie? Or Tanner? Chris or Rico? They won't be able to fight her off if they don't see her coming. She'll be an animal."

He ground his teeth as Joe put his hand on top of his. "Is Michelle stronger than I am? Stronger than Joe?"

Pappas looked wary. "Why?"

"Because if we couldn't do anything, then how can we expect her to?"

"Shit," Carter breathed. "You can't be thinking of—"

"No," Pappas said bluntly. "She's not. And if you tell her I said that, I'll deny it until the day I die. But that's not what this is about. This is a formality, nothing more. A courtesy to you. And if this Omega has deteriorated as much as you say she has, then it's already too late."

Ox nodded before he pushed himself up from the chair. "Gordo."

"Dude," Carter said, sounding alarmed. "Wait, Ox, hold on a minute, you can't just—"

"Carter," Joe said, and his brother fell silent.

Ox left the room. I did the only thing I could.

I followed him.

She was in one of the spare rooms at the top of the stairs. Kelly stood near the door, watching over his mother as she hummed quietly on the bed, the Omega in the corner, growling low in her throat. Her hair hung loosely around her face, and she was half-shifted, her eyes shining violet, her face covered in gray fur. Her right hand was a paw. Her left was still mostly human.

She saw Ox and her eyes widened. She opened her mouth to speak, but all that came out was an animalistic grunt. Her eyes darted to me and narrowed to slits before she looked back to Ox.

"What's going on?" Kelly asked nervously, picking up the waves of *blue* pouring off Ox. "What happened?"

He said, "Take your mother downstairs."

"But—"

"Kelly."

He nodded. Elizabeth didn't fight him as he helped her up from the bed. She paused next to Ox, taking his face in her hands. "Is there no other way?"

He shook his head.

"The others. They . . ." She didn't need to finish her question.

"Yes."

She sighed. "Can you show her mercy?"

"Yes."

"Can you keep her from hurting anymore?"

"*Yes.*"

She stood on her tiptoes and kissed him on the forehead. "Be her Alpha, Ox," she whispered. "She would thank you for it, if she could." Then she was gone.

Kelly gave us one last look before he followed his mother, shutting the door behind him.

The Omega whined, spittle dripping down her chin.

"I'll do it," I told him. "I've done it before. This doesn't have to be on you. You don't have to do this, Ox."

He was watching the Omega. "My father told me I was going to get shit all my life."

"I know." If he wasn't already dead, I would have hunted him down and killed him myself.

"That people would never understand me."

"Yeah, Ox."

"That I would never be able to do the right thing."

"He was wrong."

Ox looked at me. "He was. Because I have you. And Joe. The pack. I have a family. People who don't give me shit. People who understand me."

"You still don't have to do this."

The Omega snarled in my direction. For a moment I thought she was going to launch herself at me, but Ox growled at her, and she cowered back into the corner.

His hands were in fists at his sides. "Do you think it hurts? Losing your mind."

"I don't know."

"You don't?"

"Do you?"

"My mother."

Ah. "It wasn't the same for me. I didn't—my mother wasn't the same as Maggie."

"No. I don't expect anyone was the same as her. She was . . . special."

"I know, Ox."

"I felt cold. Like I had ice in my head. Everything was frozen. It ached, and I couldn't find a way to stop it. All I wanted was revenge, even if I didn't mean it. I made mistakes."

I didn't know if we'd ever get past the decisions that followed the coming of the beast. "Joe would have gone even if you hadn't said anything."

"Maybe. You lost your pack once."

Twice, but who was counting. "I did."

"They died."

"Yeah."

"It must have been like losing your mind. The bonds breaking."

And I hesitated.

He nodded, this wonderfully strange young man seeing everything I couldn't say out loud. "I wonder what you would have done to stop it."

Anything. I would have done anything.

He moved then. He'd been that kid once hiding behind his daddy's leg, staring shyly up at me as I asked him if he wanted a pop from the machine. He'd gotten a root beer. He'd laughed after he'd taken the first drink, telling me he'd never had one before and the bubbles tickled his nose.

He wasn't that kid anymore. He was a big guy now. An Alpha. Strong and brave and powerful, so much more than I'd ever thought possible. I'd seen him angry. I'd seen the rage behind his eyes when monsters came from the trees to take what was his. I'd seen him deal death with his hands.

This wasn't that.

The Omega didn't have time to react before he was on her, his hands on either side of her head, a grotesque parody of how Elizabeth had held him just minutes before.

But he wasn't angry.

All I felt was blue.

He was sad.

This hurt him.

He snapped her head viciously to the right.

The bones cracked and popped, the sound sharp in the small bedroom.

Her right leg spasmed, her foot skittering along the carpet. Her toes flexed once. Then twice. Her toenails looked as if they'd been recently painted. Elizabeth must have done it. They were pink before claws sprouted from each one.

The violet faded from her eyes.

It took only seconds for her to still.

It felt like ages.

I wasn't like the wolves. I couldn't hear the moment her heart stopped.

I wondered what it sounded like. A thundering drum that skipped some beats before falling silent.

She slumped with a low exhalation.

The claws fell away.

The hair receded from her face as her shift faded.

All that was left was a young woman.

Ox leaned forward, his forehead pressed against hers.

I closed my eyes.

He whispered, "Your pack will howl you home. All you need to do is listen for their song."

. . .

Joe took one look at Ox as soon as we opened the door and immediately pulled him away down the hall toward their room. He glanced at me over my shoulder. He didn't speak, but I understood.

Carter and Kelly were downstairs with their mother in the kitchen, huddled up on either side of her as she held a steaming cup of tea, the string from the bag resting on her fingers.

I could see Mark through the windows at the front of the house, standing outside in front of the wolves Pappas had brought. It didn't look like they were speaking, and I figured Mark was posturing, as he sometimes did.

The humans weren't at the house. As soon as we'd known Pappas was in Green Creek, we'd sent them away. Jessie had glared at Ox before huffing out a breath and stalking out the front door. The guys had followed with less attitude, which I was thankful for.

Pappas was still in the office.

As was Robbie.

"—and she sends her regards," Pappas was saying, the door not quite closed.

"That's . . . great," Robbie said, sounding uncomfortable.

"She worries about you."

"I'm fine."

"I can see that. And I'll tell her the same. Though there's always a place for you if you ever decide you want to come back home."

That irritated the hell out of me, especially since Pappas had to know I was right outside the door. They would have heard my heartbeat. Which meant he wanted me to hear.

"This is my home," Robbie said. "Ox and Joe are my Alphas. This is my pack."

"Indeed," Pappas said. He was amused. "Well. I wouldn't be doing my job if I didn't extend the Alpha's offer. You did good work for her. She was impressed. And you know she isn't impressed by much these days."

That was enough. I pushed the door open the rest of the way. "Robbie," I said evenly, "can you do me a favor and call the others? Let them know the situation's been handled."

He looked relieved, standing immediately. "Got it, boss."

"I told you not to call me that."

"Yeah. Many times. Still gonna do it, boss."

He smiled gratefully as he passed me by.

I waited until he left to close the door completely.

Pappas stayed in his chair, eyeing me curiously. He was unafraid.

"Coming to another Alpha's territory and trying to poach a member of their pack is one thing," I told him, leaning against the door. "But coming onto Bennett land? With two Alphas?" I shook my head. "That takes some balls. Or a massive amount of stupidity. Jury's still out."

If Pappas had been the sort that smiled at anything, I was sure he would have been smiling then. He wasn't intimidated. I wondered if he knew what a mistake that was. "Funny, that. Seeing as how Robbie belonged to us once."

"And here I was thinking that free will still mattered. That wolves had a choice who they belonged to."

Pappas nodded. "I was asked to make the offer. I did what I was told. Michelle, she's . . . concerned."

"About?"

"Your pack seems to be buying up a lot of the property in Green Creek. Businesses and such."

"Checking up on us, is she?"

"It's a matter of public record."

"That still needs to be searched for."

He flexed his hands. "The Bennett name seems to be tied into every facet of this town."

"We're investing."

"For?"

"The future. And it helps the local businesses. We own them. Not the banks. We can lower rent. Makes things cheaper for everyone. Keeps them happy. Michelle doesn't need to be concerned. This is our home." It was more than that, but he didn't need to know. Carter and Kelly had taken over the pack's finances and had come up with the idea to put the Bennett wealth back into the town. It did help the people who lived here, but it also tightened the pack's grip on this territory. Anyone who wanted to take it away would be foolish to try. Not with how tied we were to this place now.

"That right? Was that Thomas's plan? Before?"

"What do you want, Pappas?"

"I'm not here to force anything."

I didn't believe that for a second. "Except for the death of the Omega."

He tilted his head. "Ox volunteered."

"You gave him no choice."

"There's that word again. Choice. You must think of me as some kind of master manipulator."

"I knew Osmond." I meant the words to land with a punch, but he looked barely affected.

"A mistake."

"One that went on for *years*. Tell me. Have you figured out exactly when he turned on you? When he decided Richard Collins was worth more than all of you?"

"There were . . . signs. Things that shouldn't have been overlooked."

"And there's no one else."

"Not that we know of."

"That doesn't mean as much as it used to."

He leaned forward in his chair, hands clasped in his lap. His forehead had a sheen of sweat on it. I didn't think I'd ever seen Pappas sweat before. "What are you really asking, Gordo?"

I looked back to make sure the door remained shut so that no one could overhear us. It was. Pappas was not-smiling again when I turned toward him. He arched an eyebrow at me.

"You know what."

"Maybe I just want to hear you say it."

Fucking werewolves. "My father."

"Your father," he echoed. "Right. Robert Livingstone. After the unfortunate situation with Richard Collins, I must admit I was surprised at the . . . subterfuge. Keeping things from your Alphas doesn't seem like something you'd do, Gordo. After everything your pack has been through. It's almost as if you trust me more than them."

"You don't know the first thing about me."

And there it was. A full-on grin. It looked as if it belonged on a shark. "We know far more than you think. I report to the Alpha of all, don't I?"

"Temporary. And nothing more."

He shook his head. "Joe seems like he doesn't want to leave here. I don't blame him. This place, it's . . . unlike any other territory I've ever been to. You can feel it as you approach. It's like a great storm in the distance, all electricity and ozone. How Thomas Bennett ever

left it to begin with is beyond me. He must have trusted you greatly
to leave it in your care."

"Thomas Bennett didn't give two shits about me."

"No? How curious."

I was tired of this. Of him. "Tell me what I need to know."

He spread his hands on his thighs. I thought I saw a hint of claws,
but they were gone a moment later. "There's nothing. Or rather, nothing new. On either front."

That couldn't be possible. "I warned you that Elijah was still out
there. What her brother told me. How is it possible that a hunter of
her caliber is slipping under your radar?"

He shrugged. "Maybe she's hung up her mantle. Maybe she's
dead. Or maybe, just maybe, David King was full of shit and faced
with angry werewolves while bleeding to death, saying whatever he
thought you wanted to hear in order to save his own life."

"You're missing something. Maybe Michelle's not—are you okay?"

He was breathing heavier than he'd been just a moment before. He
closed his eyes, nostrils flaring. He reached up and wiped the sweat
from his forehead. If he hadn't been a wolf, I would have thought he
was ill. But since wolves didn't get sick—not like humans did—it had
to be something else. It was almost like he was losing control. But
that wasn't—

"I'm fine," he finally said, opening his eyes. "It's been a long trip
out here to make again in so many weeks. If I thought I could handle
a plane, we would have flown. But all those scents in such a small place
is just . . . it's too much."

I frowned. "You don't look so—"

"There have been no reports of any hunter activity in years," Pappas said evenly. "The old clans have either been dealt with or have
died out. Honestly, we have Richard to thank for that. He killed more
hunters than any wolf has in years. Regardless of what he became, he
did the dirty work for us better than we ever could. He had his faults,
but he proved useful, in the end."

"Faults," I echoed incredulously. "He murdered Thomas Bennett.
He murdered Ox's mother. He nearly killed Ox. Those aren't *faults*."

"I know it's difficult, Gordo. And while his crimes were terrible,
sometimes I don't know that you can see the bigger picture here.
You're too close."

"And my father? How does he fit into your bigger picture? How is he going to prove *useful* to you?"

"You deliberately misunderstand me."

I growled at him, scrubbing a hand over my face. "He's still out there."

"We know. But whatever he's doing, it's in shadow. He's a ghost, Gordo. You can't catch what isn't there."

"Are you even looking for him?"

"Are you? It would seem to me that if anyone had a reason for making sure he didn't hurt another living soul, it'd be you. What have you done to find your father?"

"I was just a kid," I snapped at him. "When you all came and took him away. When I was *promised* he would never hurt anyone again. And guess what? You *lied*."

"That was Osmond—"

"Fuck Osmond, and fuck you too. You should have known. About Osmond. About Richard. About my *father*. Because of you, people have died, good people. Thomas didn't deserve—"

"How human of you."

I blinked. "What?"

"Just a moment ago you said Thomas Bennett didn't give two shits about you. And yet here you are saying he didn't deserve the death he got. By implication, you're saying *you* cared about him, even though you don't feel it was reciprocated. It's such a human thing to do. A born wolf sees things in terms of pack and Alpha. Of scents and the emotions associated with them. Turned wolves tend to war with themselves, remembering both what it meant to be human and what it means to be a wolf. Humans, though. They are more . . . complex. More fallible. Your magic doesn't preclude you from this complexity." He shook his head. "It's why humans aren't often in packs. They don't have the understanding of what it means to *be* pack."

"We do just fine, thank you."

There was that smile again. "Oh, I know. Another oddity of the Bennett pack. Ox is . . . unlike anything that's ever come before. I find myself fascinated with him. We all are. He's the topic of many conversations."

I took a step toward him, slowly rolling up my sleeve until the raven was exposed. I pressed two fingers against its talons and for a moment felt the sharpness of them, the heat of them burning into my skin. I took a savage satisfaction when Pappas's eyes widened slightly. "When I was young, I sat in this room and my father carved magic into my skin. My Alpha told me I would do great things. That one day I would be his witch. Things have changed. I have new Alphas, even though I never expected to belong in a pack again. One of these Alphas also happens to be my tether." His expression stuttered. "And from where I'm standing, it sounds like you just threatened him. I don't take kindly to threats against my tether. Against my Alphas. Against my pack. If I wanted to, right here, right now, I could stuff you with so much silver, all they would have to do is strip your skin and they'd have a goddamn *statue*."

"Careful, Gordo," Pappas said, voice flat. "You don't want to burn the bridge when you're standing in the middle of it."

The raven was agitated. "When you go back, you tell your Alpha that if anything should happen to my pack, that if I get even an *inkling* of a plan against them, against *us*, I'll tear all of you apart, and I'll do it with a fucking smile on my face. Are we clear?"

Pappas nodded. "As day."

"Good. Now get the fuck out of the Bennett house. You can stay the night in town at the same motel as before, but I expect you gone by morning. We'll take care of the Omega. I don't want you touching her."

He looked as if he was going to say something more, but thought better of it. He stood and brushed by me. For a second I thought I saw something that couldn't be there.

A flash of violet.

But it had to be just a trick of the light.

The raven settled on its bed of roses, and I closed my eyes.

. . . .

The Omega burned quickly on the pyre in the woods. The stars shone above brightly. The moon was more than half-full, and I knew the wolves felt its pull.

Ox stood and watched the flames flicker toward the sky, Joe at his side. Carter and Kelly were with their mother, a shawl pulled over her shoulders. I wondered if she was thinking about the last time she'd been faced with fire, when her mate had become nothing but ash. Her sons rested their heads on her shoulders, and she hummed softly under her breath. It sounded like it was Johnny and his guitar.

Robbie stood awkwardly next to Kelly. He looked as if he wanted to reach out and put a hand on Kelly's back, but decided against it. He kept glancing at me, the expression on his face like he thought the sun shone out of my ass. It was unnerving, and I was going to nip that in the bud before it could become full-blown hero worship. I didn't need a goddamn puppy following me around.

But of course someone else noticed it too.

"Looks like you've got an admirer," Mark murmured.

I rolled my eyes. "Kid gets stars in his eyes easier than anyone I've met. He's too soft."

"What caused this newfound affection, you think?"

"Why? You jealous?"

"Do you want me to be?"

What the fuck. "What are you—Jesus Christ. I don't give two *shits* about him."

He snorted. "Sure, Gordo. Let's go with that."

"Pappas was messing with his head. I put a stop to it."

I felt Mark's gaze on me, but I watched the flames. "I never understood that. About you."

"What?"

"How the outside never matched what was inside."

I glanced at him, eyes narrowing. "What the hell are you talking about?"

He shrugged. "You aren't as much of an asshole as you want everyone to think you are. It's . . . comforting."

"Fuck off, Mark. You don't know a goddamn thing about me."

He laughed quietly. "Sure, Gordo." He reached up and squeezed my arm. I was barely able to stop from jerking it away. His hand was heavy and warm and—

Gone.

He went to Elizabeth, leaning forward and pressing a kiss against her forehead.

My stomach twisted something fierce.

I left the wolves and disappeared into the forest. I had wards to check.

Magic is a strange and expansive thing.

My father's had been more singularly focused. He was capable of great feats, of wondrous things, but he had his limits.

"I'm not like you," he'd told me once, and I wouldn't understand until I was older that he said it with a mixture of envy and irony. "Magic tends to manifest itself in odd ways. I can feel the pack. Sometimes I think I can hear them in my head. But you . . . you're different. There's never been one quite like you, Gordo. I can pass down the secrets. I can give you the tools, the symbols needed, but you will do things with them that I cannot."

The raven took three months to finish. The pain was immense. It felt like I was getting stabbed with a butcher knife that conducted electricity. I begged him to stop hurting me, I was his son, daddy please stop, daddy *please*—

Abel held me down.

Thomas put his hand in my hair.

My father bent over me with the tattoo gun, the ink in the jars on the table bursting in bright colors.

When the raven was finally finished, I felt more focused than I ever had before.

The first time it moved, I accidentally lit a tree on fire.

The wolves laughed at me.

My mother cried.

And my father?

Well.

He just stared at me.

. . . .

The wards felt thick and strong. I pushed my hand against them and they lit up, large circles with archaic symbols carved into thin air. They were all green, green, green.

My father had taught me how to make them.

But I had learned to make them more.

No one would be able to touch them.

. . . .

I'd told Ox once that magic was real. That monsters were real. That anything he could think of was *real*.

The wards were designed to keep the worst of them out.

But sometimes they kept the worst things *in*.

I blinked in a dark room, the remnants of a fading dream of a secret smile and ice-cold eyes still clinging to my skin. I turned my head, almost expecting a strong body stretched out next to mine. But he wasn't there, of course. He hadn't been for years.

My phone rang again, the screen glowing white.

I groaned before rolling over and reaching out for it.

I put it against my ear. "Hello."

Silence.

I pulled it away and squinted against the light of the screen.

UNKNOWN.

00:03

00:04

00:05

"Hello," I said again as I put it at my ear.

"Gordo."

I sat up in the bed. I knew that voice, but it was—"Pappas?"

"It . . . it *hurts*." He sounded as if he were speaking through a mouthful of fangs.

I was wide-awake. "What does? What are you talking about?"

"There's . . . something. In me. And I can't . . ." His words choked off on a growl. Then, "I didn't think . . . it would be me. It's fraying. All the little threads. They'll break. I know they'll break. I've seen it before."

I climbed out of bed. I found jeans on the floor and pulled them on. "Where are you?"

He laughed. It sounded more wolf than man. "She knows. I'm sorry, but she *knows*. More. Than you. More. Than I could say. When did they get me? When did they . . . ?"

"Pappas!" I barked into the phone. "Where the fuck are you?"

The phone beeped in my ear. The call had been disconnected.

"Motherfucker," I muttered. I grabbed a shirt from the edge of my bed and pulled it over my head.

I was out the door only a moment later.

Sheriff's deputies were at the Shady Oak Inn, the little motel at the edge of town. A cruiser was parked in front, lights spinning. I recognized one of the deputies. Something . . . Jones. He'd brought his bike into the garage with a faulty clutch. I'd knocked a few bucks off the bill, given it was easier to kiss a cop's ass than beg for leniency later.

He and another deputy I didn't know were standing with Will, the old guy who owned the motel, who was waving his hands around like he was doing an impression of some kind of Lovecraftian nightmare. I pulled up beside them, rolling down my window.

"—and then it *growled* at me," Will was saying, sounding slightly hysterical. "I didn't see it, but I heard it. It was big, okay? It sounded *big*."

"Big, huh?" Jones asked. He wasn't believing a goddamn word Will was saying. I didn't blame him. Not really. Will was drunk more than he was sober. It was well-known. Price of living in a small town. Everyone knew everyone else's business.

Most of the time.

"All right?" I asked, going for nonchalance and landing near it.

Jones turned to look at me. "Gordo? What're you doing out this late?"

I shrugged. "Paperwork. Never ends when you own a business. Ain't that right, Will?"

He nodded frantically. "Oh yeah. Just mountains of it. *I* was doing the same thing when I heard it."

He was more than likely deep in a bottle of Wild Turkey. "Heard it?"

Jones looked like he was barely restraining an eye roll. "Will here says there was some kind of animal in one of his rooms."

"Tore it to shreds!" Will cried. "Table overturned! Bed ruined. Gotta be a mountain lion or something. Big fucker too. I heard it, Gordo. I *did*. And I went to check it out, okay? Because goddamn if I was going to let another squatter come in and wreck my motel. I had a flashlight and everything. And I *heard* it."

I bet he did. "Heard what?"

His eyes were bulging, his face red. "This . . . this *growl*. It sounded like something big, okay? I swear."

"Probably just a couple of kids looking to get their rocks off," Jones said. "Will, you had anything to drink tonight?"

"*No*." Then, "Well, maybe just a couple of fingers. You know how it is."

"Uh-huh."

"You have anyone in there?" I asked, looking at the door Will had been pointing at. It hung off its hinges against the vinyl siding of the motel. Even from where I sat, I could see the claw marks in the wood.

Will nodded again, head snapping up and down. "Yes, sir. Some out-of-towners. In suits. Businessmen, looks like, though they didn't talk much about anything. They'd been here a couple of times before. Rude, if you ask me. No one was in there, though. It's empty."

"Get any names, old man?" the other deputy asked. "Or did you just take cash under the table?"

"This is a *legitimate* business," Will snapped. "Of *course* I got names. It's in the ledger. I'll show you. I don't do dirty work. And I've always said there's been something weird going on in this town, okay? No one else sees it, but *I* do. You can't tell me you don't hear the howling that comes from the forest at night. Just because other people don't talk about it doesn't mean *I* won't."

"Sure," the deputy said. "Mountain lions and howling in the woods. Got it. Let's see the ledger."

Will stomped off toward the office, muttering under his breath. The deputy followed him. I put the truck in Park and turned off the key as Jones began walking toward the motel room, flashlight out, hand on the grip of the gun.

I opened the door.

He glanced back at me. "Maybe you should stay in the truck."

I shrugged. "Wild animal, right? Probably more scared of us than we should be of it."

Jones sighed. "He's trashed."

"Probably. But what else is new."

"At least he's not behind the wheel," he muttered.

"Only because he lost his license after jumping the curb and hitting a parking meter."

"Said his brakes were faulty. Blew damn near three times the legal limit."

The gravel crunched beneath my feet as I followed Jones toward the open door.

"See that?" he said quietly, the beam of his flashlight on the scratch marks. There were four of them, scarring the door deeply. They were big.

"Still think it was a couple of kids?"

"More than a mountain lion. Could have been done with a knife."

"Sure, Jones."

We stopped on the stoop near the room. Jones cocked his head, standing stock-still. Then, "I don't hear anything."

That's because there was nothing there, but I didn't say that. "You sure?"

"Yeah."

He walked forward.

From over his shoulder, I could see the room had been destroyed, just like Will had said. Tables overturned, the walls gouged. The bed had been ripped to shreds, the mattress hanging off the frame, springs poking up through the fabric.

"What the hell?" Jones whispered.

"Kids," I said. "Drunk. Drugs. Something."

He shook his head. "Then what about that?"

I followed the beam of his flashlight.

Blood splattered the wall. It wasn't a lot. But it was there, still wet and dripping.

Jones was out in the cruiser, reporting back to dispatch. He'd changed his tune. "Animal," I could hear him saying. "Some kind of animal. Looks like it was hurt. Will's saying he had guests in the room, but their SUV is gone, so they might have already left town. Didn't get a plate number."

The phone was ringing in my ear.

"Gordo," a voice said, rough with sleep.

"Ox. We've got a problem."

"Tell me."

In the dirt, leading out of the parking lot and into the trees, were tracks. Bigger than an animal had any right to be.

"Wolves."

SHE KNOWS / THEN CAME THE VIOLET

Abel told you about tethers," my father said to me once.

I nodded, eager to please. "They keep the wolf at bay. They're the most important things in the world."

"Yes," my father said. We were sitting in the grass behind our house as we sometimes did, digging our hands into the earth to see what we could find. My tattoos felt alive. "They are. So very important. You take that tether away and all that's left is a beast."

. . .

I was in the forest, the trees around me bending in the sharp winds. I knew these woods better than almost anyone, aside from the wolves. I'd grown up here. I knew the lay of the land. How the earth pulsed.

I was breathing deeply, jacket shed somewhere farther back and left on the forest floor. The tattoos glowed brightly, and my skin felt like it was crawling.

I reached out my senses, letting them ripple through the territory around me. The wards were still intact. I flexed my hands. They flared briefly, strong and fibrous.

In the distance, I heard the howl of a wolf.

It wasn't one of mine.

It was *enraged*.

"Shit," I muttered, making a split-second decision.

I ran, feet crunching leaves, branches snapping against my arms.

I didn't understand what was happening. If Omegas had made their way into Green Creek without me knowing. If there were hunters. If somehow my father had managed to find a way through my wards. Pappas had said it was *hurting* him. What if the other wolves he'd been traveling with had turned on him? They could have been just like Osmond, worming their way into positions of power before turning around and betraying those they stood beside. I didn't know why they'd go after Pappas, or why they'd wait until they were on Bennett land to attack him.

Countless scenarios played through my head, and in my chest, the threads pulled, those bonds I had been missing for so long. The strongest was Ox, my tether. He was moving fast, shifted into his wolf. Joe was at his side, as was Carter. Mark was bringing up the rear. They whispered to me, voices melding together and saying *we're coming we hear you we need you don't be stupid gordo don't do anything without us PackWitchBrotherLove.* It sang in my head, louder than it'd ever been, and I felt their anger, their worry. And for a moment, I thought I felt Mark's *fear.* He was *scared,* his heart jackrabbiting in his great chest. It caused me to stumble, almost sending me crashing down to the ground.

I pushed back *i'm fine calm fine safe stop stop stop* as soothingly as I could, trying to get him to let up.

It worked, but barely.

He subsided, his distress a low simmer.

They were to the east.

The howl of the unknown wolf was coming from the west.

wait wait just wait please wait don't go

I went west.

Moments later I saw a pair of lights shining through the trees off to my right. I changed course and headed toward them. I broke through the tree line and hit a backwoods dirt road, one of the many that crisscrossed through the forest.

The lights were coming from the generic SUV Pappas and the two Betas had arrived in. It lay on its side, its engine still ticking. The driver's door had been ripped off its hinges and had landed in the grass at the side of the road. One of the tires was shredded. The SUV had come to rest against an old oak tree.

I pulled myself up by the doorway, arms straining, and peered down inside the SUV.

It was empty.

I dropped back down, the heat from the undercarriage hot against my face. I looked down at the dirt and saw more tracks. I turned toward the trees and—

One of the Betas was in the ditch at the side of the road, breathing shallowly. His clothes had been shredded. His body was covered with deep slashes that weren't healing. The amount of blood was immense. He stared up at the sky, mouth opening and closing, opening and closing. His eyes were faintly orange.

He was beyond my help.

His gaze was unfocused as I crouched next to him. Blood leaked from his mouth and ears.

I said, "Who did this?"

He turned his head slightly toward the sound of my voice.

A tear slipped down his cheek.

His mouth closed again.

His jaw tensed.

His teeth were bloody when he said, "Philip. He . . . lost. Control."

He laughed. It sounded like he was choking.

And then he died, the light fading from his eyes.

An angry snarl came from the woods.

I pushed myself up.

A flicker of bright orange in the trees, the crunch of autumn leaves.

I was being hunted.

It moved carefully, this half-shifted wolf. It was still upright on two legs, taking one step after another, keeping to the shadows. I couldn't tell if it was Pappas or his other Beta.

I said, "I know you're there."

It snarled in response.

There was a bright burst in my head, an angry *no gordo no run please run don't fight don't almost there i'm coming we're coming please please please.* It caused my skin to thrum electric-hot, crawling with *pack brother friend witch home home home.* I was caught in a web, the threads hooked into my flesh and pulling.

Others were there, faint but sure, the humans who by now had to know something was wrong. Stronger were Elizabeth and Kelly and Robbie, still at the Bennett house.

But it was the threads of the approaching wolves that I latched on to. The red of the Alphas, the orange of the Betas, fibrous and thick. And then there was white, a pure clean white that shot through all of them like arcing lightning. My magic, connecting to each of them.

It was a tangle of wolf and witch and *pack* and *mine* that made me grind my teeth. My head pounded, and I was hyperaware of every step the wolf hunting me took. It was growling low in its throat now, fangs gnashing together.

But it had already made a fatal mistake. It was in the Bennett territory.

And I was the Bennett witch.

My pack was still too far away, and as the wolf stalked toward me, my heart had the slightest of upticks, a natural fear response at the sight of Philip Pappas stepping out of the shadows, looking lost to his wolf.

One of the threads in my chest tightened swiftly, sending back *no gordo no run run run*, and I *recognized* that voice, *knew* that voice ever since it'd told me I smelled like dirt and leaves and rain. Mark was terrified. He was running as fast as his paws could carry him, and he was *terrified*.

Philip began to tense.

I said, "You don't want to do that."

He shot toward me, claws stretched wide.

His mouth was filled with pointed teeth.

GORDO RUN PLEASE RUN I'M COMING RUN RUN RUN

I said, "*No*," and ran toward him.

The raven took flight.

Pappas leapt at me, claws glittering in the moonlight.

I dropped to my knees at the last second, leaning back on my legs as I slid through the dirt.

My father had told me magic was an ancient thing. That it lived in the blood, constantly moving. It could be controlled through sheer force of will with the proper marks carved into the skin. But it could grow beyond one's control, he'd said. If there was no trust in it. No faith. I had to *believe* in what I could do. What I was capable of. The earth of the Bennett territory was unlike anywhere else in the world. The Livingstones were tied to it just as much as the wolves.

My father said his magic felt like a great and lumbering beast.

Mine always felt like a symphony, all these parts moving in concert. It called out my name, and at times I thought it alive and sentient, with its own free will, and it *begged* me for release. It would arc along my skin, jumping from tattoo to tattoo, zipping along the lines and shapes on my arms, spelling out ancient secrets for earth and healing and destruction and fire.

It hit hard. I felt it in the trees and the birds that sat in them, the autumn wildflowers that bloomed throughout the old growth, the leaves that broke from the limbs and fell toward the ground. It was in the blades of grass, the gnarled roots that grew beneath the surface, stretching on and on and on.

This place was mine, and this fucking wolf had made a goddamn mistake.

Pappas flew over me and crashed onto the ground behind me, rolling once, twice, before coming to a stop in a crouch. He was moving even as I pushed myself up, but before he could reach me, I held my hand up, palm toward Pappas, and I called upon the territory. The trees groaned as the air rippled around my hand. I closed my eyes and found the web of threads that bound my pack together and wrapped them around my arm, digging them into the earth. I felt the Alphas along those threads, sending pulses of *packwolf* magic. Carter joined in behind his Alphas. Mark didn't. His focus was singular, and he was singing *gordo gordo gordo.*

The tattoos were bright as they'd ever been as I opened my eyes.

I *pushed*, and earth cracked and rolled beneath Pappas's feet, causing him to stumble onto his hands and knees, and he roared angrily. But before he could pull himself back up, I took three steps and kicked him upside the head. He fell back, an arc of blood spilling from his gaping mouth. He landed hard on his side, blinking up toward the night sky.

"Stay down," I warned him.

He said, "Gordo" and "Witch" and "Help me" through a mouthful of sharp teeth. "It's wrong. Everything about this is *wrong.* I can feel it breaking. It's in my head, oh god, it's in my *head.*" Even before he finished talking, he was already pushing himself up, his claws digging into the dirt.

"Don't," I snapped as I took a step back. "I will put you down. I don't know what happened, but I will fucking *end* you if you can't find your control."

"Control," he growled, eyes bright again. "It's *frayed.* It's *breaking.* Can't you see? I didn't think—it wasn't supposed to be me. It's happening." He tilted his head back toward the sky, shoulders stiff as his jaws opened wide. "She knows. Infection. She knows about the *infection.*"

"What are you talking about?"

He jerked his head forward, orange eyes on me. He was tensing again like he was about to attack. "Omegas. All of us will become—"

A large brown wolf crashed into him, knocking him off his feet. He landed on his back, the wolf atop him, snarling down into his face. Pappas growled back up at him and, before I could move, turned his head and bit into Mark's right leg.

Mark yelped angrily, trying to jerk his leg out of Pappas's mouth. His skin tore, blood splashing down onto Pappas's face as he shook it side to side.

I didn't hesitate.

I ran toward them, the raven's wings flapping furiously. The roses in its talons were burning, the fire pulsing from the *Cen* rune on my arm. It was short for *Kenaz*, the torch. My father had whispered an old poem in my ear as he pressed it into my skin, saying *this is live fire, bright and shining/more often, it ablaze, where noble men rest in peace.*

The fire spread, and it caught the rest of the runes, burning up through my arm to my hand. Fire could be a light in the darkness, a healing that seared away scars that littered the surface. It could be warmth from the cold, a means of survival in an unforgiving world.

Or it could be a weapon.

I pressed my hand against Pappas's leg, and he *screamed*, Mark's calf coming free from his mouth. Mark moved off him, leg bloodied as he held it lamely folded up against his body. It didn't stop him from bending his head toward Pappas's throat, lips curled over long fangs, growling down at him.

But Pappas probably didn't even know he was there. He jerked on the ground, shrieking as he tried to get away from me. I knew he felt like he was burning from the inside out, and I hoped it would be enough to shock him out of whatever the hell had come over him. I held on for another beat, then two and three, and finally let him go when my Alphas came out of the trees, followed quickly by Carter.

All three of them were shifted, large and imposing and pissed off. The Alphas moved in synchronicity, one black, the other white, yin and yang. I felt Ox's anger, Joe's fury. Carter was confused, but the sight of his injured uncle caused him to whine. He went to Mark, nosed at the wound, lapped at it as it slowly healed, his tongue streaked with blood.

Pappas writhed on the ground. There was a handprint burned into his leg, charred black and smoking. He looked as if he was caught in his shift, hair sprouting along his face and neck, eyes flickering, claws lengthening, then shortening again. I knew he was trying to turn wolf because it'd make the pain more manageable, but something was stopping him.

Joe came to me, pressing his snout against my shoulder, whuffing out short, hot breaths along my skin. Questions were pushed through the bond between us, more *????* than actual words. I let it go on for a minute or two before I pushed his head away. "I'm fine."

Joe grumbled wolfishly, eyes narrowed as he looked me up and down. His nostrils flared, and I knew the moment he caught the scent of another wolf's blood as his head jerked toward the overturned SUV.

"Beta," I told him. "Dead in the ditch. Said Pappas did this to him. I don't know where the other one is."

Joe wasn't happy about that.

Carter backed away from his uncle. Mark's leg looked as if it was healing, skin and muscle stitching itself back together slowly but surely. He was starting to put weight on it again as he gimped toward me, brushing against my side. I thought about shoving him away, but the heat of him next to me was calming. I told myself it was just for this moment.

Ox shifted, the groan of muscle and bone loud in the dark. He crouched nude next to Pappas, who continued to whimper. "What's wrong with him?" he asked quietly.

I shook my head. "I don't know. He called me. He sounded out of his mind. Talking about fraying and breaking. He said *she* knows. Something about infection."

"Infection," Ox repeated. "Who was he talking—Michelle."

"Seems likely."

He looked up at me. "I don't understand. What kind of infection? Wolves can't *get* infections."

"It's not—" I stopped. Because what had he said? About—

Omegas. All of us will become—

"Ox," I said slowly. "You need to back away. Now."

He didn't hesitate. He trusted me. It was close. One moment Pappas was lying on the ground, whimpering in pain, eyes closed. The next he jerked his head forward, shifting more toward wolf than man, jaws stretching toward Ox and—

Snapped into empty air where Ox had once stood.

His eyes were orange.

Human.

Orange again.

And then, for the briefest of moments, they flashed violet.

Carter moved before I could, grabbing one of Pappas's arms in his jaws and twisting it cruelly. It broke, the pop loud and wet. Pappas shrieked.

Mark looked as if he were about to rip Pappas's throat out, but before he could, I brought my boot back and kicked Pappas in the head again. He grunted as his head snapped to the side, out cold.

"What the hell is going on?" Ox asked.

. . .

Ox carried Pappas back to the Bennett house over his bare shoulder. Carter and Joe had the Betas, the second of which had been dead in the woods, his throat torn out. Mark and I stayed behind, covering up as much of the blood as we could, his paws doing a better job than my boots. We went for the SUV next, both of us grunting as we pushed it over onto its wheels. My head was pounding, as it often did when I exerted myself heavily. Getting older didn't make things easier. I hadn't used the fire rune in a long time. There'd been no need for it.

Mark stood at my side as I called Tanner, telling him to get Chris and the tow truck to pull the SUV out of here before it was found. Rico would meet them at the garage to see what—if anything—could be done with it, or if we'd need to junk it. They knew to get rid of the plates and the VIN so no questions would be asked, just to be safe.

I hung up the phone in time to see Mark shifting.

Which, after the night I'd had, wasn't something I was ready to face.

But of course, given the way my life went, a naked Mark Bennett didn't give two shits about that.

"What the hell were you thinking?" he snapped even before the shift had faded, voice deep. "I told you to *wait*."

I felt prickly. Snappish. "You're not my Alpha."

He took a step toward me, chest heaving. "I'm not *trying* to be. I'm your—" He shook his head angrily. "All I want is to keep you safe. You were out here by yourself, not knowing what the fuck was going on. That's not what we do. That's not how a pack works."

I laughed in his face. "I can handle myself."

"That's not the *point*, Gordo. You shouldn't need to. Not when you have me to—"

"I don't have you. For anything."

His eyes narrowed. "We're pack. That counts for something. You don't have to take on this shit alone."

"Really?" I stepped forward, my chest bumping his. He didn't move. He wasn't intimidated. The air around us felt hot. "Because I had to take on *this shit* alone for years, and I still made it through. Where were you then, Mark?"

I saw the moment the words hit just as hard as I'd hoped they would. It was brief, but it looked like it hurt. It didn't make me feel as good as I thought it would. "I did what I could," he said quietly, face schooled to a blank mask. "When I could. You don't know everything. What I did to keep you—" He shook his head. "You have a pack now. You're not alone anymore. If you can't trust me, at least trust them. You could have been hurt."

"It's not about trust."

"It's about *something*."

I didn't want to have this conversation. Not now. Not out here. Maybe not at all. "It doesn't matter."

Mark sighed. "Of course it doesn't."

We stood there in the dark, staring at each other, for far longer than we should have. There were things I wanted to say to him, furious things filled with rage. I wanted to grab him by the shoulders and shake him until his neck snapped. I wanted him to put his teeth against my throat and *suck* so hard, the mark would never fade. I wanted to walk away and leave him behind. I wanted to breathe in the scent of him, warm and alive and—

He was wincing, holding his arm across his chest. It was still healing, the skin still partially shredded and irritated, an awkward lump of bone jutting up.

"Idiot," I muttered, reaching out and touching him gently. He growled at me, flinching as he tried to pull his arm back. "Knock it off, you dick. I'm helping you."

I pulled some of the pain away.

It burned.

My head pounded harder.

There was no way I was going to escape this headache.

"You don't have to do that," he said quietly. "It'll heal on its own."

"You looked pathetic. And I don't like hearing you bitch when you get hurt. You never shut up about it."

"I don't *bitch*."

I rolled my eyes. "You're almost as bad as Carter."

"That's cold, Gordo. Carter's terrible when it comes to pain."

"Exactly."

He laughed. It was such an odd sound to hear. After what we'd just been through. After everything we'd done. Here, in the dark, hearing him laugh reminded me of the way things once had been. And the way things could be if I just—

It took a moment for it to hit me. How close I was standing to him. How hot his skin felt under my fingers. How incredibly naked he was. I was used to the nudity of wolves, having been around it for most of my life. You couldn't be in a pack and *not* be.

We weren't with the pack now.

I remembered the way his nose had felt pressed against my throat in the alley. How heavy the weight of him had felt. How my magic felt like it was howling at the very thought of having him near. I'd hated him then, and I hated him now.

But the funny thing about hate is the razor-thin line that separates it from something else entirely.

Because I loved him too, no matter how hard I tried to convince myself I didn't. I always had. Even when I'd wanted to kill him, even when I felt the most betrayed, I couldn't stop. It was a twisted thing, the roots buried deep in my chest, tangled and thick. I had thought it would rot and fester, become something dark that I couldn't control, but it just stayed as it was, and I *hated* him for it. For making me feel this way after all he'd done to me and I'd done to him. I wanted him gone. I never wanted to see him again. I wanted him to hurt like I'd hurt. To burn. To bleed. I wanted to keep my hands on him, to feel the animal underneath. I wanted to lean forward and bite him, leaving my mark against his skin, tattooed so that he would never be without me on him, so that everyone would know I'd been there, and I'd been there first.

I wanted to kill him.

I wanted to fuck him.

I wanted him to tear me apart.

"Gordo," he said, ever the wolf.

"No," I said, the perfect prey.

"You don't even know what I'm going to say."

I tried to step back. I didn't move. "I've got a damn good idea."

He turned his arm over. He gripped my wrist, thumb brushing against my pulse point. "I wasn't your first."

Goddamn him for knowing what I was thinking. "Damn right you weren't."

"And you weren't mine."

I wanted a name. *Tell me who the fuck it was.* I'd find them. I'd fucking kill them. I said, "I don't care."

His eyes flickered orange. "But I swear I'm going to be your last. Fight me. Hit me. Fucking light me up. Hate me all you want—"

I bristled at that. "Get the fuck out of my head," because I could hear him whispering *gordo gordo gordo* along that thread that stretched between us. It bounced around my skull until all I could do was hear him saying my name again and again and again. He was consuming me, and I wanted him to. I couldn't stand the thought.

"—but it's going to happen. You hear me? I will hunt you down if that's what it takes. You can run from me, Gordo. But I will always find you. I let you go once. I'm not going to make that mistake again."

"Fuck you. I want nothing to do with you."

He grinned, and it was all teeth. "I felt that. In your pulse. It stuttered. It *shook*. You lied."

"Do you whisper the same things to Dale?" I asked him, jerking my arm out of his hand. "When you fuck him? Do you lean over him and tell him that he's going to be your only one?" I sneered at him. "Or does he mean nothing to you? Are you just using him to scratch that itch?"

Something complicated crawled over his face, the smile fading. I couldn't parse it because it was a jumble of too many things. "He's not—it's not *like* that."

"Does he know that?"

"Deflecting. You're always deflecting."

I snorted. "Bullshit. Just because you don't want to hear it doesn't mean it's *deflecting*."

"I don't need to—" He frowned. Closed his eyes. He grimaced, throat bobbing as he swallowed. For a moment he looked tense, muscles in his chest and arms clenching tightly.

I wanted to reach out for him. I didn't. "What's wrong?"

He opened his eyes again. "It's . . . nothing. I just—that bite must have taken more out of me than I thought. I'm fine."

He did look paler than normal. "Shift, then. You'll heal quicker. We need to get back to the house before Pappas wakes up. We need to figure out what the hell is going on."

He watched me, searching for what, I didn't know. He nodded and took a step back. Moments later a large brown wolf stood before me. He whispered his songs in my head, and it was getting harder and harder to ignore them.

He followed me back to my truck, ever my shadow, even though we weren't the same people anymore. He made a low chuffing sound as I opened the door, and I looked back in time to see him disappearing in the trees, heading toward the Bennett house.

I laid my head against the steering wheel, the leather cool against my forehead. My thoughts were chaotic, a storm of Mark and Mark and *Mark*. All the things I could have said. Like how the sound he'd made when Pappas had latched his teeth into his leg caused a red sheen to fall over my eyes. How I could have killed Pappas right then and there without a twinge of remorse. How I would have done it to anybody who tried to hurt him. Nobody hurt Mark Bennett. Especially right in front of me.

Philip Pappas was lucky I hadn't boiled him from the inside out.

If the Alphas hadn't come when they had—

I took in a breath. And then another. And then another.

There was a thrumming along the tangled web.

It came from Ox. Always Ox.

It said *home pack safe home gordo home.*

"Yeah, yeah," I muttered. "I hear you."

The house at the end of the lane was brightly lit for the late hour. Jessie's car was parked next to Ox's. Someone must have called her. She wasn't going to be happy. She had a class to teach in the morning.

I turned off my truck and opened the door. The air felt colder. I could see my breath. I wanted a cigarette, but Elizabeth didn't like when I smoked near the house. She said it made her nose itch.

Speak of the devil.

"Okay?" she asked as I came up the steps on the porch.

I nodded. "Mark get back?"

"He's inside with the others. Rico? Chris? Tanner?"

"Handling the SUV the wolves came in."

"That's good." Then, "Philip has a handprint burned into his flesh. It's not healing. I'm told that's your doing."

"I had to get him to stop."

"From hurting Mark. You must have been very angry."

Oh, she was good. "I would have done it for anyone in the pack."

She smiled serenely. "I believe you. Still. The skin is charred."

"It's magic. It always takes longer for a wolf to heal. You know that."

"Of course. Thank you."

"For?"

"Protecting Mark."

"I didn't—Jesus Christ."

"He was worried about you when he left. I don't know that I've ever seen him run as fast as he did then."

"Not the time, Elizabeth."

"Merely recounting our side of the events that transpired in your absence. In case you were wondering."

"I wasn't."

Her smile widened. "I don't believe you. Isn't that wonderful?"

For the longest time, I'd had the same contempt for her that I'd felt for Thomas and Mark Bennett. She had known, just as they had, what was coming. She had tried to warn me, even if it'd only been moments before. In my twisted thoughts, that made her just as guilty as her husband. As her brother-in-law.

It hadn't helped when she'd returned with the pack and proceeded to manipulate Ox. Oh sure, they'd say of *course* they hadn't. Of *course* they'd given him a choice. They kept the truth of it all from him for as long as they could, even if Joe had given Ox his little stone wolf without Ox understanding what it meant.

I wasn't absolved of sin. There was snowman wrapping paper and a shirt with his name stitched on the front that showed I was just as guilty as they were.

But I'd fought against it. I'd tried to keep him from all of this for as long as I could. But when she'd looked up at me, eyes wet, begging me to help her son, to help Joe, I remembered the woman who had smiled at me from her bed, asking me if I wanted to hold Carter for the first time.

There were days I couldn't stand the sight of her.

There were days I wanted to sit at her feet, my head on her knee.

There were days I thought she was just like her husband. Because wolves lied. They used. My mother had taught me that.

And then there were days like today, when I couldn't help but feel irritatingly fond toward her, even if she was doing her best to piss me off.

"I don't care if you don't believe me," I told her.

She rolled her eyes. "Well, that certainly wasn't convincing."

"Bite me."

"I'm not the one who wants to bite—"

"Don't," I warned her.

"You're quite adamant."

"Maybe because you're not getting it."

"Oh, I think I get it just fine." Her smile faded slightly. "Pappas, though."

"What about him?"

"He has a pack."

"Yeah." Michelle Hughes was his Alpha.

"Then why is he acting like an Omega? He looked as if he didn't recognize me when they brought him here."

I shook my head. "I don't know. He's . . . where is he?"

"Basement. Jessie put a line of powdered silver at the doorway. Since the walls are reinforced, he can't get out." She paused, tilting her head. "He's not talking yet. I don't know if he's capable."

I scrubbed a hand over my face. "I'll head down. When the others get here, keep them upstairs. I don't want to take any chances until we know what we're dealing with."

"Of course. Think about what I said."

"Fuck you very much."

She laughed quietly, reaching out and squeezing my hand before letting me walk away.

.   .   .

Carter was sitting in the living room, Kelly fretting above him. Robbie looked amused as Kelly tried to wipe the remnants of blood away from Carter's face. "I'm fine," Carter growled, shoving Kelly's hands away. "Would you stop fussing? I didn't even get hurt." He grimaced. "Just Mark's blood in my mouth. I don't know why I always think it's a good idea to lick open wounds when I'm shifted. I'm disgusting."

"I'll get your toothbrush!" Kelly announced frantically before turning on his heel and running out of the room.

"Is he always like that?" Robbie asked, staring in wonder after Kelly.

Carter sighed. "Not . . . usually. He's—he doesn't like it when we're separated. And then I come back covered in blood, it's—just a lot for him, sometimes." He narrowed his eyes as he looked up at Robbie. "And you are not allowed to give him shit for that. I will tear you in half if I ever hear you making fun of him."

Robbie looked horrified. "I would *never* do that."

"Just saying." Carter saw me and tilted his chin in my direction. "All right?"

"Yeah."

His nose wrinkled. "You smell like burnt skin."

"I wonder why."

"Hand of Fiery Doom?"

I glared at him. "I told you not to call it that."

He shrugged. "Eh. Remind me never to piss you off."

"You piss me off all the time."

He grinned. His teeth were bloody. "Yeah, but you like me."

I did, but he wasn't going to hear it from me. "Let Kelly take care of you. You know how he gets."

His smile softened. "Yeah, yeah."

I looked at Robbie. "And if you do *anything* to hurt Kelly, I'm going to stick my Hand of Fiery Doom so far up your ass, your throat will be on fire."

Robbie swallowed thickly as Carter laughed at him.

I headed for the stairs. I heard the low rumbles of an injured and angry wolf. When I reached the basement, I saw Jessie first, standing against the far wall, a hardened look on her face.

"Gordo," she said when she saw me. She pushed herself off the wall. "What the hell is going on?"

"I don't know. Not yet, anyway. I want you upstairs. Better yet, go home. You have work in the morning. You're not needed here now."

She tilted her head. "Are you telling me what to do?"

Jessie could be scary when she wanted to be. I faltered. "Uh. Yes? Or. Asking. I think I'm asking."

She nodded slowly. "I thought so. I will."

"Good."

"After I help burn the bodies of those Betas they brought back."

I sighed. She wasn't that little girl who'd giggled when Chris brought her into the shop for the first time. I didn't know how I felt about that. "Get Carter and Kelly to help you. After Kelly finishes shoving a toothbrush in Carter's mouth."

"I heard that!" Kelly yelled down the stairs.

Jessie snorted. "Werewolves, huh?"

"Fucking werewolves."

"The guys?"

"Doing what I told them to. Because they actually *listen* to me."

She leaned forward and kissed me on the cheek. "Sure, Gordo." She glanced at the other end of the basement before bounding up the stairs, ponytail bouncing behind her.

I turned toward the others.

The basement was the largest room of the Bennett house, and mostly sparse. The wolves tended to congregate down here after the full moons, sleeping on top of each other in piles, sometimes shifted and sometimes not. The humans had grown to need it almost as much as the wolves, with Rico loudly complaining about the amount of naked related people before usually passing out on top of a mound of overgrown werewolves.

The far side of the basement had a large room off to the side, separated by a sliding door. The door and the room itself were reinforced with steel. Abel had it built decades before for young wolves still learning to control their shifts. He would stay with them, along with their parents, in order to keep the rest of the pack safe. Thomas had hated that room, thinking of it as a prison, promising that he'd never use it as his father had. Carter and Kelly hadn't been old enough by the time the pack had left for Thomas to fulfill that promise. But Joe had, and instead, Thomas had taken the pack to the clearing.

But he'd forced something that night, regardless.

Your arms are glowing, Ox had said, eyes wide, face pale.

Ox, who now stood tall and strong, arms crossed over his chest, eyes red as he watched Philip Pappas prowl the edges of the room. Joe stood to his right. Mark was on his left. They'd all dressed, at least partially. Joe and Ox wore jeans and nothing more. Mark had on a pair of sweats and a loose T-shirt. He was still favoring his arm, though it looked as if the skin had mostly mended.

Ox said, "Gordo. Watch his eyes."

I did.

Pappas was half-shifted, but it was like he was *trapped*, like he was trying to shift completely but couldn't. He moved on his hands and feet, his claws scraping along the floor. What remained of his suit hung in tatters off his body. I could see my handprint on his leg, the skin still charred. It had only begun to heal, but it was moving slower than it should have on a wolf of his size and stature.

His eyes were dark.

And then orange.

And then dark again.

He bared his teeth at the sight of me.

Then came the violet.

It was only a second. But it was there.

"Dammit," I muttered. "I saw that earlier, but I didn't—I thought it was a trick of the light."

"I don't understand," Mark said. "It's not supposed to be like this. His tether isn't latching. Like he's lost it, somehow."

"Does he have a mate?" Ox asked. "Did something happen to them?"

"He was fine when he was here earlier," Joe said, a frown on his face. He looked so much like his father at that moment that I had to look away. "If anything, it would have been after he left."

Mark shook his head. "It wouldn't have happened this quickly. It takes . . . time."

"Tell that to my father," I said without meaning to.

The wolves all turned slowly to look at me. Mark looked shocked. "What?"

"That's . . . I don't know what that is," Ox said.

Joe squinted at me. "Did you just . . . make a joke? I don't know if I've ever heard you make a joke."

"It wasn't a *joke*. It was an *observation*."

"He can be funny," Mark said to his nephew. He frowned. "Sometimes."

"He wasn't feeling well earlier," I said, trying to get them to focus. "When I was talking to him. There was a moment when he looked . . . I don't know. *Ill.* Like he was getting sick. I didn't think much of it at the time, but . . ."

Ox was staring at me again. "When were you talking to him?"

Shit. "He was trying to poach Robbie. Told him that Michelle would welcome him back if he wanted to."

Joe and Ox immediately wolfed out. Possessive assholes.

"I already told him to fuck off," I said, rolling my eyes. "Put the claws away. You guys look like idiots. And Joe, good to know you're over the whole *back away from my man* thing. I thought you were going to piss on Ox."

Joe scowled at me. "I will bite your face off, so help me—"

"Infection," Ox said suddenly, watching me closely. "When we were in the woods, you said something about infection. You told me to get away from him right before he tried to bite me."

Gooseflesh prickled along the back of my neck. "It was something he said. On the phone. Fraying and breaking." My thoughts were jumbled as I looked into the room. Pappas was pacing along the far wall, watching me closely. When our gazes met, he snarled at me but kept his distance. "I didn't think—it's not possible."

"What is it?"

You killed him. Richard was the Alpha to the Omegas. When he died, that passed on to you. And oh, they're fighting it, I'm sure. Resisting the pull. But Green Creek was lit up like a beacon in the dark. Some can't help but seek you out. Coupled with the draw of the Bennett territory, I'm only surprised there haven't been more.

How many more do you think there could be?

Oh, I can't even begin to speculate. But they will be dealt with, no matter what. We can't afford to have our world exposed, no matter what the cost.

Philip Pappas prowled the edges of the steel room as I said, "We need to talk to Michelle Hughes. Now."

FERAL

She wasn't amused by the late hour. That much was clear. Regardless, Michelle appeared on the screen in the office as well put together as she'd always been, looking blandly indifferent at the sight of us a little worse for wear.

She said, "Alpha Bennett. Alpha Matheson. I didn't expect to speak to you again so soon."

"We wouldn't have asked if it wasn't important," Joe said. He stood shoulder to shoulder with Ox, both of them stone-faced. Robbie fidgeted awkwardly near the desk, darting glances at his Alphas and back at Michelle on the screen. Mark stood off to the side, out of sight.

"Rough night?" she asked. "The Bennett territory seems to be rather lively as of late. I wonder why that is."

"When did you last speak with Philip Pappas?" I asked her.

She blinked, caught off guard, no matter how quickly she tried to hide it. "Gordo, I'm glad you can join us, as always. May I ask why you're inquiring about Philip?"

"Answer the question."

"Two days ago. When he was on approach to Green Creek." She narrowed her eyes. "Has something happened to my second?"

"He came for the Omega."

"Of that I am aware. But there's something else."

"The Omegas. Before the girl. The others you took back. What did you do with them?"

She cocked her head. I knew she was trying to hear my heartbeat, even across thousands and thousands of miles. "Why do you ask?"

"For the sake of asking."

She nodded, eyes darting away from the screen, like she was looking at someone else in the room. It was brief, but there. "I'm afraid there was nothing to be done."

"You killed them."

"I ended their suffering. There's a difference. Ox understands, doesn't he? That poor Omega woman. He helped her."

Gotcha. "And nothing could be done to save them."

"No. They were too far gone."

"And Omegas are those wolves who lose their tethers."

"Alpha Bennett, Alpha Matheson, is there a point to all of this? Or did you ask to speak with me simply to cover topics already well known to all?"

"Humor us," Ox said.

Michelle sighed. "Yes. Omegas are wolves whose tethers are lost. Those wolves who have lost mates or packs and cannot find a way to latch on to something else."

"Richard Collins had *dozens* of them at his disposal," I reminded her.

"He did." She smiled. "The Bennett pack handled them admirably."

"Richard himself had already turned Omega before he died."

"A terrible tragedy. I wish things could have been different."

"How?"

"How?" she repeated slowly. "How what?"

"Thirty-six in twenty-nine states," I snapped at her. "Twenty-one in three Canadian provinces. That's what Pappas told us. Those are the numbers of packs that remain in North America. And it bugged me when he said it. I couldn't figure out why. But the more I've thought about it, the more I realized. Richard had *dozens* of Omegas behind him. And there were others that came here without him. How are there so many of them? Where are they coming from? Unless packs and wolves are being exterminated left and right and you haven't warned us, then how are there so many Omegas? They happen. Omegas. I get that. But not like this. Not this many."

"Where is Philip?" she asked again.

"The Omega that he came for. You just said Ox helped her. You knew she was dead already."

She sat back in her chair. "Are you accusing me of something, witch?"

"You said you last spoke with Pappas two days ago," I said coldly. "And he arrived yesterday. And yet, somehow, you knew Ox had killed her. The only way you would have known would be if you lied about when you last spoke to Pappas, or if you sent him here strictly with the orders to have Ox take matters into his own hands. To see what Ox would do. To see what he was capable of."

The room was silent.

Then, "Philip could have called me after he left the Bennett house."

"And did he?" I asked.

Her gaze was calculating, but she said nothing.

"Because I don't think he did. You see, the *reason* I don't think he did is because your second was too busy murdering the Betas traveling with him."

Michelle Hughes closed her eyes.

Goddammit. I hated being right. "He tried to tell me. He spoke of fraying and breaking. And I didn't understand what he meant. I know now. He was talking about tethers. *His* tether. Somehow he was losing it. And you knew about that."

She opened her eyes. The smile was gone. Regardless of what I thought of her, Michelle was still an Alpha. Even through the screen, she radiated power. "Not about him," she said. "Never him. He must have—one of the others. He must have found himself infected. He was careless, somehow. Dropped his guard."

"With what?" Robbie asked, sounding slightly hysterical. "What the hell could infect a *werewolf*? We're immune to almost everything!"

She sat forward suddenly, eyes flashing. "Was anybody bitten? Was any other wolf exposed? Come into contact with the blood?"

"Why?" Ox growled at her. "What would that matter if—"

"Answer me. *Was anyone bitten.*"

No. Oh fuck no, please, please, *please*—

"What did you do?" I snarled, taking a step forward. "What the *fuck* did you do?"

"Mark was bitten," Joe said, glancing worriedly around the room. "And Carter cleaned his wound."

Before I could say anything more, Mark was in front of me, eyes blazing, hands frantically running up and down my arms and shoulders. "Did he get you?" he demanded. "Did he hurt you too?"

I thought I was going to burst. "No. He didn't. Mark, he didn't. But he got—"

You.

He'd bitten Mark.

"It only matters in wolves," Michelle said tiredly. "Not witches. Even if Gordo had been bitten, it wouldn't have affected him. Not with his magic."

"What is this?" Ox said, stepping toward the monitor.

"We don't know where it came from," Michelle said. She wasn't even looking at us. Instead she was staring down at a tablet, typing furiously onto it. "Or when it started. The first that we know of was a wolf in South Dakota shortly before Thomas died. He couldn't hold his tether. He turned Omega. We thought it was a fluke. An anomaly. We had no way of knowing at the time if there were others. Not every wolf is registered or even known to us. There are outliers, packs that operate outside of our control. Omegas, too, that are packless. Loners."

"And you didn't think to tell us?" Joe demanded. "You didn't think this was information we needed to know?"

"We did," she retorted. "Thomas knew. And it was only days later that Richard came and Osmond betrayed us all. Whether or not it was intentional, it served as a distraction. And it certainly didn't help matters when you left, Alpha Bennett. You were meant to take your father's place, but you decided revenge was more important than pack."

Of course Thomas knew. Of course. "And there was nothing he could do about it?"

"That doesn't make sense," Mark said, voice flat. "All of us were injured at one point or another by Omegas. The wolves. The humans. Gordo. All of us."

Michelle glanced up from the tablet, eyes narrowing. "And nothing?"

"No," Ox said. "Nothing."

"Thomas fell *years* ago," Robbie said. "And Richard Collins died last year. Why haven't you said anything since then?"

"Because I didn't know who could be trusted," Michelle snapped. "A human Alpha? A Bennett Alpha who refuses to accept his place? You, Robbie. You who were sent to do a job and ended up *joining* the pack you were to investigate. For god's sake, there are *humans* in the pack. They *hunt* us. Tell me, exactly, at what point was I supposed to give information to a pack who seemed to exist to only serve themselves? You made a *mockery* of the Bennett name."

Joe's hands were in fists at his sides. "Say that again. I dare you."

Ox put a hand on his shoulder, fingers digging in.

Michelle ignored him. "And then there's the fact that your witch is the son of Robert Livingstone."

I narrowed my eyes. "What does my father have to do with this?"

She sighed. "Do you think it's a coincidence that when Robert Livingstone escaped custody, Richard Collins followed shortly after? Or that the wolf in South Dakota became infected? I believe in many things. I believe in pack. I believe in the strength of the wolf. I believe in the superiority of our species. I don't believe in coincidences."

"You think my father did this."

"Yes. I do. I think he's been playing a long, slow game. After the first wolf, we didn't see anything like it for a long time. It's only been . . . recently that there has been a rise, and it has become a much quicker process for an infected wolf to turn feral. Add in the fact that your father has all but disappeared. That being said, I have no proof. And since I can't be sure you haven't had contact with your father, you can see why I would be hesitant to share information with your pack."

"Don't you dare try and put this on him," Mark growled.

"By process of elimination, it's the only possible explanation. Occam's razor says—"

I was pissed. "I don't give a flying *fuck* what you think. I would *never* turn on my pack, you goddamn bitch—"

"You didn't trust me?" Robbie said, sounding hurt. "You were like my family. I never did anything to give you reason—"

"How long?"

The voice came from behind us.

I glanced over my shoulder.

Carter stood in the doorway, shoulders squared, jaw set. Kelly stood at his side, eyes wide and wet. Elizabeth was behind her eldest son, head bowed, forehead pressed against his back. "How long?" he asked again.

She had something almost akin to sympathy in her eyes. I thought it was a lie. "Two weeks. Give or take a week. But two is usually the median." She looked down at her hands. "At first there's nothing. But within a few days, you'll begin to feel it. It's like electricity underneath your skin. A low current. An itch. Like the pull of the moon. A few more days and the current will grow. The itch will intensify. You'll shift, but it won't be sated. It's like . . . bloodlust. Becoming feral is always about bloodlust. You won't be able to stop it. There will be rage.

You will lash out without meaning to. And the more you shift, the worse it gets. It's an addiction. Sometimes there's a lull, after. You'll feel better. Stronger. More in control. But that only signals the beginning of the end. You will become feral. And there is nothing you can do to stop it." She looked back up at us. "I am truly sorry that this has happened to you. To your pack. I never meant for it to get this far."

And the fucked-up thing was that I *believed* her when she said that. I doubted she ever thought her second would go feral. "There has to be a cure," I said hoarsely. "A spell. Something. If this was my father, then there has to be a way to reverse it. Whatever he's done, it can be fixed. Magic isn't one-way. Whatever he's given, it can be taken back."

She shook her head. "There's nothing that we know of. Our witches have spent two years trying to find a remedy. There's no significant changes in the blood, aside from decreased levels of serotonin and increased adrenaline and noradrenaline. The Omega literally becomes flooded with rage. And it doesn't matter the strength of the pack or the call of an Alpha. Your tether, no matter what it is, will begin to shred. Eventually it will break. You will become an Omega. You will become feral. It cannot be stopped. And the full moon coming will surely hasten the process."

"Then you don't know us at all," Ox said quietly. "Because we aren't like any pack that you've ever seen before."

"Oh, how I wish that were true, Alpha Matheson. If Carter and Mark are infected, they will turn, just as everyone else who has come before. You're right that there has never been a pack like yours before. You are . . . an anomaly. But even you can't stop this. There are those that believe lycanthropy is a disease, given that it can be spread by the bite of an Alpha. The way it alters the body down to a cellular level. Unfortunately, this . . . this *thing* appears to be similar, though it's not only cellular. It's more than that. It's metaphysical, existing only to tear the bonds away from the wolf." She frowned. "It's the perfect weapon. And who better than Robert Livingstone to inflict it upon us? He who must hate tethers most of all. For what is more poetic than a man who lost everything because of a tether to lash out at those who still have one?"

"I don't give a damn what you say," I said harshly. "There's a way to fix this, and I will find it. You may not give a shit about us, but Ox is right. You don't know the first thing about our pack. We are more than this. We are *better* than this."

"Be that as it may," she said, tapping another button on her tablet, "I must do what I have to in order to ensure the survival of our species. As with any infection, the first step is to contain it as soon as possible to prevent it from spreading. To those of you who were not exposed, I will extend an offer. Leave Green Creek. Join us. You have three days to do what is necessary."

"And what exactly is necessary?" Ox asked, taking a step toward the monitor.

Michelle barely blinked. "You know what, Alpha Matheson. Carter and Mark cannot be allowed to infect others. They must be put down."

"And in three days?" Joe asked, eyes red.

She looked at him. "In three days I will take matters into my own hands. Bennett pack, I wish things had turned out differently. But surely, if you were in my position, you would do the same. If we are to survive, then the infection must be quarantined. And then eradicated."

The screen went black.

Then Rico appeared behind the others and said, "*Oye.* Why are you all standing around looking like someone died? Oh god, someone didn't die again, did they? We just got done *burning* more dead things. I refuse to smell that again tonight. Or for the next eight months. Find someone else to do it. I refuse to be your bitch."

"Read the goddamn room," Chris muttered.

Ox snarled and smashed his fist into the monitor.

The pack dispersed throughout the house. Joe and Ox went down to the basement to check on Pappas. Elizabeth took Carter up to her room and shut the door. Robbie stood in the living room, watching Kelly pace back and forth while ranting, arms waving wildly. I didn't see where Mark went.

"This . . . isn't good," Tanner said succinctly, standing in the office, staring at the broken monitor.

"Understatement, papi," Rico said, rubbing a hand over his face. "It's a fucking mess, is what it is."

"We can figure this out, though, right?" Chris asked. He stood next to Jessie. She laid her head on his shoulder. "I mean, there's gotta be something. If it can be spread, it can be stopped."

"Something," Jessie agreed. She lifted her head. "You just have to work your way backwards. You get to the source, you might find the cure."

I stared at them. "Are you all really that stupid?"

They looked startled. "How's that now?" Chris asked.

"You need to get the fuck out of here. Right now. Leave and don't look back."

Jessie snorted. "Yeah, okay. Sure, Gordo. We'll get right on that."

"I'm being serious!"

"Oh, since you're being *serious*," Tanner said. "Guys, look. We have to listen to him now. He's being *serious*."

"That'll change my mind," Rico said, shaking his head. "Thank you, Gordo, for telling us what you think we're supposed to do. Should we ignore you right off the bat and move on to something productive, or do you want to fight us on it?"

"What the hell is wrong with all of you?" I asked incredulously. "Weren't you listening? Carter and Mark are going to go fucking *feral* unless we can find a way to stop it. They'll be just like the Omegas that came before. You remember that? When you had to fucking *kill* them? And that's not even taking into consideration the other Omegas out there that could be making their way here *right now*—"

"We remember," Chris said. "Because that was the moment we stood with our pack. Do you really think we're going to leave now? That's not what pack does, Gordo. They wouldn't leave us, so we're not going to leave them. Just because you forgot what pack meant doesn't mean we're going to."

"Too far," Rico murmured, even as I moved in front of Chris, my chest bumping his.

"I don't know that it was," Tanner said, rubbing a hand over the back of his head. "He needs to hear it at some point, right?"

"Damn right," Chris said, jutting his chin up at me defiantly.

"You're so goddamn stupid," I snapped in his face. "You're going to get yourself killed. And for *what*?"

He didn't even flinch. "For my pack. If you think we're just going to abandon them, then you don't know us as well as you think you do."

"You're *human*. What chance do you stand against—?"

"Are you leaving, then?" Jessie asked. "Because last time I checked, you're human too."

I glared at her as I stepped away from Chris. "It's not the same. I'm a goddamn witch. I have *magic*—"

"And I'm pretty good with a staff," she said. "Ox's crowbar too, since he can't use it anymore. You know, silver and all."

"Rico and me got our guns," Tanner said.

"And I've got my knives," Chris added.

"And we've been trained to fight wolves," Rico said, standing firm. "For *years*. So what if we end up having to kick Carter's ass? He deserves it for making us run laps. You know I hate running laps. I get shin splints."

I gaped at them.

They stared back at me.

"You're all out of your minds," I said faintly.

"Probably," Chris said with a shrug. "But we've stuck by you this long. And hell, we've faced crazed Omegas, a wannabe Alpha with big teeth and an even bigger ego. What's a disease that makes our friends lose their marbles in the long run? Just another thing we'll deal with."

Rico laughed but covered it up quickly with a cough. "Sorry," he said, wincing slightly. "That wasn't funny. Fear response."

"You're going to need us," Jessie said, and the others fell silent. "You most of all."

I scowled at her. "What's that supposed to mean?"

She smacked me upside the head. "Men. You're fucking idiots. Why the hell do you think, Gordo? Look. I don't pretend to know a thing about you and Mark. I don't *care* what happened to you guys or what turned you into this asshole who's so used to pretending he doesn't hurt like the rest of us that he doesn't see that we're absolutely *done* with his bullshit. If this happens, if what that bitch told us is true, you're going to need us, Gordo. We're your friends. You need us as much as we need you."

"Team Human for the win," Chris said, smiling fondly at his sister.

"We can do things the wolves can't," Tanner added. "If they're going to go feral, then they're going to need us to watch over them until we can figure out a way to get them back."

"And besides," Rico said, grinning wildly at me, "it looks good for my street cred when I kick so much ass." His smile faded a bit. "Even though I can't really tell anyone about it. Because werewolves are secret." He was frowning now. "Why the hell am I doing this? I'm already getting laid."

These ridiculous humans. How they had the hearts of wolves.

"Fuck all of you," I said helplessly.

They weren't fooled.

I was out at my truck, ready to head home to get a couple hours of sleep. I needed to rest. Facing off with Pappas had drained me. Elizabeth had offered me a bed in the Bennett house, but I hadn't slept there in years. She knew I'd say no. The guilt that had settled in my chest at Michelle's implications about my father wasn't helping. I couldn't stand Elizabeth's eyes on me, knowing the blood that ran through my veins came from a man who had helped cause the death of her husband, and potentially the destruction of her pack yet again. She didn't blame me. It wasn't who she was. But I blamed myself enough for the both of us.

I took the coward's way out.

She knew. Of course she did. She let me go with a wave of her hand.

The sky was starting to lighten. I sat in the truck, yawning as I leaned forward against the steering wheel. Joe and Ox were with Pappas, trying to figure out some way they could get through to him. I doubted it would work. Omegas could become Betas again if only they could find a tether to bring them back. I'd seen it happen before. This wasn't like that. Whatever was happening with him, whatever had caused his tether to break, it wasn't something wolf related.

It was magic. It had to be.

But I didn't know how.

I was about to start the truck when he knocked at the window.

I thought about ignoring him.

I rolled down the window instead.

"Home?" Mark asked.

"Yeah." I stared straight ahead.

"Good. You look tired."

"Getting old. Can't pull these all-nighters like I used to."

He snorted. "You're not that old, Gordo."

"Says you."

"Yeah," he said. "Says me."

I wanted to say so many things. So I picked the most inconsequential of all. "What are you doing up? Shouldn't you be—I don't know. Resting. Or something."

He leaned against the door, hands dangling inside the truck. I barely resisted the urge to touch his fingers. If Michelle was right, in a couple of weeks, he wouldn't know me at all. "Maybe. I've got some things to do first."

"Like what?"

"I— You sure you want to hear this?"

I was uncomfortable. I was also an asshole. So I just shrugged.

He saw right through me. He always did. "Going to go see Dale."

He heard the uptick of my heart. He had to. "Little early."

"Going to walk. Maybe run a little. Clear my head."

"Abby's a half hour away. By car."

"I know. But I need it. I have to."

I finally looked over at him. His eyes glittered in the low light. "Why?"

He shrugged. "Have to put an end to things."

My hands tightened on the steering wheel. "Why are you—" Then, "You fucking dick."

Mark didn't flinch. "It's not—"

"You're giving up!"

He remained infuriatingly calm. "I'm not giving up, Gordo. I'm doing the right thing. I can't take the chance that I could hurt him. And if I suddenly disappeared, he'd show up in town. Asking questions. How long do you think it'd take before he found his way out here? It's better this way. Especially if Michelle was right about the full moon. That it'll make things worse."

Goddamn him. "I'm going to fix this. I don't know how yet. But I will. We'll figure this out. There's gotta be a way. I'll find it."

"I know you will."

So many things to say. I was getting desperate. "You need to have faith in me."

He didn't hesitate. "I always do."

I thought the leather was going to crack under my hands. "Just . . . don't. Tell him you've got a business trip. Tell him you're going on vacation. Don't—just don't act like a goddamn martyr. That's not how this works."

"Because that's your job?"

All these words. It was getting dangerously close to sounding like the truth. Something he and I hadn't had in a long time. "Yeah. Right. Because that's my job. Don't take it from me."

"Listen, Gordo, it's not—"

"No," I said. "I'm not going to hear this. Not from you. You stow that shit right now, you get me? You want to break things off with him? Fine. That's your choice. But you better not start that whole *goodbye* bullshit with anyone else. Especially not me."

"Pappas—"

"Isn't you!" I cried. I didn't know if I was angry or scared or somewhere in between. I wanted to punch him in the mouth. I wanted to take him away from all of this. To force him in the truck and just drive until none of this mattered. Where we were nobody and nothing could ever hurt us. No pack. Nothing. Just him and me. "He's not you. He doesn't have what you have. He doesn't have—"

I choked.

Me.

He doesn't have me.

He reached out and put a hand over mine. My head was pounding. The bonds were twisting in my chest. There was blue, so much goddamn blue that I thought I was drowning in it. It pulsed along the threads, echoes of pain tinged with fear and anger. It wasn't just coming from him. It was coming from all of them. I felt Kelly's worry, Carter's fury. There was Robbie, little bursts of red and lapis. Joe and Ox trying to remain calm for us, for each other, but it was interwoven with a dread that was almost cobalt. Elizabeth was singing somewhere, and it was all blue. Everything we had was blue.

The bonds were aching.

And Mark. Always Mark.

He said, "Maybe it will hit me. Maybe a day from now it'll crash down upon me and I'll crack right down the middle. Or maybe it won't happen until I feel that first little tendril in my head. That pull toward the wolf that I won't be able to stop. But for now, I'm going to do what I have to. And maybe it's for the best. Maybe this is what was supposed to happen. He's not like us. He's not part of this. I don't think he was ever supposed to be. I never felt like that with him. Not like I felt with—" He sighed, shaking his head. "I'm not scared of much, Gordo. I'm not. I'm a wolf. I have a strong pack. But I never worried about losing him. It was . . . a distraction, I think. Something I didn't even know I needed. There are more important things now. Things we have to do. Things *I* have to do. To make things right." He squeezed my hand until my bones creaked. I didn't want him to let go. I hated the way he felt in my head, the whisper of *gordo gordo gordo* like a heartbeat that would never stop. "I'm not scared of much. But I think I'm scared of this. What it could mean. What I could become. Who I could forget."

I hung my head, trying to breathe through the ache in my chest.

He cleared his throat. "I know you'll do what you can. And I'll help you for as long as I'm able. But if something happens to me, if I'm—"

"Don't," I said hoarsely. "Don't do this."

"I'm scared," he repeated. "Because even when all felt lost, even when our pack split and broke again and again and again, I always had my tether. Even when he didn't want me back. And now that's being taken away from me."

He pulled away.

We breathed in and out.

I tried to find a single word to say.

There were too many. I could say none of them.

He rapped his knuckles against the door. "Okay," he said. "That's it. That's all. I just— Get some sleep, Gordo. We need you at your best."

And then he was gone.

Eventually, as the sun peeked over the horizon, I turned the truck over and headed for home.

NEVERMORE / CAN'T FIGHT THIS

I dreamed of ravens and wolves.

I flew high above my forest, my wings stretched wide.

Below me, somewhere in the trees, wolves howled. It shattered the air around me, causing my feathers to shake.

I dove for the earth.

I landed in a clearing, the ground soft beneath my feet.

There was a white wolf standing before me. It had black on its chest. On its legs.

It said, *Hello, little bird.*

I opened my beak and croaked in return, *Nevermore.*

It smiled, this wolf, this great king.

I have found you, it (*he*) said. *I'm sorry it took me so long, you prophet still, bird or devil.*

I hated it. I hated him. I wanted to sink my talons into his belly. I wanted to peck out his eyes evermore and watch the life bleed out from underneath me.

I know, he said.

Other wolves moved in the trees. Dozens of them. Hundreds. Their eyes were red and orange and violet. They were Alphas and Betas and Omegas. The woods were filled with them.

He took a step toward me.

I fluttered my wings, hopping back.

Little bird, he said. *Little bird. You fly away. Always away. I never wanted you to leave me. I never wanted to see you go. I love you.*

I didn't believe him.

He laughed, the sound low and rumbly. He said, *I know you don't. But one day I hope you'll forgive me for all that I have done to you. For all my faults. I did what I thought was right. I did what I thought would keep you safe. You are pack and pack and* packpackpack—

His eyes were red.

I croaked out, *Thomas.*

Thomas, Thomas, Thomas.

He craned his neck forward, pressing his snout against my head, and I said, *Oh. Oh, oh, oh* and—

"—and it looks as if we'll have snow early this year," the shock jock announced brightly. "Those weather jerks are calling for as much as a couple of feet throughout the Cascades in the higher elevations. Roseland could see six, Abby might get eight. You'll need to look into changing those Halloween plans, as the storm will start taking a dump late Monday night and on into Tuesday, possibly extending through the rest of the week. . . . ODOT is urging those in the mountain communities to stay off the roads if at all possible, or even to get the heck outta Dodge if you can. This looks like a big one, folks, and it's better to be safe than sorry, especially if it takes a few days for the roads in and out of the towns to be cleared. Let's go to Marnie and check in on your news around the region—"

I switched off the radio as I hit the dirt roads that led to the Bennett house. It was midafternoon, and the sky above was gray and heavy. The truck shook as I hit a pothole. My headache hadn't faded.

The front of the house should have been filled with cars. It was Sunday. It was tradition. But Team Human (god, I was never going to forgive Chris for getting that stuck in my head) had been warned to stay away, at least until they were called. Tanner and Rico were at the shop catching up on paperwork. Chris was at Jessie's house. They weren't happy about it but agreed.

Robbie was out on the porch, watching me, wearing those ridiculous glasses. He waved at me.

I nodded back.

"He's . . . coherent," he said as I exited the truck. "A little. It was a long night."

"How long?"

"A couple of hours. He's a little confused, but. I don't know. It comes and goes. I've never seen anything like it."

The steps to the porch creaked under my weight. Robbie looked pale and withdrawn. He wouldn't meet my eyes. His gaze jerked toward me, then away. Back, and away. He was nervous. I didn't know why.

"Is that it?"

He shrugged. He started wringing his hands.

I didn't have time for this. "What's the matter?"

For a moment I thought he was just going to stand there, fidgeting. I had no problem leaving him on the porch if he was going to waste my time. I had shit to do.

I didn't have to wait long.

"I didn't know," he blurted, eyes wide.

There it was. "About?"

He winced. "This. Everything. About the Omegas. About the infection or magic or whatever it is. Any of it. I didn't know."

"O . . . kay. Did someone say you did?"

He shook his head. "No, but—I'm not—I *came* from there. I was Osmond *after* Osmond."

"You're nothing like him, kid. Trust me on that. If I thought you were, you wouldn't be standing here. I don't care what Ox would say. I'd turn you inside out without a second thought."

That . . . probably wasn't the most reassuring thing I could have said. He squeaked.

"I'm not going to do it," I told him. "Because you're not him."

"Right," he said, swallowing thickly. "That's . . . good. I appreciate that. Really. Like, so much."

"Good talk," I said, turning for the door.

"But it's weird, right?"

I sighed and turned back around. "What is?"

"That I didn't know. Because Michelle knew. For a long time. Or at least, she knew *something*."

"Probably above your pay grade."

"But it shouldn't have been above Joe's. If Thomas knew, then the moment Joe became Alpha, she should have told him."

He had a point. "Those were some strange days. Things were . . . chaotic."

He pushed his glasses up his nose. "Maybe. But this past year? After Richard. We were . . . calm. Everything was fine. Mostly. Why not then? Especially since all these Omegas kept coming here. Any one of them could have bitten us. Maybe they were just regular Omegas and not the infected kind. But what if they weren't? Why would she take that chance?"

One of the many thoughts that had run jumbled through my head. "I don't know."

"I know you don't. But I think I do."

I looked at him sharply. "What?"

"Thomas Bennett was royalty," he said, shifting his weight from foot to foot nervously. "All the Bennetts are. It goes back *years*. Joe. Thomas. Abel. Even before that. Michelle was always supposed to be temporary. An interim Alpha until the Bennett Alpha could take his rightful place."

"But."

"But it hasn't happened. She's *asked* for him, but why not push more? Why hasn't she demanded Joe go to Maine to become the Alpha of all? Why haven't any of the other wolves tried to call for him either? I was told that after Abel died, there was a huge uproar that an Alpha could be killed in his own territory, especially a *Bennett* Alpha. They practically *forced* Thomas to relocate back East."

"Thomas Bennett wasn't forced to do anything he didn't want to," I said bitterly.

He blinked. "No, like, legitimately forced. He was told that if he didn't return, he was going to have to give up his title to another. Abdicate his throne, if you will. The only reason he was able to come back to Green Creek was because of what happened to Joe. And then . . . well. You know what happened after that."

History I didn't want to have to think about. "What's your point?"

"Yeah, it's like . . . okay. You're an Alpha, right? Power and pack and blah, blah, blah. But when you're Alpha of all? It's . . . more. It's incredible, or so I'm told. You're the most powerful wolf in the world. You rule over all, hence the title. Why would anyone want to give that up?"

"You think she's trying to stay right where she's at."

Robbie grimaced. "I've been thinking about it, okay? Why else would she keep the rest of this from us? Why would she send Philip here over and over again to get the Omegas, only to have us kill the last one?"

"Enlighten me."

"She's *testing* them," he said excitedly. "Or us. Joe. And Ox. Joe's a Bennett, so she thinks she knows what to expect from him. But Ox? She has no idea. None of us do. There's never been someone like him before. He was a human that somehow became an Alpha with-

out being a wolf. And Richard was able to take that from him. That shouldn't have been possible."

"Nothing about Ox should be possible."

I rolled my eyes at the dreamy quality to his voice when he said, "Right? He's just . . . awesome."

I snapped my fingers in his face. "Focus."

He jerked his head. "Uh. Sorry. What were we talking about?"

"Michelle. Testing Joe and Ox."

"Yeah. *Yeah*. She wasn't . . . lying. About what happened with Richard turning into an Alpha." *That* caught my attention, because they rarely spoke about those few moments. His gaze turned downward. "It . . . wasn't right. Feeling him. Ox is . . . light. Like the sun. Richard felt like an eclipse. It was wrong. Everything about it was wrong. But we could *feel* him. And them. All the other Omegas. They were . . . I don't know. It didn't last long, but it wasn't good. And now, with this—this *thing*. She's pushing, I think. Maybe she's using Ox. To bring all the Omegas out of hiding. Because we've been hurt by them before, and we've healed fine, so it can't be all of them. I think she knows that. She wants to see what they're capable of. What they'll do."

"In order to what?"

He looked frustrated. "I don't know. I haven't gotten that far. But it's *something*. I never—" He shook his head. "Power does funny things to people. It gets in their heads. Makes them change. She wasn't . . . she wasn't always like this. Okay? She used to be . . . different. Better. I don't—I thought, after she sent me out here, that when I came back, maybe I could be in her pack, you know? That I'd finally stay in one place. Be part of something real instead of forming these pseudobonds that were only meant to keep me from slipping."

I reached out and wrapped a hand around the back of his neck. He closed his eyes and leaned into it, humming under his breath. "You have that," I told him quietly. "Here. With us. She didn't have a damn thing to do with that."

He trembled as he opened his eyes. "I know. But what if she's trying to take that away?"

I shook him a little. "What do we do when someone tries to come for us?"

His eyes blazed orange. "We fight back."

"Exactly. They don't think of you like that. Your Alphas want you here. Your pack. Even Joe, now that you've stopped trying to slobber all over Ox's dick."

He jerked his head back. "I wasn't trying to *slobber all over*—"

"Though," I said with a frown, "you are making crazy eyes at his brother. I don't know if that's going to help things."

He squeaked again.

I took a step back. "We'll figure this out, okay? But if this *is* Michelle pulling the strings, then you need to prepare yourself for that. Because she will need to be stopped." Another thought struck me. "Do you think she would have done this on purpose?"

He blinked. "What?"

"The infection. If she sent Pappas here, knowing he was already on his way to turning Omega. As a way to get to us. To Joe and Ox."

He shook his head. "I don't—that seems too grand for her. Too big."

"You're the one that said the Alpha of all isn't something to give up lightly," I reminded him.

He looked frustrated. "I know, it's just . . . if that's the case, I can't make it fit. Why would she run the risk of infecting others? It's already spreading. Why would she want it to spread further? It could turn around and bite her in the ass." He gnawed on his bottom lip. Then, "What if it's your father?"

I narrowed my eyes. "Then I will handle it myself."

He nodded slowly. "That bugs me too."

"What?"

"How did he escape?"

To that, I had no answer.

Robbie smiled weakly. "We—I like being here. I feel . . . safe. I'm not Osmond. I'm not Pappas."

"I know."

He sighed. "Good."

I turned and headed inside. Before I shut the door, I heard, "Thanks, Gordo."

.   .   .

I heard movement in the kitchen. I looked in to see Elizabeth hugging Kelly. His head was on her shoulder. He was shaking. Carter was leaning against the counter, arms crossed over his chest, brow furrowed, mouth thin. He was staring off into nothing.

They knew I was there.

I let them be.

Mark wasn't in the house. I just knew. I didn't know how that made me feel. Maybe he'd changed his mind. I'd actively avoided thinking about how he'd said I was his tether, even after all this time. It didn't matter. Not now. We had other things to worry about. I would deal with that later if I had to.

I didn't know when I'd become such a proficient liar.

I made my way down to the basement. I saw Joe first. He was propped up against the wall, an eerie approximation of how his brother looked standing upstairs. He glanced at me and nodded before turning back toward Ox.

Ox stood in front of the open doorway. The line of powdered silver remained along the floor.

Pappas sat cross-legged in the center of the room, hands on his knees. He was nude. His eyes were closed, and he was breathing in deep breaths and letting them out slowly.

Neither of them acknowledged me.

I went to Joe first. He reached out and ran a hand along my arm, fingers trailing as he left his scent on my skin. My tattoos glowed briefly under his touch. Ox was my tether, and our packs were one, but Joe, he . . . it was different. With him. Those three years had changed us.

"I heard what you said," he told me quietly. "To Robbie."

I scowled at him. "You know I hate it when you eavesdrop."

"You're in a house of werewolves. Everyone hears everything."

"Which is why I don't like any of you."

"Lie," he said, smiling quietly. It fell only a moment later. "Ox, he's . . . trying."

I glanced at them. It was only then I noticed Ox was taking the same breaths as Pappas, like he was trying to center him somehow. "Is it working?"

"I don't know. There was a moment when I thought . . ." He shook his head. "His eyes. They're violet now. He's an Omega. I think last night was a slip. He hasn't gone completely feral. At least not yet."

"Unless we can figure out a way to fix it, it's only a matter of time before—"

"I can hear you," Pappas said without opening his eyes. His voice was deeper than it normally was, like he was speaking through a throat filled with gravel. But he sounded more in control than he had since he'd called me. I didn't know how long it would last. If Michelle had been telling the truth, he was well on his way.

Ox sighed as he looked back at us. "Thanks for that. We were getting somewhere."

Pappas opened his eyes. They were violet. "No, Oxnard. You weren't. This is a lull. I've seen it before."

Joe pushed himself off the wall and made his way toward Ox. I followed him and stood on his other side. Pappas watched us with the eyes of a monster, tracking each of our movements. It sent a chill down my spine. It was like we were being hunted.

Ox looked at me, jerking his head toward our guest.

So that's how it was going to be. "We spoke with Michelle," I said evenly.

"Did you."

"Yes."

Pappas eyed me curiously. He was speaking with a lisp. His mouth was full of fangs. "You don't say."

"She told us everything."

"I highly doubt that."

"Why?"

"Because she deals in secrets, even if they're eventually to her own detriment." He rocked his head side to side. His neck popped loudly. It caused my bones to ache. "And she doesn't trust you. Any of you, really."

"Because we're something she doesn't understand."

"Yes."

"Three days."

He blinked slowly. "Three days."

"That's how long she said she's giving us."

"Ah."

"For what?"

"I thought you said she'd told you everything."

"About the infection. How it spreads. What it entails. How your tether is shredding. Not about how she plans on containing it. To keep it from spreading."

"Your wards. What do they do?"

"They let me know when something supernatural approaches. Witches. Wolves. Omegas."

"Are they infallible?"

"Why?"

"Just a question."

"No," I said. "They're meant to protect us from those who would do us harm. It's a warning system. To give us time."

"And your pack is tied into it."

"Yes."

"Can they be modified?"

"For?"

His eyes grew brighter. "You are trying to keep things out. Have you thought about what that means you'll be keeping in? It's only a matter of time." He opened his mouth, baring his teeth. He snapped his jaws at us, once. Twice. He settled again. "I can feel it. Pulling at me. I want to tear into you. I want to taste your blood. Feel your bones crack between my teeth. I'm told I—"

"All of us?" Ox asked.

Pappas shook his head. Then, "Maybe. But it would be Gordo first."

Joe crowded in closer to me. "Why him?"

"His magic."

"What about it?" I asked.

"It hurts. It stings. It *stinks*. It's a cloud of filth that covers all of you, and it's driving me crazy. I want to tear it to pieces. I want to tear *him* to pieces."

"The Omega," Ox muttered. "The girl. She looked as if she wanted to go after you first too."

Joe stared at Pappas. "And every time you came into the room, she was more agitated."

"That's not—" I shook my head. "Shit."

"What is it?" Ox asked.

"It has to be him. My father."

"Why?"

"Magic, it—it has a signature. A fingerprint. Specific to a witch.

But amongst family, it'll be similar. Not the same, but familiar. If my father did this, if this is his magic breaking the tethers of the Omegas, his magic is in them. And they're recognizing him in me."

Joe sighed. "This sucks."

I snorted. "Yeah. Sounds about right."

Pappas stared at me. "I killed them."

"The Betas."

He growled, "*Yes.*"

"You warned me."

"I did? I can't remember."

"You called me. You said your tether was breaking. You told me about the infection. That she knew about it."

"I betrayed my Alpha," he whispered.

"You *warned* me. Us. You knew what was happening. You wanted to be stopped. It's not you, Pappas. It's something inside you."

He stood slowly. He was a big man. His skin looked as if it were rippling, like he was fighting his shift. His thighs were tree-trunk thick, and the muscles quivered as he took a step toward us.

Ox rumbled deep in his chest, a clear warning that caused my skin to crawl.

Pappas ignored him. He only had eyes for me. "Your magic," he said. "It offends me. It makes my skin itch. You would be first. I would come for you first."

"You already tried that," I said coolly. "It still hasn't healed."

He didn't acknowledge the burn mark in the shape of a hand, blackened and crisped.

Joe's fingers circled my wrist. "Maybe not piss him off even more."

"You'll have to kill me," Pappas said, coming to stand in front of us, his toes inches away from the line of silver. "Eventually."

"We don't want that," Ox said. "Not for you. Not for any of them like you. But I will. If I think you're a danger to my pack or this town, I'll do it myself."

"And Carter and Mark? What if they become the danger? What will you do then?"

To that, Ox said nothing.

"She's scared of you," Pappas said, head cocked. "The boy who ran with wolves. She doesn't know what you want. What you've become."

"The only thing I want is right here in Green Creek."

"She doesn't believe that."

Ox shook his head. "That's not my problem."

He grinned wildly. "It is now. I know—I thought I could fight it. I thought . . . I hid it. From everyone."

We stayed quiet.

"The last Omega. The man. Do you remember him? His name was . . ."

Joe said, "Jerome. His name was Jerome. He feared us, but he still came."

"Yes," Pappas said. "Jerome. He nicked me. A scratch that barely bled from one of his fangs. On the back of my hand. He . . . surprised me. He moved quicker than I expected. We had just crossed out of your territory, and he acted like we were removing him from his *pack*." His hands flexed. His claws gleamed dully in the overhead light. "I didn't know why. I thought it was nothing. I healed. And even if it was *something*, I was stronger than an *Omega*. I could fight it. I could beat it." He laughed. It was a cruel sound. "I was wrong."

"What is she doing?" I asked. "What did Michelle mean by three days? What is she going to do?"

He was up against the silver then, almost quicker than I could follow. He snarled at me, angry when his body hit an invisible wall. Spit flew and splattered the ground in front of us as he banged his fists against the barrier. The silver stayed where it lay on the floor, unmoving. Jessie had spread it, but I had shaved it myself, putting the thoughts of earth and home and pack into it. He wouldn't get through, no matter how hard he tried.

It didn't stop Ox from stepping in front of me, claws out. He saw a threat, and his instincts had kicked in. His mate and his witch were his only concern.

"Help me," Pappas gasped as he took a step back. His hands were broken, the fingers bent at odd angles. They began to pop back into place, the echo of bones snapping all around us. "I can't—I can't fight this. Not for long."

"Tell us what's she's planning and I'll help you," Ox said. "I'll do whatever I can."

"You killed her. That girl."

"Yes."

"She wanted to see. If you would."

"I know."

"She didn't think you'd—"

"Philip. What is she doing?"

"It's not the same," Pappas said, starting to pace back and forth. He moved like a caged animal, eyes on me. "It's not the same as death. When the tether breaks. It snaps clean. It's there, and then it's not. I would know. It happened to me . . . once. I loved her. She was human, and I loved her. But I was prepared for it then. This is different. This is shredding. This is the bond fraying. Piece by piece. It was *her* and then it was the *memory* of her. I can feel it. In my head. It's being taken from me. It hurts. I want to kill you. Do you get that? I can hear them. Moving around above me. After I kill all of you, I would go for her. Elizabeth. She would fight me. But I would put my teeth in her *throat*—"

Joe roared at him, eyes red, taking a step toward Pappas.

He stumbled back, cowering against the far wall, whimpering as he curled in on himself.

I heard the thundering of feet above us, the answering howls of the pack hearing the anger of their Alpha.

Pappas rocked back and forth, eyes violet.

.   .   .

"If they send wolves, we'll be ready," Ox told us, the entire pack gathered at the Bennett house. The light was failing. The moon, which would be full in less than a week, was hidden away behind a blanket of clouds. I wondered if she still missed the sun. "If they send witches, we will deal with them. We've done it before, and we can do it again. We will not abandon our home. We'll find a way to fix this. I promise. They can't have us. They can't have any of us. You are my pack. You are my family. Nothing will take any of you away from me. Thomas taught me that a wolf is only as strong as its pack. That an Alpha can only truly lead when he has the trust of those around him. There has never been a pack like ours. They want a fight? They've got one."

The wolves sang around him.

The humans tilted their faces toward the sky.

Mark's shoulder brushed against mine.

Ox was right.

Let them come.

We would tear the earth beneath their feet.

. . .

The next morning Pappas was shifted. His wolf was black and gray and white. His coat was thick. His tail swished. His paws were massive. He snarled at the sight of me. His eyes glowed violet.

. . .

Robbie called back East.

There was no answer.

. . .

The shop was closed that Monday. Most of the businesses were, ahead of the storm. The schools too.

We were in the clearing.

The air smelled of snow. It stung my nose and made my eyes water.

I moved swiftly as a shifted wolf came at me. My skin was slick with sweat. I was breathing heavily. The wolf's jaw was opened wide, but the ground split beneath its paws before it could jump, a column of rock shooting up and knocking it off its feet. It landed with a crash on the ground, skidding through grass and dirt. It pushed itself up, shaking its head as if dazed.

"Good," Joe said, standing near my side. "Kelly, shift back. Carter, you're next."

Jessie bounced on her feet in front of Tanner, her hands wrapped with white tape, as she waited for Tanner to make his move. He feinted left, then went right, broadcasting his intent in the movement on his body. He was quick, but Jessie was quicker. She stepped to the side, spinning around, fist outstretched. She knocked him in the back of the neck, sending him stumbling and falling to his knees.

"Maybe it's someone else's turn to get beat up by Jessie," he mumbled, rubbing his neck as he winced.

Rico and Chris took a step away from them.

We moved as one. We were a pack. We'd done this again and again and again. Robbie was quick on his feet. Carter was a wall of strength. Kelly could move in the shadows. Elizabeth coiled like a snake, teeth bared. Jessie could face down a wolf on her own and win. Rico and Chris could unload a single clip in seconds. Tanner's knives could pierce the flesh of even the toughest wolf.

Joe and Ox were the Alphas, and we moved in sync with them.

And then there was Mark.

The brown wolf.

He was fluid, dodging anything that came at him. He was grace and art, the muscles underneath his skin shifting as he moved. I watched as Ox came for him half-shifted. He waited, crouched, until Ox was only a few feet away before he leapt up and over him, back legs hitting the Alpha's shoulders, knocking him off-balance. He landed on his feet on the other side of Ox, whirling around, ready for when Ox came for him again.

We had trained for this.

Some of us our whole lives.

We were the Bennett pack.

Which is why it was startling when Kelly snuck up on Carter, who was distracted by Robbie's twitching tail. Kelly pounced on him, teeth bared.

And Carter responded by knocking his brother halfway across the clearing, roaring in pure fury. Kelly landed hard, dirt and grass piling up around him as he came to a stop. He groaned as he shifted back to human. "Carter, what the hell, man. I was just—"

But Carter didn't stop. He ran toward his brother, a glint in his eyes that I'd never seen before.

I shouted, "*Ox!*"

Ox moved, clothes shredding as his wolf burst forward. Kelly scrabbled backward, eyes wide at the sight of his brother barreling toward him. Carter's neck stretched outward, fangs aimed for Kelly's bare leg, and—

He let out a loud yelp as Ox landed on his back, forcing him down on the ground. Ox roared in his ear as Carter twisted underneath him, trying to knock Ox off to get at his brother. The call of his Alpha startled him, breaking him out of his shift almost instantly. He panted up at Ox, whose teeth were near his throat. "Holy shit," he breathed. "I didn't mean to. Oh my god, Ox, I didn't mean it. I didn't—"

Ox snapped at him.

He fell quiet.

Joe moved toward them, motioning for Kelly to back away. I thought Kelly was going to argue, but he did as his Alpha said.

Joe stood above his brother, his hand on his mate's side. He said, "Carter."

"Joe! I don't know what happened. Okay? I didn't mean to—"

And Joe said, "Show me your eyes."

"It's not *like* that. I swear. I just forgot for a second. I'm not—I'm not like that. I'm not like *them*—"

"Show me. Your eyes."

Carter looked stricken as his blue eyes changed color.

Orange.

Only orange, as bright as always.

Joe sighed. "Ox, let him up."

Ox stepped off him, but not before he leaned down and pressed his nose into Carter's neck, a pulse of *brother home safe home* rolling through the threads. Carter curled into a ball on the ground, a wounded noise pouring from his throat. Kelly was at his side a moment later, putting a hand in Carter's hair, whispering in his ear, telling him it was fine, everything was fine, it would be okay, Carter, I'm here, I swear I'm not mad. I'm not going to leave you, we're gonna be okay.

Robbie looked as if he was going to go to them, but Elizabeth stopped him, a hand wrapped around his wrist. She shook her head when he looked back at her. "Let them be," she said quietly.

Robbie nodded but turned back toward them, shoulders tense.

"What the hell was that?" Rico whispered.

"Dunno," Tanner said. "Do you think . . . ?"

"Does it happen that fast?" Chris asked. "I thought it was supposed to take weeks. Maybe it's the full moon?"

"Would you idiots be quiet?" Jessie hissed. "They can *hear* you."

"Right," Rico said. "Sorry about that. We'll just stand here silently, watching as two naked brothers lay on each other and cry. *Aye.* My life."

.   .   .

"Can we beat this?"

I needed to hear it from her. I needed her to say yes. I needed her to tell me so that I could be brave.

Elizabeth didn't look at me. "I don't know. If anyone can, I would expect it to be us. But sometimes strength isn't enough. We need to prepare. Just in case." Her voice broke at the end.

I wanted to give her promises I knew I couldn't keep.

But I couldn't find the words.

I left her standing in the kitchen.

⋅ ⋅ ⋅

I reached out to some old contacts. Witches without packs, as I couldn't trust those with wolves. Not when I didn't know what Michelle was capable of.

Abel had told me once the moon had missed her love. That the wolves came to be because of that. That witches were created due to a last-ditch effort to stop the sun from burning those who sang to her.

It was bullshit, of course.

Once, when magic flourished, there were more of us. Magic hadn't yet begun to fade, dying out with each passing generation. Covens existed, groups of witches that numbered in the dozens. Some were good. Some were not. Most of them burned.

There were still some of us left. They were older, far older than I.

The old witch by the sea had been one of them. He, too, had been part of a pack once. He, too, had loved a wolf. He would have been my first call, if not for his heart stopping the moment we'd left. I remembered what he'd seen in the bones.

You will be tested, Gordo Livingstone. In ways that you haven't yet imagined. One day, and one day soon, you will have to make a choice. And I fear the future of all you hold dear will depend on that choice.

I still didn't know what he'd meant. But it felt like it was happening now.

There was a woman in the north. She was borderline cliché, cauldrons bubbling, hunched over spell books that were more often bullshit than real. She claimed to speak with those who had crossed over from this life, though I didn't think she could be believed.

"Does she live in a broken-down cabin in the middle of the woods?" Rico asked me. "Like, eating children and shit? Is that offensive to witches? Are you offended? I'm sorry if you're offended."

"Aileen lives in an apartment in Minneapolis," I said.

"Oh. That's . . . disappointing."

"Livingstone," she said, her voice crackling through the phone. "I wish I could say that this was a surprise."

"I need your help."

Aileen laughed until it shattered into a dry cough that stretched on what seemed like ages. "Damn cigarettes," she finally managed to say. "Quit smoking, boyo. You'll regret it eventually, what they do to you. That I promise."

I ground out my cigarette in the overflowing ashtray.

She knew nothing. She'd never even heard of tethers broken from the outside. "I'll look," she said, but she sounded apologetic. "See what I can see. Put some feelers out there. You hang in there, boyo."

"Have you—"

"No. No, Gordo. I haven't heard anything about your father. But . . ."

"But?"

"There are whispers."

"I don't have time for you to be vague, Aileen."

"Bite your tongue, Gordo, lest I hex it from your mouth."

I sighed.

"There's movement."

I closed my eyes. "Witches."

"And wolves."

"Heading our way?"

"I don't know. But now that you've told me what you have, I wouldn't be surprised. This feels . . . different. Things are changing, boyo."

"Shit."

She coughed again. "You always had a way with words. Watch yourself. And your pack. I'll do what I can."

.   .   .

There was a man in New Orleans. He had albinism, his skin preternaturally white. His hair was a pale red. Dark, rusty freckles across his face. His voice was smooth jazz and warm whiskey. He practiced white voodoo, his magic sharp and filled with rough edges. He was a healer, and a powerful one at that. "Pauve ti bête," Patrice said quietly. "Dat's all dey got. Dem tethers."

"I know," I said through gritted teeth.

"But it's always been more with you Bennetts. Something extra. Why is dat, you tink?"

I didn't know how to answer that. Nothing about us was normal.

"You gotta reinforce dose tethers, Gordo. Dey gotta be *strong. Ou konprann*? Even when all seems dark, dey need to rememba what dey have."

"There's nothing—"

He snorted. "Dose wolves. In Maine. Dey tink dey know all. Dey tink dere way is da *only* way. It's not. Dere is more. So much more. We exist, little witch, to maintain da balance. Your place, your . . . Green Creek."

"It's different," I said quietly.

"Oh yeah. Big big. Maybe da only place left in da world like it. Who wouldn't want dat?"

The thought sent a chill down my spine. "My father—"

"Isn't you," Patrice snapped. "He made his choice. You made yours."

"The choice was made for me."

"Lies. Did you fight for what was yours? Or did you let da wolves do what dey wished?"

I didn't know what to say.

"Thomas Bennett was a good Alpha," he said. "But he made mistakes. He should've fought for you more den he did. You must now decide what he could not. What your daddy didn't understand. You must decide to *fight*, Gordo. And what you're willing ta do. What you're capable of."

"I don't know how to stop this," I admitted.

"Don't know either. I'll look. I'll pray, Gordo. On my end. But you must do all you can. *Yon sèl lang se janm ase.* One language is never enough. We need dem. Dey need us. The wolves. Never forget dat."

If only my father and mother had thought the same.

.   .   .

"Breathe," Ox said in the clearing, Carter sitting across from him in the grass. His legs were crossed, his eyes closed. Hands on his knees. He looked tired. Lines of purple under his eyes. It felt blue and bleak. "What do you hear?"

"The trees. The birds."

"What do you feel?"

"The grass. The wind."

"This is your territory."

"Yes."

"You were made to be here. It was made for you."

Carter whispered, "*Yes.*"

"Your tether," Ox said gently. "What is it?"

Carter was struggling. His throat worked. His fingers dug into his jeans. His breath was a thick plume pouring from his mouth. The air was bracingly cold, and I shivered.

"Kelly," he finally said.

"Why?" Ox asked.

"Because he's my brother. Because I'm his protector. Because I love him. He keeps me sane. He keeps me whole. He's not like Joe. He's not meant to be an Alpha. Kelly's not as strong as him. He needs me. I need him."

"And he's there, still?"

Carter nodded tightly. "Still."

But even I could see it was beginning to fray.

"It's pack," Ox said, watching Carter flee through the trees.

I waited.

"For me." He stared up at the sky. That frozen ice smell in the air was stronger still. The snow was coming. "Like it was for Thomas. It's my pack."

I wasn't surprised. "He's struggling. Already."

"I know. That doesn't mean he's weaker."

"He can't shift, Ox. If what Michelle said was true, then it makes it worse." I swallowed thickly. "Mark either. He can't—you have to tell them."

"Full moon's coming. What then? They won't have a choice."

"I don't know."

He smiled faintly. "He'll need you. Now more than ever."

I hung my head. "You know?"

"About you being his tether? Yes. I know."

I sucked in a breath. "What if—Ox, I'm not enough. For him. It—"

"You are enough," Ox said quietly. "Even if you don't believe it yourself, you have a pack that believes it for you. And a wolf who will do anything to keep his tether safe."

"We have to fix this," I said, sounding desperate. "We have to find a way to stop this from happening."

His eyes flared red. "Trust me. I'm just getting started."

I watched Mark and Ox disappear into the woods.

Behind me, I heard Robbie pleading into his phone. "Please, Alpha

Hughes. Please call me back. We need help. You can't just leave us like this. You can't do this to us. Please. Please don't do this to my family."

As the meager light began to fade outside, I walked down the stairs to the basement.

Behind the line of silver stood a shifted Omega wolf.

He snarled at the sight of me, smashing into the barrier again and again and again.

Eventually he started to bleed.

But he didn't stop.

Later, at home, I took a duffel bag out of the closet.

I unzipped the secret pocket.

Inside lay a wooden raven.

I traced the wings with my finger.

I set it on the nightstand next to the bed.

I watched it for a very long time, waiting for sleep that would never come.

The snow began to fall just before midnight.

STORM

S on of a bitch," Chris said, wiping flakes of ice from his face. "This couldn't have waited?"

"We're the only tow truck in town," Rico reminded him, pushing himself up from a crouch. "And because this idiot decided to take the curve faster than he should have means we get to go out in the cold while everyone else is sitting in front of a fire and being warm and comfortable and probably sipping a nice brandy and—"

"We get it," I muttered, making sure the hook was fixed to the front of the car. We'd been at the Bennett house under lockdown, waiting for *something* to happen. Michelle's warning of three days hadn't yet passed, and Green Creek was buried under a near foot of snow with more coming down. I hated being reactive rather than proactive, but keeping our ears to the ground had revealed nothing. Michelle Hughes and Maine were silent. Philip Pappas was more wolf than man.

I'd gotten a call from Jones—the cop at the motel—telling me some asshole had lost control of his car before smashing into a snowbank, crumpling the front fender into the tire. It'd been abandoned when Jones had come across it in his SUV while on patrol and had called me.

Ox hadn't been too happy about us leaving the safety of the Bennett house. I'd promised him we'd be careful. The wards were quiet. We'd know if they were breached. Whatever Michelle was planning we'd be ready for it. I thought the storm had come at the right time. Green Creek was essentially isolated now. Nobody could get in.

Mark hadn't been happy about us leaving either, if the look on his face had meant anything. But he hadn't said a word, only reached out and touched my shoulder before disappearing farther into the house. The guys had teased me mercilessly about possessive wolves and scent marking.

Assholes.

I hadn't had the courage to ask him yet what had happened with

Dale, though I knew something had. I tried to tell myself it was none of my business. Or that it could wait. Or that it meant nothing.

"Good?" Tanner called from the driver's seat of the tow truck.

"Yeah!" Chris shouted back. "Looks good."

The boom on the tow truck creaked as the winch whirred to life. The sedan rose, front end up toward the back of the truck.

"Thanks, Gordo," Jones said. Red and blue lights spun lazily behind him. "I know it sucks to be out here, but I didn't want to take the chance of someone else coming around that corner and running into it."

"It's fine," I grunted as the car came to a stop. "We'll get it to the shop and take care of it once the storm passes. You got a bead on the driver?"

He shook his head. He looked troubled. "No. Couldn't have been out here long. I passed through a few hours ago and it wasn't there. Had to happen since then."

Rico and Chris glanced at each other. "Where'd the driver go?" Rico asked.

"I don't know," Jones said. "Hopefully toward town, though everything is closed. It'd be just my luck if whoever it was hit their head at impact, then decided it'd be a good idea to go wandering out into the snow."

Chris let out a low whistle. "Human Popsicle."

Jones sighed. "I'm supposed to be on vacation in a few days. I can kiss *that* goodbye if there's a stiff out there. Just my luck."

"Run the plates?" I asked.

"That's the weird thing. Come look." He jerked his head toward the back of the car.

We followed him and—

"No plates," Rico said. "Huh. Maybe he . . . took them with him?"

"He hit his head and then took his plates before he walked out into the storm?" Chris asked. "That's a little weird."

"As weird as werewo—"

"Rico," I snapped.

He coughed. "Right, boss. Sorry."

Jones looked at us curiously before shaking his head. "I looked for the plates before you got here, thinking maybe they got knocked off in the crash. But there's nothing, not even any footprints. It's fine, though. I can stop by the shop after the storm and get the VIN to run that. I'll find out somehow."

"Unless that's been shaved down," Rico said cheerfully. "Maybe there's a body in the trunk."

"I don't like you," Jones said, pointing a finger at Rico. "Vacation. First time in two years. Don't fuck with me."

"Yes, Officer."

The radio on his shoulder crackled to life. Jones sighed. "No rest for the weary. You guys going to be all right getting this back to the shop? Need me to follow you in?"

I waved him off. "We'll take care of it. Call me if something else happens."

He nodded before turning back to his cruiser.

We waved as he drove by us, honking his horn before heading toward town.

"Weird, right?" Chris said, staring at the car. "You don't think it's—"

"Let's just get it to the shop," I said, cutting him off. "I want to get back to the house before this storm gets any worse. Chris, with Tanner in the tow truck. Rico, with me."

"Move your asses!" Tanner bellowed. "I'm fucking *cold*."

We moved our asses.

. . . .

It was slow going, getting back into Green Creek. The snow was coming down harder than I ever remembered seeing it. The roads had been treated ahead of the storm, but it wasn't doing much. Large drifts lined either side of the road. We followed the tow truck slowly, the light bar atop flashing bright yellow.

Rico had his phone out, set up on the dashboard, speaker on, trying to continue the conversation he'd been having beforehand. "Baby," he was saying. "Baby, listen to me. I swear I'm—"

"I don't *care*, Rico," Bambi said, voice crackling through the phone. "You were supposed to come over *here*. But instead you tell me there's a *situation* you have to handle and you won't be in town for a couple of days. And when I ask you *what* situation, you tell me it's top secret."

I turned slowly to look at him.

He shrugged. "What was I supposed to say?" he muttered.

"I heard that, Rico! Who are you talking to? Who is she? If you got some bitch pregnant, I swear to god, I will *end* you."

"Hi, Bambi," I said, dry as dust. "Rico didn't get me pregnant. I swear. And even if he tried, he'd end up knocked flat on his ass."

"Is that Gordo? Gordo, who is he screwing besides me?"

"I told you I'm not screwing *anyone* but you!" Rico cried. "You know you're my one and only."

"Like I believe that. You're a smooth talker, Rico. I see how you flirt with women. You did it to *me*, after all."

"What can I say, *mi amor*. The ladies love me."

"Probably should have kept your mouth shut," I told him.

He winced as Bambi began to let him know what she thought about *that*. I tuned them out, staring at the tow truck ahead of us. The car hooked up to the boom was shaking slightly, bouncing on the road. We passed the sign welcoming us to Green Creek, mostly covered in snow. We hit Main Street, the shops closed up on either side of us, the windows frosted in ice. The neon lights of the diner were a beacon in the white. The only time I'd ever seen them off was after Ox's mother died. The owner had shut the lights down for a couple of days to honor her, in his own way. I hadn't known how I'd felt about that, but we'd been on the road shortly after and I'd forgotten about it until now. Memory was a funny thing.

It was Halloween, and the sidewalks should have been filled with people getting ready for the trick-or-treaters. Instead, Green Creek looked abandoned. A ghost town.

There was a shriek of static as we drove down Main Street. I glanced over as Rico picked up his phone off the dashboard, frowning down at it.

"And *another* thing, I . . . that you'd . . . Rachel told me that you *talked* . . . and—"

"Bambi, you're breaking up," Rico said. "I can't hear what you're saying."

"What? I'm . . . If you're . . . I'll kill you . . . Don't think I . . . There's . . ."

The phone beeped as the call dropped.

"Huh." Rico picked up the phone from the dash and frowned down at it. "No bars." He looked over at me. "Think it's the storm?"

I shrugged. "Could be. We don't have the best cell reception up here to begin with. Surprised you lasted this long. Though I don't know that's necessarily a bad thing." I glanced down at my own phone. No service.

"Boss," the CB crackled.

I picked up the receiver. "Yeah, Tanner."

"You leave the garage door unlocked when we picked up the tow truck?"

"Yeah. Have Chris get out and open it up. We'll—"

There wasn't time to react. One moment Chris and Tanner and the tow truck were crossing the T intersection, pulling even with the diner off to their right. The next an old crew-cab truck with a black snowplow blade attached to the front slammed into the driver's door of the tow truck. Rico shouted next to me, screaming *Tanner* and *Chris* and *no no no* as the tow truck began to tip onto its passenger-side wheels. The sedan being towed fishtailed to the left, then snapped right as the truck flipped onto its side, skidding in the snow. Metal shrieked as the boom pulled the car over along with the truck. It smashed into the diner front, glass breaking as the truck went *into* the diner.

I swerved hard left even as a bright burst of *something* exploded in my head, the old truck groaning as it began to slide on the slick surface. The steering wheel jerked in my hands as I struggled to hold on to it, gritting my teeth against the onslaught rolling over my body, my tattoos feeling like they were on fire. I thought we were going to tip over too, but somehow we stayed upright, coming to a stop yards away from the intersection.

Red blazed in my chest. The tangled roots were *writhing*.

"What the fuck!" Rico was screaming, voice breaking. "Gordo, what the fuck!"

The crew cab began to back away slowly. I groaned, bringing my hands up to my head, trying to focus, trying to clear my vision and—

"What do we do?" Rico asked frantically. "What do we do?"

"Something's wrong," I ground out as I looked back up. "Something's—"

The passenger door on the crew cab opened.

A man rose from inside, standing against the door. He was wearing Kevlar, a balaclava covering his head and face. Goggles over his eyes. All I could make out was the tip of his nose, the white flash of teeth.

In his hands he held a semiautomatic rifle.

He pointed it directly at us, elbows resting on top of the door.

I grabbed Rico by the neck and shoved him down as gunfire erupted. The windshield shattered. Rico cried out, but I didn't think he was hit. I couldn't smell blood.

The raven spread its wings even as something tried to cage it.

I slammed my hand to the floor of the truck. The frame rattled as the pack bonds flared brightly, blue, ice blue, and red, red, red. I was buried in my fury, I was *reveling* in it, and deep in my head and heart, the roots of the threads that bound us together *roiled* like a den of snakes, thrumming and writhing.

But it felt different.

I couldn't pick out the wolves.

I couldn't *hear* them.

I was pissed.

The road cracked beneath the truck as I *pushed*.

I gritted my teeth as the pavement slid apart, shaking the truck around us as Main Street split right down the middle. The gunfire cut off, and I heard the man yelling *back back back*, and all I could think about was Chris and Tanner, Chris and Tanner, knowing they had to be hurt, knowing they had to be *scared*, and I wouldn't stand for it. I wouldn't stand for any of it.

"Stay here," I growled at Rico.

"What? Gordo, no. We have to—"

I ignored him. I reached up and snapped off the rearview mirror. Cold air and snow blew in through the shattered windshield. Glass littered the dashboard.

I threw open the driver's door. It creaked on its hinges.

I stepped out of the truck, leaning my back against the door. The storm swirled around me. No one approached from behind us. I held up the rearview mirror above me at an angle, twisting it until I could see in front of the truck.

I could make out the tow truck on its side in the diner. The back tire was still spinning. The boom had snapped off, and the car they'd been towing had slid away from the diner. The driver's door was still closed, which meant that Chris and Tanner were probably still inside. I tried to feel them, tried to reach along the threads, but it was as if they were *muted*, and I couldn't find them, couldn't hold on to them.

"Shit," I muttered.

I turned the mirror.

The crew cab had fallen into the crack in the middle of the street and lay, nose first, at a sharp angle. The rear of the vehicle pointed up toward the gray sky. I couldn't see the man with the rifle.

I looked back in the truck. Rico was staring at me with wide eyes. He had a gash on his cheek, and blood was trickling down his jaw. "To me. You stay right by my—"

A bright lance of pain roared through my head. It was as if long, spindly fingers had reached inside my skull and were *gripping* my brain, squeezing tightly, digging in. I gritted my teeth as a wave of nausea rolled through me, vertigo causing my stomach to swoop. The wards. Someone was fucking *raping* my goddamn wards.

I heard Rico saying my name, telling me to get up, I had to get up, please, Gordo, please, and somewhere in the furthest reaches of my mind, I heard *gordo gordo gordo*, and I *knew* that voice. I *knew* the wolf behind it. He was furious, and he was coming for me. I tried to tell him no, no, no, to stay away, to stay *back*, but I couldn't focus. I couldn't find the thread that connected us, lost in a haze of the storm that raged in and out of my head.

Then, from behind us, a voice in the snow.

At first I couldn't make it out. What it was saying. It sounded bigger than a normal human voice should have. Amplified, somehow. I was on my knees in the snow, bare hands cold and wet on the ground in front of me. I tried to lift my head, but it was so heavy.

"What is that?" Rico asked, voice cracking. "Gordo, what is that?"

I breathed and breathed and—

"—and this town has been marked by God as an *unholy* place, in need of a cleansing. Your sins are many, but you are human. You are *fallible*. It is to be expected. The blessed waters have receded from the earth beneath your feet. And do you know any better? Do you understand the depths of what hides in the forest? It is unfortunate, truly. You walk the streets of this town, cowering behind the abominations that have infiltrated your very lives. Their shadows stretch long, blocking out the light of the Lord. You tell yourselves that your eyes are playing tricks on you, that you don't believe in the twisted depravity. But you *know*. Each and every one of you *knows*."

I lifted my head.

There, walking down the middle of the road toward Green Creek, was a figure. At first it was nothing but a black smudge against the white of the storm, fat flakes swirling around it. But with every step the figure took, it came more into focus.

It was a woman.

She was speaking, her voice booming and echoing around us.

Behind her was a line of vehicles like the one that had crashed into the tow truck, the tires crunching in the snow, snowplow blades on the front. Some had light bars across the top, rows of LED bulbs shining bright.

And there, on either side of her, was something I did not expect.

Two shifted wolves.

The one on the right was red and white, its coat thick and long. Its teeth were bared in a silent snarl, a thick line of drool hanging from its mouth.

The one on the left was gray and white and black, like a timber wolf. But it was bigger than any wolf I'd seen before, its back almost to the woman's *shoulders*, its massive paws looking bigger than the spread of my *hands*.

Both of them had chains wrapped around their necks, silver links that looked as if they had been *embedded* into their skin.

The woman was holding the ends of the chains.

Like they were leashes.

The eyes of the unknown wolves flared.

Violet.

Omegas.

The woman spoke again. Her voice carried through the storm, blaring from the vehicle directly behind her. "The cities of the plain knew sin. They knew vice. They were Admah. Zeboiim. Bela. Sodom. Gomorrah. All in the land of Canaan. And God sent three angels to Abraham in the plains of Mamre. The Lord revealed unto Abraham the egregious sin that was Sodom and Gomorrah. And Abraham, the prophet, *begged* the angels to spare those in the cities of the plain if fifty righteous people could be found. And the Lord *agreed*. But Abraham *knew* what the people were. He knew what they were made of. And he returned to the Lord again and again, asking that the number be lowered. From fifty to forty-five. Forty-five to forty. To thirty. To twenty. To *ten*. To find *ten* people. Out of *thousands*, who could be righteous. And God *agreed*. He said *yes*. Find just *ten* righteous people and the cities would be spared."

The wolves at her sides growled. Their nostrils flared.

Rico's breathing was quick and high.

The woman wasn't dressed like the man that had fired upon us from the crew cab. She didn't have a Kevlar vest or a balaclava. She wore a heavy coat, the collar pulled up around her neck and face. Her skin was pale, her lips thin. She had a scar on her face, starting on her forehead, crawling down *over* her eye and onto her cheek. She was lucky she hadn't been blinded. Something with large claws and teeth had tried to kill her. And she had survived. I wondered if she now wore that wolf's skin over her shoulders, the head of which rested on top of hers, the length falling behind her like a cape.

She hadn't had that scar the last time I'd seen her, sitting across from me in the diner when I was a kid, asking if we could pray.

Meredith King.

Elijah.

She was older now. She had to be in her early fifties. But she moved easily, artfully, like a much younger woman. She held the heavy chains in her gloved hands, and the wolves kept pace with her, matching their steps with hers.

She said, "Two angels were then sent to Sodom to investigate. There they came upon Abraham's nephew, Lot. And while they broke bread with Lot, the sinners of Sodom stood outside Lot's door. 'Where are the men that came in to thee this night?' they asked. 'Bring them out unto us so that we may *know* them.' And Lot refused, because he knew what these men meant. He knew what they were asking for. In their black hearts, they thought to *defile* the angels of the Lord. Lot, in order to appease the lust of the growing crowd, instead offered his two virgin daughters. The offer was refused. The crowd moved toward the house, intent upon breaking down the door. The angels, having seen there was no good left in Sodom, struck the crowd with blindness and told Lot of their decision to destroy the city. For there were not fifty righteous men. There were not twenty righteous men. There were not even *ten* righteous men in the city of Sodom. They harbored the monsters of man, the sins of the world. The angels told Lot to gather his family and leave. 'Look not behind thee.'"

The fingers wrapped around my brain gripped tighter, and I cried out in pain, my head feeling like it was breaking apart.

"And they fled," Elijah said. "They fled, even as fire and brimstone began to rain down from the sky. For God is a loving god, but He is also a *vengeful* god. He will smite from the world the wickedness that festers like disease. The cities of the plain were destroyed. And even though she was *told* not to look back, Lot's wife did just that, and she paid the price for being a nonbeliever, becoming a pillar of salt. And when the fire ended, all that remained was a smoking wasteland, a dead and ruined land kept as a reminder of the power of sin. Of *abomination*.

"Green Creek is the New Sodom. You have monsters in your woods. There was a cleansing here once. At least, an attempt at one. God brought down his righteous fury through me, but I wasn't strong enough. The wound was cauterized, but still it seeped. And soon it began to fester." She stopped walking. The trucks behind her eased to a halt. The wolves brushed against her, shifting side to side, eyes filled with murderous violence. "I doubt there is even one righteous man in this place. One person capable of standing with God as I have." Her voice echoed through the snow. "Green Creek is a gateway to Hell. Where beasts have crawled up from the burning fire and shoved their teeth into the earth. I failed once. And I paid the price for it." She reached up with one gloved hand, the chain rattling. She touched the scar on her face, the eye underneath it foggy white and unseeing. "I will not fail again. All outside communication has been cut off. Your phones. Your internet. All the signals have been jammed. The town of Green Creek is under quarantine by order of God and the clan of the Kings. I am but a messenger, here to make sure the word of the Lord is carried out." She smiled a terrible smile. "This place will know the light of God, or it will be nothing but a wasteland."

She dropped the chains.

"Oh shit," Rico breathed.

Elijah said, "Sic 'em, boys."

The Omegas roared forward.

I rose quickly, slamming the door to the truck. "Don't fucking move," I snarled at Rico, ignoring the *pull* I felt in my head, the spindly fingers having become *hooks* as the wards *shifted*, becoming something twisted and rotten. My legs felt weak, and I stumbled with the first running step I took, somehow managing to keep myself upright. I heard the snarl of wolves behind me, the sounds of their paws in the snow, the heaving breaths in their chests.

The raven was struggling to flap its wings, exerting more force than should have been necessary. The roses felt like they were rotting, shriveling until I thought they were *dying*. The thorns were blackened and cracking.

I ran for the upturned crew cab still stuck in the remains of Main Street. I could see the men inside, slumped forward and unmoving. I glanced over my shoulder in time to see the red wolf leap *over* my truck, its chain trailing behind it until it landed right behind me. It hit the ground hard, its paws sliding out from underneath it. It slammed into the earth with a low whine, snow piling up around it as it landed on its side, heavy chain dragging behind it.

The bigger timber wolf didn't follow. It came around the driver's side of the truck, claws digging in as it course-corrected toward me. The red wolf was struggling to rise to its feet as the timber wolf ran past it. I'd been around wolves for most of my life, and I recognized when the wolf began to lower itself toward the ground, muscles coiling in its legs. I was almost to the crew cab when the wolf leapt toward me.

I kicked my legs out in front of me, falling to my side, sliding through the snow and *under* the angled truck. Ice and gravel tore at my skin. I flipped over in time to see the timber wolf smash into the side of the crew cab, the metal groaning, truck shifting after me, scraping along the broken pavement. The wolf was dazed, mouth open as it lay on its side, tongue lolling out into the snow, breathing heavily, eyes unfocused.

I stood—

here and here and here and here is another ward twist it twist it twist

—and *screamed* as a voice filled my head, the spindly fingers digging even deeper. The wards around Green Creek were shredding as if being pulled apart by some force greater than I'd ever felt before. It was—

strong they're stronger than we thought than we expected twist them break them

—too much for me to take, it fucking *filled* me up, and I was sure I was burning from the inside out, and even though I hadn't heard his voice in decades, even though I had been a *child* the last time I'd laid eyes upon him, I *knew* that voice. I knew it down to my very bones.

The red wolf was on its feet and—

I was surrounded.

On either side of me stood Alpha wolves, shifted and snarling.

Behind me, pressing his snout against my back, was a brown Beta. I could feel the low thrum of the song he was singing, but it was buried under the roar of the broken wards and the voice of my father.

Another, but he remained hidden, moving behind the buildings to the right.

And others. Our pack. All of them.

"Chris, Tanner," I said through gritted teeth. "In the tow truck. Rico in my truck. They need help."

Joe rumbled lowly and disappeared into the divide that split Main Street.

Mark huffed a hot breath against the back of my neck.

The red wolf shrank back against the growl of a pissed-off Alpha, a low whine in the back of its throat. Its ears were flattened, its shoulders low to the ground. Its tail was curled up behind its hind legs as it backed away slowly. For a moment its eyes flickered, the violet fading to brown before going back again.

The timber wolf had lifted itself to its feet. Its violet eyes narrowed at me, teeth gnashing as it took a step, chain dragging alongside it. Behind it, I could see Rico in the truck, peeking his head over the door.

The timber wolf coiled and—

Carter launched himself out from an alleyway. He collided with the side of the timber wolf, knocking it off his feet. Fangs and claws dug into flesh, the burst of blood shocking against the white snow. The timber wolf snarled in anger as it landed on the ground, turning its head to try and close its jaws around whatever part of Carter it could get. It was bigger than Carter, but Carter was faster. He twisted, avoiding the fangs snapping in his direction. Carter's back left paw hit the chain, and he yelped in pain, a thin wisp of smoke curling up.

Ox darted toward my truck and Rico. The red wolf scrabbled backward, trying to get away from the charging Alphas. Even through the storm in my head, I could hear Ox saying *get pack get pack get pack and run run we run we don't fight not here not now we run* and even before their words finished echoing, the raven began to move. It felt caged still, like something was trying to *stifle* the bird, but it wasn't enough.

I crossed my arms, hands grabbing the opposite wrists. I dug my fingernails into my own skin and *scraped* down, sliding my hands until I was palm to palm, slick with blood.

The timber wolf craned its neck farther to try to get at Carter, and there was a brief moment when I thought it *hesitated*, nostrils flaring as its nose came into contact with Carter's side, but it didn't matter. My blood dripped onto the earth, and the chains wrapped around the necks of each of the foreign wolves *jerked* up, pulling the wolves up by their necks. The legs of both the red wolf and the timber wolf kicked, trying to find purchase on the ground, but I gritted my teeth, palms pressed against each other, and—

they're breaking they're breaking they're BREAKING

—took a stumbling step forward, feeling like my head was splitting right down the middle. It wasn't just the voice of Robert Livingstone in my head. No, it was a goddamn *chorus* of voices ringing out as the wards turned against my magic, being taken away from me and made into something else.

I pushed through the haze that had started to fall over my eyes.

The feral wolves were snarling as they hovered ten feet off the ground. Mark stood at my side, pressed against me, tail curled around my hips. He was grounding me, trying to burst through the cacophony of voices in my head. He was here, he was *pack gordo pack here LoveMateHeart*, and whatever was happening with the wards was pushed to the background. The scene in front of me snapped back into startling focus.

Carter's head snapped toward me as a wave of my fury rolled through the threads between us.

I ignored Rico as we walked by the truck, the door open, Ox gently biting him on the hand and pulling. I heard him gasp as we passed by, but it didn't matter. He was safe. His Alpha would see to that.

Mark stayed by me with every step I took.

The snow stuttered and shook around us as if it were reacting to the unseen force of the magic burning in my chest.

I squeezed my hands into fists. The blood squelched between my fingers.

The chains jerked up, wrapping themselves around the feral wolves.

They yowled as the silver burned their flesh.

There, standing a dozen yards down the road, was Elijah.

Hunters had surrounded her, the doors of their trucks opened behind them.

All had guns trained on us.

Elijah looked up at the wolves floating ten feet above the ground, writhing in pain as their skin burned. She smiled, then turned her gaze back on me. "Gordo Livingstone, as I live and breathe. You certainly have grown up well. But I suppose we were all younger then. Lord knows I certainly was. But that is the way of things. Time stops for no man." Her smile widened. "Or woman." She glanced up again at the wolves. "Those are mine. My pets."

"What the fuck are you doing here?" I growled at her.

The hunters behind her laughed as Elijah cocked her head. "Didn't you hear anything I've said? Gordo, this town, this *place*, has been judged. It has been found guilty. I am here to mete out the punishment for the sins of Green Creek. The blight must be eradicated. For too long, the beasts here have infected these woods. We came here once. We were unprepared. We won't make that mistake again."

Mark growled next to me, ears flattened and teeth bared.

The snow fell around us.

A pulse rose behind me. And even though the storm in my head thundered, it didn't compare to the strength of my pack.

Carter arrived first, moving until he stood next to Mark, shoulders brushing together.

Some of the hunters took a step back.

Ox came next. His eyes burned furiously.

Rico pressed his hand against my back.

Joe's paws crunched the snow as he came up on our left. Chris and Tanner stood on either side of him, Chris bleeding from a gash on his head and Tanner limping. But they were defiant.

More wolves came.

Elizabeth and Robbie, both shifted and growling, tails swishing as they stood next to their pack.

Jessie brought up the rear. She tapped Ox's crowbar against her shoulder.

The hunters were scared. The barrels of their rifles shook. The first one who fired was going to be the first to die. I would see to it myself.

"The Bennett pack," Elijah breathed. "How . . . expectant. Allow me to introduce myself. My name is Elijah. The wolf pack that came before you killed most of my clan. I am here to make sure that never happens again." She glanced at me. "I'm told my brother, may he rest in peace, warned your witch of me."

The feeling of *blue* threatened to overwhelm me. It came from Elizabeth. I realized then that aside from myself and Mark, she was the only one who had faced Elijah before. Had seen what she was capable of. She had survived only to live in the aftermath of the destruction of most of her pack.

And I had kept Elijah's existence from her.

But that wasn't—"How did you know what your brother said?" I demanded. "The only person I told was . . ." No.

No, fuck, please no.

The wolves were confused, but it was lost to my horror.

"Philip Pappas," Elijah said, the smile fading from her face. "Who in turn told Michelle Hughes. Michelle Hughes, who asked my clan to return to Green Creek and eradicate the infection spreading amongst the beasts that haunt this town. I must admit, it wasn't exactly ideal, forming an alliance with the wolves, but she promised me I would have my revenge. I just had to wait. But as a prophet of the Lord, I understood that one day, my time would come. The enemy of my enemy is my friend, after all." She lifted the wolf head up and off, letting it rest back on her shoulders. She'd shaved her hair down close to the scalp. The scar on her face etched its way up the side of her head. Snow landed on her skin and trickled down her face like tears. "We have a code. No humans are to be harmed unless they actively assist the wolves. As long as the people of Green Creek stay out of my way, they will not be touched. As for the traitors standing with the wolves, I will afford them this once chance. Walk away. Leave this pack behind. At the borders of your territory stand witches prepared to allow you through the wards they have commandeered from Gordo

Livingstone. You have until the full moon, when I'm told that part of your pack will turn feral. If you do not accept this offer, you will be shown no quarter and hunted as if you were a Bennett."

It was Jessie who spoke. "We're already Bennetts, you cunt. And if you were taken out once like you say you were, then it can happen again."

The wolves rumbled around us.

Elijah's mouth was a thin line. "I see. I was warned of your . . . loyalty. I've witnessed it before. The way wolves assert their control over humans. It is unfortunate that you can't see what you've become."

There was the telltale snap of muscle and bone, and Oxnard Matheson stood upright slowly, nude, snow falling onto his shoulders.

"Alpha," Elijah said, nodding in deference. "I'm told you're unusual, even for a wolf. The mate of the boy who would be king. A human Alpha who gave in to the sin of the wolf." She reached up and touched the skin of the wolf hanging off her back. "Yours would be an impressive pelt to own. I think I shall have it."

"It appears you've been told many things."

"A necessary thing in warfare."

"You have already made a mistake," Ox said quietly, taking a step forward. The rifles tracked toward him, the hunters beginning to murmur their unease.

"Oh?" Elijah asked, voice cool. "And what would that be exactly?"

"You came into my territory uninvited," Ox said, "with the intention of hurting my family. Omegas came once, intending to do the same. We were smaller then. Unsure. Scared. We thought ourselves alone." His eyes flared red. "Only a few of them crawled away. The rest had their throats ripped out. Their blood drenched this earth, and I swore then and there that I would do whatever it took to keep my pack safe."

Elijah's eyes narrowed. "I don't fear you, wolf—"

"No," Ox snapped. "But your clan does. I can smell it. The sweat dripping down the backs of their necks. The way their heartbeats stutter and trip. You may not be scared, but they are *terrified*."

"They will do as they're told."

ready be ready run protect the humans get back to the house home safe home

"Then they're already dead," Ox said, and it was now, it was now, *it was now—*

An electronic sound chirruped loudly behind us.

"You there!" a voice called out from a loudspeaker. "Stand down. I repeat, *stand down.* Lower your weapons and—holy shit, are those *wolves?*"

Jones.

Many things happened at once.

Ox: *move safe home now*

and,

the wolves in the air above us screamed as the chains tightened

and,

Rico and Chris and Tanner and Jessie running

and,

the raven broke free of its cage, wings spreading as I *hurled* the feral wolves at the hunters, their jaws gaping as they snarled, Elijah's eyes going wide, the hunters shouting,

and,

two shots fired.

A bullet whizzed by near my ear.

The second bullet caused Ox to grunt as it hit him high in the shoulder. I *felt* it, a burst of *it hurts it hurts oh my god it hurts*, and he took a step back.

Elijah jumped out of the way as the feral wolves slammed into the group of hunters that had gathered behind her.

Joe roared angrily, even as Ox fell to his knees, his shift taking over. The muscles in his back rippled as black hair sprouted along his skin. His hands became great paws, his face elongating as the wolf emerged.

Mark pushed against my legs, forcing me away from the screaming hunters, who were scrabbling back from the snapping pain of the hurt wolves.

We ran.

I glanced back over my shoulder before we disappeared into the swirling snow. Elijah had picked herself up and was staring after us. She caught my gaze and raised her hand, wiggling her fingers at me.

We passed by the cruiser.

Jones was inside, eyes sightless.

A trickle of blood slid down from the hole in the center of his forehead.

ENOUGH

M y lungs were burning by the time we reached the house at the end of the lane. The wolves had stayed behind the humans, making sure they didn't stop. Chris and Tanner were flagging. Elizabeth and Robbie kept them upright, allowing them to lean on their backs, pushing them on.

We passed the blue house, Kelly leading the way, shifting toward human, feet slipping in the snow as he reached the porch of the Bennett house. His eyes were wide and fearful as he looked back at us in time to see Ox fall to the ground, sliding in the snow, leaving a trail of blood behind him.

Rico took a step toward him. "What's wrong with Ox?" he asked, voice high-pitched. "Is he okay? Why is he—"

"Silver," I grunted, shoving him out of the way. "The bullet was made of silver. Jessie. In the house. A knife. We have to get the bullet out. I don't have the strength to do it myself."

She didn't hesitate, hitting the stairs at a full run, the door to the Bennett house banging open as she disappeared inside.

Elizabeth shifted back to human, grabbing on to Chris and Tanner, pulling them away from Joe, who stood above his mate, growling angrily. "It's okay," she said, face ashen. "He'll be okay. We need to get you seen to. Rico, Robbie, I need your help."

Rico nodded, even as Tanner and Chris protested loudly.

Carter stood in front of Kelly, pacing back and forth, nostrils flaring. Robbie looked conflicted, glancing back and forth between Ox and Elizabeth. It took Elizabeth saying his name sharply before he herded the humans toward the house, snapping at their heels.

"Joe," I said, hands up in a placating gesture. "I need to help Ox, okay? You know me. You know I won't do anything to hurt him further."

For a moment I thought Joe was going to lunge for me, but Mark was at my side, lips pulled back over his teeth, growling lowly in his throat. The wolves were singing in my head, and all their songs were blue and filled with hurt and confusion and *alpha alpha alpha*. The other voices I'd heard back in the street had quieted. I didn't know what that meant. I couldn't feel the wards anymore, at least not as they'd been before.

That had to wait.

I needed to help Ox.

My hands shook, the blood on them still wet.

I could see the moment the metallic scent of it hit Joe's nose, because he whined in my direction, torn between his mate and his hurt witch. "I'm okay," I told him. "I'm okay. But I need to get to Ox."

Jessie came flying back out of the house, a large kitchen knife in her hand. She jumped down the steps and landed gracefully at the bottom. Her cheeks were reddened, her breaths coming hard and quick.

Joe jerked his head toward her, crouching low over Ox as if he thought she was a threat.

She reached out with her free hand and smacked him upside the head. "Knock it off," she snapped. "Let us do what we need to. If you're not going to help, then get the fuck out of the way."

"Maybe not piss off the angry Alpha," I muttered.

She rolled her eyes. "We don't have *time* for mystical moon magic bullshit. Either he moves, or I make him move."

Joe huffed out a breath, steam curling around his face.

And he stepped aside.

I went to my knees beside Ox. He was trembling, but his eyes were open and aware. I could see where his hair was matted with blood, but it would be easier if—"Ox, I need you to shift back, okay? I need to see the wound better. I don't have time to shave down the hair."

"Won't the shift cause the silver to enter his bloodstream quicker?" Kelly asked, sounding gut-punched. "It'll make it—"

"It's not near his heart," I said. "If I move fast, it won't matter."

Joe leaned down, nuzzling against Ox's head. It was *please* and *help* and *OxLoveMate*. Ox shuddered on the ground in the snow, and the long whine turned into a dull groan as he shifted back to human. He gasped as the hair melted away, leaving nothing but white skin and a bloody, ragged hole in his shoulder, roughly the size of a quarter, that looked as if it was *smoking*.

His back arched off the ground. "Fuck," he said through gritted teeth. "Jesus Christ, that *hurts*, Gordo, it's—"

"You have to hold him down," I said. "Kelly. Carter. I need you to—"

Kelly was there, pushing down on Ox's shoulders.

Carter took a step toward us, still a wolf. His eyes blazed orange. He screwed them shut, and I could *feel* him trying to force his shift, but something was wrong. He opened his eyes again, and for a moment I swore I saw—

Mark appeared, human and kneeling at Ox's feet. He put his hands on Ox's shins, forcing them down into the snow. He looked up at me and nodded.

"It's going to be quick," I warned Ox. "Stay as still as you can. The more you move, the longer it'll take."

He nodded, eyes red, nostrils flaring.

I didn't hesitate.

I took the knife from Jessie and sliced the skin around the bullet wound, making the opening wider. Ox's hands closed to fists and his toes curled, but he turned his head toward Joe, who pressed his nose against his forehead.

"You ready?" I asked Kelly and Mark.

They nodded.

I put my hand over the wound, close but not touching. I was exhausted, but I pushed through it. It took a moment for me to find it, the bullet of silver embedded in his shoulder. But once I did, I latched on to it and *pulled* it up. Ox screamed as it slowly rose out of him, keeping to the same path it'd used to enter him. The smell of burning flesh filled my nostrils, but I was so fucking close to—

The bullet slid from the wound. It was really the smallest of things.

Ox gasped as it left him, throat working as Joe rumbled in his ear.

I put my hand over the wound again, this time pressing down against his skin.

I tried to pull as much of the pain as I could. My vision started to swim only seconds later, and I heard Mark say, "Gordo, that's enough. Gordo. *Gordo.*"

Arms wrapped around me, tugging me away. I fell back against a warm chest.

"It's okay," Mark whispered in my ear. "It's okay. Look. He's already starting to heal. You did it. Gordo, you did it. It's okay."

I nodded, unable to find the strength to open my eyes.

I didn't remember much after that.

I woke in a room that was not my own. The light was dull. I was warm.

I blinked slowly, muscles stiff and sore. My tattoos felt burnt-out, weak. I wanted nothing more than to close my eyes and drift away again.

But then I remembered everything.

"Fuck," I groaned, turning my head into the pillow.

"Sounds about right."

I sighed. Of course. I didn't look at him. "How long have I been out?"

"A few hours," Mark said from somewhere in the room.

"Ox?"

"Healing. He'll be fine."

I closed my eyes again. I knew where we were. The pillow smelled of him. I would know that scent anywhere. It'd been burned into me since I was a kid. "You're a fucking asshole."

Mark snorted. "Glad to know you're feeling better."

"You shifted. Carter too."

"You were in trouble."

I ground my teeth together. My jaw hurt. "You heard what Michelle said. It makes it worse. Is that what you want?"

"You were in trouble," he repeated.

"I had the situation under control."

"Against Elijah, you mean."

"Yes."

"Who you apparently knew about."

Goddammit. I should have known this was going to bite me in the ass. I opened my eyes again and turned my head. Mark stood near the window to his room, silhouetted against the dim light coming in. Frost covered the glass. Outside, snow still fell in fat flakes. His eyes glittered in the shadows. A thought struck me, harsh and biting. "I wasn't—I didn't know about Michelle. I didn't know about Pappas. Elijah. I'm not my father. Mark, you gotta believe me. I'm not my—"

"I know. We know. Joe . . . wasn't happy. But Elizabeth got through to him, I think. Aside from her, and you and me, no one else knew about Elijah. What she was capable of. But she told the others. About what happened last time."

I pushed myself up to a sitting position with a groan. I was shirtless, my skin pebbling in the cool air in the room. Someone had gotten me out of my clothes and into a pair of sweats while I'd been unconscious. I had a good idea who it was. "The guys?"

Mark tilted his head slightly. "Bruised. A little bloodied. But nothing serious. They got patched up. They were very lucky. All of you were."

I popped my neck, stretching the stiff muscles. "And the hunters?"

"Haven't approached the house. They're staying away. For now."

"Of course they are," I muttered, sliding my feet to the floor. "Fucking melodramatic assholes." Elijah said she was giving us until the full moon. I didn't know what that meant. But it didn't matter. She would be dead by then. I would see to it myself. "I can't believe I didn't see this coming. Michelle. She betrayed us."

"I don't know that you could have," Mark said slowly. "Wolves working with hunters? She's playing a dangerous game." He paused, considering. "But she's not the only one keeping secrets."

I winced at the dig. I deserved that. "David King."

"What about him?"

"He's the one who told me that his sister was still around."

"And you didn't think to say anything?" There it was. The first hint of anger.

"I didn't think—I don't know what I was thinking."

"You never do."

I rolled my eyes. "You're not funny."

"I'm not trying to be." His eyes flared orange briefly. "And whether or not we should have seen what Michelle would do, you still should have told us."

"I know."

He scoffed. "Do you? Because I don't believe you."

I glared up at him. "I fucked up, okay? I know that."

"You don't trust us. You don't trust your pack."

Now I was getting angry. "Go to hell, Mark. You don't know what the fuck—"

"It took me a little bit to figure out why."

"And now you're going to tell me, aren't you."

He ignored me. "You don't trust us. Even after everything we've been through. You don't trust us because you think this is all temporary. That your pack is going to leave you again."

"Gee, I wonder where I'd get *that* idea."

He scowled at me. "Can you be serious for once?"

I laughed. It wasn't the nicest sound. "Bullshit. You brought it up, Mark. If your pseudopsychobabble bullshit was true, if I didn't trust my pack, it would be because of people like you."

"I told you before. I would always come back—"

"But you *didn't*," I snapped at him. "You fucking *left* and—no. You know what? I'm not doing this now. Or ever. There are more important things we have to worry about."

"You don't trust us," Mark said, as if I hadn't spoken. I gave very real thought to calling on my magic and knocking him through the window. I was pretty sure he'd survive the fall. "And I'm to blame for that. Me. Elizabeth." He swallowed thickly. "Thomas. And I will regret for the rest of my life not fighting harder."

"He was your Alpha," I muttered. "Kinda hard to say *no* when he could make you do anything he wanted."

"He wasn't like that."

"Sure."

"Gordo."

I sighed. "I know." Because no matter the complicated feelings I had toward Thomas Bennett, he wasn't . . . He had never taken away the free will of his pack. They may have made decisions he hadn't liked, but he would always listen to them.

"Do you?" Mark asked me.

"Yeah."

Mark shook his head. "It was—anything I could say to you about him, it would be the truth. You wouldn't have to believe me, but I have never lied to you, Gordo. Not once. Not ever."

I nodded, unable to speak.

"It killed him to leave you here. To leave you behind. He fought fang and claw for you. Against those in Maine. You were his. You belonged to him just as much as he belonged to you. He was your Alpha, Gordo. You were his witch. We were all young. We were all surviving. And we were all grieving those we'd lost."

"He could have stayed here," I said hoarsely, looking down at my hands. "But instead he left a child alone so he could go be king. A child who also had almost everything taken away. Thomas just finished the job."

"That wasn't—" Mark's jaw tensed. "It wasn't like that. He—if there was no Alpha of all, then there was a chance the wolves could have descended into chaos. He had to weigh the needs of the few with the needs of the many."

"And we know where I fell in that decision, don't we?"

"He was so angry, Gordo."

"So was I."

"Jesus *Christ*," Mark snarled. "Can you *listen* for once in your goddamn life?"

I snapped my head up. Mark was always cool. Calm. And collected. But right now he was fucking furious. "I didn't—"

"I'm trying to have an honest conversation with you, the first one we've had in *years*, and you're being an asshole."

The raven closed its talons around a stem of thorns. A rose felt like it was blooming.

"He fought for you," Mark said, voice hard. "Those speciesist assholes hated that you were human. They were still terrified of what had happened to the Bennett pack because of the hunters. Humans weren't—it wasn't like it was in our pack. My father thought humans were the strength behind the wolf. Everyone else thought they were a weakness. A liability. Witches were the exception, because they had *magic*."

"Then what the fuck was their—my father."

Mark nodded. "You were your father's son. That's all they saw. You weren't your own person. Your father lost control. You were a *child* when my father made you his witch. And then hunters came, and it was . . . compounded. It was too much. And Thomas knew, he *knew* that there would be anarchy unless he accepted his place as Alpha of all. I hated him for it. Elizabeth did too, at least a little bit. But nothing compared to the hate my brother had for himself. We had lost our father. Our aunts and uncles." Mark bowed his head. "Our little cousins. It was—we were lost, Gordo. I don't think even Thomas knew how lost we were. But I believe Osmond did. And I think he played upon that. Whether he was already working with

Richard Collins by then, I don't know. But it was Osmond who convinced Thomas to return. And it was Osmond who said you needed
to stay." He looked back up at me with an unreadable expression.
"Thomas didn't lie to you. He was always going to come back for you.
It just took him longer than he thought it would. And by the time we
came home, you didn't want anything to do with us. With wolves."

"I didn't know what else to do. You left me, Mark. You fucking *left*
me. Thomas told you to follow him, and you just—"

"I almost broke bonds with the pack. Because of that."

"What?" I asked, startled.

"I almost left the pack."

"Why?"

He chuckled bitterly. "Why. *Why.* So I could stay here, you idiot.
So I could be with *you.*"

"I asked you. I *begged* you. And you told me no. Because you would
be an Omega."

"Doesn't matter now, does it? It's already happening."

I was in front of him before I realized I was moving. My chest
bumped his. He breathed in sharply, nostrils flaring. His eyes flickered orange. There was a low rumble in the back of his throat. "Don't.
You're not going to be an Omega. I won't let it happen."

"Gordo," he growled, and I swore I saw a hint of fang.

"Shut up. You've had your time to talk. It's my turn. You hear me?"
He nodded slowly.

"I hated you. For the longest time. All of you. You. Elizabeth.
Thomas. All of you. You fucking left me here. And all I wanted to do
was hurt you as best as I knew how. And then you all came back to
Green Creek, acting like it was *nothing.* Like you didn't need me. Like
you didn't even *remember* me. And then you fucking tried to take Ox
and—"

"Pretty sure that was Joe."

"I *know* that was Joe," I snapped at him. "And you know when the
first time I heard from Thomas was? It was *because* of Joe. It wasn't *I'm
sorry, Gordo.* It wasn't *I never meant to leave you behind.* It was because
he needed me to help his son. He needed me to help Joe. After all these
years, he came for me because he wanted to use me."

They don't love you, my mother had said. *They* need *you. They* use
you.

"He came to you," Mark said in a rough voice, "because you were the only one he trusted enough to help his son."

I sucked in a sharp breath. Through the bonds between us, all I felt was the blue sorrow.

"After . . . after we found Joe, after we took him back from Richard, he wasn't the same. Not until Ox and he found his voice again. And even then, he would wake screaming in the middle of the night. About the monster who was coming for him. The monster who would take him away again. Thomas didn't know what else to do. Those full moons before Joe achieved his shift were . . . harsh on him. His wolf was there under his skin, and it was tearing him apart. Thomas came to you because you were his pack, even if he wasn't yours."

I bowed my head, laying it on Mark's shoulder. My eyes were burning, my body trembling. A hand came to the back of my neck, fingers in my hair. It was grounding. It was familiar. It was oh so dangerous.

His mouth was near my ear when he said, "I wanted to do it. For you. Maybe I would have turned Omega. Maybe not. You were my tether, even then. It might have been enough, but I was too scared to find out. You're my mate, Gordo. Dirt and leaves and rain."

I shuddered against him. "I hate you."

"I know. Even though your heartbeat says otherwise. I think you believe it. And I'm sorry for that."

"Goddamn you."

"I know that too."

I lifted my head but didn't pull away. He didn't drop his hand. Every breath I let out, he took in. His eyes searched mine. He glanced down briefly. His lips twitched as his gaze met mine again. "I like the tattoo."

I didn't understand. "What are you talking about? You've seen all my—"

Except he hadn't, had he? No. He hadn't seen the one I'd gotten after he left. The one that had been just for me. To remember.

He hadn't seen the wolf and the raven inked into the skin above my heart.

"How long have you had that?" he asked, teeth razor-sharp.

I said, "It's not about you," but even I felt the stutter in my heart.

"Sure, Gordo."

"It's not."

"Okay. So you know a lot of wolves that look like me when I shift, then?"

"Asshole," I muttered as he laughed quietly.

He dropped his hand.

I took a step back, though I wanted nothing more than to press myself against him. Things were changing, and at the worst possible time. I felt pulled in a million different directions.

He understood. He smiled sadly at me. "I have things to say to you, Gordo. So many things. Things you might not be ready to hear. But I will mean every word of them. If it gets to the point where I start to go feral—"

I shook my head furiously. "No. No, I won't let that happen. I won't—"

"I know," he said gently. "I know you won't. But sometimes things happen that we don't expect. Like finding a boy with magic in his skin who is everything." He closed his eyes. "Or losing my mind."

My hands curled into fists at my sides. "If this is my father, then there has to be a way to reverse it. I'll find it. I've—"

"It's already begun."

I took a step back, eyes wide and wet. "What?"

"Carter."

"What about Carter?"

"He's . . . it took him a while. To come out of his shift. It was harder for him than it should have been."

I scrubbed a hand over my face. "Did he hurt anyone?"

"No, though he did snap at Robbie for getting too close to Kelly. Ox was able to get between them in time."

"Why is it happening so fast? Michelle said—"

"Even if we could believe a single word she said, it could be any number of things. It could be the coming moon. Or the stress on the body because of the shift. The anger toward the hunters. Or Michelle could be lying to us about how long it takes."

I didn't want to know the answer, but I had to ask. "And you?"

He looked away. "It's . . . there. It's quiet. But it's there. I can feel it." He shrugged awkwardly as he let out a shuddering breath. "I don't want it to happen, Gordo. I don't want to lose this. This tether." His smile was shaky. "It's the only part of you that's ever been mine."

There were days before, long days, where the very thought of this wolf standing before me filled me with rage. I would have given anything to never hear the Bennett name again. To leave the world of wolves behind and try to forget that they had done the same to me.

But now I was only filled with anguish. With remorse.

I had wasted time. So much time.

I took a step toward him.

He never looked away.

He inhaled as our knees bumped together.

His eyes glittered in the dark.

I pressed my forehead against his.

His fingers trailed along my arms.

He exhaled.

I inhaled.

It would be so easy. Now. Here, at the end. To take what he was offering. What he'd always offered.

His breath was hot against my lips as I—

His head jerked to the side.

I sighed.

"Ox," he said quietly. "It's Ox. He wants us downstairs."

I was going to murder my Alpha.

I moved to step away from Mark.

He held on to my hand. "Hey."

I looked up. He was smiling at me shyly. "We'll . . . can we talk about this later?"

I said, "Yeah," and my voice was hoarse.

"Okay," he said. "Okay."

For now, it was enough.

It would have to be.

We had a goddamn war to fight.

.   .   .

We descended the staircase in the Bennett house, Mark walking close behind me. The wooden steps creaked underneath our feet, and the buzz of conversation stopped at the sound.

Fucking werewolves.

They were in the great room. All of them. Our pack.

Rico sat on an oversized sofa, Jessie perched on the arm. Both of them watched every step I took. Rico's wounds weren't as bad as they looked in the truck.

Chris and Tanner were battered and bruised. Chris's forehead had been cleaned, and there was a small row of black stitches across the top. It'd leave a scar, but one I knew he'd wear proudly. Tanner's knee was slightly swollen and wrapped in a brace, but he had a determined look on his face.

Team motherfucking Human.

Elizabeth sat on the couch, her legs curled up underneath her. Kelly was at her side, pressed shoulder to shoulder. Carter sat at their feet, head tilted back, eyes closed as he breathed in slowly, held it, then let it out through his nose. Kelly's hand was in his hair.

Robbie stood behind the long couch, wringing his hands. His glasses were perched awkwardly on his face, but I couldn't find the strength to tell him they looked ridiculous. He must have been growing on me.

And the Alphas.

They stood near the windows, upright and rigid, their backs to the pack. An aura of power surrounded them. There were the threads, yes, the ones between all of us. Wolves. Humans. A witch. And there was the ever-present tinge of blue echoing along them. But it was overwhelmed by Joe. By Ox. They were furious, though that fury didn't seem to be directed toward anyone in the house.

I wasn't a wolf, but I still understood the urgent feeling of an invading force in our territory. Couple that with the betrayal of a woman who, while we didn't trust her, we hadn't expected to throw us to a group of hunters. Especially not Elijah, who had been here once before and taken almost everything. It was a knife in our backs, twisted cruelly.

If we survived this, if we survived the hunters and the infection spreading in two of our own, Michelle Hughes was going to pay.

I would see to it.

And even though we felt blue, there was green. Still. Now. The green of *relief*, because we were here. We were together.

We were *packpackpack*.

Carter broke the silence.

"You know," he said, voice a little hoarse, "I hope you guys are on your way to working out whatever the fuck is going on between the two of you. I mean, it was really gross to watch my uncle carry you

up the stairs in his arms like some damsel in distress and snarl at
anyone who tried to go into his room to check on you."

I turned slowly to look at Mark, who suddenly found the wall very
interesting. "You did what?"

He was frowning. "Shut up."

"No. Seriously. You did *what*."

"Went all wolfy caveman," Rico said. "I thought he was going to
bite my head off when I knocked on the door. He clubbed you upside
the head and then took you to his den. You should probably ask if
he licked you while you were sleeping. You know, to clean you and
stuff."

"What happened to Dale?" Tanner whispered to Chris. "Is he still
a thing we don't talk about?"

"Would you stop saying his name?" Chris hissed back. "You're
going to ruin their mystical moon magic."

Jessie sighed. "I really wish I hadn't said that. It sounds so ridiculous now."

"Ignore my son," Elizabeth told me. "It was really rather sweet the
way Mark wanted to take care of you. I highly doubt he would have
licked you in your sleep."

Carter opened his eyes. They were a normal pale blue. "You said
once that you woke up and Dad was sniffing your hair."

Kelly groaned, tilting his head back on the couch.

Robbie reached down and awkwardly touched Kelly's shoulder.
Surprisingly, Kelly didn't try to shrug him away. Robbie blushed
slightly, pushing his glasses up his nose, but he didn't move his hand.

"Those clothes look big on you, papi," Rico said to me. "As if
they're not your own. Kind of like a certain wolf gave them to you so
you could smell like him."

I scowled.

Mark preened.

I scowled harder.

"They're out there," Ox said, and we all fell silent. "I can feel them.
It's like . . . a shadow. Covering the earth."

He was staring out the window, watching the snow fall. It didn't
look as if it was letting up. The light was already fading, which meant
it was late afternoon.

Joe looked over at him, studying him in profile, but he didn't speak.

Ox spoke again. "This . . . Elijah. Gordo. I'm told she is known to the Bennett pack. Those who came before."

I nodded, though he couldn't see me, as I tried to find the words to explain to my friend, my Alpha, this boy who had become more than any of us thought possible. "I . . . yes."

"Okay," Ox said, exhaling slowly. "I've already heard from Elizabeth. What she knows. Of what happened to your pack. I would hear from you now. Why."

Ox was angry.

"He wasn't—" Mark started, but I took him by the hand and squeezed tightly. He looked over at me, and I shook my head slightly. He frowned but didn't speak.

This was on me.

Maybe Mark had been right with what he'd said in his room. About trust. About secrets. I was in this pack. I was the witch to the Bennetts. My family had been intertwined with theirs for generations. It was a long history twisted so deeply into my bones that even when I thought I could, I would never fully be free of it.

And I didn't want to be.

Thomas Bennett was a wolf.

But he'd also been human.

He made mistakes, yes. Like his father. And mine.

The difference between Thomas and Abel and my father, however, was great. The wolves did what they thought was right.

My father had given in to his grief.

This wasn't about Mark, at least not all of it.

When we'd been on the road, the Bennett brothers and me, it'd been different. We'd done what we had to do to survive. I'd told myself it had nothing to do with seeking vengeance for Thomas Bennett. I was there because Joe had asked me to follow him. They needed someone to watch over them.

I didn't think that was true anymore.

Part of me had gone because of Thomas Bennett. He'd sunk his claws into me deep when I was a kid, and no matter how complicated our relationship had become, he'd been torn from me just the same.

Quoth the raven, I thought.

Nevermore.

I said, "Pappas."

"Feral," Ox said. "The man he was is gone, I think. There's only the wolf."

"Okay."

He turned to face me. I had a queer moment when I remembered a little boy hiding behind his daddy's leg. He'd never had root beer before. "Do you think he's complicit?"

I shook my head. "No. Not completely. I think . . . I think Michelle Hughes kept things from him. How much he knew about the infection is one thing. The hunters, though. Elijah? He couldn't have."

"But he knew *of* her," Ox said.

"Yes."

"Because you told him." It wasn't an accusation, though it felt like one.

"Yes."

"Why?" Joe asked. "I mean . . . I don't understand, Gordo. How long did you know about her?"

"Since we found David King in Fairbanks."

Joe's eyes flashed. "And you didn't think to say anything?"

"I didn't tell any of you about David King until long after he left," Ox reminded him. "Not yet. Remember?"

Joe looked at him, a frown on his face. "That's not—"

"And then when Richard came. He came for me. And I still said nothing."

"That's because you're a self-sacrificing asshole," Rico said. Then, "No offense, *alfa*. Okay. Maybe some offense."

"You did it because you were trying to keep us safe," Joe argued. "And even then, Gordo saw right through it."

"Then it's possible that Gordo was trying to do the same, isn't it?"

They all looked at me.

Goddammit. "I . . ."

Mark squeezed my hand. I hadn't even realized I was still holding it.

"I thought it would be enough," I said. "If they knew. We'd . . . everything here. Everything we'd been through. It was too much. Thomas. The years we were separated. Richard. I'd hoped that by telling Pappas, and by him telling Michelle, that they'd do something about it. For all I knew, she was already gone. I didn't want to make things bad again. Not when we were still healing. We— I didn't know how to be pack. Not like it was before. Not with everyone here. It's not that I didn't trust any of you. It's more that I didn't trust myself. And I thought if something came of it, if need be, I could take care of it on my own."

"Men," Jessie said, sounding pissed off. "You're all bunch of asshole martyrs. No wonder Elizabeth and I are the smartest people in the goddamn room."

"I concur," Elizabeth said, staring up at me. "They're lucky to have us."

"They'd probably run off half-cocked without a single idea about what they're doing," Jessie said.

Elizabeth nodded. "And get themselves infected."

"Oh," Rico said. "Can we joke about that now? I wasn't sure if it was still too soon or what. Because if you think about it, it's funny because—yep, from the looks I'm getting, it's still too soon. Shutting up now."

"There's more," I said, wincing slightly.

"Of course there is," Chris said. He knocked his shoulder against Tanner's. "Remember the days when the weirdest thing in our lives was when Gordo tried to grow that pussy-tickler mustache?"

"Those were the days," Tanner sighed. "We made that Wanted poster with his mustache face on it and posted them all over town, telling everyone to protect their children."

"You tried to grow a mustache?" Mark asked me.

"Gross," Kelly said, nose wrinkling. "We can smell that, Uncle Mark."

"What is it, Gordo?" Ox asked me.

Best to get it over with. "You felt it too. The wards. When they were corrupted."

He nodded slowly. "Elijah said there were witches. Which means they aren't trying to keep anything out. They're trying to keep us all in."

"Yeah. But I also felt something else. Heard something else."

"What?" Joe asked.

"My father."

Silence.

Then, "Great," Carter groaned. "We've got a weird religious chick who wears skins of her kills on her back and who has pet feral Omegas on chains, one of which tried to sniff me and kill me at the same time. Witches who have the town surrounded doing creepy magic to keep us in. Michelle Hughes is some kind of stupid evil chick, and Mark and I are slowly going nutso. And *now* you're saying that your dear old dad is talking in your head? Fuck this day. Fuck this entire day."

I couldn't agree more.

We slept that night together.

All of us.

The couches and chairs were moved away.

Thick, heavy blankets were spread out on the floor. Piles of pillows.

The Alphas were in the middle. The rest of the pack surrounded them. Even Rico did it with minimal complaining, though he said he was thankful that everyone was wearing clothes this time.

I lay with my head pressed against Ox's leg, failing to resist the urge to be close to my tether.

Mark must have felt the same, because he never went far. We lay facing each other in the dark, his ice-cold eyes ever-watching. There was a moment before I drifted off to sleep, hearing the voices of my Alphas singing in my head, when Mark reached up and traced a finger over my cheeks. My nose. My lips and chin.

A kiss was pressed against my forehead.

And then I slept.

The phones didn't work.

The internet was down.

We were cut off.

Pappas prowled the length of powdered silver on the ground. He snarled at the sight of me, hackles raised.

Ox roared at him with everything he had.

His violet eyes flickered, and I thought maybe he—

No.

They flared again.

He was lost.

"We'll have to deal with him," Mark told me later, staring off into nothing. "We can't risk him hurting anyone or spreading whatever's in his bite. We'll have to deal with him. Soon."

I wanted nothing more than to burn the world down.

We made our way through the snow. The trees were heavy in white around us. Ox and Joe had shifted, leaving large paw prints behind them. Mark walked on two legs beside me as we trailed behind the wolves.

It was still snowing, but it wasn't coming down as hard as it'd been the day before. The sky above was a dark gray, and the morning sun was hidden somewhere behind the clouds. I knew the moon was there too, widening toward fat and full. I wasn't a wolf, but even I could feel it.

Carter had complained about being left behind, saying he was Joe's second, therefore he should go to face the witches. Joe had looked as if he were about to give in, but Elizabeth intervened, and without her saying a word, it was understood that Carter wasn't going anywhere. He'd sighed but slumped back against Kelly, who hadn't gone more than a few feet from his brother since they'd woken up.

Robbie volunteered to accompany us, but Ox had told him to stay. He didn't want Michelle's people to play games with his head.

Birds called out, singing in the trees.

The ice crunched underneath our feet.

Our breath billowed around us.

Mark said, "Your father."

"My father," I muttered, stepping over a tree that had fallen years before.

"In your head."

"Right."

"Is that normal?"

I rolled my eyes. "Oh, sure. Wolves going crazy. Jesus-freak hunters. Betrayal from on high. Dear old Dad in my head. Sure, Mark. Everything about this is normal."

"Why, though?"

"Why what?" I asked, watching the massive wolves walk ahead of us, their tails brushing together.

"Why is he in your head?"

"Because he has boundary issues?"

Mark squinted at me. "I can't tell if you're joking or not."

"I don't fucking *know*, Mark. I haven't seen him since I was a kid and he murdered sixteen people along with my mother after *she* murdered the woman he was having an affair with."

Mark snorted. "So. Pretty normal, then."

I gaped at him. "Are you seriously deciding that *now* is a good time to try and find a sense of humor?"

"I've always been funny."

He was such a liar. "No, I don't know why he's in my head. I don't know what it means. I don't even know if it was *real*. Or if he's even in Green Creek. If there's a bunch of Michelle's asshole witches here, do you really think he'd try and show his face?"

Mark rubbed his jaw. "Unless he's also working with Michelle."

I glared at him. "Don't. Don't you fucking say that. You're going to jinx us, and I will fucking light you on fire without a second thought."

He grinned at me. "Nah. I don't think you would."

I liked him better when we despised each other. "He would never do that. Not like Elijah. It would be beneath him."

"Because he hates wolves. That's what you told Michelle. He would blame them for . . . everything."

"Yeah."

Mark grabbed my gloved hand. I turned to look at him, a question on my face.

He was studying me thoughtfully, and it made me uncomfortable. I was so used to hiding everything from him, and this shift between us, this *thing* I'd spent most of my life ignoring, wasn't something I had prepared for. I was dizzy with it.

He said, "You're not him."

I tried to tug my hand away, but he held on tight. "I know."

"Do you?" he asked. "Because I don't know if—"

"Jesus fuck, Mark. I told you I didn't want to hear your bullshit about—"

"He made his choice," Mark said, "to do what he did. And even though you could have done the same, even though you had every right to hate us with everything you had, you didn't."

"I *did*," I retorted, suddenly angry for reasons I didn't understand.

"I *did* hate you. And Thomas. And Elizabeth. I hated wolves and packs. I hated *you*."

"But part of you didn't," Mark said, sounding sure. "Your story, it—" He shook his head. "You could have become the villain, Gordo. And it would have been within your rights. Instead you just chose to be an asshole."

"Are you . . . complimenting me? Because if you are, you're doing a really bad job at it."

He smiled his secret smile, but it faded almost as soon as it appeared. "You're not your father."

"I know that."

"Do you?"

I jerked my hand away. "That's not what this is about. It's about some jackasses that think they can come into our territory and fuck with us. It's about the fact that I haven't gotten to kill anything in *weeks*, and it's starting to piss me off."

"You do get grumpy when that happens."

"Right," I said, scowling at him. "So maybe stow the introspective shit until later, okay?" He opened his mouth to respond, but I cut him off. "And I swear to god, if you say there may not *be* a later, I won't be responsible for what happens next."

The smile returned. "Your threats don't sound so bad now that I know you've got my wolf tattooed on your chest."

"Bite me," I snapped, stalking off after the Alphas.

Mark chuckled behind me. "Oh, I will."

Fucking werewolves.

. . . .

Once there had stood an old covered wooden bridge that crossed over a stream along a dirt road leading out of Green Creek.

Then Richard Collins had come with Osmond and the Omegas, and it had been destroyed in everything that followed.

The bridge, it was said later, had been too old. It hadn't been maintained as well as it should have.

Many were surprised it hadn't fallen sooner.

A donation had come to the town by a notable family. Elizabeth Bennett, on behalf of her late husband, had given fifty thousand dollars for it to be rebuilt.

There had been a ceremony the following summer. A ribbon-cutting where Elizabeth Bennett had stood with her sons, all three dressed smartly in perfectly tailored suits. The rest of the pack had watched with a rather sizable crowd as the mayor made a canned speech of appreciation. The ribbon had been cut, and people had cheered.

The new bridge was almost an exact replica of the old one, though far sturdier. It was part of the charm of Green Creek, the town council who had approved the design said. A gateway to a small mountain town.

The only real difference was the plaque on the Green Creek side of the bridge, six words etched into metal:

May our songs always be heard.

People had been perplexed at the legend.

But we knew. Oh, how we knew.

The bridge now looked like a postcard, red wood barely visible through heavy snow.

And there were people standing in front of it.

They were dressed well for the cold weather. There were four of them, and though I didn't recognize a single one of them, I knew them as witches the moment I set eyes on them. I'd told my Alphas that magic had a signature, a fingerprint. The feral wolves knew that more than anyone, which was why I was convinced my father was behind the infection.

And I could *feel* the wards in front of us, though they were no longer my own. Pappas had asked me if the wards were infallible. How much he'd known at the time, I doubted we'd ever find out. But I thought maybe that was his way of trying to warn us. I hadn't listened. Or at the very least, I hadn't understood what he'd been trying to say.

But the wards *weren't* infallible. I was strong, and my magic was expansive, but even my wards in the Bennett territory couldn't survive the onslaught of multiple witches bent on manipulating them. Magic wasn't wish fulfillment. It was harsh and rough, pulling from the blood and bones of the witch, focused with the ink etched into my skin.

The witches—three men and one woman—looked wary as we approached. They eyed the Alphas, who stopped just short of the wards. The wolves couldn't see them, not like I could, but they could *feel* them. Ox told me once that the scent of magic made his nose itch like he was about to sneeze. It smelled ozone-sharp and smoky.

"Alphas Bennett and Matheson," the woman said stiffly. She was trying to be deferential, but we were so far past standing on ceremony, it was ridiculous. "We are honored to be in your presence. Alpha Hughes sends her regards."

"Yeah," I said dryly. "Maybe take your honor and shove it up your—"

Ox growled at me.

Mark decided to take over, which was probably better for all of us. He knew diplomacy, where I only wanted to break some bones. "What our witch meant to say was we aren't exactly here to receive regards from Alpha Hughes. So take your honor and shove it up your ass."

Maybe not so diplomatic.

Joe growled at him.

Thankfully I remembered I was a hard-core thirty-nine-year-old redneck before I swooned a little. It was close, though.

The witches weren't pleased. The woman addressed the Alphas. "She has done what she must in order to ensure the survival of the wolves." She glanced at Mark. "And since the Bennett pack has found itself with infected members, you must be contained. Surely, if our roles were reversed, you would do the same."

"See," I said, "I don't know if that's true. We would find a way to fix this. And we are."

The woman cocked her head at me. "Like the Omega you fixed in Montana?"

I blinked. "What the hell are you—"

And you just had an Alpha's claws around your throat and lived to tell the tale. You went to my home and were shown mercy. But I am not a wolf. And I'm not exactly human. Veins underneath the earth. Sometimes so deep, they will never be found. Until someone like me comes along. And I'm the one you should be scared of. Because I'm the worst of them all.

"That's right," the woman said. "The Omega you killed in an alleyway. A team Michelle had dispatched to track Richard Collins found him before the humans did. The stench of your magic was all over him, Livingstone. So do not speak to us of fixing anything."

"He was an Omega," I growled at her. "Who worked for Collins. He wasn't—"

"And what happens when Mark Bennett turns Omega?" she asked. "Will you do the same for him? When the bloodlust descends and he is lost to his animal?"

The wolves growled as I stepped forward. The strength of the wards bowled over me, causing me to grit my teeth. It felt as if a thousand tiny needles prickled along my skin, not going deep enough to draw blood, but close. They were good. Much better than I expected them to be.

To their credit, the witches looked worried, taking a step back as if they thought I would burst through the wards regardless. Either that or they didn't like the sound of pissed-off Alpha wolves. They were smarter than they looked.

And it should have ended there. We would have threatened them, they would have retorted uselessly, and then we would have left. The whole point of showing ourselves, Ox had told us, was to make sure Michelle Hughes understood we knew about her. That we wouldn't be cowed. That she had brought this fight to our door, and once we were done here, once we'd found a way to cure Carter and Mark and had taken care of the hunters, we were going to come after her.

But instead, a figure appeared on the bridge.

For a brief moment I thought it was my father, and my heart stumbled in my chest.

Mark heard, and he crowded close to me. My Alphas brushed against me, tails twitching dangerously.

But it didn't *feel* like him. I would know my father's magic. It wasn't in these wards. It wasn't in these witches. Whoever they were, they didn't belong to him.

It didn't stop the fear, however brief it was.

A fear that soon changed to disbelief when I saw who it was.

A disbelief that turned to *rage* when Mark stiffened beside me.

"Dale?" he asked, voice choked.

Dale walked out from the bridge, snow crunching underneath his feet. "Mark," Dale said, nodding in greeting. "Hello."

"What the fuck are you doing here?" I snapped.

Dale glanced at me coolly. "I'm here as the witch to Alpha Michelle Hughes. To make sure the wards hold. It's my job." He reached up and tapped against them. A deep pulse bloomed in my head as the wards *burst* in color, and I felt just how far around us they stretched. They didn't encompass the entire territory, but all of Green Creek was surrounded.

Before I could stop him, Mark half shifted and launched himself at Dale, fangs bared, eyes blazing orange. He crashed into the wards, which echoed brightly with the deep sound of a heavy bell. He fell back into the snow.

The Alphas snarled as they paced back and forth in front of us while I knelt down beside Mark. He groaned, eyes fading into ice blue. "You idiot," I said, helping him up. "Are you okay?"

He shook his head. "Fine." He glared at Dale. "How the hell are you a witch? I didn't smell magic on you."

Dale shrugged. "There are ways to hide one's true self, Mark. It's not that difficult. Isn't that right, Gordo?"

"When we get out of here," I promised him, "I'm coming for you first." I didn't know how he'd managed to get inside my wards without me knowing, but it didn't matter now. He'd made a mistake in revealing himself.

Dale wasn't impressed. "Michelle gave you the opportunity. She told you what would happen if you allowed the infected wolves to live. We do what we must to survive. Surely you can appreciate that."

"All this time," Mark said, sounding dazed. "You were working for her all this time."

Dale looked almost regretful. "I did care about you, Mark. More than I thought I would." He glanced at me. "Even if your mind was . . . elsewhere. If that offers you any sort of solace. To be that close to a Bennett, to know you intimately." He shook his head. "I wouldn't change that for anything in the world."

Oh yeah. He was going to be first.

There was the familiar snap of muscle and bone, and Oxnard Matheson and Joe Bennett stood nude in the snow.

Now the witches took a step back.

Even Dale.

"You're here because of Michelle Hughes," Ox said slowly. "Because she told you to come."

"She wanted—"

"That was rhetorical," Joe growled.

Dale's face took on the color of the snow.

"Your Alpha," Ox said, voice deadly calm, "has sent hunters. Into *our* territory. To take out *our* pack."

The female witch bristled. "They are under strict orders to only handle the infected Omegas—"

"And you really think that's where they'll stop?" Joe asked coolly. "Don't you have any idea who they are? They came once. They killed my grandfather. They killed *children*. You think they're going to stop at two wolves?"

The woman turned to Dale, eyes wide. "She sent in the *Kings*? Dale, what on earth is she—"

"She knows what she's doing," Dale snapped, and the woman fell silent. He looked at Ox. "They won't hurt anyone else."

And I said, "They've already killed a human cop."

"Shit," one of the other witches muttered. "I knew this was a bad idea."

Dale looked tense. "If there was a reason—"

Joe wasn't having any of it. "The *reason* was that he was in the wrong place at the wrong time. They murdered him. They spilled innocent blood, and that's on your Alpha. His death is on her hands."

"Dale," Mark begged, and Christ, I hated hearing it. "Listen to me. Please. If there was any part of you that cared about me, you need to let them out. My pack. Leave Carter and me here, fine. But you need to get everyone else out of here."

"Yeah," I said, taking a step toward the wards. "Open up the wards. Come on. You cared about him, right? Do it. See what happens."

"Gordo," Mark said.

"No," I retorted. "Absolutely not. You really think I'd leave you here by yourself? Fuck that, and fuck you." I turned back to Dale. "Open it up. Do it now. If you do, I'll give you a head start. If you don't and I get out of here, you're not going to like what I do." I looked at the other witches behind him. "That counts for all of you. You think this can hold me? It might take me some time, but I'm a Livingstone in Bennett territory. I *will* get out. And there is nowhere you can run that I won't find you."

For a moment I thought one of the witches would break. The men looked worried, the woman fearful.

But in the end, it was Dale who stepped forward.

Mere inches separated us, but they were filled with a wall of magic. I could see the wards clear as day. I could see the magic they used, the swirling archaic symbols that were lock and key.

"You know what must be done," he said quietly, though he had to have known all the wolves could hear him. "The infection will be contained."

"And you think that if we do as you ask, if we just . . . kill Mark and Carter, that this will all be over? You can't possibly be that stupid."

He glanced over my shoulder, then looked back at me. "It could be. My Alpha is not the monster you make her out to be."

I laughed bitterly. "She aligned herself with the hunter clan that murdered most of the Bennett pack. The same clan that killed *children*. And then she sent them *here*. If you don't think that makes her a monster, then you've got some seriously fucked-up morals, my friend."

He wasn't fazed. "She has given the Bennett pack ample warning. This isn't on her. This is on all of you."

"We have Pappas. I will kill him as soon as we get back to the house."

"Alpha Hughes is aware that Philip Pappas is lost to her. It's regrettable, but casualties always are."

I slammed my hands against the wards. My tattoos felt like they were burning. Dale barely blinked. "I'll kill you. I'll fucking kill you."

"Empty threats, I'm afraid," Dale said. "The wards will hold—"

Mark said, "If you promise me that everyone else will be safe, I'll come with you right now. I won't fight, I swear I won't fight," and *I* said, "You shut your goddamn mouth. I won't let you, I won't *let you*."

Mark looked at me with sad eyes. "Gordo. It's—"

"No," I said, shaking my head. "I'm goddamn sick and tired of the fucking martyrs in this pack."

"That's rich coming from you," Mark said, taking a step toward me. He winced as he got closer to the wards. "But if it means—"

"And Carter?" Dale asked.

"He would do the same," Mark said over the protests of his Alphas. "I know he would. As long as you can promise me right here and now that no one else will get hurt. That the hunters will leave Green Creek and never return."

Dale nodded slowly. "That sounds reasonable." And before I could figure out how to punch his teeth down his throat, he continued. "The problem with that, though, is that we don't know who else in your pack is infected."

"There's no one," Mark said. "There's no one else."

"Yes," Dale said, not unkindly. "So you say. But how can you prove it? For all we know, your entire pack is infected. All the wolves. Can we really take that chance?"

It hit me then. I should have seen it before. But I'd forgotten. "He's lying."

He looked startled. "Lying about what?"

I looked to my Alphas. "Mark went to Dale. Right after we spoke with Michelle. He went the next morning. He said he was going to end things with him."

"Mark?" Ox asked.

Mark turned his head slowly to look at me. "Yeah. I did. It was . . . He said he was—that he understood. It was easier than I thought it would be."

"And if he wanted to," I said, thoughts spinning furiously, "if Michelle actually gave a shit about feral wolves, Dale could have killed him right then and there. But he didn't. It's not about the infection. It's not *about* Mark and Carter. It's about the entire pack." I turned back to Dale. "Michelle Hughes is using the infection as an excuse. To take us out. All of us. She knew. Before. About Pappas. Even though Pappas didn't think she did. She knew. And she sent him here anyway, knowing what could happen."

Dale didn't speak. He just stared at me.

"Dale?" the woman asked, sounding unsure. "What's he talking about?"

"It's never been about the infection," I said, staring right back at Dale. "She doesn't want the Bennett pack. She doesn't want Joe. She wants the territory. She wants Green Creek. She sent the hunters here to wipe us all out. Everything else was just ancillary. How did she do it? Did she find my father? Did she make him do this?"

Dale laughed. "Oh, Gordo. No matter how far you run, no matter how you try and hide, you will always have the shadow of being a Livingstone covering every inch of your skin. It's something you will never escape. No. No, she has nothing to do with Robert Livingstone. And nor do I, before you ask. He is . . . we don't know where he is. For all we know, he's dead."

"But the rest?" Joe asked, eyes red.

Dale didn't cower. "The rest is as it is. You run to this place. You always have. Green Creek was a refuge for the Bennetts long before any of you were even a thought. Alpha Hughes understands this. And since you cannot seem to accept your place in this world, she will take it from you."

The woman said, "This was never part of—"

Dale didn't even turn to look at her when he said, "Another word and you will end up in there with them. Understood?"

The witches didn't speak.

"She wrestled with this," he said, having the audacity to sound apologetic. "It hurt her. It caused her great pain. Especially . . . especially about Pappas. He was her second. She cares for him. But she knew that in order to protect all wolves, a choice had to be made. And in the end, she was strong enough to make that choice. She is the Alpha of all. Yes, she has underestimated you in the past. She won't do that again. The hunters are the final solution."

"Because we'll take each other out," I said slowly, the last piece falling into place. "And Green Creek will be left open for the taking."

"You're smarter than most give you credit for," Dale said, and I couldn't believe Mark fell for his shit. "This place is different. Alpha Matheson can attest to that. Whatever magic is in the earth led to him becoming a human Alpha out of necessity. There was no Alpha here, and the territory *needed* one. You were here, Gordo, as a gatekeeper, but even you left eventually. There was a pack, but no one to lead them. And so Ox became what was needed." He shook his head. "I can't even begin to imagine the power in this place. And I can't wait to find out just how deep it goes."

The wolves stepped forward until we stood shoulder to shoulder in front of the witches, in front of Dale. He didn't back down, not like those behind him, who stepped back. I heard the fury in my head, the songs of the wolves who wanted to sink their teeth into the flesh of those before us. Through the threads, the rest of the pack was howling their anger.

"Michelle played her hand too soon," Ox said, voice low and

strong. "You want a war? You've got one. Because once we're done with the hunters, we'll come for you. And as my witch said, there is nowhere you can run that we won't find you."

And he turned and walked away, heading toward the trees.

Joe spat on the ground in front of the witches before he followed his mate. I heard the sounds of them shifting behind me before Ox howled, the sound shattering the still air around us.

Even Dale flinched at the sound.

"You done fucked up," I said, smiling tightly. "Maybe I'm just a small-town hick who works in a garage. But I've got a long memory, and I will remember each of your faces. You would do well to start running now. Because the last time someone came for our pack, he ended up getting his head torn off. And you can sure as shit bet that'll be the very *least* I do to you."

I turned and followed my Alphas.

I'd only made it a few steps before I looked back over my shoulder.

Mark stood in front of the witches. His hands were in fists at his sides. He wasn't speaking, and neither was Dale, but I couldn't help but feel a slick twist of anger on his behalf. Maybe Dale hadn't meant much to him, not in the long run, but he'd meant *something*. Dale used him. I swore to myself it was going to be one of the last things he ever did. "Mark," I said sharply.

Mark nodded at Dale before he turned and walked toward me.

His eyes were blazing orange.

I wanted to say something, *anything* to make it all right again, to make it how it'd been the night before, but words failed me.

So instead, I did the only thing I could think of when he was about to pass me by: I reached out and took his hand.

The tightness around his eyes eased. He looked down at our joined hands, then back up at me.

He arched an eyebrow.

"Shut up," I muttered. "If you make a big deal about this, I'm going to give you to Dale myself."

He squeezed my hand.

And then I led us home.

COME AND GET ME / TUG OF WAR

"Motherfuckers," Chris growled. "Those goddamn bitches. Who the hell do they think they are?"

"Bastards," Tanner said, sounding furious. "All of them. Can I shoot them? Please? Please say I can shoot them."

"In the nuts," Rico spat. "I'm going to shoot them in the nuts, and while they're screaming in pain, I'm going to shove my fist down their throats until I reach their stomachs. And *then* I'm going to pull their stomachs *out* of their mouths and spill the *contents* of their stomachs on their faces, and I'm going to *like it*."

We all turned slowly to stare at him.

"What?" he asked. "They're in our *garage*."

We were hunkered down across the street, hiding behind what remained of the diner. The snow was still falling, the lull having passed. It was thick again, this storm. Robbie had found an old radio in the blue house. Ox said it'd belonged to his mother, and they'd danced in his kitchen to the music it played. We'd managed to find a station out of Eugene, which said the storm was expected to last a few more days.

The tow truck was still lying on its side in the diner, propped up precariously by the boom. A thin layer of ice covered the driver's side and the hoist from the snow blown in by the wind. It didn't look as if anyone else had been inside the diner, and I thanked god for small favors. Either the storm or the warnings blared by the hunters had kept people indoors. I didn't know how long it would last.

The King clan had taken over the garage.

We could see them inside, moving about. The lights were on, and one of the garage doors was open. They'd parked their trucks around the front like a barricade, bumper to bumper. A few hunters looked to be on patrol, moving around the outside of the garage. One stood on top of the cab of one of the trucks, keeping watch.

Jones was gone, as was his cruiser. I didn't know what they'd done with his body.

I wanted to launch a full frontal assault. To take them out. To get

rid of as many of them as I could. But Ox had said this was recon-
naissance only. And, if need be, a distraction.

Because the wolves were on the move.

"They better not be touching my tools," Chris muttered. "That
shit is expensive."

Jessie snorted. "Way to have your priorities straight."

"Hey! Do you know how long it took me to—"

"Shut up," I growled, lowering my binoculars. "All of you."

"Oh, sure," Tanner said, as bitchy as I'd ever heard him. "Look at
boss man over here. Sounding all tough and shit. I saw the way Mark
kissed your forehead before we left and the gross look on your face
when you watched him walk away."

"Seriously," Rico groaned. "Is that what we're going to have to put
up with now? I mean, we already get enough of that with Ox and Joe.
You were supposed to be the asshole forever. How am I supposed to
act now that you're the asshole with the heart of gold? It's fucking up
my worldview, man. Not cool."

"Don't you do the same thing with Bambi?" Chris asked.

"I like her boobs. And the way she makes me think. It's not some
mystical moon magic bullshit. It's carnal passion of the body and the
mind."

"She does have a great rack," Jessie said, reaching up to wipe the
condensation from the window.

We all turned slowly to look at her.

Jessie rolled her eyes. "What? She does. And at least I don't sound
like a creep when *I* say it."

"That doesn't make it any better," Chris said, eyeing her warily.

Goddamn Team Human.

"It doesn't matter," Rico said with a sigh. "She's probably going
to break up with me anyway. I mean, getting everyone we can into
her bar with as little explanation as possible? That's not going to go
well."

It'd been Carter's idea. The Lighthouse was as far away from Main
Street as someone could be and still be in Green Creek. The town it-
self was small, with only a few hundred people counted as residents.
Many of those lived in homes spread out miles around Green Creek.
Fewer than a hundred lived in Green Creek proper, and quite a few
of them had already left ahead of the storm. The more hard-core had

stayed to batten down the hatches. We didn't know the extent of what the hunters were here to do, and we didn't want to take any chances.

The wolves were moving quickly through the town, gathering as many people as they could and taking them to the bar. Mark hadn't been pleased at the idea of the humans being in charge of locating the hunters and making sure they stayed where they were, but as soon as Carter had pointed out he needed to stop thinking with this dick, he had backed down.

Well, mostly. He had backed down after he tackled Carter and held his face in the snow until his nephew literally cried uncle.

He wouldn't look at me after.

I didn't know what to do with that.

The Bennetts were known, and I didn't think they'd have a hard time convincing people to go, especially in light of what Elijah had said upon her arrival. The story being spun was one of meth-head hillbillies bent on causing trouble. Robbie seemed sure it was believable and would convince people to stay away. "Either that or it'll make them come running with their guns," he'd said, pushing his glasses back up his nose. "People get weird when it comes to meth-head hillbillies."

The wolves could move quicker than we could.

And there were the feral Omegas to worry about. The ones Elijah had called her pets.

I knew that if another wolf had approached the garage, they'd be scented almost immediately. But we were human, and the storm was thick. Even if the Omegas had parts of their minds intact, we would be less noticeable than the rest of the pack.

Which is why we had been hunkered down in the diner for going on an hour.

It was fine.

Everything was fine.

"I feel like we should talk about the elephant in the room," Tanner said.

"You mean Dale?" Chris asked.

"Exactly. I mean, do we give Mark shit for ignoring the mystical moon magic and sleeping with the enemy? Or do we put this on Gordo for ignoring the connection with the wolf who wants to take him carnally underneath a full moon?"

Everything was not fine.

"Guys," Rico said, pulling his coat around him tighter as he shivered, "this isn't the right time to be talking about this."

That surprised me. "Thank you, Rico—"

"Because *before* we can talk about whether to blame Mark or Gordo, we need to figure out if Dale put some kind of *brujo* mind-control whammy on Mark that *made* him bone Dale."

Fuck them. Fuck every single one of them.

"Huh," Chris said, rubbing his jaw. "I never thought about it that way. Hey, Gordo."

I ignored him.

"Gordo."

I glared at him. *"What."*

He had no sense of self-preservation. "Did Dale put some kind of mind-control whammy on Mark to make him sexually subservient?"

I ordered Jessie to control her brother.

She cocked her head at me. "Why? I want to know too. Now that you and Mark are going to be—"

"We're not going to be *anything*," I growled at her.

They all turned slowly to stare at me.

"Gordo," Jessie said. "You do realize that you're a liar, right?" She looked at her brother. "He knows that, right?"

Chris sighed. "Gordo doesn't know how to deal with all his feelings. He needs to pretend to be a prick, but really he's thinking about Mark's thighs wrapped around his neck."

Tanner grimaced. "Now *I'm* thinking of Mark's thighs wrapped around his neck. Ugh."

"Heart of gold," Rico said solemnly.

"I hate all of you," I mumbled, raising the binoculars again, hoping that would be the end of it.

It wasn't.

"We're going to figure this out," Chris said softly. He put his hand on my arm. "You know that, right? You're allowed to be happy. He's going to be fine. So is Carter. We're going to beat this."

And that was it, wasn't it? I hated how well they could read me, even if they didn't necessarily know about that almost-kiss in Mark's room. Part of me wished I'd been stronger, that I'd turned around and walked away, leaving him standing there. But even that was nothing compared to the long-ago memory of the way his mouth felt against mine. The way he'd felt against me. The feeling of his hands on my skin. I'd kept it locked away for so long, put into a box and strapped with chains, shoved into a dark corner to gather dust.

But the chains had broken now, the box cracked right down the middle.

For the longest time, Mark had been nothing but a ghost. Even when he stood in front of me, even as we'd fought side by side, I had rarely let myself think of what we'd once been. What we could have had if it wasn't for pack and wolves and fucking human stubbornness.

Of course it would take until the world was crashing down around us.

He was acting strong. And brave. But I was as much an expert in Mark Bennett as I'd been the first time we'd kissed.

He was scared.

It went beyond the idea of becoming an Omega, beyond the idea of losing his tether.

I had lost my pack. Again and again and again.

But so had he.

I'd forgotten that.

In my anger. In my grief.

Here he was, faced with losing it again.

And I still didn't know how to stop it.

Jessie's hand pressed against mine, and it was only then that I realized I was shaking.

I took a deep breath and let it out slow. "I'm fine," I said gruffly. "Don't worry about me. There are other things—"

There.

Through the open garage door.

Two feral wolves.

The red wolf's head was low, nose to the ground.

The timber wolf was upright, ears twitching.

The long chains had been removed, though they still had silver links around their necks, like a collar. It looked as if the silver had been embedded into their skin.

"Shit," I muttered. "Omegas. Both of them. Still inside."

Rico groaned quietly. "Is it too much to ask for evil werewolves to die when they're thrown across the road by a witch?"

"Elijah?" Jessie whispered.

I shook my head.

"How many of them are there?"

"Twenty. That I can see."

"Can't you just . . . I don't know," Tanner said. "Kill them? Somehow? Freeze the air in their lungs or something? The full moon is in two days. We're running out of time. I don't understand why we just don't take them head-on."

"Ox and Joe said this was recon only," Chris reminded him. "He didn't want us doing anything to bring attention to ourselves."

"I know that, but why can't we just get the pack together and make the streets run red with their—and holy *hell*, I've become a rage monster." Tanner shook his head. "That's probably not a good thing."

"You know why," Jessie said, wiping the window again. "Jones already died because of them. We can't take the chance of someone else getting hurt. Not until we know more."

The timber wolf's ears twitched. Its head turned in our direction.

"Down," I hissed.

We all hit the floor of the diner.

The wind howled outside.

The air was cold.

My heart was racing.

In my head came the wolves in a burst of color, of *PackBrotherLoveWitch*. I sent back soothing waves of calm, though it felt like a lie. I didn't know if they believed me.

"Stay down," I whispered to them. "Don't move unless I say."

"What is—" Chris started, but I shook my head, and he fell silent.

I took a deep breath and held it in my chest.

I pushed myself up.

I peered over the diner counter out the window.

The men still milled inside the garage. The few outside moved back and forth in the snow.

The timber wolf stood with its back to us, looking farther into the garage.

The red wolf was nowhere in sight.

It was probably just in the garage.

I let out the breath I was holding. "Okay. All clear. We're—"

A low growl off to my right.

I turned my head.

There, head bowed low to the ground to peer at us from under the other side of the tow truck, was the red wolf.

"Well, fuck," I said.

The wolf's lips quivered over sharp fangs.

Its ears flattened to the back of its head.

There wasn't enough room for it to get to us. At least not yet.

Chris gasped behind me.

I held up my hand at them without looking away from the wolf.

Its violet eyes glittered in the snow.

"Slow," I said, voice even. "Back the way we came. No sudden movements."

Tanner said, "Gordo," but I just shook my head.

"Now."

I heard them moving. The wolf's gaze darted over my shoulder, but I snapped my fingers, bringing its attention back to me.

It growled lowly.

I didn't look away.

The others were moving behind me. I knew we didn't have much time. Either the wolf would try to come for us or the hunters would be alerted. Our pack was too far away.

But I'd faced worse.

I'd seen the monsters in the dark.

This asshole didn't know who the *fuck* he was dealing with.

I grinned at the wolf. "I'm going to kill you. All of you. Just you wait and see."

It growled louder as it took a step forward. Its shoulders hit the tow truck, which creaked ominously, the boom scraping against the floor, the frame shuddering. It didn't like that sound, backing a step or two away.

"Come on," I said under my breath. "Come on."

The raven fluttered its wings.

The wolf crouched low and began to crawl toward me, black claws digging into the snow.

"That's right," I said. "Come and get me, you fucker."

I backed away slowly.

It snarled at me.

Flakes of snow blew in from a broken window.

Men laughed across the street in the garage.

Glass crunched underneath my feet.

The wolf was all the way under the truck, claws digging into wood and ice as it pulled itself toward me, jaws open wide.

Nevermore.

The raven flew.

The pack knew. They knew. I felt it. All of them.

The Alphas were there. In me. In my head.

gordo gordo gordo

And Mark.

Always Mark.

I pulled on those threads. The ones that connected us all.

And pushed.

There was a shriek of metal as the boom twisted, the tow truck shaking.

The wolf opened its mouth, tilting its head back to fucking *howl* and—

The boom snapped to the side, the linoleum floor underneath it splitting apart.

The boom landed outside of the diner in the snow.

For a moment, the tow truck hung suspended.

The wolf's howl cut off even before it began as the tow truck collapsed on top of it. I heard a wet *crunch* as six tons of metal met bone and muscle.

I didn't hesitate.

Even as the hunters began to shout in warning, I pushed myself up and ran toward the back of the diner. The door we'd come in was hanging open, snow falling. A wave of cold air washed over me as I passed through the doorway, looking over my shoulder on the off chance the wolf had survived the truck falling on top of it and was coming after me.

It wasn't.

"I think it's dead," I said to the others. "I think it—"

I bumped into someone.

I turned.

Chris. I had stumbled into Chris. Rico was to his left. Jessie to his right. Tanner stood on the other side of Jessie.

They weren't moving.

"What the hell are you stopping for?" I demanded, pushing my way through them. "We have to—mother*fucker*."

In the back alley behind the diner, in front of Team Human, stood the timber wolf.

I hadn't had much time to parse out its details when it'd come for me the day Elijah had arrived in Green Creek. I knew it was big, almost bigger than any wolf I'd seen before, but now, here, up close, I understood just how massive it was. Before Ox, Thomas Bennett had been the biggest wolf I'd ever seen. Before him, his father, Abel. Carter was bigger than his brothers, even Joe, his Alpha, but none of them compared to the size of the Omega in front of us.

Its eyes snapped to me.

I took a step back.

Its nostrils flared, and there was a brief moment when the violet in its eyes faded into a deep, muddy brown that I thought almost looked *familiar*, but then the violet returned bright as ever.

Only two ways out of this.

Through the alley behind the wolf.

Or back the way we'd come through the front of the diner.

Toward the hunters.

Tanner and Rico had their guns drawn but stood down, knowing gunfire would bring the attention of the hunters.

The knives hidden under Chris's sleeves popped forward.

Jessie tapped Ox's old crowbar against her shoulder.

The wolf wasn't impressed.

It took a step toward us and—

"Fuck this," Jessie said.

And before I could stop her, she pushed past me, took three running steps, and swung the crowbar upside the feral wolf's head.

The crowbar that was inlaid with silver.

The wolf yelped in pain as its head jerked to the side, a burning gash alongside its muzzle and cheek and up to its eye, which was squeezed shut and bleeding. It brought its head down toward the ground, pawing furiously at the smoking wound that hadn't yet started to close.

"Come on," she spat at us, dancing out of the way as the wolf tried to snap at her, missing by a good foot.

Rico and Tanner followed her, giving the injured wolf a wide berth. It tried to whirl on them, but Chris was there on its other side, slicing along the wolf's back as he ran in the narrow space between the Omega and the brick wall of the hardware store next to the diner. The wolf turned its head, snapping its fangs after him, but he was already past it, running after the others.

Red dripped onto white.

The wolf turned to me.

It took a step toward me.

I raised a hand, the roses blooming underneath the raven, ready to end this now.

But then it *faltered*.

The wolf snorted, shaking its head violently side to side. The chain around its neck barely shifted, the links deep into its skin. It blinked its one good eye rapidly and lowered its face to the snow, pushing down into it, leaving streaks of blood behind it.

And I . . . I couldn't do it.

"Gordo," Rico shouted. "Move your ass!"

I moved.

The Omega barely glanced in my direction.

"What the hell is wrong with it?" Chris asked me as soon as I reached them, coming out the other side of the alley behind the diner.

I glanced back at it. The Omega was pawing at its face again. "I don't know."

"Why didn't you kill it?" Jessie asked me, already moving away from the diner.

I didn't answer.

. . . . .

Halfway toward the Lighthouse, we met up with Mark and Elizabeth. She came to me first as Chris, Tanner, and Rico shared with Mark their outrage about the hunters being in the garage.

"All right?" she asked me, and I remembered Thomas telling me there was never anyone else for him.

"Yeah," I muttered.

"He took out one of the Omegas," Jessie told her, glancing at me curiously. "The red one. We got a few hits in on the bigger one, but it's still upright last we saw."

"And Elijah?"

Jessie shook her head.

Elizabeth touched my arm. "Gordo?"

I blinked. "I'm fine."

She didn't look like she believed me, but she let it go. She glanced over her shoulder at the others before lowering her voice. "We got as many as we could. They're at the Lighthouse."

"Something's wrong," I said, because I *knew* her.

She sighed. "Mark."

My stomach flipped. "What about him?"

She shook her head. "It's . . . there was a man. Jameson? I think his name is Jameson. Lives in the trailer park." Her nose wrinkled. "Smells terrible."

"Big guy? Mustache?" Jameson was an asshole on a good day, and these weren't good days.

She nodded. "He didn't want to come with us. Told us to leave him alone. Mark, he—he didn't take that well. He was angry. I thought he was going to shift right then and there. Mark scared him. I could smell it, though he tried to hide it."

"He stayed behind?" I asked, not liking where this was going.

"No," she said. "He agreed to go when Mark put a fist through his trailer wall."

"Jesus Christ."

"It's the moon, I think. It's pulling on him. It's getting stronger. Whatever it was, he snapped out of it almost immediately. It's happening, Gordo. Carter. And now Mark."

Even with all that had happened, I was surprised I was still capable of feeling gutted at the sound of *fear* in Elizabeth Bennett's voice. "We'll figure it out," I said, though I felt like a liar.

·   ·   ·

"I'm fine," Mark said as we approached the Lighthouse, snow crunching under our feet. The power was still on, and the Lighthouse was lit up like it was a Friday night.

"You sure about that?"

He rolled his eyes. "He was pissing me off."

"Jameson."

"Yeah. Wouldn't listen."

"So you punched a hole through his house."

"He listened after that."

"Mark."

"Gordo."

I grabbed him by the arm. "Would you stop? For fuck's sake. You can't hide this. Not from me."

"That's almost funny coming from you. Talking about hiding things."

That stung, though I deserved it. It wasn't Mark, though. He didn't *dig* at open wounds. "Don't be a dick."

He winced. "Sorry. I don't—I don't know where that came from."

He was lying. We both knew exactly where it'd come from. "I need to know if you're in control. You can't go into a room full of humans if there's a chance you'll turn on them."

For a moment I thought he was going to pull away. He breathed in through his nose as the others went inside. As the door opened voices poured out, some of them angry. I wasn't looking forward to facing the people who had remained in town. Hopefully they'd bought the bullshit story being spun.

"I'm not going to hurt them," Mark said, a scowl on his face.

"Show me your eyes."

"Gordo—"

"Do it, Mark."

He flashed his eyes.

Orange. Just orange.

I breathed a sigh of relief. "Just—stay by me, okay?"

His lips twitched. I saw the hint of teeth. "Gonna keep everyone safe from the big bad wolf?"

"Christ. That's not going to be a thing. Ever. You hear me? In fact, you say that again and I'll kill you myself. I think I liked it better when we hated each other."

He took me by the hand. "I never hated you, Gordo."

I looked away. I wanted to tell him the same, but I couldn't. Because I had hated him. I had hated all of them. It'd taken me a long time to figure out how to stop. And I didn't know if I was all the way there yet.

He sounded sad when he said, "I know. It's okay, though. It only took my ex being an evil witch and me losing my mind to get you to come back to me. Worth it, if you ask me."

"That's not funny," I said hoarsely.

"A little funny."

"When this is over, we need to have a long talk about this thing you call your sense of—"

He moved then, almost faster than I could follow. One moment he was in front of me, his hand in mine. The next I was shoved behind him as he began to shift, growling low in his throat.

I looked over his shoulder.

The timber wolf stood in the middle of the road.

Its face still hadn't healed, not completely. The silver in the crowbar was strong, and the wolf was an Omega. Its power to heal had slowed. The wound was knitting itself back together, but its muzzle was caked with blood, and its right eye was swollen shut.

And it was pissed off.

"Get inside," Mark growled at me.

"Fuck you," I retorted. "I'm not going to leave you—"

"If it's like the others, it'll come for you first. I can't hold it off if I'm worried about—"

"I don't *need* you to worry about—holy *fuck!*"

I tackled Mark to the side as the feral wolf launched itself at us. We fell into the snow, Mark hitting the ground first. I landed on top of him as the wolf sailed over us, teeth snapping, missing my neck by inches. Its hot breath stank, and I could almost feel the *weight* of it in the air above us.

"You just wanted to lay on top of me," Mark said from beneath me.

"Seriously," I snapped, pushing myself off him and standing. "Now is *not the time.*"

The wolf had landed near the Lighthouse, skidding in the snow but managing to stay upright. Its ears pricked toward the bar, and I knew it could hear probably dozens of heartbeats inside. Its eyes flickered violet, and it took a step toward the bar door, and—

"Hey!" I shouted at it, trying to get its attention. "Over here, you goddamn mutt!"

It slowly turned its head toward me.

I swallowed thickly.

It really was a big werewolf.

Mark was at my side, half-shifted, and before I could chew him out for *that*, the timber wolf crouched low, ready to attack.

Screams came from inside the bar.

We all hesitated.

And then Carter burst out of the Lighthouse, the door slamming against the wall, the wood splintering. He, too, was half-shifted, and it hit me then that the people inside the bar *had seen it,* but before I could even begin to process this monumental fuckup, he'd tackled the timber wolf from behind.

It went down hard, slipping in the snow. Carter's face elongated, hair sprouting along his cheeks, and he was snarling at the wolf beneath him. The timber wolf pushed itself up quickly, knocking Carter off its back and into the snow.

He landed, orange eyes wide, exhaling heavily.

The timber wolf rose slowly above him, lips pulled back, teeth bared.

I touched the rune on my arm, ready to light the motherfucker on fire, and Elizabeth stood in the doorway, eyes blazing, ready to attack whatever was going after her son, and Ox and Joe roared from inside the Lighthouse, their Alpha song bowling over us because one of their pack was in danger, one of their *pack* was about to—

The timber wolf stopped snarling.

Its eyes narrowed.

As the wolf lowered its head, Carter raised his claws, ready to swipe at it, to gouge its eyes out just as he'd been trained to do, but—

It didn't happen.

The timber wolf just . . . sniffed him.

Its eyes were violet, and its hackles were raised, but it put its snout against Carter's chest and *inhaled.*

"Um," Carter said, lisping through a mouthful of fangs. "Guys? What the hell is going on?"

"Carter," Elizabeth said. "I need you to—"

Joe and Ox appeared behind him, ignoring the cacophony of voices rising behind them. Their eyes were red, and when Joe saw his brother on the ground with a strange wolf above him, he tried to push past his mother. The timber wolf heard him coming and turned its back on Carter, snarling at Joe. It began to back away slowly, crowding Carter until he was forced to scoot back in the snow.

"What the fuck is going on?" Carter squeaked, startled out of his shift as he got a face full of tail.

"Joe," Elizabeth said sharply, causing her son to stop before he could reach the timber wolf. "Don't."

Joe looked surprised as he glanced back at his mother. "But it's going to hurt him."

"I don't think it is," Mark said thoughtfully at my side. "It's . . . protecting him."

"From *what*?" Joe asked.

"From you. From all of us. Step back, Joe."

"But—"

"Joe."

Joe did as his uncle asked.

The timber wolf eyed him warily, standing above Carter. Once it was sure that Joe wasn't a threat, it turned back around and put its snout against Carter's chest again, rumbling low in its throat.

Carter tried to shove its face away, but it snapped at his fingers, growling a warning. "What the hell is its *problem*?" Carter asked, sounding annoyed.

"I think it likes you," Elizabeth said mildly.

"Oh, gee, Mother, *thank you* for your input! I don't know *where* I'd be without you!"

"You wouldn't be born without her," Joe said, helpful as ever.

"Ox!" Carter cried, trying unsuccessfully to shove the wolf away from him. "Do your I'm-So-Special Alpha thing and get this fucker *off* me."

"You seem to be doing just fine on your own," Ox said, stepping out of the bar and into the snow. The timber wolf glared back at him over its shoulder. Ox made sure to give them a wide berth as he approached us, much to Carter's outrage.

"What happened?" Ox asked us in a low voice. "Rico said the hunters were in the garage?"

I scowled. "As if I didn't want to kill them already, they're touching my stuff."

"He focuses on what's important," Mark told Ox, and I gave very real consideration to blasting him across the bar parking lot. But I didn't think it would do well for whatever was going on between us, so I didn't.

"I don't like it when people touch my things."

"I'm sure Dale would agree with that," Ox said, because even though he was an Alpha, he was still a bitch.

Mark started choking.

I hated everyone. "Killed the red wolf. Crushed it under the truck."

"You followed?"

I shook my head. "The guys and Jessie made sure our tracks were covered most of the way here."

"And what's that about?" he asked, nodding toward the wolf that now had the collar of Carter's coat between its teeth and was trying to drag him away. It wasn't going so well for the timber wolf, seeing as Kelly had burst out of the bar with an impressive battle cry, grabbed his brother's leg, and was pulling him in the opposite direction.

"I couldn't even begin to tell you."

"Kelly!" Carter shouted. "Save me!"

"I *am*," Kelly yelled back.

The timber wolf jerked its head back roughly, trying to pull Carter away from Kelly as it snarled a warning.

"Are we playing tug-of-war with Carter now?" another voice said. I looked up to see Team Human crowding around Elizabeth, even as the shouts in the bar grew louder. Rico had his hands on his hips, and his head was cocked, eyes squinted. "Because I don't know if that's going to endear the general population of Green Creek now that they've seen half of the Bennetts—who they assumed were just rich weirdos that lived in the woods—suddenly turn into monsters right in front of them." Something shattered inside the bar, and he winced. "Bambi's probably not going to like that. Or the fact that I've been keeping this from her."

"I can talk to her for you," Jessie said, patting his arm. "Give it a woman's touch."

"You stay away from her," Chris said, glaring at his sister. "You already think she has a nice rack. It's not cool to try and steal Rico's girlfriend."

"Or is it?" Rico asked, eyeing Jessie up and down. "I mean, as long as I can watch, I wouldn't mind— *Ow, vete a la verga, culero*, my arm isn't supposed to *twist* that way. Stop it!"

Jessie waited a beat to prove her point, but then let Rico's arm go.

Chris and Tanner laughed.

Jessie glared at them.

They backed away from her slowly.

"Um, guys?" Robbie said, coming up behind them, looking frantic. "As fun as this is, I think we've got a problem."

He pointed over his shoulder back in the bar.

Pressed against the windows were many, many faces, eyes wide, mouths open as they watched a wolf the size of a horse trying to steal Carter from his brother, both of whose eyes were glowing brightly.

Will, the drunken owner of the motel, spoke first. "I *knew* it!" he shouted, eyes rheumy and bloodshot. "Fucking *animals*. No one believed me, but they came and stayed in my motel! Mountain lion my *ass*. Look at the size of that fucker! Shape-shifters! We're surrounded by shape-shifters!"

"Fuck," Ox said succinctly.

IMPERFECT

They were . . . loud. The people inside the bar. Some of them cringed away from the Bennetts, trying to get as far from them as possible while still remaining in the Lighthouse.

Will, the bastard that he was, tried to tell anyone who would listen that he knew something had been going on in this town, had been going on for years, and everyone had called him crazy. "Who's crazy now?" he said, laughing wildly. "*Who's crazy now?*"

"I could do it again," I told Ox under my breath. "Alter their memories. Like I did with the people after Richard."

Ox shook his head slowly. "You were off your feet for a few days after that. And there were only a handful. There's almost fifty people in here. I need you strong."

He had a point. Expending that much energy would make me next to useless for at least a week. And we didn't have time for that now. "There's always after."

"Maybe." He looked at the people standing before us. They were starting to get loud again. Jameson, the owner of a brand-new hole in his trailer wall, was staring at Mark as if he expected Mark to shift and eat him right then and there. It would have been funny if the situation weren't so fucked. Especially since Mark seemed on the verge of doing exactly that. I stayed close, trying to get him to calm.

Others were still at the window, staring out at where Kelly and Robbie were keeping an eye on Carter. The timber wolf hadn't been too pleased when Carter had tried to follow us inside, growling at him until Carter stopped trying to get away. I had a good idea what was going on there, and I thought Elizabeth did too, if the knowing look on her face meant anything. The others were . . . too young. Too inexperienced. Even Joe and Ox seemed perplexed. I didn't know if it would matter in the long run. The wolf was an Omega. If it was like Pappas, I didn't know if there was any turning back. It was best if Carter didn't know. At least not until we could be sure.

He was in for a rude awakening, at any rate.

"What are we going to do?" Mark murmured. He was breathing

in and out through his nose, and I knew he was doing it to keep his heart rate slow. I didn't know if it was working. "We can't—Ox. There's a reason packs are kept hidden."

Ox tilted his head. "Why, though? Because the Alpha of all says that's the way it's supposed to be? She betrayed us. Or is it because it could bring hunters down upon us? They're already here. And we're trapped inside with them because witches have surrounded Green Creek and taken our wards away from us. These people are in danger. Don't they have a right to know why?"

Mark paled. His voice was rough when he spoke. "Do you even know what you're saying? What you're risking? It's not just about us, Ox. If this gets out, if this spreads beyond our borders, then it puts other packs at risk. People are scared of what they don't understand. And they won't understand us."

"I get that," Ox said lightly. "I do. But we can't live in fear. If we're going to have hope for a tomorrow, then we have to deal with it today."

Mark shook his head. "You don't—you weren't *there*. You didn't see what they did to us. What the humans did to our family. They came in and—there were *children*, Ox. They were just *kids*, and they—"

Ox wrapped a hand around his neck, bringing his forehead to Mark's. "Breathe," he whispered, eyes flashing red, and Mark's nostrils flared. "I need you to breathe. I know it hurts. I know it does. We will stop it, okay? We're going to find a way to stop it."

Mark reared back, breaking out of Ox's grasp. For a moment I thought he was going to lash out. "You don't *get* it," he growled, deeper than any human ever could. The people closest to him backed away slowly. "You're *fine*. You don't have this—this *thing* inside of you. You still have your tether, and it's *intact*. I can feel it, Ox. Every fucking second, I can *feel* it. Just because you still get to keep everything you love doesn't mean you get to spout your Alpha bullshit on me. That's not fair. None of this is fair."

Blood began to drip from his hands where his claws had popped into the fleshy part of his palms.

"Mark," Ox warned, eyes blazing. "I need you to calm down. Listen to me, okay?" He reached for Mark again. "We're right here. Your pack is here. Gordo is—"

"Don't," Mark said, chest heaving as he took a step back. He bumped into a woman, who gasped and almost fell back. She was caught by Jameson, who glared at Mark. "Don't tell me to calm down. Don't talk to me about Gordo."

"Mark," Joe said, coming to stand next to Ox. "You're scaring people. This isn't you. This isn't who you are."

Mark laughed bitterly. "You don't know the first fucking thing about me. You left, Joe. My brother died. He was cut to ribbons, and you *left*. You didn't even have a second thought about it, and even if you did, was it about me? Or your mother? Or was it just about Ox? Was it just about your fucking mate?"

Joe's throat clicked as he swallowed, jaw tight.

"*That's* right," Mark said, voice hard. "All I wanted was to keep everyone safe. That's all I ever wanted. And then those fucking hunters came, and they took everything away from me. And then Thomas took what was left of my shredded heart and put it beneath his heel, telling me I didn't have a choice. I had to leave. And just when I thought I could finally forgive him, when I thought it would all be okay again, he *died*." Ice blue gave way to orange. "And then you made the same mistakes he did."

"Mark," I snapped, stepping forward. "Knock it off. You're getting yourself worked up. That's not going to help—"

"You're scared?" Mark snarled, whirling on the people in the Lighthouse. "You should be. You want to see what you're so afraid of? Let me show you."

He started to shift.

Before I could step forward, Elizabeth was there behind him, hand on his shoulder.

I didn't have time to react.

He spun, hand out. He backhanded her across the face, and as she fell into her Alphas, as the sound of a small bone snapping filled the room, Mark Bennett's eyes flickered. Blue. Orange. Blue.

Violet.

And then it faded.

Mark looked horrified as he lowered his hand.

The room exploded around us as people began shouting. Jessie and Chris ran to Elizabeth's side and helped her up. Tanner and Rico stood in front of them, arms across their chests as they glared at Mark. Elizabeth was muttering that she was fine, she was *fine*, even as the bone in her cheek began to heal. Ox looked furious, Joe murderous, and I thought I heard the wolves outside roar in anger.

A gun fired.

I jerked my head toward the sound, sure the hunters had found us, that we were all fucking *trapped* in here and—

Bambi stood on top of the bar, pistol pointed up. Bits of plaster sprinkled down on her from a hole in the ceiling. Her eyes were narrowed and her voice cold when she said, "You touch her again and I'll put a bullet in your head. Maybe it won't kill you, whatever the fuck you are, but I bet it'll slow you down."

Mark was stricken. He raised his hands in front of his face. His fingers were trembling, claws sinking back down. "Elizabeth," he whispered. "I didn't—I didn't mean to. I didn't—" He took a step toward her.

Bambi pointed the gun at him. "I mean it, Mark Bennett. Another step and we'll see if the color of your brains matches the décor."

"Holy shit," Rico whispered. "I'm *dating* her."

"Not the time," Tanner whispered back. "But seriously. Props, man."

They fist-pounded without looking away from Mark.

"I'm *fine*," Elizabeth said, knocking Joe's hands off her. "He caught me by surprise. Joe, stop growling at him. You know as well as I do that I can take Mark in a fair fight any day."

"Ox," Mark said, eyes wide and pleading, "it wasn't—it was an accident. I swear. I'm in control. I promise. I promise. *I promise*—"

"You stay here with everyone," Ox told Joe. "Try to keep everyone calm. I'll take Mark and—"

And I said, "No."

Ox closed his eyes and sighed. "Gordo, if he's . . . if this is him turning, and if it's like the others, he'll go after you first. You have to know that."

"I don't care," I said, stepping between Mark and the rest of the pack. His hands curled in the back of my shirt, his forehead pressed against my neck. He sounded close to hyperventilating. "There's nothing more you can do that you haven't already tried."

Ox's eyes narrowed. "What are you going to do?"

"I don't know," I admitted. "But I'll figure out something. I always do. Just . . . I need you to trust me, okay? This isn't because he's my . . . it's not because of that."

Elizabeth snorted, her cheek bright red. "I don't know if that's exactly true. Just ask Carter about that right now."

"What?" Joe asked. "What the hell does this have to do with Carter?"

"I'll explain later," Elizabeth said, patting his hand.

"You always say that, and you never do," Joe muttered. "I'm an *adult* now. I'm your *Alpha*."

"And I'm still your mother," Elizabeth said sharply. "I brought you into this world. I will take you out of it, Alpha or not."

Joe groaned. "Did you have to say that in front of everyone? Jeez."

"Fine," Ox said after staring at me for a long moment. "Take him back to the house and—"

I shook my head. "I'm taking him to mine."

"Gordo—"

"Ox."

He was frustrated with me, but there was nothing I could do about that now. "Just . . . stay there. Okay? Don't go after the hunters. When we move against them, we move together. Understood?"

I nodded.

"Go, then. I'll send Carter back to the house just to be safe. Kelly and Robbie can go with him to keep an eye on him and to check on Pappas."

"Don't forget about the other wolf," Elizabeth said. "I highly doubt he'll let Carter get very far without him."

Ox growled in annoyance. "Yes. And the other wolf. The rest of you will stay with me and see what we can do about—" He nodded toward the others in the bar, who were all watching us silently.

"Better you than me," I muttered, turning and grabbing Mark by the hand. I thought he was going to protest, because he resisted when I tried to pull him away. His gaze was trained on Elizabeth. She smiled at him, though she winced when she did so.

"Go," she said quietly. "I'll see you soon."

He nodded tightly and let me pull him through the door and out into the snow.

Robbie and Kelly were standing near the door. Carter was still trying to get up, but the other wolf wouldn't let him. Its front paws were on his chest, holding him down. It turned its head toward me, eyes flaring violet at the sight of me. Its nose twitched, and I was again hit with a wave of familiarity. Like I should *know* this wolf. It was possible I'd met it (*him*) before it'd turned Omega, but for the life of me, I couldn't remember ever seeing a wolf like it before. I would have remembered a shifter that size.

"All right?" Kelly asked, voice strained.

"We're okay," I said smoothly. "Go back to the house. Take Robbie and Carter too. Stay there until you hear from Ox. Don't be seen."

Kelly nodded slowly. "Mark?"

Mark didn't speak.

"Kelly," I said. "Now."

Robbie took Kelly's elbow in his hand, tugging him gently toward Carter, who was yelling at us to tell him what was going on, and why we were splitting up, and would *someone get the fucking wolf off of him for fuck's sake?*

. . . .

Mark didn't speak as I led him home. He held my hand tightly, so much so that I was sure there'd be bruises. But I didn't try to get him to ease up. I didn't want him to.

I avoided the deepest drifts as best I could as we trekked the mile or so to my house. It was still snowing and didn't seem to be letting up anytime soon.

I was sweating by the time we reached my door. The driveway was empty, and it was only then I realized we'd left my truck behind when Elijah had come. I hadn't seen it in the road this morning. They must have moved it. Jones's cruiser had been gone too.

He'd only been two days away from his vacation, he'd said.

"Christ," I muttered, pulling Mark up the driveway. My keys were still in the truck. There was a spare, and I had to let Mark's hand go to bend over and dig for it. He stared down at the ground.

I dug through the snow until I found the rock with the key underneath. I opened the screen door, unlocked the door, and shoved it open. I stood aside, glancing back at Mark. "Inside."

He looked dazed as he lifted his head. "What."

I jerked my head toward the open door. "Move your ass."

He hesitated. "Gordo, if I'm—if this is happening, then I need to be as far away from you as I can be."

"Get in the house."

His eyes narrowed. That was better. I could deal with him being pissed off at me. It put us back on even ground. "Are you stupid?" he growled.

"I swear to god, if you don't *get into this fucking house*, I'm going to lose my shit, and you won't like it when I do."

He scowled.

I waited.

With a huff, he pushed past me and went into the house, muttering under his breath about bossy fucking witches.

I looked out into the snow.

It was quiet.

I knew it wouldn't last long.

I followed him inside and locked the door behind us.

.   .   .

He was in the kitchen by the time I came out of the bedroom, changed into dry clothes. I felt centered, being in my own house, head clear for the first time in what felt like days.

He stood in front of the sink, staring out the window into the white. He didn't turn, though he knew I was there. He always did.

"I put clothes out for you," I said quietly. "On the bed. They might be a little tight, but it's better than having the smell of wet dog in my house."

He snorted, shaking his head. "Asshole."

"Not going to argue that. Hope you weren't expecting something more romantic from me. This is pretty much all you'll get. I don't do shit like that."

He turned his head slightly. "Romantic?"

Yeah, I hadn't meant to say that. "Shut up. Forget I said anything."

"I don't know if I can. Be still my heart."

"Mark. Change your fucking clothes."

He huffed out a breath as he turned around. He looked at me, searching for what, I didn't know. He seemed to be in control, at least more than he had before. I didn't know how much longer that would last. The full moon was less than two days away. We were running out of time.

He nodded and started out of the kitchen. But before he went down the hall to the bedroom, he paused. "You knew."

"What?"

"To bring me here instead of to the pack house."

I felt his eyes on me, but I couldn't bring myself to look back. "I don't know what you're talking about."

A beat of silence. Then, "I think you do. At the house, you don't have . . . you stay, sometimes. But not like the others. You always come back here. You're pack, but this is your home. It smells like you. This place. The weight of you, it's . . . everywhere. You knew that bringing me here would help."

"Go change, Mark."

He went.

I listened to the sounds of him moving slowly through my house, the wood creaking under his feet, his fingertips dragging along the walls, leaving his scent behind. I knew what he was doing. I knew what we were headed toward, and I didn't know if there was anything I could do to stop it. I didn't know if I *wanted* it to stop. When was the last time he'd been here? When was the last time he'd felt like he was *welcome* here?

My skin felt too tight. The ink on my skin was thrumming with something I couldn't quite name. Either that, or I didn't want to face it. There was something here, some precipice we were standing on, and I didn't think there was any turning back after this. If we tried, I didn't know if there'd be enough pieces of us left to put back together.

Once, there was a boy.

An extraordinary boy.

And as an Alpha held him down, this extraordinary boy's father whispered in his ear while taking a needle to his skin, etching ink and leaving a trail of magic in its wake.

Once, there was a wolf.

A brave wolf.

And as this brave wolf grew, he followed the scent of dirt and leaves and rain, his Alpha telling him that he had found the one to make him whole.

The boy had loved this wolf.

But it hadn't been enough.

Once, the moon had loved the sun.

But no matter how hard she tried, the sun was always at the other end of the sky, and they could never meet. She would sink, and he would rise. She was dark and he was day. The world slept while she shone. She waxed and waned, and sometimes disappeared entirely.

Once, an old blind witch had spoken words of choice, of truth and prophecy.

He said, *You will be tested, Gordo Livingstone. In ways that you haven't yet imagined. One day, and one day soon, you will have to make a choice. And I fear the future of all you hold dear will depend on that choice.*

I was tired of being angry.

I was tired of the whispers in my ear, telling me the wolves didn't love me, that they only wanted to use me.

I was tired of always being at the other end of the sky, of waxing and waning and disappearing entirely.

Roses bloomed.

The raven's talons tightened amongst the thorns.

I pushed away from the counter.

And I did what I should have done a long time ago.

I followed my wolf.

The bedroom door was open.

I couldn't hear him moving.

It felt like this was a dream.

Like even after all this time, it couldn't be real.

I'd been here before. Dreaming of him.

Waxing and waning. Waxing and waning.

He stood with his back to me. He had peeled off his coat and shirt, and they lay discarded on the floor in a wet heap.

The muscles in his back rippled. His head was bowed, and I didn't know why.

"Mark?" I asked, my voice barely above a whisper.

He breathed, but he didn't speak.

I took another step toward him, reaching out in the bond that stretched between us. I thought I was too late. That coming here had been a mistake. That I'd be met with nothing but a wall of violet rage and that he'd turn, teeth bared, skin shifting, and no matter what I said, no matter how hard I tried, he wouldn't know me. He wouldn't remember me.

But instead of violet, I was drowning in blue. So much blue.

I stopped.

I said, "Mark?"

His shoulders shook. "You."

"Yes."

He didn't raise his head. I didn't know what he was looking at. "I told myself that you—that you'd forgotten."

"About what?"

He laughed, though it cracked right down the middle. "This. Me. Everything."

"I don't—"

He raised his hand so I could see it over his shoulder.

Clutched in his fingers was a raven made of wood.

The raven I'd left on the nightstand after taking it out of the secret pocket where it'd stayed hidden for over three years.

The raven he'd given to me when we didn't know any better.

He said, "It took me weeks to do this. To make this. To get it just right. I nicked my fingers more times than I could count. The cuts always healed, but sometimes the blood got into the wood, and I would rub at it until it was ingrained. I didn't—I didn't like the way one of the wings looked, and I couldn't figure out how to fix it. So I went to Thomas. He smiled at me when he took it in his hands. He studied it for a long time. Then he handed it back to me and said it was perfect the way it was. And I remember being so *angry* with him. Because it *wasn't* perfect. It was crude. Clumsy. Do you know what he said to me?"

I shook my head, unable to speak.

"He said, 'It's perfect because it's imperfect. Like you. Like Gordo. Like all of us. It's perfect because of the intent. Of what it means. He'll get it, Mark. I promise you he'll understand.'"

I blinked away the burn.

Mark shook his head. "And I remember being so irritated with him. It sounded like something our father would say. A bunch of Alpha nonsense. Because it *was* imperfect. It was flawed and misshapen. It took me a while to see that was the point. And you kept it."

I opened my mouth, but no words came out. I cleared my throat and tried again. "I took it with me. When we left."

He turned slowly. The shadows played along his bare skin. The hair on his chest trailed down to his stomach and disappeared into the top of his pants. He held the raven in his hand gently, as if it were something to be revered.

"Why?"

I looked away and remembered his words when we'd last been alone. "Because it was the only part of you that's ever been mine."

"That's not true," he said, voice rough. "That's *never* been true. Gordo, everything I have, everything I am, it's *always* been yours. You were just too goddamn stubborn to see that."

"I was hurt."

"I know."

"And angry."

"I know that too. And I would give almost anything to take that back. I would. I swear. To make Thomas see he was wrong. He should have fought for you more." He closed his eyes. "I should have fought for you more."

"But you didn't."

"No. I didn't."

"I was here, Mark. I was fifteen years old, and my mother was dead. My pack was *dead*. My father was gone. And then you—*he* just . . . you said it was the hardest decision he ever had to make. You said it nearly killed him. But then why did he never come back? Why did he never come for me?"

Mark opened his eyes. They were orange and then blue and then *violet*, and I didn't know what to do. I didn't know how to stop it. "He wanted to," Mark growled. "God, Gordo. He wanted to. But there was always *something* that kept him away. And he would send me, and there were times I thought you wanted me here, and then times where I thought you never wanted to see me again."

"It wasn't enough," I snapped. "Parts of you. *Pieces* of you. It wasn't fair. You couldn't be here for days and then leave for months. I would be left here *again*, and you would go back to the pack, with your *family*. Jesus Christ, I fucking hated you for that. I fucking hated all of you for doing that to me."

His eyes glowed. He popped his neck side to side. The veins in his thick biceps pulsed. "I know you did. And when I came back that last time and the stench on your skin was of some goddamn stranger, I was barely able to restrain myself. I wanted to fucking kill him. I wanted to knock you to the side and find whoever it was and tear him to shreds. To spill his blood. To break his bones. To make him suffer for having the goddamn *audacity* to think he could ever touch you. That he could even *think* of touching you."

"You weren't here," I said, a nasty curl to my lips. I was playing with fire, and I didn't care. "You weren't here and he was. It had to be someone. Might as well have been him. I don't even remember his name. But at least he wasn't afraid to touch me. At least he wouldn't hurt me. At least he wouldn't fucking *betray me*."

"Don't," Mark warned. "Gordo, don't. Don't make me angry. I can smell it. Your magic. It's—"

"*Fuck* my magic," I snarled at him. "Fuck the pack. Fuck my father and your father. *Fuck* Thomas. This is you and me. This is you and me, and fuck you if you think I'm just going to let this go. Let *you* go. I'm not scared of you. I never have been, and I never will be."

He shook his head. "It's too late. Gordo, can't you see that? It's too late. I—I can feel it. In my head. It was just a whisper, and it was just *scraping* along my skin. But now it has hooks, and it's digging in. It's digging in, and I can't make it stop. Gordo, I can't make it—"

Once, the moon had loved the sun.

Once, there was a boy who had loved a wolf.

Once, an old witch had spoken of choice, of truth and prophecy.

And it was blue, so much of it was blue, but I was tired of it. I was tired of feeling this way, of being alone, of being scared, of thinking that I couldn't have what I wanted more than anything in this world.

And so I made my choice.

I chose the wolf.

I took three steps forward, my hands going up to Mark Bennett's face. He flinched, eyes flaring, but it was already too late to stop it.

I kissed him. There, in the darkened room while snow fell outside.

At first he didn't respond, and I thought I'd misunderstood. That I was too late. That the gulf between us was too wide to ever be crossed.

But then he sighed and slumped against me, his hands on my hips, the raven still clutched between his fingers. I felt the sharp press of its wooden wing against my side. He sang a song in my head of *gordo love mate please love*, and though it was tinged with blue and blue and blue, there was a thread of green shot right through the middle, of relief and hope. It was like I was young again and there was this boy, this tall, gangly boy sitting against a tree in summer, his feet bare in the green, green grass, and he was my *shadow*, following me everywhere, telling me he was trying to keep me safe from bad guys. I'd sat up on my knees and kissed him because it felt like the right thing to do. Everything about Mark Bennett had felt right, even then in the summer when we hadn't known just how sharp teeth could be.

We weren't young anymore.

But it still felt like we could be.

It still felt like this could be a first time.

And then it changed.

The green began to tinge toward red, like fire spreading along the grass. The blue started to *swell*, an ocean rising. It hit the fire and *mixed* until the sea burned violet, and it was there, just lurking underneath the surface.

Claws, near my skin.

I groaned against him, mouth opening. His tongue slid against mine as he growled, the rumble crawling in his chest and up his throat. He felt like he was *vibrating*, and as I slid my hands down from his face to his chest, my tongue scraped against the tip of a fang. It should not have turned me on as much as it did.

And then it was gone.

He was gone.

One moment he was pressed against me, his mouth on my jaw, my neck, and the next he was standing on the other side of the room, chest heaving, eyes wide, jaw clenched.

I blinked slowly, trying to clear my head. I reached for him.

He took a step back. "Gordo. You—I . . ."

I shook my head. "No. Enough."

"We can't do this."

"We *can*."

"I could *hurt* you," he snarled at me, eyes orange and bright in the dark room. "Don't you get that? Haven't you been *listening*? I'm losing my fucking *mind*. I'm turning Omega. I already hurt Elizabeth. I can't take the chance that I could—" He choked.

"You won't," I told him. "You won't."

"You don't know that. It's happening, Gordo. It's happening, and there's nothing we can do to stop it."

"Then *fight* it!" I shouted at him. "Goddamn you, you *fight* it. You aren't allowed to give up. You aren't *allowed* to leave me again. You hear me? Fuck you if you think I'm going to just let you go again. Not now. Not because of this. Not because of something as fucking *stupid as this*."

"Why?" he cried. "Why the hell are you doing this? Why do you even care? Is it guilt? Is this your way of getting back at me? Do you really hate me that much? Why the hell are you doing this, Gordo? Now, after all this time, why are you doing this?"

"It's because I'm scared," I said, voice breaking. "I love you, and I'm so scared I'm going to lose you."

The wolf responded then. The wooden raven fell from his hands and the wolf came rushing forward. I didn't have time to react. If he was truly lost to me, if the tether had finally snapped, then I didn't know if I wanted him to stop.

I closed my eyes.

But then I was lifted, hands under my thighs, pulling me up. My back slammed against the wall behind me, almost knocking the breath from my lungs as the plaster cracked. I wrapped my legs around his waist, and his mouth was on my neck, teeth scraping against my skin. He was rumbling lowly in his throat, and I *felt* it, the way he vibrated. The way he shook. My hands went to the back of his head, forcing him to look up at me.

Orange and violet and that ice-cold blue flickered back.

I kissed him, pressing his lips back against his teeth. His fingers dug into my thighs, claws piercing the thick pants I wore, dimpling the skin. He rolled his hips, grinding against my dick. I groaned into his mouth as he sucked on my tongue. Bright flashes went off in my head, and they were him, they were coming from him, and I was *shocked* at the level of desire I felt, the animalistic urge that roared through him, demanding that he bite. That he fuck. That he claim.

And I—

I knew what I had to do.

"Mark," I gasped as he latched on to my throat again, beard scraping my skin raw. "Listen to me."

"No," he growled, worrying a mark on my neck. "Busy."

"I need you to fuck me."

"I'm *getting* there."

"No, listen to me. Just—Jesus *fuck*, do that again—no. Stop. Mark, listen."

He pulled away, eyes dazed. His lips were swollen and slick with spit, and I wanted nothing more than to pull him back to me. A drop of sweat dripped down the side of his neck and onto my thumb. "Did I hurt you?" he asked.

I shook my head furiously. "No. You didn't. Do you trust me?"

"Yes."

"Do you want me?"

"Yes."

"Do you love me?"

And he said, *"Yes."*

Because I have never seen a wolf love another as much as he loved you.

I am here as your Alpha. And I have received a formal request from one of my Betas.

I thought of a boy with eyes of ice telling me that he loved me, that he didn't want to leave again, but he had to, he had to, his Alpha was demanding it, and he would come back for me, Gordo, you have to believe I'll come back for you. You are my mate, I love you, I love you, I love you.

I leaned close and whispered words in his ear. Words I once said to him when he stood outside my door and my heart was breaking. "You can have me. Right now. Here. Choose me. Mark. Choose me. Stay here. Or don't. We can go anywhere you want. We can leave right now. You and me. Fuck everything else. No packs, no Alphas. No *wolves.* Just . . . us."

He pulled his head back.

His eyes were the brightest orange I'd ever seen.

"You want this?" he whispered. "With me?"

"Yes. I do."

"But—"

"Maybe it'll stop it. Maybe it'll slow it down."

The orange faded slightly. "If you're only doing this because of—"

I kissed him. "No," I mumbled against his lips. "Not because of that. Not just because of that. Because of everything else."

"There's no going back. After this."

"I know."

"And it might not work. Gordo, it might not do anything at all."

"I know that too."

"And you would still? For me?"

"Yes. Yes. Always for you."

It was blue. Of course it was. The ocean always was. It was vast and filled so deeply with melancholy that I thought I would choke on it.

But through the ocean, through the violet fire that burned on top of it, the green grew again.

He kissed me reverently, his grip softening, as if he never thought he would hear such words from me. It was soft and sweet, and I ached from the very thought of it.

I reached down between us, fumbling with the buttons to his pants as my skin flushed. I'd thought of this before. In those late nights when I couldn't sleep, though I'd never admit it to myself the next morning. I wondered how he'd feel pressed against me, how the muscles in his arms and chest would feel under my tongue. I'd thought it weak and foolish, angry with myself how much it hurt.

But this was real now. I could smell him. Taste him. Touch him. He turned and carried me to the bed, setting me down gently before he crawled on top of me, letting his considerable weight push me down into the mattress. I was engulfed by him, and everything was Mark and Mark and *Mark*, and there was an answering song in my head, a howl coming from deep within him. It rocked me to my core, the sheer *joy* of it causing my hands to shake as I wrapped them around his neck, urging him on.

He pushed himself up, hands on either side of my head, muscles in his arms straining. He leaned down and kissed me as I felt his legs jerk. He toed off his boots, which fell heavily to the floor. I ran my hands through the hair on his stomach before I reached the top of his pants and shoved them down as far as I could get them. His cock sprang free, smacking up against his stomach. I used my bare foot to push his pants the rest of the way down. They, too, fell to the floor.

He was all hard lines and edges perched above me. I remembered who he once had been—who we *both* had been. Nervous and hormonal and awkward.

My shadow protecting me from bad guys.

We weren't like that anymore. Gone were the boys who thought the world was a safe and mysterious place. We'd been hurt, and we'd hurt each other, but everything had led to here, now. This moment.

He sat up, knees on either side of my arms. His balls rested on my chest, and he reached up and stroked his dick slowly, staring down at me.

I burned at the sight of him.

I tried to move, needing to get my hands on him, but he squeezed his thighs, pinning my arms at my sides.

I was trapped by a wolf on the way to losing his mind.

And I didn't care.

His voice was low when he said, "Open your mouth. Stick out your tongue."

I did as he asked.

He grunted, moving forward slightly, ass rising but still holding my arms in place with his legs. His cockhead bumped into my chin before it hit my tongue. I closed my eyes at the taste of skin. "That's good," he said quietly. "That's real good, Gordo." His balls rested in the hollow of my throat. His dick pressed against my tongue. My lips. I tried to catch it in my mouth, but he wouldn't give it to me. I opened my eyes to glare at him, but he paid me no mind. He fisted the base of his cock, and he watched as he rubbed it against my face. He lifted it and smacked it against my tongue, heavy and fat.

"I'll give it to you," he said. "I promise. Is that what you want?"

He was driving me crazy, and all I could do was nod.

"Okay," he said. "Okay."

He lifted his hips as he grabbed the headboard above me. The shadows played along his nudity. His nipples were hard, gooseflesh prickling along his skin.

He was gentle when he fed me his dick, canting his hips down, the muscles in his legs flexing against me. I swallowed him, breathing through my nose, barely able to keep my eyes from rolling back in my head. He pressed down on the top of his dick, keeping it in place as he thrust shallowly. I was overwhelmed by him, my heart stumbling in my chest. My throat worked around him as he pushed in deeper, my tongue running along the underside of his dick.

Mark growled above me as he fucked my face. Everything was him. His eyes were narrowed, and he kept saying, "That's good, Gordo, that's real good, you're so good," just under his breath, like he couldn't help himself. It was thrumming between us, the thread, the bond. It wasn't about *packpackpack*. It wasn't about anyone else. It was him and me. It was just us.

He pulled out of my mouth. My jaw hurt, but I tried to raise my head to chase after him. He sat back against my chest, still holding me in place. He cupped the side of my face, thumb tracing over my bottom lip. I couldn't figure out the look on his face, but it was akin to awe.

"Are you sure about this?" he asked.

"Yeah," I croaked out.

He leaned down and kissed me, slow and sweet.

Later, I groaned his name, spitting curses at him as he pressed my knees against my chest, folding me in half. His hands were on my ass, holding me apart, and his tongue inside me. The raven fluttered around on my arm on a bed of blooming roses. The petals were red like the eyes of our Alphas, and their leaves were green, green, green with relief that I could have this. That I could finally have the one thing I needed most.

He licked up my ass until he reached my balls, taking one in his mouth and then the other. My dick was flat against my stomach, so hard it *hurt*. I told him to fuck me, you bastard, Jesus Christ, just *fuck* me, but he only laughed against my skin before running a finger over my asshole. He brought his hand up to my mouth, telling me to get his fingers wet. He pressed down on my jaw until I opened wide. I sucked his fingers as best I could, rolling my tongue around them. He pulled them out with a wet pop before he brought them back down between us.

I winced when he pressed a single finger inside. It'd been years since I'd been with anyone else, and even longer since I'd been fucked. I hadn't much liked the thought of someone above me, fucking into me. It felt wrong.

It didn't feel that way now.

He turned his face and kissed my knee as he added a second finger. I gasped at the sensation as he slowly worked my hole. He looked down at the sight of his fingers disappearing into me, eyes blown wide with lust.

"Pervert," I muttered.

"Yeah. I guess I am. You're taking it, though. You're taking it so good."

I flushed at the praise. It'd never been like this before.

But then, it'd never been him.

He had worked a third finger in before I snapped that he either needed to fuck me or I'd do it myself.

He laughed. "I'd like to see you try."

I wrapped a hand around his throat.

The vines around the roses tightened.

I shoved him to the side, rolling with him as my magic burst along my arm. He grunted in surprise when he landed on his back. I straddled his hips, his cock under my ass. I ground down against it, and he groaned as he thrust up. "Impatient," he said.

I ignored him, reaching over to the nightstand to grab the slick I kept in the drawer. The wooden raven rattled across the surface, tilting to the side on its wing.

Mark was watching me when I sat back up, having found what I was looking for. I met his gaze after I poured the slick onto my hand, sitting up and reaching behind me. I wrapped my hand around his dick, getting him wet. He swallowed thickly, eyes fluttering shut as I stroked him. The angle was awkward, and he was thick, but I couldn't wait any longer. I wiped the remaining slick against my asshole as I tossed the bottle onto the floor.

I put one hand flat against his chest as I reached behind me again and rose. His eyes opened, his hands coming to my hips. I pressed his cock against my asshole, breathing out slowly as I bore down on him.

Claws popped against my skin.

His chest rumbled as I sank down.

One of his claws pierced the skin on my right side.

I breathed in the blue and the green and the *violet* and—

My hips were flush with his.

"Gordo," he breathed, my name like a benediction through sharpening teeth.

I waited, holding myself in place, hands in his chest hair. "Yeah," I sighed. "I know."

"I need to move," he said, sounding desperate. "You need to let me move—"

I glared down at him. "You need to hold the fuck up."

He snapped his teeth at me, eyes flaring violet.

I brought my hand back to his throat, wrapping my fingers around his neck. The skin dimpled where my fingertips pressed down.

He growled up at me, claws digging in.

The raven stretched its wings.

I watched as roses began to bloom down my arm. They covered the runes and symbols my father had given me. They'd never been like this before. So free. So wild. The grew until they covered every inch of skin, the vines stretching down toward my hand, leaves sprouting, the thick black thorns curved sharply.

The roses burst along the back of my hand, the red as bright as it'd ever been. The vines stretched down the lengths of my fingers, and for a moment, brief though it was, I swore they began to spread along his neck underneath my hand. That part of me was now etched into him.

The violet in his eyes faded away.

All that was left was blue. Clear, clean ice-cold blue.

I rose slowly, holding my hand in place, before falling back down on him. He groaned as I clenched my ass. His claws retreated, and I felt a thin trickle of blood roll down my side as his fingers gripped my hips. I rose again and was met on the way back down by his hips. He moved until his feet were flat against the bed before he fucked up into me harder, his skin slapping against mine.

I bowed my head, my hair falling into my eyes. The raven shrank as it flitted down my arm toward my hand, its wings scraping against the rose petals. It spread its wings when it reached the back of my hand, and Mark groaned my name as I held on tight. He pushed his hips up again harshly.

This had to work.

It had to.

I bent down over him so my head was just above his, tilting it to the side, exposing my neck. The rumble in his chest turned into a full-fledged snarl, and the song in my head become a cacophony of *gordo* and *yes* and *PackLoveMateMine*.

"Do it," I told him. "Fucking do it. I want you to. Christ, I want you to put your teeth in me—"

The wolf came forward. Claws dug in again, and fangs snapped, eyes orange, muscles tensing. I fell against him, the juncture between my neck and shoulder resting against his lips. My cock was trapped between us, rubbing against the muscles in his stomach.

I came first, and the petals of the roses shuddered and shook.

He fucked up into me one final time, legs trembling, and—
Mark Bennett bit down.

Pain flashed through me as his fangs sank into my skin. I gasped as it rolled over me, skin shredding, tendons crunching. The roses shriveled up, sinking back down into buds, the vines retracting, the raven opening its beak and screaming *nevermore, nevermore, nevermore.*

But then it—

here here here i could see i could see through a wolf's eyes everything bright and

i was young

i was a kid i was a

pup

i was a pup and my father said he loved me he loved me he loved me

he says your brother will be alpha but that doesn't make you any less special

you are good mark you are good you are kind you are loving and wonderful

thomas thomas thomas will be alpha but you will be

thomas said richard will be his second

not me

not me at all

i understand

don't i

i'm a wolf i'm a good wolf because my daddy said so

but thomas is

dirt and leaves and rain

there is

DIRT and LEAVES and RAIN

follow

save

protect

i must protect

from bad guys

bad wolves

gordo gordo gordo gordo and it's

gone it's all gone everything is gone because everything is blue

i could hear them

they were screaming
the pups the pups were screaming saying no please no please no
daddy daddy daddy
hurts it hurts oh my god it hurts
where where where is gordo where is
DIRT and LEAVES and RAIN and and and
gone they're gone thomas says they're gone but he is alpha he is
alpha he is my
hunt i must hunt for him biggest animal biggest i can find
so he knows
he knows i can provide
keep him warm
keep him safe
and
no please thomas
please don't make me go
please don't take me away from DIRT and LEAVES and RAIN and
thomas says
thomas says i have to
he says i have to go
gordo is gordo is gordo is HUMAN
they are scared of HUMANS
thomas says i can come back i can come back we will come back it
will not
it will not be forever
it will not be the end
why does it feel like the end
i love him
please don't let me go
please wait for me
please love me back
please please please
and he tells me
he tells me i have to go
tells me he doesn't want me
tells me he doesn't love me
tells me i'm like the others
like all the other wolves

it hurts
it hurts
it hurts but he's right
i didn't do what i could
didn't do more
he's
he's
he's

It was there, all of this. Everything. Jumbled and broken, more wolf than man. Everything he'd felt. Everything he'd thought. There was pain and wonder, sweet joy and dark jealousy. He'd been close, the last time he'd come to my house, the scent of another man's spunk on my skin. He'd been close to pushing right by me and finding the owner of the scent and sinking his claws into his throat until blood arced against the walls. He'd wanted to hurt me. He'd wanted to hurt me so badly.

Instead he'd walked away.

He didn't come back until after Joe had been saved from the beast.

And there'd been a moment, a brief and shining moment, when he'd seen me walking on the street, had heard my heartbeat again from inside the diner where Joe had put french fries under his lips and pretended to be a walrus. He'd told himself to stay away, had told himself that keeping his distance was the right thing to do, but he couldn't help himself.

And even though I'd been angry, even though I'd wanted nothing to do with him, just standing in front of me again after all these years—inhaling dirt and leaves and rain—had centered him like he hadn't been in years. He'd struggled for a long time with his tether. Thomas had told him for years (though never unkindly) that it might be best to change it, to find something else to latch on to.

Mark had *hated* his brother for that, even though he knew Thomas was right. He knew Thomas was only looking out for him, knew that Thomas was aware just how deep his grief ran. But he couldn't stop the anger he felt, and they'd *fought* then, fought like they'd never done before. It started out verbal, Mark's voice rising until he was *shouting* and Thomas remaining furiously calm like their father had always been.

Mark threw the first punch.

It landed with a crunch on Thomas's jaw, his Alpha's head snapping back. Later, much, much later, after his brother was nothing but smoke and ash, Mark would realize that Thomas hadn't moved. Thomas hadn't even *tried* to dodge. He'd taken it. He'd taken the hit as if it were penance. Mark had needed a focus for his anger, and Thomas had known that. Had *goaded* him into it. He had to have known the reaction he'd get. Gordo had been a topic they did not discuss.

Mark ended up on top of Thomas, hitting him again and again and again.

Thomas just took it.

By the time Mark finished, Thomas's face was a bloody mess and two of Mark's fingers were broken, jutting out awkwardly. He fell to the side, chest heaving as he lay next to his brother. They stared at the ceiling as their bodies healed, cuts closing and bones resetting.

"I'll never give him up," Mark said quietly.

"I know," Thomas said. "I know."

They never told anyone about it. That moment.

So, yes. Standing in front of me again after years was something he treasured, no matter what my reaction had been.

And it went on for *years*, after. But it didn't matter to him, not really. Oh, sure, it'd hurt sometimes, being so close and yet kept at such a distance. But he felt settled in ways he couldn't explain. Maybe it was being back in Green Creek. Maybe it was having Joe with them again.

Or maybe it was the fact that his mate was only a few miles away on any given day.

Until he wasn't.

The beast came, and Mark's Alpha lay on a pyre in the woods, wolves howling their songs of mourning around them, and he'd thought about that day again. That day where he'd gone after his brother, the rage that had long simmered below the surface finally boiling over. Thomas should have done more. Fought harder. For Gordo. For him. For all of them. He was the Alpha of all, yes, but he was the *Bennett* Alpha too, and there was a Bennett wolf whose heart was broken, and he'd just *taken* it. Even when his nose had snapped, even when his cheek had shattered, he'd lain there and *taken* it. Mark had been shouting down at him, telling him it was his fault, it was all his fault, how could he do this, how could Thomas do this to him.

After they'd healed and wiped away the blood to hide the evidence from Elizabeth (who, in the end, would still be able to smell it and would glare at the both of them without saying a word), Thomas had said, "I'll make this right. I don't know how. I don't know when. But I promise you, I'll do everything I can to make this right."

And I could *feel* it now. All of it. How ridiculously *proud* he was at this moment to have someone such as me as his mate, the love he felt, the dark, animalistic part of him reveling at his cock still up my ass, spunk dripping down the length. He wanted to roll in the scent of our sex that was thick in the room, covering us both in it until everyone knew what we'd done.

He was scared too. Oh Jesus Christ, was he scared. Scared that he'd finally gotten what he wanted and wouldn't be good enough. Scared that he wasn't brave enough or strong enough. Scared that he was going to lose all of this. That his tether and mate would disappear into the wolf when he turned Omega.

Because he didn't know what to do.

How to stop it.

It was there still, low and vibrating. Even now he could feel it. It wasn't as loud as it'd been before, but it was there.

And it terrified him.

This wolf.

This foolish, wonderful wolf.

I blinked slowly down at him. He stared up at me, a look of reverence on his face. My hand was still wrapped around his neck, though I wasn't holding on as tight as I had been.

He reached up, pressing his fingers against my face. "I never thought—" His voice broke. He shook his head before he tried again. "I never thought it could be this way. Feel like this. You—I saw things. Gordo. You—I'm so sorry. About everything. All of it. I'm so sorry."

I turned my face and kissed the palm of his hand. "You can't leave me."

"Never, never, never."

"I won't let you."

"I know."

"I'm too old for this shit."

And my god, how he *smiled* up at me. "Move good for an old man." He jerked his hips, causing my eyes to roll back in my head.

"Fuck," I muttered.

"Yeah." His fingers fell from my face to the bite mark between my neck and shoulder. It would scar, I knew. I'd seen Joe's and Ox's. Elizabeth's, though hers wasn't as pronounced as it'd once been.

Blood had trickled down from the wound onto my chest, bisecting the tattoo of the wolf and the raven. He ran his thumb down the wet stripe, smearing it into the ink.

The others were there. In my head. But they were faint. They would know what had happened. Know what we'd done. At least Ox and Joe would. They would know to stay away. Mark wouldn't want them coming here so soon after.

I moved my hand from around his neck and—

My eyes widened. "Holy shit."

"What? What's wrong?"

I coughed, a lump suddenly in my throat. I never thought of this. What it would mean for him. I wasn't a wolf. I couldn't bite him. Not like he'd done to me. It would have healed quickly, no matter the intent. He would not have carried my mark, not like I carried his.

I should have known it'd be something else.

There, embedded into the skin of his neck, was a raven, a near twin to the one on my arm.

It was no bigger than the width of my hand. Its wings spread to either side of his throat. Its head was bowed, resting over his Adam's apple, and when he swallowed it looked as if it was moving. Its talons and the fan of its tail feathers stretched toward the hollow of his throat.

I had his mark on me.

And now he had mine.

I reached down and touched the wings. They felt warm beneath my fingers.

"What is it?" he asked again, tilting his head back to allow me better access. "My throat is—it feels strange. Did you bruise me?"

I shook my head. "My magic, it—everyone will know now. Here. The tips of the wings go to here." I ran my finger along the length of the feathers. "And the head is here. The tail feathers here."

"A raven."

"Yes. I didn't—I didn't know that would happen."

"Does it look like yours?"

"Exactly like mine."

He pulled me down and kissed me, deep and slow. There was blue there, still. I thought maybe it was part of us. But it was quiet under all the green. "Good," he whispered against my lips. "Good, good, good."

OPEN THE DOOR / MAKE THEM PAY

I woke to a furious pounding on the door.

I opened my eyes slowly. It took me a moment to remember where I was. And what had happened.

My body was sore. My neck throbbed. Muscles ached.

But it was *more* than that. There was an undercurrent to it all, something wild that I couldn't get a grasp on.

It was dark. Snow lashed against the window.

I reached for Mark and—

The space next to me in the bed was empty.

And cold.

There again came a knocking at my chamber door.

"Nevermore," I muttered, groaning as I pushed myself up and out of the bed.

I found a pair of sweats on the floor and slid them on. The air was cool. My skin pebbled.

That undercurrent grew stronger.

I took a step and—

gordo can you hear

—I took a breath, groaning as the pounding in my head intensified, and I reached for the door, the chamber door, the bedroom door, the doorknob hot underneath my hand, and I *twisted* it, twisted it as hard as I could, throwing my shoulder against it and—

It opened.

But not into my house.

The sun was shining early morning light through a window off to my left.

The room I was in was small and tidy, the carpet underneath my feet cream-colored and thick. There was a kitchen off to the right, and a teakettle bubbled on the stove. I—

"Gordo."

It was like I was moving underwater. My limbs felt weighted and heavy. It took ages for me to turn my head to the right to see—

A witch sat in a high-back chair. His eyes were milky white, and his lips were moving quietly, mumbling words I couldn't quite make out. A tear trickled down his cheek.

Patrice.

The albino witch.

Next to him stood an older woman. One hand was on Patrice's shoulder. The other held a lit cigarette, the smoke curling up around her fingers.

Aileen.

"Can you hear me?" she asked.

I tried to say *yes, yes, I can hear you*, but it came out garbled, as if I were speaking through a mouthful of rocks.

"We don't have much time," she said, and one moment she was next to Patrice, and the next she was in front of me, blowing a thick ring of smoke in my face. "Patrice is barely holding on as it is. The witches around Green Creek are strong."

"What is this?" I managed to say.

The ember on the tip of her cigarette burned. Smoke leaked from her nose. "This is the last chance, boyo. I told you things were changing. I just didn't know how much. A wolf came to me. Stood right in this very room. He was white. Brighter than I'd ever seen before. Do you understand?"

No. I didn't. I didn't understand any of this. I didn't—

I was in my bedroom. There was—

Aileen slapped me across the face. "*Gordo*. Focus."

Everything was blue. Everything felt *blue* and *red* and oh my god, there was *violet*—

I grimaced at the throbbing in my shoulder. I reached up and pressed against the mark in my neck. The pain was heavy, and it grounded me.

Aileen shook her head. "You certainly don't do anything halfway, do you? There was a wolf, Gordo. He came to me. I knew him. Even though I'd never met him in this life, I knew him. Gordo, he said you have to open the door. You have to throw it wide open if you expect to survive this."

"The . . . door?"

"Yes," she said, and she sounded *frantic*. Patrice started seizing behind her, spit dribbling down his lips, hanging in a long string. "Shit. They've found him. Gordo, it's the *door*. You have to open the goddamn *door*. We're coming, okay? We'll do what we can, but he said you have to open the door. He said you'd understand. That I had to tell you nevermore and you'd understand. Thomas said *nevermore*—"

Thomas.

Thomas.

Thomas, Thomas, Thomas, because he was Alpha.

He was *packpackpack*.

The floor opened up beneath me and I—

I opened my eyes.

I was in my room.

My shoulder throbbed.

The bed next to me was empty.

I blinked, slow and sure.

The bedroom door was open.

The house was dark.

The light outside the window was weak, the snow still falling.

That undercurrent was still there, garbled and *strange*. It felt familiar, it felt like mine, it felt like *PackLoveMateHome*, but it was *twisting*, it was *twisting*, and I couldn't do anything to stop it.

The door, Aileen had said.

I have to open the door.

I didn't—

A creak of a floorboard from somewhere inside the house.

"Mark?" I whispered as I rose from the bed. I found a pair of sweats on the floor and quickly threw them on. "Mark, is that—"

I wasn't dreaming. I couldn't be dreaming. Not again.

If that had even *been* a dream.

I moved through the house. Everything seemed to be in its place. Nothing had moved.

Mark stood in the kitchen. His back was to me. He was nude, and his head was bowed. In his right hand he held the wooden raven.

"Mark?" I asked. "What's—"

He said, "*Gordo*," but it came out sounding harder than I'd ever heard him speak my name before. Animalistic. Meaner, filled with—

No. No, oh god, please no—

"You need to run," he said, his shoulders shaking. "I can't—I can't fight it. It's—"

There was a sharp *crack* as the wooden raven splintered. One of the wings fell to the floor.

The shift came over him slowly. Thick black claws grew at the tips of his fingers and toes. The muscles under his skin began to ripple. Chestnut-brown hair sprouted over his shaved head.

This wasn't supposed to happen. It wasn't supposed to end like this. Not now. Not after we'd come this far. Not when I wore his mark just as sure as he bore mine. It wasn't fair. It wasn't fair. It wasn't—

I took a step back.

He turned his head sharply, chin touching his right shoulder. I could make out one of the wings of the raven on his neck. He flexed his hands, and the carving he'd made for me when we hadn't yet known how much a heart could break fell to the floor in pieces.

He inhaled deeply.

I could see the fangs in the low light.

He opened his eyes.

They were violet.

It hadn't been enough.

I hadn't been enough.

He said, "Run, Gordo, please run, run so I can chase you, so I can *hunt* you, so I can find you and *taste* you and *fuck you with my teeth*—"

I was already running.

He howled behind me, the song reverberating through the bones of the house around us. I felt it deep in my skin, flashes of pain as if I were held down by an Alpha and my father was whispering his poison in my ears.

Outside. I needed to get outside.

Before I could reach the front door, it *imploded*, the wood cracking as a shifted Alpha burst through, eyes blazing red. He landed in front of me and my hands went into his fur, digging in deep. Ox, it was Ox, it was—

Ox knocked me to the side even as he began to shift toward human. There came the snarl of a feral wolf, angry and crazed, and I hit the floor, turning my head in time to see Ox catch Mark by the throat. His hand completely covered the raven on Mark's skin.

Mark tried to claw at him, tried to rip his skin apart. He kicked up with his feet to get at Ox's stomach, meaning to eviscerate and cause as much damage as he could. He missed, barely, as Ox raised him high above his head as far as he could stretch, before he slammed Mark onto the ground. The floorboards that the guys from the shop had helped me lay one long, hot summer years ago cracked loudly as Ox pushed Mark *through* them. Mark grunted painfully, and I knew his bones were already trying to put themselves back together.

Ox's eyes burned like fire as he roared in Mark's face.

The song of the Alpha, even as he bled onto the Omega wolf below him.

It startled Mark. His violet eyes widened and he cried, "Alpha. Alpha. Alpha."

Ox loosened his grip.

Mark immediately snapped his head toward me, violet flaring brightly, snapping his teeth.

Oxnard said, "I'm so sorry for this," and let go of his throat before bringing a closed fist down on the side of Mark's head.

Mark grunted and his body went slack.

And in the ruins of my living room, all we felt was blue.

He told me. How he felt it. How he felt it when Mark bit me. Felt it when we mated. It was a surge of power that rolled through him. Through Joe. Through the pack.

But it hadn't lasted.

"It started to splinter," he said quietly as we trekked through the snow. Mark was slung over his shoulder. "It started to fray. It was like . . . it was being poisoned. Shriveling. I hadn't felt it like that before. Not since they were infected."

The snow whispered down around us. It crunched under our feet. Somewhere above, hidden away behind the clouds, the moon grew fatter, calling out for her love, who always ran from her. She would be at her fullest soon enough.

"I thought," I said in a choked voice, "I thought it would help. I thought it would . . ."

"I know," Ox said, though he wouldn't look at me. "I know you did."

Thankfully he didn't say what we were both thinking.

That instead of slowing it down, we'd sped it up.

I followed my Alpha home.

Wolves waited for us at the house at the end of the lane.

They knew, of course. They had to. They could feel it just the same.

Carter stood off to the side, arms across his chest, face pinched and lined. Kelly was at his side, whispering in his ear, much to the consternation of the timber wolf that circled around them slowly, tail twitching. The moment it caught my scent, its hackles rose and it moved in front of Carter, trying to herd him away from me. Its violet eyes tracked every step I took.

Carter snapped at the wolf, trying to stand his ground. But the wolf was having none of it, watching me warily as I approached. I gave them a wide berth.

Joe stood with Elizabeth on the porch, arm around her shoulders. Her eyes were wide and wet, but no tears fell as she watched us come to stand in front of the house, a twisted inversion of the day her sons and I had returned to Green Creek.

I didn't know what to say to her. To them.

"Jessie?" Ox grunted.

"Down with Pappas," Joe said quietly. "Spreading another line of silver." His glanced at me before looking back at Ox. "She'll be ready."

"Dude," Carter said off to our right. "Would you knock it off? What the fuck is your *problem*?"

The timber wolf grumbled at him, still trying to push him away from me.

Ox nodded, hoisting Mark back up on his shoulder from where he was about to slip off. Mark's arms hung loose down his back.

"Did he hurt you?" Elizabeth asked, and for a moment I thought she was talking to Ox.

She wasn't. She was looking directly at me.

I shook my head, words stuck in my throat.

"Good. He . . . he wouldn't be able to forgive himself if he had. He's always been that way about you."

Goddammit.

"He didn't bite you, did he?" Joe asked Ox, and though he was trying to keep his voice even, it came out strained and high. He sounded like a kid again, the boy who Ox had called his tornado.

"No," Ox said. "He tried, but no."

Joe nodded tightly.

Elizabeth moved down the stairs as Ox approached. She ran a hand over Mark's bare back, trails of melted snow running down toward his shoulders. I saw the exact moment she became aware of the raven on his throat, her lips thinning, hand closing into a fist. The wooden steps creaked under their combined weight as Ox carried Mark into the house.

Joe turned to follow them, but he stopped before he reached the door. He looked like he was working himself toward something, and I dreaded whatever came out of his mouth next.

He said, "Carter."

Kelly hung his head.

Carter sighed. "I know. I just . . . I just wanted to be outside. For a little bit longer."

He tilted his head back toward the sky. Snow fell on his eyelashes, and he blinked it away. He took a deep breath and let it out slow. It streamed up around his face. Kelly reached out and took his brother's hand, their fingers interlocking. Carter looked over at him, expression softening. "It'll be all right. You'll see."

Kelly nodded jerkily.

"Hey," he said. "None of that now. Look at me. Please."

Kelly did. His bottom lip was trembling.

"It'll be okay," Carter whispered. "I promise."

"You can't know that."

Carter shrugged. "Yeah, but it sounds good, so. Go inside and help the others. Can you do that for me?"

Kelly's eyes narrowed. "Why?"

"I just . . . I need to talk to Gordo. I'll follow you in a second."

Kelly looked at me suspiciously. I kept my face blank. He dropped his brother's hand without another word and headed for the house. His mother touched his arm as he walked by. She leaned over and whispered something in his ear. He stood stiffly by her side until she finished speaking and kissed his cheek. She let him go, and he disappeared into the house.

Carter took a step toward me, but before he could get any closer, the timber wolf grabbed him by the coat, biting down and trying to pull him away. Carter slipped on the snow, turning over his shoulder to glare at the wolf. "Dude, I'm going to kick your wolfy ass if you don't leave me the fuck alone. I don't know what your deal is, but I don't like weird fucking ferals getting all up in my shit."

The wolf growled at him, jerking on his coat again.

"I need to talk to Gordo."

The wolf didn't think that was a good idea.

"Jesus *Christ*. Look, just . . . back off for a second, okay? This is my pack. No one here is going to try anything. Stop it, or I'm going to make Gordo blast you with his Force lightning."

The wolf let go of Carter's coat and snarled at me.

I rolled my eyes. "I don't have Force lightning. Why do I have to keep telling you all that?"

"Whatever," Carter said dismissively. "That's not the point. Stop trying to undermine my totally credible threats to this stranger wolf who doesn't understand the concept of *personal space*."

He took another step toward me.

The wolf growled at him.

He smacked it upside the head.

For some reason, it subsided.

"Of all the things I have to deal with now," Carter muttered, but the wolf stayed where it was as Carter approached me.

Elizabeth remained quiet.

Carter stood in front of me. He wasn't . . . The road had changed him. He'd become harder. Toward the end, we all had. But being back home, he'd softened, at least a little. Not as much as his brothers, but enough. He hadn't been who he once was, but none of them could be. Not after their father. Not after everything they'd seen.

But in the past year, he'd settled, somehow, in his skin. He was his Alpha's second, this brave boy who was fiercely protective of those he loved.

And now this.

I knew why Joe had called for him now.

Jessie wasn't just making a cage for Mark.

She was making one for Carter too.

He studied me, and I didn't know what he was looking for. He said, "It's . . . you felt it. I know you did. When we were on the road. You tried to fight it. I didn't know why, at first. I didn't understand. Everything you'd been through. And maybe I still don't know it all.

But somewhere along the way, you became pack. To me. To us. And I trusted you then to watch over my brothers and me. And when we got home, to watch over the rest of us. You didn't want it. This burden. And I'm sorry for that. But you have it anyway. Because you're family. My family." He shook his head. "And I need you to promise me something. Because I can't ask anyone else to do it."

"Carter—"

He held up his hand. "Just—listen. Please? This is hard enough as it is. I need—if you can't turn us back. If you can't . . . fix this, then I need you to promise me that you'll be the one. To—"

"Fuck you," I said hoarsely. "Fuck you, Carter."

He blinked rapidly. "I know. But I can't have . . . my mom and . . . Joe, just. And Kelly? Oh god, Gordo. Kelly is so . . . he's not like us. He's not an Alpha. He's not a second. He needs . . . just, please. Please just do it. For me. I can't be like that. I can't take the chance that I'll hurt anyone. It's not—"

I hugged him.

He was surprised. I'd never initiated anything like this before. Not with him. He felt . . . strange, pressed up against me, and I remembered the look on Elizabeth's face when I'd gone into her room that first time after he'd been born.

Would you look at that, she'd said. *He likes you, Gordo.*

And I'd promised him something then. As his little fist curled in my hair, I'd made him a promise.

You will be safe. I'll help keep you safe.

His arms came up around me, and he hugged me back.

Eventually he let me go.

He rolled his eyes as the wolf snarled behind him. "Yeah, yeah, you asshole. Shut up already."

He kissed his mother on the cheek as he headed toward the house, a gigantic feral wolf trailing behind him.

Only Elizabeth and I remained out in the snow, the morning light weak around us.

I didn't know what to say to her. What was right. What was wrong. Her son had just asked me to end his life if it came down to it, and she'd stood silent in the face of it.

In the end, it didn't matter. She spoke first.

She said, "The others are at the bar still. Robbie too, though he wasn't very happy to let Kelly out of his sight."

"Of course he wasn't," I muttered. "How are the humans taking it?"

"Disbelief, I think. Most of them. I think they're trying to convince themselves it wasn't what it appeared. Some of them, though. They're not . . . afraid. They're curious. Bambi especially. I think I like that girl."

"Rico's got his hands full, that's for sure."

"Quite. But they're handling it, for now. No one is trying to leave the Lighthouse, and there haven't been any threats against us. If anything, we had to stop them from trying to leave to take on the hunters themselves. I don't know what it is about this place, but it certainly fosters men to behave like fools. Robbie argued with Ox about being separated from Kelly. Threatened him, even. I'm not sure Kelly knew what to do with that."

"Kid is kind of an idiot that way."

"He's not the only one."

"Yeah, about that. How long do you think it's going to be before Carter figures it out?"

A little smile appeared on her face. "Oh, I expect it'll take some time. I love my children, but they can be a bit naïve when it comes to certain things. But I wasn't talking about Carter."

I scowled at her. "Do we really have to do this now?"

"You're Mark's mate. Of course we do."

"I didn't— I thought it would— I didn't mean to—"

"I know," she said. "But leave it to you to wait until the last possible second to pull your head out of your ass."

"He's . . . he didn't mean it. When he hit you. He would never—"

"Of course he didn't," she said, not unkindly. "And once everything is good again, I will make sure to have my revenge."

I deflated slightly. "He's all I've got left."

She huffed out a breath. "I know you're stupid, Gordo, but you can't possibly be *that* stupid."

I snapped my head up and glared at her. "I don't—"

"Do you remember what I told you before you left with my sons?"

"You told me you trusted me with your sons."

"Yes. And I meant that."

"You also said you would rip me apart if I betrayed that trust," I reminded her.

"And I meant that too," she said, eyes flashing orange. "But that was the only way you would have understood me, Gordo. If I'd said it any other way, you wouldn't have believed me. For the longest time, you dealt only in threats. For the pack. And then against us. Against yourself. Thomas . . . he was to blame for that. Maybe not completely, but a large part. And that is something he never forgave himself for. He loved you, Gordo. He loved you. He came to you when he needed you most. With Joe. He knew that even though you were so angry at him, that you had such rage in your heart, that deep down, you were still the Bennett witch, even if neither of you could say it out loud. Men are stubborn that way. Ridiculous and stubborn."

"He threatened me. Told me if I didn't help, he'd—"

"Because that's the only thing you would have responded to," she said. "But you're not that person anymore. You haven't been for a long time. You protected my sons. You brought them all home. You made yourself a pack, and even if you didn't believe it, they believed in *you*. None of us, Gordo, none of us would be the same without you. And Mark? Mark has loved you since he knew what love *was*."

"But I couldn't," I told her, needing her to understand. "In the end, I couldn't protect them. If this is him, if this is my father, then he's doing this because of me. Carter and Mark and—"

"You are *not* your father," she said fiercely. "You're so much more than he could ever be. You have a pack, Gordo. You have the strength of the wolves behind you. You have the humans, those wonderful humans who would follow you anywhere. Can't you see? What my son just asked of you wasn't because he thinks you'd be the only one who could do it. He—he asked you because he knew he could trust you. In the end, he asked you because there was no one else he trusted more. Just like his father. Just like me."

I bowed my head.

She cupped my face. "You are not alone, Gordo. You haven't been for a long time. It's only now you're finally seeing that. You've felt this way for too long, and I'm sorry for that. I'm sorry for everything."

She wiped away the single tear that trickled down my cheek. She tilted my face up until I could look her in the eye. "But I know something they don't. And I think you know it too. Don't you?"

I nodded slowly.

"We're not going to let it get that far, are we?"

"No."

"Because this is our town. This is our pack. And no one is going to take that away from us. Not again."

The roses on my arm began to bloom. I felt their petals expanding on my skin. "Never again."

Her eyes were shining orange. "Not witches. Not hunters. Not an Alpha who wants what has never belonged to her. And not your father."

"No. None of them will."

She nodded slowly. "You know something, don't you? I can feel it. Through the bonds. It's dark under all that blue. But it's there."

And I hesitated.

"Gordo?" she asked. "What is it?"

There was a wolf, Gordo. He came to me. I knew him. Even though I'd never met him in this life, I knew him. Gordo, he said you have to open the door. You have to throw it wide open if you expect to survive this.

We're coming, okay? We'll do what we can, but he said you have to open the door. He said you'd understand. That I had to tell you never-more *and you'd understand. Thomas said—*

"Nevermore," I breathed.

"He used to say that about you. When we were alone." Elizabeth Bennett looked upon me with the wolf crawling underneath her skin. "'Tell me, I implore!' / Quoth the Raven 'Nevermore.'"

And all I felt buried in the deep, deep blue was *pack* and *pack* and *pack*.

.   .   .

Jessie said, "It's happening, isn't it."

She was leaning against the wall near the cellar door. She looked as tired as I felt, but she was carrying herself high and proud. Like a wolf.

"I think so."

She nodded slowly. "Can we beat this? All of this?"

"I don't know. But we're going to fight like hell."

She pushed herself off the wall, leaning forward to kiss me on the cheek. "I'm glad you got your mystical moon magic mate."

I scowled at her.

She wasn't fooled.

"Elizabeth is waiting for you outside. Get to the bar. Bring the rest of the pack home. Stay out of sight."

She eyed me curiously. "What are you going to do?"

I looked at the cellar door. I could hear the sounds of wolves beneath us. "What I have to."

.   .   .   .

"We don't need the wolves," my father had told me once. "They need us, yes, but we have never needed them. They use our magic. As a tether. It binds a pack together. Yes, there are packs without witches. More than have them. But the ones that *do* have witches are the ones in power. There's a reason for that. You need to remember that, Gordo. They will always need you more than you could ever need them."

My father had never understood. Even when he had pledged himself to Abel Bennett, he hadn't understood. What it meant to be tied to a wolf. What it meant to be pack. It wasn't about necessity.

It was about choice.

He hadn't given me one.

Neither had Abel Bennett.

Thomas Bennett had. In the end. I was just too blind to see it through the fury I felt at everything that was being taken away from me.

He'd been wrong to do it the way he had.

But in the end, I'd been given a choice.

I'd said no.

He had threatened me. I wasn't lying when I'd told Elizabeth that.

But there'd been more. After fang and claws and red, red eyes.

"My son," he'd told me. "Please, Gordo. It's Joe. It's my *son*. Please help me."

He'd fallen to his knees then, tilting his head back, exposing his neck.

The Alpha of all, *begging* me to help him.

I'd almost turned and left him there, on the ground.

And I half think he expected it.

But it was there, wasn't it?

Deep down, buried in an ocean of blue.

That *spark* that demanded my Alpha.

I'd forgotten how bright it burned.

"Get up," I'd told him roughly. "Get up. Get up, and I'll help you."

I chose him then. Chose to help him.

Even after everything.

It wasn't about necessity.

We were pack because we chose to be.

And I wasn't going to let that go without a fight.

I knew now what needed to be done.

I just hoped they would be able to forgive me.

Pappas prowled along the line of silver spread out in front of him, boxing him in. The metal wall behind him was scored with thick claw marks. He snarled at the sight of me, throwing himself against the invisible wall that held him in.

Carter and Kelly stood face-to-face, the silver running between them on the floor. Kelly reached up and pressed his hand against the wall. Carter hesitated before doing the same. The timber wolf was trapped inside with him, pacing behind him, tail flicking dangerously.

And Mark.

Always Mark.

He sat nude in the middle of the floor, eyes closed. He was awake, and his hands were on his knees, digging into his skin. The raven on his throat fluttered every time he swallowed. Ox was crouched on the other side of the line of silver before him, watching him intently.

Joe touched Ox's shoulder, causing him to look back. He stood as I approached, nodding toward Mark. "It's like it was with Pappas," he said quietly. "The lull before . . ."

I nodded tightly.

Joe squinted at me. He reached out and pressed his fingers against my forehead. "It's in here, isn't it? Something's happened."

I nodded, and his hand fell away. "I . . . might have a plan. But it's going to take all of us, I think. And you're not going to like it."

Joe frowned. "What is it?"

"It's . . . we need to wait. For the others. Elizabeth and Jessie, they'll . . . We just need to wait. I only want to say this once."

Ox stared at me. "Will it help them? Carter. And Mark."

"I don't know," I said truthfully. "But it's the only thing I've got.

Tomorrow's the full moon. There's not time. I just . . . can you give me a moment? I need to . . ."

Ox and Joe stepped back.

I took a deep breath and turned to Mark.

I sat down on the floor, mirroring his position. My eyes burned when I looked at him, but I couldn't do anything to stop it.

"Mark," I said. His name on my tongue broke into pieces, and I cleared my throat.

He opened his eyes. The violet had faded. All that was left was the frozen blue. "Gordo," he rumbled. "I—I'm sorry. I tried to fight it. I tried to—"

"It's okay. I'm okay. You didn't—you didn't hurt me."

He looked stricken. "If Ox hadn't been there—"

I snorted. "I don't need Ox to kick your ass, you overgrown mutt. I can handle myself just fine."

His jaw clenched. "This isn't a joke, Gordo."

"Good thing I'm not joking. If you think you can take me in a fight, you're even dumber than I thought you were."

"I wanted to hurt you," Mark said. "I saw you lying in the bed next to me sleeping and I wanted to tear your throat out. I wanted to stain my teeth with your blood. It was close, Gordo. You don't know how close it was."

"But you didn't."

His claws extended, digging into his knees. "Because it burned."

I frowned. "What did?"

He tilted his head back slightly, exposing the raven. "This. I thought—it felt like it was flying in the sun, and it *burned*."

"That's because I'm your mate, jackass. You're bonded to a Livingstone now. The only way you get out of this is if I kill you myself, just like dear old Dad."

"Do it, then. Kill me."

And I said, *"No."*

His eyes flashed violet.

"Gordo," Ox said as he took a step toward us.

I turned and glared at him over my shoulder. "Don't. Stay back."

Ox looked like he was going to argue, but Joe put his hand on his arm, and he nodded.

I looked back at Mark. His knees were bleeding from his claws. "Do you trust me?"

"Yes," he growled. "But I can't trust myself. It's here, Gordo." He reached with a bloody claw, tapping the side of his head. "It's taking you away from me. I can feel it. It hurts. It hurts like nothing I've ever felt before. And I'm trying to hold on. I'm trying to hold on to it as best I can. But it's slipping through my fingers. I want you. I want you so bad." He snapped his teeth at me.

I said, "Let go."

That startled the violet out of his eyes. "What?"

"Let me go."

Ox said, "Gordo, you need to—"

I held my hand up over my shoulder, and he fell quiet. "Give in to it."

Mark snarled at me. "You would like that, wouldn't you? Mated to me for less than a day and you're already looking for a way out. You running again, Gordo? Just like always. Things get rough and Gordo Livingstone just fucking *runs*."

I tilted my head to the side, trying to remain calm. "I'm not going anywhere. Listen to my heartbeat. Tell me if I'm lying."

He stood slowly. His knees popped. His chest heaved. His eyes flickered between ice and violet.

Pappas threw himself at the line of silver again. I thought I heard a bone snap.

Carter stood stock-still, nostrils flaring as he stared at me. The timber wolf stood at his side. Kelly was watching me with a look of horror, as if he couldn't believe what he was hearing.

"Why?" Mark demanded, pacing back and forth. "Why are you here? Why are *any* of you here? You don't want me. You don't *need* me. I'm losing my goddamned *mind*, and you're just sitting there like it's *nothing*."

"I don't need you."

He rushed forward, and I had to fight to keep from flinching. "Why!" he shouted at me. "Why! Why!" Each *why* was punctuated with a fist against the barrier.

I stood slowly.

He tracked my movements, ever the predator.

I stood before him. Only a few feet separated us.

"Because I chose you instead," I told him quietly, and he reared back. "We never needed each other to survive. If we did, we would have both been dead a long time ago. It's never been about that, Mark. We're here now because we chose each other. In the end, it's always been about choice. We chose to fight each other until we chose to fight together. You chose me a long time ago. And now I'm choosing you back."

Conflicting emotions battled on his face: incredulity, sadness, anger, and hope. "I don't—"

"You broke the raven you made for me."

His face crumpled and his shoulders shook. "I know. I know, and I will never forgive myself for—"

"Do you still have it?"

"It's *broken*, Gordo, it's on the floor and it's *broken*—" Coherency dissolved, words becoming garbled snarls.

"The stone wolf. The one you gave me a long time ago. And the one I gave back. Do you still have it?"

He looked up at me, eyes wet and wild. "I . . . yeah. Yes." His chest hitched. "I still have it. It hurts, Gordo. It hurts."

"You're going to give it to me, okay? When all this is done, I'm going to ask that you give it back to me. And if you think that's all right, if you think that's the right thing to do, I promise you I'm going to take care of it for the rest of our days."

He pressed his hand flat against the barrier. "Show me," he said through a mouthful of fangs.

I knew what he meant. I tilted my head to the side and stretched the collar of my coat until he could see the bite mark. It was throbbing angrily, and I relished each pulse of pain that shot through me.

"I'll give you my wolf, witch," he growled. "If I don't kill you first."

I grinned at him nastily. "I'd like to see you try."

The ice-blue was gone.

All that was left was violet.

"What are you doing?" Ox asked me angrily. "What the hell are you doing, Gordo?"

I stared at Mark as his half shift came over him and he began to prowl along the line of silver, narrowed gaze trained on me. "I'm going to make them pay. All of them."

SHATTER

It was midday before the others returned. I'd stayed down in the basement, watching Mark as he descended. It was slow going, and painful, and I knew that if this didn't work, I probably wouldn't last long enough to live to regret it.

Kelly was furious with me, daring me to do the same with Carter, daring me to try to make his brother feral. Joe barely held him back. I ignored them both, focusing everything I had on Mark. Kelly had broken down in tears, and Carter had tried to console him, but he was breathing heavily, tense and stiff. The timber wolf with him kept pressing against his shoulder until Carter snarled at it to stay the fuck away from him.

Ox hadn't moved, and I could feel him staring at the back of my head. Jumbled emotions poured through the bonds between us. He was angry with me and saddened at the sight before him. But he *knew* me, knew I wouldn't do what I'd done without a reason. He was still holding on, still trusting me, and I hoped it was enough.

"They're here," Ox said, and a moment later, there came the sound of a door being thrown open at the front of the house. Footsteps thundered overhead, heading toward the stairs. Ox's eyes flared brightly. "But not all of them. Something's wrong."

Robbie came down first, looking frantic. He must have felt Kelly's anguish, because he looked like he wanted to shred the cause of it. I hoped Kelly wouldn't sic him on me. Granted, it would have given me an excuse to break his glasses, but I'd hate to have to hurt the kid right off the bat.

He stood in front of Kelly, reaching up like he wanted to touch him, but he closed his fingers into fists and brought them back to his sides. "Are you okay?" he asked in a hushed voice. "I tried to get here as fast as I could, but Elizabeth said we needed to move together, and she wouldn't let me shift, and then we got attacked and—"

"I'm fine," Kelly said through gritted teeth. "What do you mean *attacked*?"

"Hunters," Robbie said, face pale. "They found us when we were halfway here. I should have—but I was trying to get back here and I didn't hear them. I didn't *hear them*. I'm sorry. I'm so sorry."

My blood ran cold. "Who?" I managed to ask. "Who did they—" Elizabeth came down next. And she wasn't alone.

She had an arm wrapped around Rico's back, trying to hold his weight up. Jessie was on his other side, arm around his waist. Rico's face was pinched and he was gritting his teeth. His left pant leg was soaked with blood.

Ox and Joe were in front of them before anyone could speak. Elizabeth and Jessie handed him off to the Alphas. "I'm fine," Rico muttered, trying to put on a brave face. "Just clipped me. Looks worse than it is."

"Those bastards," Jessie growled, hair hanging in wisps around her forehead. "I'm going to *kill them*."

"We'll get the hunters," Joe told her, kneeling in front of Rico. "We'll—"

"Not the hunters," she snapped. "Although you bet your ass we will. I'm talking about Chris and Tanner. I'm going to fucking *murder* them."

I looked back at the stairs, waiting for them to appear. "What did they do now?"

She whirled on me, looking furious. "They—they—goddammit, what is with the men in this pack? Why are you *like* this?"

"They told us to run," Robbie said quietly, looking down at his hands. "Told us to get away. They . . . the hunters surprised us. A group of them. Elijah wasn't there, but . . . Rico was hit, and Chris took Rico's gun and told us to run. That we needed to get Elizabeth away from them." He took in a shuddering breath. "Chris said he didn't want Elizabeth to ever be hurt by them again."

Elizabeth reached up and wiped a sweaty lock of hair from Rico's face. "They were very brave. They gave us time to get away."

I barely knew I was speaking. "Are they . . . are they still alive?"

"Yes," Ox said, watching as Joe tore Rico's pant leg. "They're still alive. I didn't . . . I was so focused on Mark and Carter that I didn't even feel them being taken." He breathed heavily out his nose. "They're alive. And angry."

"The Lighthouse," Carter asked, voice harder than I'd ever heard it. "Do the hunters know about the Lighthouse?"

Rico shook his head, groaning as Joe pressed his fingers around the wound on his leg. "Don't think so. We were far enough away. Covered our tracks. Bambi, she—anyone tries to come for them will get a face full of buckshot. She's hard-core like that."

"It's not bad," Joe told Ox. "Winged him. Took a chunk out, but the bullet isn't in him."

"Told you," Rico said as he grimaced. "Lucky shot, anyway. If Chris hadn't taken my gun, I would have shot the bastard between the eyes. *Pendejo*. Had sideburns. You know how I feel about sideburns."

"Jessie," Ox said, "get the med kit. We need to get this cleaned and wrapped."

Jessie nodded, turned, and ran back upstairs.

"Great," Rico muttered. "Because that's going to feel good."

"Shut up," I told him, nudging Joe out of the way. "It'll scar. Bambi seems like the type that likes scars."

He perked up at that. "You think? Because if she gets over the whole I-run-around-with-werewolves thing, that'd be pretty cool and—oh my god, why are you *touching* it? I'm *bleeding*, Gordo!"

I pressed my palm flat against the wound. The raven's talons tightened around vines and thorns as I pulled the pain as best I could. It rolled through my arm and into my chest, wrapping itself around my heart and squeezing.

And then Elizabeth said, "Mark?" and I hung my head.

Mark growled in response.

"What happened?" she asked, and everything felt blue coming from her. "Why is he—"

"It was Gordo," Kelly spat, sounding furious. "Gordo made him like this. Gordo made him turn into an Omega and—"

"That's *enough*," Ox said, and everyone fell silent. Jessie came back down the stairs, white box clutched against her chest. The mood had shifted drastically in the few seconds she'd been gone, and she kept her mouth shut as she knelt next to me. She moved my hand, and Rico hissed as the pain returned. I stood slowly, letting her take over.

Elizabeth was watching me with an inscrutable expression. "Gordo?" she asked. "Is that true?"

I took a deep breath. "It is."

Her eyes flashed orange, but that was all. "Why?"

Kelly glared at me as Robbie stood at his side, looking confused. Carter paced behind them, the timber wolf acting as his shadow. Pappas was sitting in a corner, mewling loudly. Ox and Joe stood side by side. Rico yelped as Jessie did *something* to the wound on his leg.

And Mark.

Mark stood in the center of his cage. He was caught in his shift, though he was still more man than wolf. His bottom lip was bleeding from where a fang had pierced it. And his eyes were violet. So violet.

"Do you see the mark on his neck?" I asked her.

She nodded tightly. "The raven."

"Do you know what that means?"

"Yes."

"Then you know I would do anything for him."

"Would you?" she asked. "Why now? Why after all this time?"

"Because if this is the end," I said as honestly as I could, "he needed to know that I never stopped loving him."

My heartbeat, though accelerated, remained steady.

And she knew it.

Kelly scoffed. "You *forced* him to turn Omega. You told him to let go. How the hell can you say that you—"

Elizabeth said, "Kelly," and he subsided, though he still looked murderous. I hoped he would forgive me for what I was about to do. "Why?"

I swallowed thickly. "You know why."

"Not good enough," she said, and oh, she was *angry*. "After everything we've been through, that's not good enough, Gordo Livingstone. You will say it. Now."

I knew what she was asking for, and it was the least I could give. "Because he's my mate."

She wiped her eyes. "You were his choice. You always were. Even when—even when he thought you would never choose him back. Even when you thought otherwise, he always chose you."

"I know."

"Did you choose him back? Or was this all part of a plan? Are you using him?"

You can't trust a wolf.

They don't love you.

They need you.

They use you.
The magic in you is a lie.

Except it wasn't. My mother hadn't understood. But that hadn't been her fault. She had been fooled by my father, just as the rest of us had. And in the end, she did the only thing she could.

"I chose him," I told her. "And I would do it again. And if this works, if this will do what I think it will, then we may still have a chance. *They* may have a chance. The hunters, they—they gave us until the full moon. And they have our friends. Our pack." Those crazy, brilliant men. "We're outnumbered. Maybe we could take them head-on. Maybe we could win. But the weapons they have can put down a wolf in seconds. We need to even the odds." It was now or never. "We need to open the door."

They were confused. I expected that. They weren't thinking like I was. They didn't know what I did. And the idea was so abstract that it was a struggle to even understand it to begin with.

Ox understood first. He knew what it would mean. "The door," he repeated. "Are you sure?"

I nodded.

Joe looked between us, eyes narrowing. "What are you—no." He took a step forward. "You can't possibly be thinking of—"

Ox put a hand on his shoulder. "We need to listen."

"What's he talking about?" Kelly demanded, ignoring Robbie when he tried to soothe him. "What does he want to do?"

"The moment before Richard Collins died," I said. "After he . . . hurt Ox, he became an Alpha. But before that, the Omegas had already gathered behind him. Whether or not some of them were infected, I don't know. But I have to believe some of them were. He was . . . like Ox."

The wolves growled.

I raised my hands, trying to placate them. "Not . . . look. Ox was an Alpha without even being a wolf. We know that. Richard was . . . not the same, but it was close. Two sides of the same coin. The Omegas followed him. He *controlled* them. An Alpha without actually *being* an Alpha. Until he took it from Ox. You know what happened then."

"Mierda," Rico muttered as Jessie finished wrapping his leg. "It was bad. Like a storm in my head. Could feel them. Bugs crawling on my brain."

I nodded. "Because Richard became your Alpha."

"Until I killed him," Joe said. "And gave it back to Ox."

"And I took them with me," Ox said, glancing at Joe before looking back at me. "The Omegas. Until we closed that door."

"We locked it tight," I agreed. "Some still managed to make it through. It was why Omegas showed up here every now and then. They felt Ox pulling them, even when he wasn't meaning to. Michelle Hughes wasn't wrong when she said that Green Creek became a beacon. But she doesn't know just how far it goes. Just how bright it could be."

"So, what," Kelly snapped. "You want to unlock the door? Are you out of your mind?"

"No," I said coolly. "I don't want to unlock it. I want to shatter it to pieces. Ox needs to become Alpha of the Omegas."

The only sounds came from feral wolves.

Then Rico said, "Okay, like. No offense, papi. You know I love you. Bros for life, and all that. But did you go a little nuts in your head from the mystical moon magic? Because it seems like you went a little nuts in your head from the mystical moon magic."

"Try it, witch," Kelly said, eyes flashing. "You just try it."

Robbie said, "Kelly—" but the wolf snapped, "*No.* No, no, I won't let you. I won't let this happen. Can't you see what will happen? It'll *pull* on them. On the Omegas. On Mark. On *Carter.* It will force them further. They will both be completely feral. I don't care if it's magic. I don't care if it's something else. You can't do this." His voice broke. "You can't take them away from me. You can't have Carter."

"Hey," Carter said, taking a step forward. He growled angrily when he bumped into the line of silver, unable to reach his brother. "Kelly. Come on, man. It's not—"

"Don't," Kelly said hoarsely. "Don't do this. Please. Not you."

Carter shrugged awkwardly. "It's—I'm already losing it, here." He tried to smile, but it collapsed before it could reach his eyes. "I'm holding on, but it's a losing battle."

"No," Kelly said, shaking his head furiously. "There has to be another way. I'll find it. I don't know how, but I will. I won't let you do this. I won't."

"I know you're scared—"

"You're damn *right* I am!" he cried, slamming his fists against the barrier between them. "What if we can't fix this? Carter, what if you—what if you can't come back?"

"I will," he said. "I promise. Ox, or Joe, or Gordo. One of them will find a way. I know it. But it's . . . it's already taking you away from me. But if Ox can still be my Alpha, even if I'm an Omega, then we have to take that chance. Because if he's still my Alpha and he's yours too, that means we're still connected, even if I can't feel it anymore. You'll still be a part of me. And I have to believe that will be enough to bring me home."

The tears spilled over, and Robbie wrapped an arm around Kelly's shoulders, holding him as he sobbed.

I looked away, my own heart breaking. If this didn't work—or even if it did—and I couldn't find a way to bring them back, Kelly would never forgive me. And I wouldn't blame him. I would never forgive myself.

"You mean to use them," Ox said, and I was very tired. "The Omegas. You want to call them here. To Green Creek. To weaponize them."

"You said we were in a war," I told him quietly. "And if that's the case, then we need an army."

"And after the hunters? What then?"

"I don't know," I admitted. "But if we don't do something about the hunters now, about Elijah, then there will be nothing left *to* worry about."

"I don't like this," he said.

"I know."

"Do you? Because you're asking me to do the same thing Richard Collins did. You're asking me to take control of a group of wolves who won't be able to say no. To *use* them."

"You're not him. You never have been."

His clenched his jaw. "You said we were the same. Sides of a coin."

"Yeah. But the difference is you aren't trying to take something away. You're trying to protect what's already yours." I shook my head. "Look, Ox. I can't pretend that this isn't messed up. Because it is. You see everything in black and white. As good and bad. And that's what makes you the Alpha that you are. But I can't do that. I can't. I'm not like you. I never have been, and I never will be. My conscience can't be as clear as yours. I've—done things. Things I'm not proud of. But I would do *anything* to keep my pack safe. To keep my *family* safe. And I'm asking you to do the same. Because it won't end with the hunters. There are always going to be more who try and take what doesn't belong to them. Witches. Michelle Hughes." I sighed. "My father. It won't—what would you do? To protect those you love?"

"Everything," Ox said, though I knew it hurt him to say. "I would do everything."

"I need you to trust me on this."

He sighed and closed his eyes. "The wards. Witches. Won't they keep the Omegas out? Can you even change them back?"

"Maybe not by myself. But others are coming."

Joe blinked. "What? What others? How can you know that? We're cut off from the outside."

I shrugged. "Magic." It was easier than telling him his dead father appeared in a vision to a witch in Minneapolis and she told me so in a dream. Maybe when things were all said and done. Maybe never.

Rico snorted. "Magic. Magic, he says. *Ay dios mío.* Our lives, man. Bambi is never going to forgive me, even with a sexy scar."

"I'm sure you'll figure it out," Jessie told him, patting him on the hand. "I've got faith in you." She frowned. "Maybe."

"Hey! I've been *shot*. You're supposed to be nice to me."

"You were grazed. And then let women carry you back."

"That's because I'm a feminist."

Jessie sighed.

"Can you do this?" Joe asked Ox.

Ox started to shake his head but stopped himself. "I don't—I think so. I'll need you." He reached out and took Joe's hand. "I'll need all of you. Especially if I'm going to . . . control them."

"Won't they go after Gordo?" Robbie asked, still standing close to Kelly. "If they're like the others, can you stop them from attacking him?"

"I'll do what I can," Ox said. "But it's not going to be easy."

"I can handle myself," I said.

"I can't believe you," Kelly said, and it *hurt* to hear the betrayal in his voice. "Any of you. That you'd do this to them. To Mark. To Carter."

Carter sighed. "Pretty sure I'm still in my right mind here. Well.

Mostly in my right mind. I can speak for myself." The timber wolf pressed its nose against his shoulder, and he shoved it away.

Kelly laughed bitterly. "Only because you're scared and don't see any other way."

"Kelly."

"Fuck you."

"Look at me."

Somehow, Kelly did.

"I am scared," Carter admitted, and I remembered them singing along with the radio, windows rolled down and a breeze blowing through their hair as we traveled farther and farther from our home. "Scared as I've been in a long time. Maybe ever. But you want to know what scares me even more than turning Omega?"

Kelly shook his head, lips in a thin line.

Carter smiled, though it trembled. "Losing you. That might scare me more than anything else in this world. If there's even a chance that we can beat this, even a chance that I can keep you safe for at least one more day, don't you think I'm going to do it? And I know you'd be doing the same for me if it was you in here. Don't try and tell me otherwise."

"You can't leave me."

Carter's smile widened. "Never. I still need to threaten Robbie some more. Did you know he sniffs you when he thinks no one is looking?"

"I do *not*," Robbie said, though he was blushing furiously and looking down at his feet.

Kelly glanced at Robbie, scandalized, before turning back to his brother. "You promise?"

"That he sniffs you? Yeah, man. He does it—"

"Carter."

Carter's expression softened. "Yeah, Kelly. I promise. I'll always come back for you."

"Elizabeth?" Ox asked.

She stood in front of her brother-in-law. He was almost against the barrier, growling lowly. He tapped his claws against his bare legs. The raven on his throat twitched with the tensing of his neck muscles. He watched her with violet eyes.

This was her family.

This was all she had left.

And when a wolf mother was backed into a corner, there was nothing she wouldn't do to protect what was hers.

Elizabeth Bennett said, "Do it. Shatter the door."

. . .

Kelly and Joe stood in front of Carter. The timber wolf wasn't pleased to have them so close, but it kept back behind him. They spoke quietly to each other, Joe's arm wrapped around Kelly's shoulders. Carter was trying to get Kelly to smile, but Kelly wouldn't look at him. I didn't know if he'd ever forgive me.

Robbie was at my side on the other end of the basement, away from everyone else. I knew he was working himself up to something, so I was giving him the time he needed. He was going to threaten me, and I'd let him. He had Kelly's back, after all.

So I was surprised when he finally said, "You're doing the right thing."

I grunted, because I didn't know what else to say.

"He might not see it, and maybe he never will, but you are."

"I don't give a shit."

Robbie rolled his eyes. "Yeah. Okay, Gordo." He pushed himself off the wall with a sigh. "If it makes you feel any better, I'll pretend to believe you."

He started to walk away.

I called after him.

He looked over his shoulder.

"You don't need those glasses," I said. "Take them off. You look stupid."

He grinned at me. "Love you too."

Idiot.

. . .

I looked away when Elizabeth stood before her son.

He tried to be brave. He really did. But when he couldn't reach her, when he couldn't touch her skin, his smile trembled and broke, and he—

"Fuck this," Jessie muttered, and before anyone could stop her, she was next to Elizabeth, using her foot to break the line of powdered silver.

Elizabeth threw herself at her son. He caught her, nose going to her throat as he inhaled deeply.

Jessie looked back at the rest of us defiantly.

No one said a word.

They left to give me time to center myself. To give me a moment to breathe.

Pappas prowled back and forth, tracking my every movement.

The line of silver in front of Carter had been restored. He sat on the ground, legs crossed. The timber wolf sat curled around him, tail on his legs. Carter looked down at it, resigned. He shook his head. "You know," he said, "I never thought . . . well. I don't know what I thought."

"About?"

He shrugged. "Everything."

"That's . . . vague."

"Right? I'm having hard time focusing."

"It's getting worse."

He nodded. "Yeah. Has been all morning. I . . . I didn't want Kelly to see. You know how he is."

"Yeah."

"You gotta take care of them for me, man. Just in case I—"

"I will."

He nodded and closed his eyes, leaning back against the feral wolf behind him. "It's been good, you know? Even through all the suck-age, we've got a good pack. I'm very lucky to have had that."

I looked away.

"Do what you need to do, Gordo. While you still can. He can hear you. I know he can."

I did too. It was violet, the bond between us, and it felt like it was hanging in tatters, but it still held, no matter how stretched thin it was. The bite mark on my neck throbbed as I came to stand before him.

He watched me, Mark did. My wolf.

The raven was ink black against his throat.

His eyes burned.

"I'm sorry," I told him quietly. "That it took me this long to get here. I should have—I should have done things differently. I didn't know how."

He cocked his head, sharp teeth bared.

"But we didn't come this far just to lose it now. And if you try to leave me after everything we've been through, I will hunt you down myself."

Carter sounded like he was choking.

I turned slowly to glare at him.

He shrugged. "Just . . . way to be romantic, you know? I don't know why I'm so surprised that you tell him you care about him by threatening him. You guys are ridiculous."

I rolled my eyes. "You'll learn about it soon enough."

His brow furrowed. "What? What are you talking about? I'm going to learn about what soon enough?"

I ignored him.

Mark took a step toward me.

I waited.

He tilted his head back toward the ceiling, exposing the raven. His nostrils flared as he tried to catch my scent through the silver. The violet in his eyes pulsed. He reached up and pressed his hand against the barrier.

"Gordo," he said, voice a deep rumble.

I smiled sadly at him. "Yeah. It's me."

"Gordo. Gordo. Gordo."

And deep in my head, along the frayed thread that stretched between us, I heard a wolf howling a song of the lost, trying to find his way home.

.   .   .

It was late in the afternoon when Ox sat on the floor in front of me in the basement of the house at the end of the lane. Behind him sat our pack, though we were down two members. Joe was immediately behind Ox, head bowed, forehead pressed against the back of Ox's neck. Behind him were Rico and Jessie, each with a hand on his shoulder. Elizabeth, Kelly, and Robbie sat closest to the wolves behind the lines of silver, each of them touching the humans in some way.

Mark was agitated, moving back and forth.

Carter still sat against the timber wolf, struggling to control his breathing.

Pappas was snarling, angrier than I'd ever seen him. I wondered if he was already too far gone to save.

My knees bumped against those of my Alpha.

It hadn't been like this when we'd shut the door and locked it. It'd been only the Alphas and me. I'd kept the others away because I didn't want the distraction.

I needed them now.

I needed all of them.

I took his hands in mine. He watched me carefully, always trusting. He wasn't that kid who'd never had a root beer before. He was my Alpha.

My brother.

My friend.

My tether.

He was afraid, though. It was small, and well hidden, but it was there. It was *you're gonna get shit for the rest of your life*. It was *you're not good enough*. It was *you're not strong enough*.

It was ghosts. It always came back to ghosts.

They don't love you. They need you. They use you. The magic in you is a lie.

And maybe they would always haunt us. Maybe we would never truly be free.

But their words were buried under the call of *packpackpack*.

I turned his hands over, palms up.

I pressed my own down against his.

He wrapped his fingers around my wrist.

I did the same to him.

We breathed in sync.

And I *pushed*.

The raven spread its wings.

The bonds between us all flared to life.

I heard them.

Even the ones who weren't with us. They whispered in my head, telling me they were here, they were here with us, with *me*. That no matter what happened, no matter what came down upon us, we were Bennetts, and this was *our* territory. This was *our* home. And no one was going to take that away from us.

We were the goddamn Bennett pack.

And our song would always be heard.

I pushed through everything, even as the vines and thorns began to tighten around my arm. I saw it—

heard it felt it touched it yes touched it because he is me and i am
him i am
  wolf
  i am
  alpha wolf
—and it was stronger than I expected it to be, stronger than it'd been before. There was Dinah Shore singing about how she didn't mind being lonely when she knew my heart was lonely too. There was Joe, Joe, skinny little Joe, saying it was pinecones and candy canes, it was epic and awesome. There was the quiet hum of an SUV underneath us, tires spinning on the road, and boy-wolves talking about how when they got home, there'd be mashed potatoes and carrots and roast, and all of us ignoring the tears on their faces. There was a woman, a wonderful woman, a *sweet* woman, saying there was a soap bubble in his ear, and they were *dancing*, oh god, they were *dancing* and everything was fine and nothing hurt. It was—
  too much it was too much it was too much for me for me for me to
  take
  i can't take it
  i can't do this
  i can't
  it's
—brighter then, and heavier, and there were brothers lying on top of each other, breathing each other in after being apart for so long. It was the feeling of a body heavy with child, a hand on the wide curve of a stomach, whispering sweet nothings of warm love. It was the way the humans felt amongst the wolves, like they'd once been lost but had finally found their way home. It was a wolf who didn't belong anywhere finally finding *somewhere* he could stay, somewhere he could call his own. It was so big, it was so much bigger than I thought it could ever be, so much—
  more
  i need
  more
  gordo gordo gordo
  pack
  brother

friend
love
mate
give him
more
give him
everything
more
more
more
—expansive than it should have been. It was the way we trained together, the way we laughed together, the way we ate together on Sundays because it was tradition. It was how we loved each other and would die for every single person in this pack pack pack.

It was a wolf who one day whispered to a wide-eyed boy *it'll be you and me forever* and *we are going to be our own pack* and *I will be your Alpha, and you will be my witch.*

You are my family.

This wolf.

This great white wolf.

They had held me down, yes. An Alpha. My father.

They had held me down while magic was etched into my skin.

I hadn't been given a choice.

My mother had seen that, in her own way.

And there.

There through the *they don't love you, they need you, they use you* spinning furiously around us all, stood a door.

It was strong, because I had made it that way. This was my Alpha and tether. My friend and brother.

It'd held.

I pressed my ear to the door.

On the other side, something scratched against it, snarling angrily.

Many somethings.

I stood upright.

I looked over my shoulder.

Behind me stood my pack.

All of them. Even Chris and Tanner, though they flickered in and out. I didn't know what it was costing them to be here, but I loved them more than I could ever say.

Here. With me. My people.

Whole and healthy and strong.

Chris said, "It's okay."

Tanner said, "We can feel it too."

Jessie said, "All of us."

Rico said, "Right here, papi. Right here with you."

Robbie said, "We won't stop."

Kelly said, "No matter what."

Carter said, "Because that's what pack does."

Elizabeth said, "That's what family is supposed to do."

Joe said, "We fight back."

Ox said, "And we never stop."

Mark leaned forward and kissed me sweetly. I closed my eyes, and it was dirt and leaves and rain and he said, "I love you, I love you, I love you."

And I believed him.

I believed all of them.

Because I was feral strong and wolf proud. There was magic coursing through my veins, singing as loud as I'd ever heard it.

I was Gordo Livingstone.

I was the witch to the Bennett pack.

I turned back toward the door.

In between the door and me stood a white wolf.

I hated him.

I loved him.

I was so angry with him.

And somehow I let it all go.

Somehow I forgave him.

"I'm sorry," I told him.

His eyes flared red as he *whuffed* in response.

"I need you now. Please."

He leaned forward, pressing his nose against my forehead, and I said, "*Oh.*"

I opened my eyes.

The wolf was gone. There was only the door.

But I could still feel him under my skin.

He was with us.

He would always be with us until the day we stood in a clearing and were together again.

But if I had my say, it would be a long time before that happened.

I didn't reach for the doorknob. It was useless to me. I wasn't going to open the door.

I was going to *break* it.

With the strength of the pack behind me, I pressed my palms flat against it.

Little pinpricks of light shot through the grain of the wood. They were Alpha red and Beta orange and Omega violet. There was the blue of all we had lost and the sweet green of relief that it had finally come to this.

My arms were covered in roses, an unkindness of ravens.

The roses bloomed.

The ravens flew.

And I *pushed*.

The door vibrated underneath my hands. The growling and scratching on the other side grew louder.

I pushed harder.

The door rattled in its frame, and I gritted my teeth as a bright pain lanced through my head, sharp and terrible. It was fighting back against me, the magic in my blood curdling.

It said, *I know what you're doing.*

I know what you think you'll achieve.

And maybe . . . maybe you'll win.

You are stronger than I thought possible.

But this is just a battle, Gordo. One tiny little fight.

There is still the war.

I will bring it to your doorstep.

I will take what is rightfully mine.

And there is nothing you can do to stop me.

You will lose, in the end.

You will lose everything.

I looked up at the door, and between my hands, between the pinpricks of light, the wood began to warp outward. I didn't understand what I was seeing, at least at first. I knew that voice. God, how I knew it. Once, while an Alpha wolf held me down, the same voice had told me it was going to hurt, it was going to hurt like nothing I'd ever felt before.

You'll think I'm tearing you apart, and in a sense, you're right. You have magic in you, child, but it hasn't yet manifested. These marks will center you and give you the tools to begin to control it. I will hurt you, but it's necessary for who you're supposed to become. Pain is a lesson. It teaches you the ways of the world. We must hurt the ones we love in order to make them stronger. To make them better. One day you'll understand.

One day, you'll be like me.

The wood *stretched* out between my hands, and it took shape. There was a nose and lips, and wooden eyes, and it blinked again, and again, and then the mouth moved. The face of my father said, "I see you. I see you, Gordo. I knew you would be something special."

I cried out as the pain in my head grew worse, as my father's *hands* appeared in the wood, reaching up and covering the backs of mine, squeezing until I thought my bones would turn to dust.

But my father had always underestimated a wolf pack. And I had mine behind me.

They howled. All of them. Even the humans.

My father's wooden eyes widened as his face split with a sharp *crack*, the door splintering.

He opened his mouth to speak, and I said, "*No.*"

The door shattered underneath my hands.

I was bowled over by a wave of violet rage, of rapacious violence.

And there, on the other side, stood—

I opened my eyes.

The others did the same, blinking slowly.

All except for Ox.

He breathed in and out. In and out.

I could feel them. All of them. My pack.

And more. So many more.

It was tornadic in nature, a self-contained storm that swirled in our heads and chests. I tried to find the edges, tried to find a way to contain it, but it was big, bigger than I thought it would be.

In the end, it didn't matter.

Because he was here.

A boy who had become a man.

He who had become an Alpha even before he felt the pull of the wolf underneath his skin.

Oxnard Matheson.

The Alpha of the Omegas.

Behind him, a choking sound.

I looked over his shoulder.

Kelly had crawled on his knees toward his brother.

Carter was on all fours, his palms flat against the stone floor. His head jerked side to side as his chest heaved.

"Carter?" Kelly asked, voice trembling.

Carter looked up, face elongating, eyes violet.

"Kelly," he growled. But it was the only thing he said before he shifted into a wolf.

It looked painful, probably more so than it'd been since the first time he turned.

The claws grew as his clothes shredded, bones popping, muscles shifting. He howled toward the floor as his back arched, hair sprouting along his skin under his tattered shirt.

It took only a minute, but it felt like it stretched on forever.

And when it was done, Carter was gone.

In his place stood an Omega.

But . . .

Somehow he was still *there*. With us. In our heads. Oh, his bonds that stretched out between all of us were tenuous, and they were *wracked* by the storm, but they held.

And next to him, in his own cage, was a large brown wolf with eyes of violet.

No one stopped me as I rose.

No one said a word as I walked between them toward the wolf behind the line of silver, the bite on my neck pulsing.

He watched me as I approached, eyes narrowing, fangs bared.

I stood in front of him, separated by an invisible barrier.

"I can feel you," I whispered. "You're still here. It's not the same, but you're still here."

I toed the silver, breaking the line.

He moved almost faster than I could follow.

But before he could reach me, Ox was at my side, half-shifted and roaring, catching Mark by the scruff of his neck and slamming him back down to the ground.

Mark tried to bite at him, tried to scratch and wiggle free.

Ox bent over him until they were almost face-to-face.

He growled and flashed his eyes, which swirled with a mix of red and violet.

And Mark just . . . stopped.

He was still filled with rage, roiling and mean, but it poured into Ox and was *muted*, like a feedback loop where the volume was lowered on one side.

Ox stood up slowly, letting Mark go.

Mark pushed himself up from the floor.

When he was shifted, when he was a wolf with eyes of orange or ice, I could still hear him in my head, singing my name, thinking thoughts of a wolf, however primitive.

That was gone now.

Everything from him was primal.

Feral.

His nostrils flared as he looked at me, growling lowly.

But he didn't come for me.

"Okay," I said. "Okay."

We stood in front of the house at the end of the lane.

The blue house across from us was dark.

Ox watched it without speaking.

I said the only thing I could think of. "She would be proud of you. Of who you've become."

He turned his head slightly to look at me. He was still Ox, but there was something *more* about him now. Something bigger. I had known Alpha wolves my entire life. It'd never been like this. He radiated a power larger than any other wolf I'd known. He was containing it, somehow. All the Omegas. They would hear him. They would listen.

And yet he smiled quietly at me. "I wonder sometimes. If that's true."

"You don't have to wonder. I know it, Ox. Maggie." I swallowed, forcing the remaining words out. "Thomas. Both of them. They knew before everyone else, I think. Who you were. And who you would be."

"I heard him. Your father."

I looked away, eyes stinging.

He took my hand in his. "Maggie was my mom. Thomas was my dad. I am who I am because of them. Because of Joe. Because of this pack." He squeezed my hand. "And because of you. You are more than you think, Gordo. And I have never been happier to say that your father is not proud of who you've become. That's a good thing, in case you didn't know."

I laughed wetly. "Yeah?"

"Yeah."

"Thanks, Ox."

He looked back at the blue house. "Will this work?"

"It has to."

He nodded. "What now?"

I glanced over my shoulder, hearing the rest of the pack exiting the house. Jessie and Rico came down the stairs first. Rico batted her hands away as she tried to help him. She rolled her eyes and muttered about not helping him if he fell down the stairs.

Robbie came next, holding Elizabeth's hand. She was pale, but she carried herself regally. Her eyes were orange. She was ready to fight.

Joe came next, taking a moment to breathe in the cold air. The snow had finally stopped, and the clouds were beginning to clear. Above, the light in the sky was beginning to fade. Stars appeared like chips of ice. The porch steps creaked under him as he descended, coming to stand next to his mate. He kissed Ox's shoulder but stayed silent.

Kelly and Carter followed, Kelly's hand pressed against his brother's back. Carter was skittish, eyes continually flashing violet. The timber wolf trailed behind them, crowding against Carter, trying to keep him away from the rest of us. Carter snapped at him, but the wolf remained by his side.

Mark was last. The muscles under his skin shifted with every step he took. His claws dug into the wood of the porch as he stood above us. His eyes never left me, always watching. Waiting. I wondered if I were to push the hair around his throat away if there would still be a raven there, hidden away. I wasn't going to take the chance of trying to look, as he seemed confused as to whether he wanted to rub against me or kill me.

Two of us were missing.

But we would get them back.

The hunters had made a mistake in coming here.

Michelle Hughes had made a mistake in sending them.

And my father had made the gravest mistake of all.

His time would come. One day.

"Gordo?" Ox asked. "What now?"

I looked at our pack before I turned back to him.

I said, "Now you howl. As big and loud as you've ever howled before. Bring them here. The Omegas. Bring as many of them here as you can. They'll hear you. And they'll come running."

He studied me for a moment, eyes glittering. Then he nodded.

He turned his face toward the sky.

He exhaled a stream of white smoke.

Above, the clouds shifted, revealing the moon.

It was almost full.

His eyes were red and violet.

The Alpha of the Omegas opened his mouth.

And howled.

HEAR YOUR VOICE / CRY HAVOC

It was close to dawn when Oxnard Matheson looked at me and said, "They're here."

I smiled.

. . .

The moon was bright overhead as we trekked through the snow. The clouds had mostly cleared, and the air was cold. The stars were blinking against the black sky. On the eastern horizon, the night was beginning to fade toward day.

Ox led the way. I was behind him, stepping in the paw prints he left in the snow. Joe was behind me, snout pressing every now and then against my back, huffing out a warm breath. Mark growled every time he did it, a threat Joe ignored. Carter was behind Mark, and Elizabeth brought up the rear.

Somewhere in the trees, the timber wolf prowled, never letting Carter out of his sight.

Kelly had tried to come along, had all but demanded it, but Ox had asked him to stay behind, to help Robbie guard the house with Jessie and Rico. He hadn't been pleased with being left behind but did as his Alpha asked.

He wouldn't look at me before we left.

It was different now. In our heads. Before, when the packs had been split and Richard had lost his head, it had only affected those under Ox. Joe, Carter, Kelly, and I hadn't felt it. The Omegas. We weren't a part of them.

We were now.

Ox took the brunt of it, and in turn Joe. But even though we had two Alphas holding it together, there was still the undercurrent running through all of us. It was like wasps trapped in our heads, building a thick nest in our brains. I felt their wings fluttering, their stingers scraping.

I felt wild and savage.

Feral.

The tattoos on my arms hadn't stopped glowing since I'd woken up after shattering the door.

I snorted, shaking my head.

Ox looked back at me, a question in the form of *????* pushing through the bond between us.

I sent back a memory of when we were younger, buried under the wasps—

Does it hurt?

What?

The colors.

No. It pulls and I push and it crawls along my skin, but it never hurts. Not anymore.

—and I knew the moment it hit him, the moment he remembered, because he responded in the voice of an overgrown boy who was about to find out that monsters were real, that magic was real, that the world was a dark and frightening place because it was all real and—

shiny arms you have shiny arms gordo

—I choked on a laugh at the absurdity of it all.

"Yeah," I told him. "Shiny arms. That's it."

His tongue lolled out of his mouth, and I heard Joe huff behind me. "Yeah, Yeah. We're going."

. . .

They were waiting for us, as they'd been before. As if they knew we were coming. They probably did. They just didn't know what was coming for *them*.

The wooden bridge loomed behind them. The dirt road was covered with snow that crunched beneath our feet. The same people waited for us. Three men. One woman. All witches.

Dale was absent.

I wasn't surprised.

He'd probably left Green Creek right after we'd met.

He wouldn't have thought we'd come to this point.

If we survived this day, I'd show him just how wrong he was.

The witches looked nervous as we approached, though they tried hard to cover it. Problem was, they weren't very good at it.

The wards felt sticky and hot, the magic foreign.

Maybe they'd been telling the truth before. That my father had nothing to do with this. That Michelle wasn't working with him.

It didn't matter now.

They were the same to me.

They weren't with us. Which meant they were against us. That much was clear.

Ox shifted, just as he'd said he would. He stood nude in the snow, the shadows crawling along his skin. The others remained as they were.

"Alpha Matheson," the woman said, voice defiant. "We didn't expect to see you again so soon. Have you given further consideration to what Alpha Hughes has—"

"I stood here once," Ox said, and a chill went down my spine. "When I was human. And right where you are were Omegas who had come to take what belonged to me. They had a member of my pack, though we didn't know that she was then. She was scared, but she was strong. So much stronger than they expected. They tried to use her as leverage against me."

The witches glanced warily at each other. The woman said, "I don't see what a history lesson has to do with—"

Ox didn't let her finish. "They thought because we'd been broken, because we were hurting and scared, we would just . . . fold. That I would let them take away everything I had left without a fight. I asked a question that night. One question that I wanted answered. Many things could have ended differently if they had just told me what I wanted to know. I want you to remember that, because I'm going to give you the same courtesy. I am going to ask you one question."

"We *won't* be intimidated like feral dogs," one of the men spat. "You have nothing that can—"

And Oxnard Matheson asked, "What are your names?"

The witches were startled. They hadn't been expecting that.

Ox waited.

The wolves stood stock-still.

In the trees, I heard the crunch of snow as a timber wolf prowled.

"What does it matter?" the woman asked.

Ox shook his head. "That's not what I asked. What are your names?"

A man shoved the woman to the side, a scowl on his face. "I'm fucking sick of this. I don't give a shit what Alpha Hughes said. I'm going to end this—"

"How many are you?" I asked.

The man narrowed his eyes at me. "What?"

"Around Green Creek. I mean, you guys have us surrounded, right? How many witches? You four. Is there another dozen? Two dozen?"

"Thirty of us," the man said, a nasty smile on his face. "Spread around the perimeter of your territory. All volunteers. They couldn't *wait* to come here. Nothing gets in and nothing gets out."

"Dale?"

He rolled his eyes. "His work was done. He fucked your mate, didn't he? Wasn't needed anymore. Ran back to Alpha Hughes like the good little lapdog."

Oh, I was going to enjoy this. "And you won't leave? Like, leave right now. Turn around and walk away. Any of you."

He bristled at that. "Of course not. Why the fuck would we do that?"

I whistled lowly. "That's going to be a blow. There aren't many witches left that I know of. Ah well. We'll make do somehow."

"What the hell are you *talking* about—"

"I am going to give you one last chance," Ox growled. "What. Are. Your. *Names.*"

The man in front spat on the ground at the Alpha's feet.

That was the wrong move.

All I felt was *packpackpack,* but it was so much bigger than it'd been before.

So much angrier.

So much more *violet.*

"In a minute," Ox said, and I'd never heard him speak so coldly, "there's going to be yelling. Probably some screaming. Things are going to get confusing. Blood will be spilled. I want you to remember something for me when that happens. All I wanted to know was your names."

The woman said, "Look. Oh my god, look."

I followed her trembling finger.

She was pointing at the wolves behind us. They stood in a row, almost shoulder to shoulder. Joe was the farthest left, teeth bared. Elizabeth was on the right, and her ears were flat against her head.

And between them were Mark and Carter, eyes Omega-bright.

Behind them, the feral timber wolf prowled back and forth, dwarfing them all.

"They're feral," one of the men said. "They've already turned. How are they not—"

The woman stepped forward. The wards burst brightly as she neared. The echoing ping stretched far down either side of us. She was sending a warning. That was okay. It was already too late. They just didn't know it yet. "What are you doing?" she asked. "Why aren't they attacking you? That's not possible. They're *Omegas*. They're *monsters*." She looked at Ox, eyes wide and wet, like she knew it was almost the end. Her voice broke. "How are you doing this?"

"I am Oxnard Matheson," he told her. "I am the Alpha to the Bennett pack, like my father before me." His eyes began to glow. Red and violet. "And I am the Alpha of the Omegas."

The witches took a step back.

They should have told Ox their names.

Behind them, on the banks of the creek that ran under the covered bridge, violet eyes began to glow.

At first there were only a few of them, blinking slowly in the dark. And then came more. So many more than I ever expected. They stretched along the creek, going down as far as I could see.

Some were shifted completely.

Others were caught in between.

A few were still human.

They were in the bridge, eyes glowing in the dark.

Two stood *on top* of the bridge, the wood creaking underneath their feet as they stepped forward.

One of the men at the rear heard them first. He turned slowly, his breath coming out in great gasps as his chest heaved. "Oh no," he whispered.

The other witches whirled at the sound of his voice.

And then they froze.

"This moment," I told them. "This is the exact moment you realize why no one fucks with the Bennett pack."

The man with the nasty smile was the first to move. He stumbled back toward the wards, eyes wide. The line of wolves behind us snarled angrily, and he slipped in the snow, trying to stay on his feet. "You can't do this," he said, sounding breathless. "You *wouldn't*. You're an Alpha. You're supposed to *protect*."

Ox leaned forward, face almost pressed flat against the ward in front of him.

The man cowered.

The Alpha wolf said, "All I wanted to know was your name."

In the end, it was swift. The Omegas surged forward, moving quick and sure. Some leapt over the creek bed and took off down either side of the wards, heading for the other witches just out of sight.

Others shifted in the covered bridge, their claws digging into the wood as they tilted their heads back and howled.

The two on top of the bridge jumped down and crouched low in the snow, fangs bared at the witches trying to hurt their Alpha.

The witches fought back. There were flashes of light as the ground split beneath the feral wolves. Some were knocked off their feet, crashing down hard on the ground. One of the men clapped his hands together in front of him, and a burst of compressed air flew out around him, slamming into the approaching waves of Omegas. They flew back.

Most got up immediately.

The witches were hopelessly outnumbered.

In the distance, I could hear the shouts and screams of the other witches in the woods, could see light bursting in the trees.

The man with the nasty smile was the first to fall, throat torn out, blood gushing onto the snow. He was on his knees, head tilted back as he gurgled. A blood bubble burst from his mouth, red mist landing on his face. He turned his head toward me, eyes locking with mine, pleading silently.

I didn't react as another wolf descended on him, and he was no more.

One of the remaining men tried to run.

He didn't get very far before two half-shifted wolves landed on his back, fangs and claws tearing.

The last man turned and ran toward us, *through* the wards. He wasn't afraid.

He was going for Ox.

He didn't make it.

Joe moved in front of his mate.

The man tried to stop, but he slid in the snow right into Joe's open jaws. He barely made a sound as the jaws shut tight.

The woman was last.

Her arms moved.

Her fingers twitched.

One of the shifted Omegas, a thin and mangy creature, rose in the air in front of her. She twisted her wrist, muttering under her breath, and it *folded* in half, the sound of its back breaking loud and wet. It writhed, feet kicking, and she *threw* it at a small group of approaching Omegas. They yelped as the wolf collided with them.

A half-shifted wolf came running at her from her left, but she raised her leg at an angle before slamming it down against the ground in the snow. The ground split beneath the Omega, swallowing it down to its hips before closing around it. It struggled to pull itself out, but then it tilted its head back and *screamed* as it began to thrash. Whatever was happening below the ground was hurting it, and it took only seconds before it slumped over, violet fading from its unblinking eyes.

But that was as much damage as she could do.

Another Omega jumped at her, and she stumbled backward through the wards.

Directly into Ox.

She whirled around, the Omegas behind her throwing themselves against the wards, trying to get through to her, to their Alpha.

Ox wrapped a hand around her throat, lifting her off the ground.

Her feet kicked uselessly.

She clung to his bare arm as he lowered her face toward his.

She said, "My name is Emma," and Ox stopped.

The feral Omegas growled along the wards. There were so many of them.

"My name is Emma," she said again, voice frantic. "Emma Patterson. I am Emma. I am Emma. I am *Emma*."

Ox's half shift faded.

He blinked slowly up at her.

And then—

He set her down on the ground.

She wheezed as he let go of her neck.

"Emma," Ox said. "Emma Patterson."

She nodded. "Yes. Yes. Yes. You said you only wanted my name. You asked me for my *name*—"

She was smart. We were distracted. Violence and bloodshed spread out before us, and this woman, this tiny woman, was sobbing her name, telling us to please spare her, her name was Emma and she didn't want to be here, this wasn't even her idea, she only went along with it because she had to, she thought she *had* to.

It was only at the last second that I saw her reaching into her coat. The moonlight caught the blade, causing it to glitter in the dark. The knife was long and curved, looking as if it were made of pure silver.

They couldn't see it. Not like I could. She was bent away from them.

I ran toward her. Toward my Alpha.

She spun on her heels, bringing the knife out in a flat arc and—

I reached out to grab her wrist and overshot.

I saved my Alpha.

But there was nothing I could do about my hand.

There was a wet *thunk* of knife hitting bone, before it continued on. Continued *through*.

I felt nothing at first. I fell against Ox, and his arms came around me. I was breathing, I was breathing, I was *breathing,* and I looked up at him, frowning at his expression of *horror*.

"What's wrong?" I tried to ask, but was hit with a wave of pain like nothing I'd ever felt before. I screamed in my Alpha's arms as I looked down, trying to find why it hurt, oh god, it *hurt*.

I saw my hand.

Lying in the snow a few feet away, fingers curled up toward the sky. The snow underneath it was turning red.

I raised my arm to see where my hand had once been. It was a clean cut, the skin barely ragged. Blood was spilling from it down my arm, mixing in with the roses.

There came the roar of an enraged animal.

Through the red-hot sheen of pain I saw a brown wolf leap forward and land on top of Emma. Her hands came up to ward him off, but it was too late. His jaws closed over her throat and twisted viciously. Her neck snapped loudly, blood gushing around wicked sharp teeth. She barely made a sound.

"No," I heard Ox muttering above me. "No, no, no, stay with me, Gordo, you need to stay with me—"

There came a groan of muscle and bone. I heard Joe. He said, "Holy shit, what the fuck, we need to bite him, Ox, we need to bite him—"

Elizabeth said, "You can't, you can't, he's a witch, a powerful witch, it would kill him, it would kill him, he can't be changed into a wolf, it would *kill him.*"

A brown wolf stood in front of me, eyes violet and searching. He whined lowly, leaning his head forward, pressing his nose against my cheek.

"Hey," I said, feeling floaty and disconnected. "It's okay. It hurt, but it's not that bad anymore. I probably won't be as handy as I was before, ha, ha, ha—"

"Jesus *Christ*," Joe said, sounding strangled. "Did he just—"

The wolves all growled angrily, louder than I'd ever heard it before. It sounded like there were hundreds of them. But I was safe, safe, safe in my Alpha's arms, and I knew he would never let anyone hurt me again.

I wanted to close my eyes.

"Alpha Matheson!" a shrill voice called. "Please, if we're to help Gordo, you need to let us through. We are here because of him. We can break the wards. There are enough of us. My name is Aileen. This is Patrice. We're here to help. We're here to—"

Ox howled above me. It reverberated down to my bones. It felt like it was a part of me.

I heard strange voices sounding like they were chanting in unison from somewhere far away. The brown wolf licked my cheek, and I couldn't even be bothered to try to push him away. There was a pulse of something heated on my shoulder, and I remembered I was marked by the one I loved. It calmed me, knowing that no matter what happened, everyone would know I belonged to a wolf.

I screamed as I felt the wards break, body electrified as my back arched.

Ox whispered in my ear, telling me I was safe, I was safe, and he would always watch over me, please, Gordo, please, please listen, listen to me, can you hear them? Can you hear us? All of us, Gordo. All of us, because we are—

pack, the wolves and humans whispered in my head, *we are pack-packpack and you are BrotherFriendLoveMate you are witch you are life you are love and we will protect you.*

"Hold him down," a voice said, the words lilted and smooth. "Dis is gonna hurt."

Tears leaked from my eyes and rolled down my cheeks. I stared up at Ox, who still held me in his arms. He reached up and brushed the wetness from my face. He said, "I've got him. I've got him."

"Patrice?" I heard Aileen ask. "Can you help him?"

"Petèt. Maybe. Won't be like it was. Dat hand is gone. Dat's over with now. But he won't need dat. *Maji.* The magic in him and dis pack. It's big. It'll compensate. *Parè.* Get ready, Alpha. You in dis as much as I am. Whole pack. We have help. *Lalin.* The moon."

I was floating away, away, away, and I was higher than I'd ever been before, and I swore I could see all of Green Creek, all of the territory that the *packpackpack* called home, and it was alight with a deep violet, all moving toward a group of witches and wolves hunched over a bleeding body and—

I was slammed back down as the pain returned with a vengeance, ferocious and clawing. I howled a song of agony as the raven stretched its wings, a hand that felt like it was made of molten steel closing over the gushing wound and—

·   ·   ·

I opened my eyes.

I was in the clearing.

A man sat across from me. His back was to me. His head was tilted back toward the sky. The moon was full. The stars looked like wolves.

Around us, in the trees, prowled great beasts.

The man said, "I was foolish. Proud. Angry. I tried not to be. I thought being an Alpha meant—I don't know. That I could be above all that. That I wouldn't be so . . . human. But as it turned out, I had so much to learn. Even at the end."

I couldn't speak.

"I hear you," the man said. "All of you. When you sing your wolf-songs. Even the humans. They—I always thought they made us better. Made us whole. Reminded us who we were supposed to be. Call it tethers or something more, it doesn't matter. They . . . it's something others don't understand. They don't see it like we do." The man bowed his head. "I should have fought harder for you. And for that, I am sorry. You were my family. And I should have remembered that above all else. I failed you."

My breath hitched in my chest, and my voice was just a whisper when I spoke. "Thomas?"

He turned his head slightly, a small smile on his face. "Gordo. Oh, I do love to hear your voice."

"I'm . . . I don't—"

"That's okay." He turned to look back up at the moon.

"Is this real?"

"I think so."

"I'm hurt."

"Yes. Protecting your Alpha. I'm so proud of you."

My eyes burned as I hung my head. I didn't know until that very moment how much I longed to hear those words from him. "Mark," I choked out. "He . . . he's changed. An Omega."

"I know. But he is not lost. None of them are. You are so much more than what they think, Gordo. All of you. My wife. My sons. My pack."

I crawled toward him, almost falling face-first into the ground when I went to put my right hand down only to realize it wasn't there anymore. It was a smooth stump, looking fully healed. There were barely even scars.

I didn't let it deter me.

Not now.

Not from him.

Not ever.

I reached him, and for the first time since I could remember, I could feel him. My Alpha. I pressed my forehead against the back of his neck, and he said, "Oh. Oh, Gordo. I'm so sorry. I am. But it's you, okay? One day it'll be you and me forever. We are going to be our own pack again. And you will *always* be my witch."

And as the wolves sang their songs around us, I kissed the skin of my Alpha's neck and pulled away to—

I took in a great gasping breath, sitting up quickly.

My head hurt.

My arm was throbbing.

I was cold.

And surrounding me, moving in a slow circle, were dozens of Omega wolves.

"It's okay," a voice said near my ear. I turned my head slightly to see Ox still holding on to me. "They're . . . they won't hurt us. I have them. It's . . . heavy. But I've got it. All of you are helping."

Two people moved in front of me, crouching down. The brown wolf crowding my side growled angrily at them, eyes flashing, but he made no move toward them.

Aileen looked older than I remembered, the lines on her face deeper. But her eyes were knowing, always knowing. She reached out and pressed two fingers against my heated forehead. Almost immediately, the clouds in my head began to part.

Patrice looked startling against the snow and the blood that had soaked into it. His skin was as white as the snow around us, his freckles like little spots of fire on his skin. He was ethereally beautiful.

He was frowning as he reached toward me. He took my arm gently in his, lifting it up.

My hand was gone.

But the stump was on its way toward healing, far more than it should have been. Gone was the open wound. In its place was a mass of red scar tissue that felt warm and achy. It looked months old rather than minutes. He held my arm gently, twisting it this way and that as he studied it. "It'll do," he said with a sigh. "Best I got." He set my arm down carefully before he looked up at me. "Foolish witch," he said, not unkindly.

"You are lucky we were here, boyo," Aileen snapped. "And that it was only your hand. She could have taken your head off with that thing, and where would you be then?"

"Headless," I muttered, and heard Ox choke behind me.

Aileen rolled her eyes. "Don't get smart with me, Gordo. I have had just about enough excitement for one day, and we've only just begun."

I struggled to stand up. Ox tried to help me, but Mark growled at him. Ox backed off as I glared at the wolf. He pushed himself against me, snout nosing under my good arm until I lifted it around him. He rose fully to his feet, pulling me up with him. Vertigo swam through me for a moment, but it passed.

The Omegas continued to move in a wide circle around us. They kept their gazes on all of us, darting back and forth but lingering on Ox. They didn't seem to be paying me any attention. It was almost as if I wasn't even there.

Except for Mark. He stood pressed against me.

Ox was in control. Somehow, he was in control of all the feral wolves.

I shook my head. "I don't know how I'm going to—" I had to stop and swallow past the lump in my throat. I tried again, voice rougher than it'd been before. "I don't know how I'm going to be any use now. I can't use—"

"Bah," Patrice said dismissively. "Dat won't matter much. It's a hand, Gordo. Not where your magic came from. It's in your marks. *Boustabak*. Dat raven. It'll hold. You have pack. You have a mate. You'll learn."

"That's not—"

"It is, boyo," Aileen said sharply. "In the end, it's not going to matter much. Not to who you are. Only thing it's going to be a problem for is if you were right-handed to begin with. I'm sure Mark will help you learn how to jack off with the left."

"Jesus Christ."

She coughed. It sounded harsh in her chest. "Now that that's out of the way, you gotta get moving. Those hunters. They aren't going to wait. Things are changing, Gordo. Whispers in the wind. I can hear them. It's not the same. Not anymore. It's going to come to a head sooner rather than later. These feral wolves were just the first step. The hunters yet another. It's escalating, I think. Michelle Hughes is going to tighten her grip. She's had a taste now. And soon she's going to know exactly what you all are capable of." She glanced at Ox before looking back at me, a grim look on her face. "There's never been anything like the Bennett pack. Or this place. She's going to do whatever she can to find out why. And she will try to take it."

"And the Omegas?" I asked. "The infection?"

Patrice shook his head. "Dat don't matter. Your Alpha here, he's got 'em. In dere heads. You can feel it. I know you can. Hell, *I* can feel it, and I'm not even in your pack." He turned to Ox. "I don't know where you came from, boy, but I don't tink I've ever seen someone like you before."

"I can bring them back," Ox said quietly. He was looking at the Omegas that moved around us. "After. When this is done. They'll . . . still be Omegas. The infected ones. But I think it'll hold. Until . . ."

"Until you kill Robert Livingstone," Aileen said grimly. "This is deep magic. Deeper than I ever thought anyone could go. We can't fix it. Not until we know what he's done. And if he dies, there's a chance his spell dies with him. That's what I got from Thomas when he—"

"Thomas?" a trembling voice asked.

I turned. Elizabeth Bennett stood nude, eyes alight in the dark. She was staring at Aileen, an indecipherable look on her face.

Aileen sighed. "Yes. It's . . . it wasn't clear. The visions never are. I see . . . I think he knew. That we would be needed." She glanced at me before looking back at the mother wolf. "It was faint. And quick. But we—"

I couldn't stop myself. I didn't know if I wanted to. She had to know. They all did. "I've seen him. Before. At the door. And here. Now."

Joe made a wounded noise, bowing his head, wrapping his arms around his middle.

Elizabeth took a step toward me, her bare feet sinking into the snow. Her skin was pebbled with gooseflesh, but she moved with great deliberation until she stood before me. She trailed her fingers along my injured arm, running along the tattoos. The runes and roses glowed under her touch. She looked up at me, and there was never a moment in my life I wanted to protect her more than I did right then. "He found you again."

I nodded, unable to speak.

"Did he speak to you?"

"He said he loves us," I said quietly. "Loves you. And that I was his witch."

Carter tilted his head back and howled mournfully. The timber wolf whined and rubbed against his side. The Omegas seemed agitated at the sound, but they stayed away, still moving slowly in a circle around us.

"You see now, don't you?" Elizabeth asked, reaching up to cup my face. Her hands were warm and kind.

"I think so. It . . . hurts. To know what I've lost. What *we've* lost. It hurts."

"And it will. Maybe forever." Her thumbs brushed over my cheeks. "But it will become a part of you, and one day it'll be bearable." A single tear fell from her eye. "But you will never forget your Alpha."

"He said he was proud of me," I whispered, fearing that saying it any louder would make it untrue.

And oh, how she *smiled*. "He is, Gordo. As am I. As we all are. You were lost, I think. For a long time. But you have found your way home. Though it was not without consequence."

I winced. "That might be an understatement."

"I know. But we will figure it out. We always do. You're not alone, Gordo. And I promise you that you never will be."

She stepped away, dropping her hands from my face. I watched as she shifted in front of me, and I remembered being told that it was easier to deal with grief as a wolf. Human emotions were complex. Wolf instincts were not. She was blue, so blue, but mixed in was green, wrapping around her, keeping her safe. She nosed Mark's throat before she went to stand back next to Carter, who licked one of her ears.

"We will stay here," Aileen said quietly. "Clean up what remains. There are enough of us who have come to Green Creek to rebuild your wards while you do what you must. Nothing will escape, not while we stand watch. You have many allies, Alpha Matheson, whether you realize it or not. You must remember this, because there will come a time when it'll seem that the whole world is against you. You have powerful enemies. But I can see your strength. I will pray that it is enough to do what you must."

Ox nodded. "Thank you. For coming for my witch. For us."

"Peace, Alpha. May your pack one day know peace." She stepped back.

Patrice reached up and rubbed his thumb over Ox's forehead. A little trail of light formed a symbol on Ox's brow, an inverted *S*. The Omegas rumbled around us. Carter yipped. Mark growled at my side.

Ox breathed in deeply. His eyes burned. "What did you do?"

"Focus," Patrice said. "Dat's focus. Dere tied to you, Alpha. All of dem. It'll pull harder den you ever imagined. Tightened those bonds a bit. Not much, but it's da best I can do."

Ox bowed his head in deference. "Thank you."

The witches moved away from us. The Omegas parted, letting them pass through without incident. They moved toward the bridge.

"Gordo."

"Oxnard."

"I—you need—"

"Shut up, Ox."

He frowned. "It's not—"

"Would you do the same for me?"

"Always."

"Then shut up."

He sighed. "Only you wouldn't accept gratitude after getting your hand cut off."

"We have bigger things to worry about now. We can talk about it later, when I come off my inevitable meltdown."

"He'll wait on you hand and foot," Joe said. "Or maybe just foot, now."

We turned slowly to look at him.

He blinked at us. "Too soon?" He nodded. "Yeah. Too soon. Sorry, Gordo."

Ox took a step forward.

The circle of the Omegas broke. They amassed in front of him. Some were half-shifted. Most were wolves. There had to be at least sixty of them. All their eyes were violet. It was more than Richard Collins ever had.

Oxnard Matheson said, "I called you. And you came. I have made mistakes in the past. I cut myself off from all of you. I closed that door, even though you needed me. I have no right to ask anything of you, but in the end, I must. There are people here. Hunters. They have come into Bennett territory uninvited. And they have come to take away everything I hold dear. They already have two of my pack, and I will not accept that. If you help me, if you stand with me, then I promise you, I will do everything in my power to bring you back. To put your minds back together, no matter how long it might take. You are the forgotten. The lost. But if we survive today, I will find a way to bring you home."

The Omega wolves tilted their heads back and howled for their Alpha. The sound rolled over us, causing me to shake down to my bones.

It was loud and angry.

Feral and harsh.

I hoped Elijah and her hunters heard it too.

They were waiting for us when we arrived back at the house at the end of the lane. The sky was nearly cloudless, a cold, clear blue. The sun was bright. And the moon was full and pale, but visible. I remembered the story Abel had told me about her love.

Rico was standing on his own, eyes wide as he watched us approach. He was muttering something I couldn't hear.

Jessie was next to him, tapping the crowbar on her shoulder, eyes narrowed.

Robbie stood at the bottom of the stairs next to Kelly, who was wringing his hands. He looked as if he didn't know whether he wanted to step in front of Kelly and snarl, or pull him back into the house. He did neither. Instead he said, "That's a lot of Omegas."

Elizabeth went to them first, shifting as she approached the house. Jessie reached down to a pack at her feet, pulled out a robe, and tossed it down the stairs. Elizabeth caught it midshift and wrapped it around her shoulders as the wolf melted away.

"What happened?" Kelly demanded. "We felt—I don't *know* what it was. But it was awful. It was like someone died, but—"

"Gordo?" Rico asked. "Why are you holding your arm like that? Did you break it?"

"Not exactly," I muttered.

"Gordo saved Ox," Elizabeth said. "He was hurt, but it'll be okay."

"I don't understand," Robbie said, sounding confused. "It was like—"

I held up my arm.

Silence.

Then:

"What the *fuck*," Rico squeaked.

"Who did that?" Jessie growled. "And please tell me they're already dead."

"How is it healed already?" Robbie demanded, eyes flashing.

Kelly came first, Kelly who had stood in the doorway of a dilapidated motel in the middle of nowhere, watching me shave my head, and told me I had to do it to him next, had to make him look like me. I thought he'd been my pack first, before Joe and Carter, because of that. His hands had been gentle when they pressed against my shoulders, and he hadn't fidgeted when I'd done the same to him. I remembered how prickly his scalp had felt when I'd run my fingers over it after I'd finished. He'd still been a child then, a grieving child far away from home.

That child was gone now.

The man he'd become stood before me.

And he leaned forward, pressing his forehead against mine, eyes open and staring at me.

I didn't look away.

"You idiot," he said. "You stupid idiot."

"Had to get you to stop being angry with me somehow."

He choked on a laugh. "Oh, I'm still mad at you. But now it's for entirely different reasons. I'll probably need to come to the shop to give you a hand now. I don't know the first thing about cars."

"Too soon," Joe muttered, sliding into a pair of jeans Jessie had given him. "Already tried it."

I shoved Kelly away. "Asshole."

He shook his head as he went to his brother. The timber wolf didn't seem pleased to see him again, but Kelly ignored it, falling to his knees in the snow, wrapping his arms around Carter's neck.

"I'm fine," I told Jessie and Rico, who were starting to fuss.

"Yeah, sure you are," Rico snapped. "I get shot, and you just had to go and try and one-up me. I'm going to have a sexy scar, and you're going to be able to get a sexy hook. Pirates *always* beat scars, Gordo. You *know* that. You stay away from Bambi. You don't get to try and take her away from me when you already got a wolf."

"Why does it feel like this is a conversation you guys have had before?" Jessie asked us suspiciously.

"Weed is a hell of drug," Rico told her. "Though it does make more sense that Gordo would be the pirate instead of me."

"Why would that be?" Jessie asked.

"Because I'm straight," Rico explained. "And Gordo likes to plunder the booty."

"I hate you so fucking much," I told him.

"Nah. That's a lie. Don't even try it. And, as a sidebar, is it almost time to kill the bad guys and get Chris and Tanner back? Because I'm going to need them here with me to help me get over the trauma of getting shot and having a one-handed boss. They'll help me come to terms with this brave new world we find ourselves in."

"Men," Jessie grumbled. "You're all fucking idiots."

"Hey! This has hands down—sorry, Gordo—been one of the worst days ever. Show a little respect!"

I loved them more than I could ever say. "Yeah. It's almost time."

"Good," they muttered in unison, sounding more wolfish than the actual wolves. The hunters should never have come to this town.

And because he was the only one left, and still stood near the porch looking ridiculously unsure, I waved Robbie over.

He came, trying not to stare at my arm but failing miserably. "Who did this?" he asked, voice hushed.

"A witch."

"Is she dead?"

Mark growled as I said, "Very."

Robbie nodded frantically. "Great, that's great, that's—"

"Kid, you need to calm down. Take a breath. We're fine. We're all—"

He surprised me by leaping forward and throwing his arms around me. I grunted at the impact, and Mark snapped at him, fangs flashing but not actually sinking into skin. "I'm glad you're okay," he whispered into my neck.

I rolled my eyes and wrapped my good arm around his back. Kid was soft. "Yeah, yeah. Enough with the feelings, all right? We've got bigger things to worry about."

He stepped back, and his eyes were orange. "We're going after her, aren't we? Eventually."

He wasn't talking about Elijah. "Yeah. We are. You going to be okay with that?"

He didn't hesitate. "This is my home. This is my pack. I'll do whatever it takes."

I reached up and squeezed the back of his neck. "We're lucky to have you, Robbie. Even if you insist on wearing those fucking glasses."

He grinned at me.

Ox said, "Do it."

I kicked away the line of silver.

Pappas jumped forward, ready to bite and tear and—

Ox roared.

Pappas stopped.

He blinked, tilting his head toward Ox.

His eyes were violet.

Ox rumbled deep in his chest.

And Pappas listened.

gordo gordo gordo

"I know," I told Mark, squatting in front of him. "I know."

He pressed his head against my shoulder and breathed me in.

gordo gordo gordo

I was not a wolf.

But even I could feel the pull of the moon.

When I'd been alone, when all the wolves had left me behind, I hated it. I hated the way it stretched my skin tight. The way I always felt it overhead.

Eventually the bonds broke.

Eventually I didn't feel the moon anymore.

But it wasn't done with me. Not by a long shot.

Here, now, I felt it, maybe more so than ever before.

I was not a wolf.

But I was a part of them.

They were a part of me.

And the moon *pulled.*

We stood in front of the house at the end of the lane, snow still drifting down around us. Nine members of the Bennett pack. A timber wolf. Pappas.

And all those Omegas.

The full moon was here.

"Cry 'havoc,'" I whispered as the wolves sang their songs around me, "and let slip the dogs of war."

PACK

When I was a child, a woman named Elijah had held my hand in the diner as she prayed.

And then, even as she slipped a needle into my skin, much like my father had done before her, she rained fire down upon us.

Hunters came to Green Creek and took away almost everyone I loved.

We weren't ready.

We paid the price for that.

All that remained was a smoking crater strewn with death.

She survived, somehow.

And she had come again.

She meant to finish what she'd started.

She had taken two of my pack away from me.

She thought she had the upper hand, that she had us beat.

But after all she'd brought upon us, after all she was capable of, she still didn't understand there was one thing that should never be done.

Back a beast into a corner.

Because that's when it has nothing left to lose, and it will do everything it can to survive.

      .   .   .

"I trust you," Ox told me.

"I know."

"They have Tanner. And Chris."

"I know."

"And they're still alive. Still fighting."

"*I know.*"

Ox nodded. "Which is why you will go to them. We will come in from the front. Distract the Hunters. Distract Elijah. Pick them off one by one while we can before going full-bore. And that's when you will come in from the rear. With any luck, they won't even know you're there until it's too late."

"Divide and conquer."

His smile was all teeth. "It's how wolves hunt in the wild. They separate the flock."

"And you're sure they're in the garage? Chris and Tanner."

"Have I ever told you what it was like? When I opened my eyes as a wolf for the first time?"

I shook my head. He'd hinted at it, but then we'd realized just how wide open that door was, and everything was focused on shutting it and making sure it was locked.

"I could feel you. All of you. My pack. But it was more than that. I could feel *all* of them. The people here. In the territory. I felt the grass. The leaves. The birds in the trees. Everything. You know this place, Gordo. I know you do. You are in touch with it in ways that most others are not. But I think it's more than that for me. You are the earth and I am the sky. So yes. I know they're in the garage. I know they're scared. I know they're hurt. I know they're as stubborn as they've ever been. And we're going to make the Kings pay for all they've done. Their names don't matter to me."

"Dirt and leaves and rain," I muttered.

He cocked his head at me.

"I—it's something Mark tells me." I looked away. "It's what I smell like to him."

"I will bring him back to you," Ox said, and I closed my eyes. "To all of us."

"You can't promise that," I said through gritted teeth.

"Watch me," Ox said.

.   .   .

"I love you," Joe told us from the porch, Ox at his side. "I love all of you. You are my pack. And this is our town. It's time to take it back."

.   .   .

Nevermore. Nevermore. *Never—*

I moved through the back dirt roads of Green Creek, snow crunching underneath my feet. Mark was on my right and Elizabeth on my left. It wasn't until after Ox had told them to go with me that I realized what he was doing. He was trying to keep those who remembered the last time Elijah had been here away from her. Carter had been too young. But the three of us were not. I didn't know whether to thank him or be pissed off.

It didn't matter.

We could deal with it later.

The stump that had once been my right hand was wrapped with a bandage, and a sock placed over it. Jessie told me that while she trusted my magic, she didn't know these other witches. We couldn't know if there was nerve damage. I needed to avoid frostbite. "We're going to have to get that checked," she told me, fitting the sock over the stump. "And somehow figure out how to explain how it happened, and how it already healed."

"Half the town already knows about wolves," I reminded her. "I saw the doc in there too. What's a magically healed amputation in the face of that?"

"This is going to explode in our faces."

"Maybe. But if it does, we'll deal with it then."

The forest felt unnaturally quiet, as if it and the nearby town were empty. Rico and Jessie had made their way to the Lighthouse with orders to keep everyone safe in case the hunters somehow found their way to it. Jessie looked like she was going to argue, but Ox told her that he was trusting her to keep the rest of the humans safe. Rico sighed but agreed. "I mean, if I'm going to get shot, it might as well be by my girlfriend. At least I'll expect it coming from her."

It was slow going, even though we kept to what were normally dirt roads. The snow was deep, and the drifts even deeper. I stumbled a few times, but a wolf was always there to keep me upright.

gordo gordo gordo.

"Yeah, yeah," I muttered, putting my remaining hand on Mark's back.

He was there, somehow. Mark. The bonds between us were frayed and tenuous, but they were holding. Because of Ox or because I bore my wolf's mark upon my shoulder, I didn't know. I believed Ox when he said he would find a way.

It was *gordo gordo gordo* and *MateWitch* and some wolf-blue song of *mine* and *mine* and *mine*. He was echoing in my head, agitated and twitchy, but I held on to it as best I could. It meant there was hope.

He helped me up again, and I was about to take a step forward when Elizabeth froze, ears perking, tail curved up behind her.

Mark growled lowly next to me before he herded me against a large tree.

It took a moment to hear what they did.

Voices.

They were faint at first. But they grew louder as I breathed shallowly through my nose. The vines on my arm began to tighten under my coat, pulling against my skin. My magic was wilder than it'd been before, and I felt a phantom sensation where my hand had once been, like I still had fingers that could curl into a fist.

Elizabeth moved a few feet away from us and began to dig in the snow, the powder and ice piling up behind her. Her claws scraped, and I worried she was going to give us away before she finished, lowering herself into the indentation she'd created. She blended in with the snow and trees.

I put my back against the tree trunk, Mark standing in front of me, not even trying to conceal himself.

"Idiot," I said quietly, reaching up and running a finger between his eyes.

He pressed against my hand and breathed in deeply.

"—don't know why we had to wait," a voice said as it got closer. A man. "What the hell is she doing?"

"I think she likes it here," another voice replied. A woman. "Don't know why. This place gives me the creeps. Being in an Alpha's territory is one thing, but *two* Alphas? She's going to get us all killed."

Oh, how right she was.

They were closer.

"I don't give a fuck what she likes," the man said. "And just because she thinks the ferals are going to do the job for us doesn't mean they're not going to come for us after. I mean, there were already two of them. What if it's the whole pack by now?"

"They're easier to put down," the woman muttered. "Feral wolves don't think. They're nothing but animals. It's the nonferal wolves I'm worried about. She should have just let us burn down the goddamn house. Circle the whole thing with silver and just be done with it."

The man snorted. "Did you see the look on her face when Grant told her that? I thought she was going to shoot him right there."

Closer.

"We're hunters," the woman said mockingly. "We're supposed to *hunt*."

"Right? I get off on killing these things as much as anyone else, but goddamn, she's getting careless. This isn't like it was in Omaha. Or West Virginia."

"Bennetts," the woman said. "I don't necessarily agree with the way she's going about this, but can you imagine what it's going to be like for us when we get to say we took out the Bennett pack? We're going to be *legendary*."

Closer.

"As long as we get paid, I don't care about—"

Mark looked at me with violet eyes.

gordo gordo gordo

I stepped out from behind the tree.

They were young.

Almost kids, really. Maybe younger than Joe.

Such a waste.

They both had their rifles slung over their shoulders.

They hadn't expected me.

They stopped, eyes wide.

"Hello," I said.

They took a step back.

Mark rounded the other side of the tree, lips pulled back against his fangs. His tail swished side to side.

They took another step back.

"Your mistake," I told them, "was talking about killing a pack when a mother wolf could hear you."

The man snapped, "What are you—"

Elizabeth rose from the snow off to their left.

The woman said, "Oh, please, no."

They barely had time to reach for their guns before Elizabeth was on them.

It was over without a shot being fired.

Birds took off in the trees, wings frantic as a predator took down its prey.

Hunter blood had once again been spilled on Bennett land.

And we had only just begun.

When Elizabeth lifted her head, red droplets clinging to her whiskers, her eyes flashed orange.

pack, she whispered in my head. *packpackpack.*

We came in on the opposite side of town, near where we'd found the abandoned car.

Our tire tracks had long been buried by the storm that had since dissipated into flurries.

I wondered what they'd done with Jones. His body. When all was said and done, I would make sure he got a proper burial.

We stayed off the road as we approached Green Creek, the buildings rising up out of the snow. In the distance, I could see the remains of the diner, the tow truck still on its side. I didn't know if they'd tried to move it to get at the body of the red wolf underneath or if they'd just let it be.

Farther down Main Street, one of the traffic signals was blinking yellow. Beyond it was the garage.

The hunters' trucks still surrounded it. It didn't look like they'd been moved since we'd been there last, hunkered down in the diner. I could make out someone moving on the roof. Still others near the trucks. Halogen lights had been set up around the garage, casting a harsh glow in every direction. The power in the town was still out, but the garage was lit like a beacon.

I was uneasy. Elijah wasn't stupid. We couldn't underestimate her. She had waited until the full moon for a reason. Whether it was to justify the killing of werewolves under the thrall of the moon, or to wait and see if the feral wolves would either infect or kill the others before she descended, I didn't know. But the fact that she hadn't tried anything further since coming to Green Creek was unexpected. I hadn't believed her when she'd said the humans of the town were off-limits. She was waiting for something, but what, I didn't know.

But she had Chris and Tanner.

That was more than enough reason for us to descend upon her.

The sky above had begun to darken almost an hour before. The moon was growing brighter through breaks in gray clouds.

We hit the town line, staying out of sight behind the buildings in the shadows.

There were no other hunters this far south. What those two had been doing in the woods, I didn't know. Maybe they were on patrol. Maybe they were looking for us. It didn't matter anymore. They couldn't hurt anyone again.

We were a few blocks away from the garage when we stopped. I leaned against a brick wall. The building had once housed a post office before it'd been closed and moved to Abby. It was now a seasonal gift shop that had closed early for the winter ahead of the storm. The shop owner brought her ancient Buick in for an oil change every three months like clockwork. I hadn't seen her in the Lighthouse. I hoped she had escaped before the hunters had come.

We waited.

It wouldn't be much longer.

The wolves sat in the snow on either side of me, huddled close to keep me warm.

I said, "If this doesn't go well—"

Elizabeth growled.

"If we don't make it out—"

Mark growled.

"I'm trying to—"

They both growled.

I sighed. "Fine. I won't be that guy. But never again can you tell me to stop being an asshole when the both of you are just as bad. Especially you, Elizabeth. I don't know why more people can't see how much of a bastard you are."

She snorted.

Mark pawed at the snow.

I reached up to rub a hand over my face, only to remember at the last second that the hand was gone.

"Fuck," I muttered hoarsely.

gordo gordo gordo

"It's not—"

BrotherLovePack

"It's not going to be the same. None of this will be."

Mark nosed at my stump.

Elizabeth crowded closer.

"I'm going to need you both," I said, and it was easier than I expected it to be. I didn't know why I couldn't see that before. "I'm going to need all of you."

yes yes yes yes
gordo gordo gordo
"Okay. Okay. We'll—"
It came then.
A surge that rolled through us.
The strength of our Alphas.
It was time.
A moment later a lone howl rose over the town, echoing down the empty streets.
I knew that wolf.
I knew where it'd come from.
The earth around us pulsed, recognizing its call.
It fell away.
Shouts of alarm rose from the garage down the street from us.
The wolves were coming.
And there was nothing they could do to stop it.
"Here we go," I whispered.
Elizabeth and Mark stood at the same time.
I pushed myself up off the building.
I cracked my neck side to side.
The raven spread its wings.
It wasn't like it'd been before. My hand was gone. My magic felt untethered.
I wondered if this was what it felt like to be feral. To be Omega.
The howl rang out again. It was louder this time. And for a moment, it was still alone. But even before it could start to fade, another wolf began to sing, almost like it was harmonizing with his mate.
Oxnard.
Joe.
And then came the others.
Carter. Robbie. And farther away—much, much farther—Rico and Jessie, howling in our heads. Chris and Tanner, laughing hysterically at the sounds of their pack coming for them.
And then all the wolves began to sing, and it was unlike anything I'd ever heard before. All the Omegas howling with their Alpha, singing a song of war.
It was time to end this.
Even before we rounded the back of the building, the first sounds

of gunfire split the air. It echoed through the town, sharp cracks above the shouts of men.

There were little bursts of light in my head, little flashes of pain, and I knew almost immediately it was Omegas being struck. They weren't pack, not like the others, but they belonged to Ox just as much as we did. It was in the periphery, and I hoped he would be able to forgive himself one day. Forgive me for telling him to bring them here. Whether it was too late for them or not, whether we could find a way to bring them back when all this was said and done, this was going to weigh on him. On all of us.

We moved swiftly and surely. We knew what we had to do. We knew the plan. Divide and conquer. Even as we kept to the shadows, my breath harsh in my ears, I knew the first wave of Omegas would be breaking off into the town, feinting onto the side streets, small groups led by a member of my pack. They'd draw the hunters away. Even as we got closer, I heard the loud shouts of the hunters, and then their trucks fired up and tore off through the snow, giving chase.

It was working.

Ox and Joe would be the most visible, eyes on fire, making sure the hunters could *see* that there were Alphas there. And if the Alpha was killed, then the pack would flounder, be easier to take out. They had the largest targets on their backs, and they would make sure the hunters saw them first. Especially Elijah. She would be leading the charge.

There was a pull in my head, and it was cleaner than it'd been in days. The witches around Green Creek had finished constructing the wards. I didn't know how many had come with Patrice and Aileen, but they'd done what they set out to do. Nothing further would get in.

And the Omegas wouldn't get out.

It was a prison, but one we now controlled.

The hunters just didn't know it yet.

The halogen lights were harsh as we neared the garage. I kept out of sight, the wolves crouching low beside me. A hunter stood on the roof, firing a rifle with quick precision. Another pinprick of pain flashed in my head—silver entering an Omega wolf—but there was nothing I could do about that now. It wasn't one of my wolves.

The garage had three work bays. One of the doors in the rear had been raised, and light spilled out from inside. I heard the chugging rumble of a generator.

Two hunters stood there, backs flat against the wall.

"There," I whispered. "Take them. I've got the guy on the roof."

Mark wasn't happy about separating, but we didn't have a choice. We needed to clear out as many as we could before we went inside.

Elizabeth whispered in my head, and the blue was gone. She was hunting.

Mark stared at me with Omega eyes.

"Go."

They went, disappearing into shadow, crouched low.

A metal ladder was attached to the side of the garage. Marty had had it installed not long after I'd come to live with him. One of the guys—Jordy, dead by cancer less than a year later—had almost fallen off the old rickety wooden ladder they'd normally used, and Marty swore up and down that he sure as shit wasn't going to see his premiums go up because of a goddamn worker's compensation claim. He shelled out a couple hundred bucks to have the ladder installed on the side of the building.

It was this ladder I went to now. I reached to grab a rung and—

"Shit," I muttered as my stump knocked against the metal, sending a sharp burst of pain through my arm. I gritted my teeth and grabbed the ladder with my left hand, hooking my arm into the rung above, and pulled myself up. The metal was cold and slick. My hand went numb almost immediately. Above me, the sound of gunfire continued.

I was sweating profusely by the time I neared the roof. The sweat dripped into my eye, causing it to burn. I lifted my head until I could see out onto the roof.

The hunter stood on the opposite edge, firing his rifle again and again and again. It wasn't scoped, and I hoped that meant he was missing more than he was hitting. I pushed myself up as quietly as I could. The snow that had accumulated on the roof had turned to slush from so many people walking on it.

I breathed shallowly as I stood.

The hunter hadn't heard me.

He fired again.

Between us was a row of skylights, long windows that led down into the garage and were used for ventilation in the hot summers. The snow had been cleared from the glass.

Below me, I heard the grunt of men surprised, but it was the only sound they made before their throats were torn out.

The hunter fired once more, and then came a dry *click*.

He cursed and stepped back to reload. He reached into his coat pocket and—

I was moving even before he could pull his hand back out of his pocket. He heard me in those last few feet. He started to turn, rifle swinging toward me, but I was on him before he could face me completely.

I knocked the barrel of the rifle down, not wanting to take a chance that it had misfired and could still cause damage.

He opened his mouth like he was ready to shout in warning, but it came out as a gurgle after I punched him in the throat. Something gave way with an audible *crunch*, and his eyes bulged as he struggled to breathe. I wrapped my hand around the back of his neck, forcing his head down as I raised my knee up into his face. Bones broke, and blood dripped into the slush.

He raised his head again, and Jesus Christ, he was just a *kid,* just a kid like those two in the woods. I didn't know where Elijah had gotten them, how she had recruited them, but she'd gone young. They couldn't be Kings. Most of them were dead.

But they were here to hurt my family.

I backhanded him across the face, and he fell onto his back, sliding near the edge of the roof. He blinked blearily up at me as I stood above him.

I said, "You shouldn't have come here."

He raised his leg to kick out at me, but I deflected it easily. The roses burst to life, and I swore right then and there I felt my hand again, like it was made of flowery petals and thick vines. I trusted it, my magic, and I followed it. I knelt and pressed my stump against the roof.

The slushy snow around us began to crawl over him like it was sentient. He opened his mouth again to scream, but the dirty snow went *into* his mouth, pouring down his throat, causing him to gurgle.

I twisted my stump against the roof, grinding my teeth.

A surge of frigid air surrounded us.

I stood back up slowly.

The man's face was frozen solid, his mouth open, ice jutting out between his lips and teeth.

His eyes were wide and unblinking.

The raven was flapping its wings, struggling to calm. It hadn't been like that since I was a kid, the ink still fresh on my arm.

I'd have to deal with it later before it became a problem.

I went to the rear of the building, peering down over the ledge in time to see Elizabeth and Mark dragging the bodies of two men away from the garage and into the dark, leaving behind twin streaks of blood in the snow.

I turned around to head toward the ladder and—

"Hello, Gordo," Elijah said, standing right in front of me. "What happened to your hand?"

Before I could react, she lashed out. I saw stars as she smashed her fist into the side of my head, knocking me to the side. My vision swam as I fell to my knees. My ear went numb, a loud buzzing echoing in my head. Before I could react, she spun in a tight circle, bringing her leg up and then smashing the heel of her foot against the side my neck. My teeth snapped together, biting into my tongue. Blood flooded my mouth as I landed on my back.

I stared up at the night sky, dazed.

The moon was blurry.

She gripped my hair as she dragged me across the roof toward the skylight. I could hear the wolves screaming for me, singing in terror. Howls ripped through the night air, and the raven tried to take flight, but it was confused; it didn't know where to go. It didn't know what to do.

We reached the skylight, and she pressed my face flat against the glass.

"Look, Gordo," she said, her mouth near my ear. "Look and see what happens to humans who run with wolves."

I opened my eyes.

Twenty feet below us was the garage floor. And against the far wall were Chris and Tanner.

They'd been beaten within an inch of their lives. Their arms were chained above them, their heads bowed. Every part of them seemed to be covered with blood. Tanner's arm looked like it'd been broken. Chris's face was so swollen, I doubted he could see.

I waited for them to move.

To show me they were here.

That they were alive.

That they hadn't left us.

Left me.

please please please please please

They heard me.

Tanner raised his head and looked straight up at me.

His eyes widened.

Chris coughed, blood spilling out onto the floor.

"They are strong," Elijah said quietly. "I'll give them that. They didn't give you up, even when their bones broke. Even when I made them scream. And Gordo, how they *screamed* for you. Begging you to come save them. They believed you would come for them. All of you. And here you are. I see their faith in you wasn't misplaced. It's . . . endearing. Misguided, but endearing. I will save them for last. After your pack is dead and the fire of God has cleansed this place from evil, I will return and absolve them of their sins. It has been made abundantly clear that nothing in Green Creek must remain as it is now. I don't know how it was done, but Omegas have overrun this territory. It will need to be cleansed. The people here cannot be saved. My vision is clear, and I can see."

She let me go.

Chris and Tanner screamed for me as I turned over on my back.

The moon was so bright. I didn't think I'd ever seen anything more beautiful.

Elijah reached behind her shoulders and pulled the skin of the wolf over her head again. In my dazed mind, I thought I was safe. That the wolves had come for me, and I was safe.

Her hand went into her coat. For a moment I saw a flash of *something* that looked like it was attached to her chest underneath her coat, but then she pulled out a gun.

And pointed it at my face.

It was larger than anything I'd seen before.

The end of the barrel looked like a gaping tunnel.

I grinned up at her. My teeth felt slick with blood. "Would do it again."

She cocked the gun. "I know you would. And that's why Green Creek will be purged. I spared you once because you were just a child, and I hoped that by freeing you from the chains of the wolf, you would see the errors of your ways. I won't make that mistake again."

I said the only thing I could. "Nevermore."

She blinked. "What?"

"*Nevermore.*"

The raven flew.

The ink in my skin felt scorched, the bonds within me burning brighter than the sun.

gordo gordo gordo

The wolves were with me.

It was all I could ever ask for. Here, at the end.

I would take her with me, and they would be safe.

I slammed my arms against the glass underneath me.

The roof rumbled as it cracked, metal and concrete and plaster shifting. Elijah took a stumbling step back, eyes going wide as the roof shook.

She was off center, which was the reason the bullet missed its target.

It didn't hit me.

Instead it shattered the glass of the skylight I lay upon.

Weightlessness, only for a moment, as the glass gave way beneath me.

I fell through the skylight, head rapping against the metal frame, feet scraping against the cracks in the roof.

I remembered him.

Mark.

Standing in front of me, telling me I smelled like dirt and leaves and rain.

Telling me he needed to protect me.

The way he'd tasted on a summer's day, his bare feet in the grass.

The look of betrayal on his face as he stood on my doorstep.

The way my hand had felt on his throat as I left a raven on his skin.

I wished I'd gotten to tell him I loved him. One last time.

I fell.

The glass spun around me.

And from below me came the sound of a furious wolf.

I turned my head in time to see Mark burst into the garage.

Everything felt slow.

His muscles coiled before he jumped.

And then he began to turn.

The muscles and bones shifted underneath his skin. The thick hairs on his body receded. The paws outstretched in front of him spread and became fingers, the claws black and wicked sharp. As he became human, as his violet eyes flashed, the raven on his throat ruffled its feathered wings and—

Strong arms wrapped around me as a heavy human body collided into me. The breath was knocked from my chest as he curled himself around me, taking the brunt of the impact with the ground as we rolled. I ended up tucked into his side as the glass shattered.

And then silence.

I opened my eyes.

Mark was staring down at me.

His eyes were violet, but he was here. He was human.

I reached up and touched his face.

"Gordo," he growled through a mouthful of fangs.

"I don't understand," I whispered. "How are you—"

"As romantic as this is," Tanner said hoarsely, "and it's really very sweet, I would like it if my arms weren't chained to the fucking ceiling anymore."

"Yeah," Chris said, coughing wetly. "What he said."

Mark snapped his head up, nostrils flaring.

I pushed myself up away from him, struggling to get to my feet, body aching. I looked up at the skylight, expecting to see Elijah staring down at us, gun pointed in our direction, but all I could see was the moon.

Elizabeth ran into the rear of the garage, shifting violently. Her eyes were blazing orange as she stood.

"Hi, Mrs. Bennett," Tanner said.

"Nice to see you, Mrs. Bennett," Chris said.

Her eyes widened at the sight of Mark standing next to me, his hand still on my arm. "How did you—" She shook her head, moving toward the others. "Elijah escaped. I saw her jumping from the roof, but she was gone before I could get back around. She left a scent trail." She stood in front of Chris and Tanner, reaching out her hands to cup their faces. "I'm so happy to see you again. You are safe now. I promise you. I won't let them touch you again."

Chris sighed and leaned into her touch. "I'm okay," he said, words lisped through swollen and split lips. "It looks worse than it is. Get Tanner down first. They broke his arm this morning, those assholes. I'm going to fucking kill—holy *shit*, Gordo, where the fuck is your *hand*?"

"Long story," I muttered. "Later. We need to figure out what Elijah is going to do." I looked up at Mark. He was watching me. His eyes were still violet, but he wasn't struggling with his shift. "How are you doing this?"

It looked like it cost him greatly to speak. His words were rough. "You. You. It was you. Pack. Strong. Helped us. Gordo safe. Keep Gordo safe."

"Yeah. Okay. Safe. We're safe."

Tanner cried out as Elizabeth broke the manacles around his wrists. She held him against her as he cradled his arm, her hand on the back of his head, fingers in his hair as he sobbed. "I've got you," she whispered. "I've got you."

"Gordo," Chris said, "you gotta help them. She's going to—" He grimaced, turning his head and spitting a thick wad of blood onto the ground. "Elijah. She's not going to let anyone go. She knows. About the Lighthouse. We saw her. Packing it. Wearing it. Gordo, she's got a bomb strapped to her chest. And it's filled with silver. Ball bearings. It's—"

After your pack is dead and the fire of God has cleansed this place from evil, I will return and wash them of their sins. It has been made abundantly clear that nothing in Green Creek must remain as it is. I don't know how it was done, but Omegas have overrun this territory. It will need to be cleansed. The people here cannot be saved. I see that now. I will deal with them myself.

"Jessie," I breathed. "Rico."

Elizabeth moved in front of Chris. "I will stay with them. Gordo, you need to get to the Lighthouse before it's too late."

I turned to Mark.

His eyes were blazing,

I leaned forward and pressed my forehead to his. "Are you with me?"

His breath was hot against my face. *"Gordo."*

MOON

The streets of Green Creek were awash with blood.

Men and women—all hunters—stared sightlessly at the sky, eyes reflecting the full moon.

Their guns lay scattered in the snow.

There were Omegas. Full wolves. Some half-shifted. One whined at me as we passed it by, reaching its hands toward me. Its lower half had been crushed as if it'd been rolled over. Nothing could be done to save it.

Mark had shifted back into a wolf.

He stood above the Omega, head cocked down at it.

It reached up and ran a single hand through the hair on his throat.

It was over quick. Mark reached his head down and snapped its neck.

It didn't move after that.

He returned to my side.

We came to an overturned truck on fire, flames sputtering out into the snow. A pair of legs stuck out from beneath the cab. Another hunter had tried to crawl away but had been caught by a wolf. I didn't know where his arm had ended up.

From out of the trees stepped Robbie Fontaine, shifted and tense, followed by a small group of Omegas.

He came to me and pressed his nose against my hip. He huffed out a breath, leaving his scent upon me. I ran my hand between his ears. He leaned into the touch. There was a question sent, and I said, "We have to move. She's going to hurt everyone."

Robbie stepped away, turning over his shoulder to growl at the Omegas behind him. They flattened their ears. One hissed back at him, jaws stretched wide, but it subsided when Robbie let out a rough bark.

He fell in step beside me, and we moved on.

Kelly and Carter were next. They came out from between two houses, their muzzles caked with blood. Carter snarled at the sight of us, his hackles raised, beginning to coil like he was going to strike.

Kelly moved in front of him, throat rumbling almost like he was purring. Carter's eyes flickered between his normal blue and violet, and he whined, sounding confused. The timber wolf came up behind him, rubbing against his side. Carter allowed it for a moment before he turned his head and snapped at the wolf. It bared its teeth back at him, not moving away.

They surrounded me. Kelly and Robbie moved side by side. Carter and the timber wolf were to my left, next to Mark. More Omegas came out from the trees. All were shifted. One looked as if its leg had been severely broken. I saw the flash of wet white bone as it held the leg up against its stomach.

I could feel them.

My pack.

The Omegas.

A violent thrum that made my head ache.

The Alphas were waiting for us at the top of a hill, surrounded by feral wolves who seemed to want to get as close to Ox as they could. They were whining and barking in low, coarse tones, their songs running through us like a storm.

Behind them were the bodies of more hunters, mouths agape, arms stiff and hands frozen above them, as if they were still trying to ward off wolves, even in death.

I felt no pity for them.

They had brought this on themselves.

Joe looked over all of us, asking a question without making a sound.

"She's fine," I said. "With Chris and Tanner. She'll keep them safe. Elijah. She's—we have to help them. Jessie. Rico. The town."

The Alphas tilted their heads back and howled.

In the distance, we heard the sounds of gunfire.

·   ·   ·

She was waiting for us in front of the Lighthouse.

Her gun was in her hand, at her side.

She sat in the snow, cross-legged.

The bodies of six Omegas lay at her feet, all with smoking wounds, the silver burning its way through them.

She had pulled the wolf's head back, letting it rest on her neck.

Her coat was open.

On her torso, attached to a thin Kevlar vest, were long glass cylinders. Eight of them in total. Each had two wires fixed to the top, green and red. The cylinders were packed full of silver ball bearings, just as Chris had said. Between her Kevlar and the cylinders were small bricks of what looked like black putty.

Behind her, the Lighthouse stood darkened.

Rico and Jessie must have heard her coming and turned out the lights. Hopefully they were keeping everyone down on the floor and quiet. I was about to look away when Rico peered out the window, eyes wide. He saw us approaching and disappeared. Christ, I needed to keep them safe.

Elijah slowly rose at our approach. The moon caused her shadow to stretch out grotesquely onto the Lighthouse.

She wasn't scared.

Her hands did not shake.

She smiled.

She said, "Alphas. Monsters. Beasts. A blight on the skin of the world." She spat onto the bodies of the Omegas at her feet. "Paul the Apostle gave warning. He pleaded with his elders to keep watch over the Lord's blood-soaked flock. He told them that after his departure, fierce wolves would come among them, not sparing the flock. They did not care, these wolves, about righteousness. About piety. They were devoted only to the rage that called from the moon. And Peter— he knew this too. He told them of false prophets who would rise amongst the people." She raised her voice. "Just as there will be false teachers among you, who will secretly bring in destructive heresies, even denying the Master who bought them, bringing upon themselves swift destruction. And from among your own selves will arise men speaking twisted things, to draw away the disciples after them." She looked at Ox. "You. You are the false prophet. The false teacher. The abomination. You, who found a way to become an Alpha even before you gave in to the sins of a wolf. Beware the wolf in sheep's clothing. It will come to scatter the flock. But the Lord is my shepherd, and I shall not fear the wolf."

"It's over," I said. "You're outnumbered, Elijah. Your people are dead."

Her smile widened. "A necessary sacrifice which proves everything I've said. Everything I've believed. This town has a curse upon it. The land has been poisoned. We came here once, hoping to cleanse the earth so that it could heal, free from the chains of the beast. My God walked with me that day, steadying my aim." She tilted her head toward the sky. "Especially when it came to the smaller ones. The little wolves. They . . . tried to run from me. I was a shining light in the darkness, and they could not escape."

"They were just kids," I said hoarsely as the wolves growled around me, all of us blue and blue and blue.

"Little wolves grow into big wolves," she said. "And big wolves know nothing but the taste for flesh and blood. They were already lost the moment they took a breath in this world. Either they must be put down, or their spirit broken until they become nothing but a pet." She glanced at the timber wolf, who flinched and tried to crowd closer to Carter. "But even then they disappoint you."

Mark took a step forward, growling dangerously.

Elijah didn't recoil. If anything, that made her angry. "But we couldn't take them all. I watched as my family fell around me. I saw their skin tear. I heard their screams. I was a *child*, but I saw it all from the trees." A tear fell from her eye and onto the knotted tissue of the scar on her face. "My family. Aunts and uncles. Cousins. People who believed such as I did. The wolves didn't know I was there. The blood was too thick in the air for them to notice me. My father, he . . . lost his way, after that. He didn't understand why God had forsaken him. Why he had abandoned us when we needed him most. He couldn't see what I could see. He didn't know what I knew. We hadn't been abandoned. We had been *tested*. It's always been about the strength of faith. He is a just God, but he is a demanding God. He needs proof of our convictions. My father had lost sight of that. He spoke of walking away. Of just letting them *go*. And no matter what I said to him, no matter how much I begged and pleaded with him, he wouldn't listen to *reason*. He had fallen from his faith." She raised her gun and put the barrel to the side of her head. "I told him that I was sorry." Her voice broke. "That I wished it didn't have to end like this. But I couldn't have his discord spread to the others. In the end, he, too, was a wolf in sheep's clothing, trying to take down the flock one by one." She put her finger on the trigger. "God commanded Abraham to sacrifice Isaac, his son. On Moriah. To prove his faith. He took his son to the mountain, bound and gagged, and placed him atop the altar. And just as he was about to show God how much he loved him, an angel came, telling him that God knew just how much Abraham feared him now. A ram appeared, and Abraham was able to sacrifice that instead, and God was *appeased*." She put the slightest amount of pressure on the trigger. "I knew that I was being tested, just as Abraham was. I knew what God was asking of me. Because I had faltered. In this place. I had *failed*. So I went to my father while he slept. And I put my gun to his head, and I put my finger on the trigger, and I *waited* for the angel to appear, I *waited* for a sign to tell me that I had proven myself, that I was who God wanted me to be."

gordo gordo gordo

"Nothing came," Elijah said. "And I did what I had to. I didn't cry when I shot my father in the head. I didn't—I felt peace. I knew that I had done the right thing. What had been asked of me. It was necessary. My father had failed. And I could not. It was . . . simple, in the end." She lowered the gun back down to her side. "I buried him under an old oak tree. I carved his initials into the trunk. He would have been proud of me for that. My brother, Daniel, he—he didn't see it that way. I buried him next to my father."

"You won't leave here," I told her. "This is the end, Elijah."

She nodded. "I know. I always knew that coming back would be the last thing I ever did. I prepared myself for that, even if I felt my skin crawl at being ordered by one such as Michelle Hughes. Standing in front of her and not filling her with silver was one of the hardest things I've ever done. And she thought we agreed for the sake of protecting the wolves from sickness. From infection. It was never about that. It was finally time to return to this place that had taken so much from me. It was about doing what I was born to do. What I was instructed by God to do."

"I won't let you hurt them. I'll kill you before you can—"

She laughed. "I don't fear death, Gordo. I will be rewarded after for all that I've done. A plague has fallen upon the beasts, and I will stop it before it spreads further. Calling the Omegas here was something I didn't expect, but in the end, you have done the work for me. You have brought them all to this place, and I will smite every single one of them. I stand before an Alpha of the Omegas and the boy who would be king. Their deaths will signal the beginning of the end of the wolves, and I—"

Pappas came then. He was quick. I hadn't even heard him approach. He growled from on top of the Lighthouse, eyes violet and bright in the dark. He leapt from the roof directly toward her. He had the high ground, and I knew this was it. It was finally going to be over—

Except Elijah was an old hunter. Years and years of experience. She had killed dozens—maybe even hundreds—of wolves. She knew them. She knew how they moved. How they hunted.

Divide and conquer.

I had time to wonder if this had been her plan all along. This moment.

She spun on her feet, the skin of the dead wolf hanging off her back flaring around her, kicking up snow as she dropped to her heels. Pappas missed her by inches, crashing into the ground in front of her, sliding in the snow.

He had barely begun to push himself to his feet when Elijah raised her gun and pulled the trigger.

The *crack* of gunfire echoed in the forest around us. Philip Pappas's head snapped to the side, an arc of blood in the air as he fell.

He was dead even before he hit the ground.

The wolves started to advance on her.

"Don't," she said coldly, but instead of pointing her gun at us, she raised her *other* hand. In it was a small black rectangular box, her thumb pressed against the top.

"Dead man's switch," she said. "Anything happens to me, seven pounds of C-4 explosive will send six hundred silver ball bearings at speeds greater than three hundred miles per hour. Nothing—not humans, not wolves—will survive the blast."

Ox and Joe shifted almost immediately.

The Omegas whimpered around them.

Ox said, "You will not hurt them. The humans have done nothing wrong. You want the pack? Fine. You have us. But you can't hurt innocent people. Your fight is not with them. It's with us."

Elijah's eyes narrowed. "Innocent? What does a wolf know of *innocence?* They have sided with *animals*. They—"

"We didn't give them a choice," Joe said. "We held them captive. All they want is to be free. You're right. They're lost. They need to have someone to show them the way."

She glared at him. "You *lie*."

"You spoke of the failings of a father," Ox said, taking a step toward her. "I know exactly what you meant. I, too, had a father who lost faith. In himself. In my mother. In me."

Elijah took a step back. "Stop."

"He told me that I would be nothing. That I was going to get shit all of my life."

"You don't know *anything*—"

"And I believed him. For the longest time, I believed him. Until I found myself a place in this world. We're not that different. You had your clan. I have my pack. You're not a wolf, but I know you have felt the bonds between your people. It's—"

She shook her head furiously. "No. No, no, no—"

"And I'm sorry that it has come to this," Ox said, taking another step. The raven was agitated. I didn't know what it was going to do. "But you gave me no choice. I would do anything to keep my family safe. You forced my hand. All we wanted was to be left alone."

"I don't believe you," she said. She brought the gun up and pointed it at Ox's head.

"Ox," Joe warned.

Mark bristled at my side.

"I know you're scared," Ox said quietly. "And I know you think you have no other choice, but you *do*. Would your God really ask you to do this? Would he really want you to hurt people who have done *nothing*?"

He stopped in front of her.

She pressed the barrel of the gun against his forehead.

"We're not animals, Meredith," he said quietly.

Her face scrunched up, and incredulously, I thought it had worked. That Ox, crazy, beautiful Ox, had somehow gotten through to her. That he would take the gun from her, that she would back down and this would all be over. Oh, I was going to kill her the moment she let her guard down, but the fact that an Alpha wolf had pierced through the broken fury of the hunter Elijah was nothing short of extraordinary.

And then she laughed.

A chill ran down my spine.

"That was good," she said. "I'll give you that. But it wasn't good enough. Go to hell, Alpha."

Her finger tightened on the trigger.

I was already moving, but it was too late. The hammer rose and then fell back with an audible *snap*.

There was the dry click of an empty gun.

"Well, shit," Elijah said, and then she smashed the gun upside Ox's skull.

His head jerked to the right.

The wolves howled.

She spun and ran toward the Lighthouse.

She was up the stairs right as I reached Ox.

She hit the door hard.

It splintered around her, and she fell inside the Lighthouse.

"Gordo," Ox shouted, and the terror in his voice broke my heart. *"No!"*

I was at the bottom of the stairs when she lifted her head to look back at me. She raised the hand with the dead man's switch.

"Please," I breathed.

The raven flew.

She smiled.

And lifted her thumb.

She exploded in a bright flash of fire. I felt a wave of heat, but I was lost to the petals of roses, to the prick of thorns, to the furious storm of an unkindness of ravens. My mother had told me they didn't love me, they needed me, they would *use* me, and that the magic in me was a lie.

She had been wrong.

My wolves loved, and I loved them in return.

I was pack and pack and *packpackpack—*

BrotherLovePackFriendMateMateMate

A great wall of ice rose in front of us, even as Ox put his hand on my shoulder, as Mark pressed against my side. Through the thick blue sheen, fire roared as the Lighthouse blew apart. The ice began to crack as balls of silver smashed into it, boring through with such force that I thought they'd break out the other side and hurt my pack.

In my head, I heard them all—my pack, the Omegas—and they were *pushing* against me, *pushing* and giving me their strength.

And suddenly the roses began to bloom *in* the ice, the flowers thick and fibrous. The wall burst into vibrant life, as wild and fierce as my Alphas' eyes. Ravens flew along the vines, grasping them in their talons and pulling them up higher, until the wall in front of us was completely filled with roses. The fire burned behind it, making the garden look as if it was alight.

A single silver ball bearing made its way through the ice. There was a small *crack* as it came out the other side. It fell into the snow at my feet even as debris from the Lighthouse rained down around us. Wolves climbed on top of me, pressing me down into the snow as they shielded me from flaming debris.

I could barely breathe.

Those people.

All those people.

Rico.

And Jessie.

And it'd been my fault. All my fault.

"No," Ox whispered in my ear, "no, Gordo, it wasn't," and I realized I'd been saying that aloud. "Gordo, you saved us. You need to listen to me. I need you to listen to me."

gordo gordo gordo

Mark grunted as a heavy piece of *something* hit his back, but he wouldn't move. He wouldn't leave me.

I couldn't breathe.

I couldn't breathe.

I couldn't—

The raven flew again.

The wolves were knocked off me with a furious burst of magic, Joe shouting in surprise, Mark snarling as he hit the ground. I pushed myself to my feet even before they could move. I pressed my hand against the rose ice wall, cursing in anger when I realized I didn't *have* a fucking hand anymore, but it didn't matter. The wall shattered, and I cried out as heavy chunks of ice filled with blooms landed on my head, my shoulders. I pushed through it, needing to get to Jessie, needing to get to Rico. I remembered when Tanner had brought me a little sandwich while I was buried in grief at the loss of my mother at the hands of my father, and how he'd brought Rico a taquito, a motherfucking *taquito,* and Rico had told him that was racist, that was racist, and how *dare* he. I had brought them into this life I had tried so hard to keep them away from, because they were my *normal*, they were my *safety*. They were there when everyone had left me behind. And now look at them. Chris and Tanner had been hurt, they'd been *tortured* because of me, and now Rico was—oh Jesus, Rico was—

The Lighthouse had been leveled to its foundations. Wood burned, hissing when it hit the wet snow. The bar top was gone, and tiny bits of glass shone like stars in the firelight littering the floor.

Elijah was—not much of her remained. The wolf skin had been shredded, and the head was burning. Elijah herself had mostly been destroyed. One of her legs remained. Her arm. I thought I saw what was left of her gun, the iron blackened and smoking.

I stepped over her, choking on smoke, trying to push my way into the Lighthouse, needing to find them, needing to see for myself that they were gone because of me. They were gone, and there was nothing I could do about it.

Except . . .

There was nothing there.

Even through the smoke, even through the storm that raged in my head, *there was nothing there*.

Strong hands wrapped around me, pulling me away, away, away.

I fell down into the snow outside the Lighthouse. My eyes burned from the smoke. I coughed roughly, on my hand and knees, head bowed. I struggled to take a deep breath, but my lungs hurt.

Mark knelt before me, once again human. He took my face in his hands and lifted me toward him.

His eyes were violet, but his touch was soft and forgiving. The raven on his throat stood out bright in the moonlight.

"Gone," he said through gritted teeth. "Already gone. Out. Escaped."

I didn't understand. I was exhausted. What remained of my strength was rapidly diminishing. I'd pushed too hard in the end. To save them. My pack.

Mark look frustrated, mouth a thin line, like he couldn't find the right words.

My heart ached.

Joe came then. He put his forehead on my shoulder. "Rico and Jessie. They got everyone out the back in time. While Ox kept her talking. They're fine, Gordo. Everyone is safe."

I closed my eyes and sagged against Mark.

He held me tightly.

"Pappas?" I managed to ask.

Joe said, "No. He . . . he didn't make it."

"Okay," Mark whispered, rocking me back and forth. "Okay. Okay. Okay."

I opened my eyes to the sound of an approaching vehicle.

There, on the road, heading straight for us, was one of the trucks belonging to the hunters, light bar across the top lit up.

I struggled to push myself up, needing to get to whoever it was. It never ended. It never ended, and I couldn't—

"Elizabeth," Mark grunted in my ear, arms tightening around me as he held me against his chest. "Tanner. Chris."

"What?" I croaked out.

"Pack. Pack. Pack."

The truck stopped, and through the windshield, I could see Tanner and Chris staring out in horror at the sight before them. Elizabeth said something and pushed the door open, sliding from the driver's seat. She had found some clothes to wear, and though they looked big on her, she was still intimidating as fuck. Her eyes were orange as she approached, her hand going to the tops of her sons' heads as Carter and Kelly fell in step beside her.

"Is she gone?" she asked, voice hard. "Elijah."

"Yeah," Joe said wearily. "She's—Gordo. He saved us. He saved all of us."

"What happened to him?"

"Just tired," I muttered, though my words came out in a slur. "Give me a few. I'll be up to kick some ass again later."

"Jesus *Christ*," I heard Chris say. "You let her blow up the bar? Oh my god, where the hell are we supposed to drink *now*? Mack's? His beer is all foam, man."

"I told you two to stay in the truck," Elizabeth scolded Chris and Tanner as they approached. Chris looked worse than before, and Tanner's face was pale as he held his arm against his chest. "You can't be moving around much until we get your injuries checked out."

"Oh, man," Chris said. "Please tell me my sister's okay and that she didn't hear me bitch about the bar before I asked about her well-being."

"Every word," another voice said. "When you get healed up again, I'm going to kick your ass."

I turned my head against Mark's chest.

Coming out of the dark on the other side of the bar was Jessie. And Rico. And they were leading a group of wide-eyed people, most of whom were staring in shock at the devastation before them.

The Omegas growled at them, but Ox flashed his eyes and they flinched away, trembling against each other in the snow.

Chris moved toward Jessie, smiling even though it obviously pained him. He limped, right leg dragging behind him. She met him halfway, wrapping her hands around him. He grunted in pain, and when she tried to pull away, he just held her tighter.

"This kind of sucks," another voice said, and I looked to see Bambi standing with her hands on her hips, glaring at what remained of her bar. "Good thing it's covered. Though I'm probably going to have to commit insurance fraud, because I don't think it's going to go over very well if I tell them the reason my bar exploded was because hunters came to kill my boyfriend's werewolf pack."

"I love you so much," Rico breathed. "I'm going to do so many things to you after I get over the mind-numbing PTSD of almost getting murdered by evil humans and feral werewolves."

"Werewolves!" Will cried, and he looked soberer than I'd seen him in a long time. "I always knew something was going on with that family. Always hiding out in the woods. And you all said it was *coyotes* we heard howling. Looks like I'm owed apologies from all of you!"

The townspeople murmured behind him, huddling together. Some of them watched the feral wolves. Some of them were watching the fire burn.

But most of them were watching Oxnard Matheson as he approached.

"Maybe he should think about putting on some pants," Rico muttered, hanging off Bambi. "If he's going to tell them more than we did, they should probably hear it without his dick hanging out."

"It's a nice dick," Bambi said.

"Oh my god, would you *please* not stare at my *alfa's* junk?"

"He's pretty good with it too," Jessie said.

Joe growled at both of them as he followed his mate.

Bambi laughed as Jessie flipped him off.

Elizabeth kneeled in front of me. Mark tightened his grip around me, and I rolled my eyes.

"All right?" she asked, leaning forward to put a hand to my forehead. It was such a motherly thing to do that I had to swallow past the sudden lump in my throat.

"Yeah," I managed to say. "All right."

"Saved us," Mark grunted from behind me. "Gordo saved us."

Elizabeth glanced at him before looking back at me. "I know. It stinks of magic."

"Not much I can do about that," I said, trying to keep my eyes open.

There was a pulse under her hand, and I felt *green green green* come through the bonds. "Thank you," she whispered. "For keeping them safe."

I sighed. "Promised you I would. And then you threatened to kill me."

And she *laughed*. "Oh, Gordo. How I love you so."

The other wolves came then, and the humans. Bambi looked confused when Rico kissed her forehead and left her standing next to the bar. He went to Tanner and Chris first, and though I could hear them complaining about being too manly for such a thing, they hugged for a long, long time, Rico first kissing Chris on the cheek and then turning his head and doing the same to Tanner, muttering something that I couldn't hear to each of them.

Elizabeth sat in front of me, her hands on my legs.

Carter and the timber wolf lay on my left, Carter's nose pressed against my thigh, breathing in my scent. Kelly and Robbie came on my right, trying to get as close to me as they could. Jessie's hand was in my hair, and Chris, Tanner, and Rico stood behind us, always the protectors of their pack.

Oxnard Matheson and Joe Bennett stood in front of the people gathered near the remains of the bar. He looked over all of them, and Joe reached over, taking his mate's hand in his, holding it tight.

"You've known me," Ox said, "for a long time. I was just a kid when I came here. My mother, she . . . she did her best in the face of everything. She raised me. She loved me with every piece of her soul. She laughed. She danced. And one day she gave her life so that I could live mine. A monster came and took her from me. He also took my father, Thomas Bennett. I didn't—I didn't know if I would survive after that. But it was because of my family that I survived. You see, one day I met a boy. A boy who talked and talked and talked of things like candy canes and pinecones. Epic and awesome. A tornado who would never let me go. And he helped me be brave and strong. Even when my heart was breaking, I remembered that. Remembered him. And . . . my pack. I'm a mechanic. I'm the guy that lives in the house at the end of the lane. I eat with you. I laugh with you. I *live* with you. I bleed, and I hurt, and I love this town. This place. Thomas taught me there is nothing like Green Creek anywhere else in the world. It doesn't matter if you're human. Or a witch. Or something more. Like an Alpha." His eyes flared red and violet, and the people gasped. But none of them backed away. None of them tried to run, which, given it was a full moon and they stood before a pack of wolves, was probably a good thing. They were scared, even I could see that, but it was out-weighed by something more. "I am the Alpha of the Omegas."

"And I am the Alpha of all," Joe said, squeezing Ox's hand.

"And this is the Bennett pack," Ox said. "Our pack. And I promise you, no matter what happens, we will always be here to keep you safe. If you let us."

No one spoke.

The fire burned.

My pack breathed around me.

Then Bambi spoke. "You gonna bite us?"

And because he just couldn't help himself, Rico said, "That's my job."

Bambi glared at him. "Consider correcting what you just said."

Rico blanched. "Yes, my queen. You are the light in my life. Without you my world is cold and dark and celibate."

She looked back at Ox and arched an eyebrow.

"No," Ox said. "I will not bite you. I will not harm you. Any of you. We will protect Green Creek with everything we have."

"And what about them?" she asked, nodding toward the Omegas prowling behind us. "If what Rico and Jessie told us is true, they're sick. They're hurting. And you don't know how to fix it. How can you guarantee they won't turn around and attack someone when you're not looking? You can't be everywhere at once, Ox. No matter how strong you are."

"That's where we come in," another voice said.

I turned my head.

On the road stood Aileen and Patrice. Behind them were a group of people.

Witches. All of them.

Aileen smiled. "I have an idea."

RAVENSONG

This has to work."

I turned my head, fumbling with the cigarette in my left hand. Ash burned my fingers as I blew smoke out my nose. Maybe it was time to quit.

I looked back out at the front of the house at the end of the lane. Omegas prowled in the snow. Some were sleeping. Others were grooming. Still others crashed in the forest around us.

Mark lay at the bottom of the steps, ears perked up, paws crossed in front of him, watching the feral wolves.

Carter was running with the timber wolf at his side. I could make him out in the distance, weaving in and out of the trees.

"I don't know," I muttered, stubbing out my cigarette and dropping it into an old coffee canister.

Oxnard didn't say anything more.

He didn't need to. We were all thinking the same thing.

It'd been six weeks since the full moon. Things had changed yet again, and I couldn't help but feel like we were barely in control. The people who'd been at the Lighthouse the night Elijah had come for them had formed somewhat of an uneasy truce with us, led by Bambi and, surprisingly, Will. Granted, he seemed to take pleasure in telling anyone who would listen just how right he'd been, but still. People who thought he was crazy before didn't think that now.

We hadn't been able to escape scrutiny. A cop had been shot in the head. Green Creek had been torn apart. People were dead.

A tale was spun. Of a militia group who had come to Green Creek under the cover of a storm. They hadn't been happy, Elizabeth Bennett had told authorities, about a land deal that had been in the works with her husband before he died. He'd been planning on pulling out but had had his heart attack before he could do so. It'd been left to a grieving family to inform the Kings that any negotiations that had been in place before Thomas Bennett died were over.

The Kings had come then. Armed to the teeth. They'd murdered Jones, dumping his body in the woods. They'd almost killed Chris and Tanner, first by knocking them into the diner, and then, later, by holding them hostage and torturing them. They'd destroyed the bar.

They'd been led by Meredith King.

Meredith King who, in the end, had blown herself up in the Lighthouse.

As for the others, well. While everyone had been trying to hide, there must have been some infighting. There'd been gunfire. That was all anybody knew.

Oh yes, there'd been dogs with them, now that you mention it. Big dogs. Dogs that almost looked . . . feral. The Kings had brought them when they tried to take over. No one seemed very surprised that the dogs would have turned on their masters. You raise a hand to an animal enough, and eventually it will either cower or fight back.

It looked as if these dogs fought back.

No, no one saw where the dogs went. The area was rural. The forests stretched for miles and miles into the mountains. They probably took their pack and fled. They'd be long gone by now.

It was shaky, held together by thin strings. It had holes large enough to drive a truck through. It was national news, the tiny mountain town under siege by a group of redneck militants. Oregon seemed to breed them. There'd been that group the year before in Eastern Oregon who'd taken over a wildlife refuge to protest the Bureau of Land Management. Granted, they'd gotten off free in the end, hadn't they?

The Kings didn't.

It'd lasted days. Cameras and reporters with wide eyes and breathless voices, speaking into microphones about the Terror in Green Creek, as the chyrons all said across the bottoms of screens. And while it started off as a major story, the media quickly became frustrated at how *no one* wanted to speak about it. No one wanted to be interviewed. They all just wanted to move on.

Sometimes howls could be heard coming from the trees. "Coyotes," Will told reporters who'd stayed in his motel. "Maybe a couple of wolves. Best stay of out of the forest if you know what's good for you. If I was a betting man, I'd wager they don't take kindly to outsiders."

They left as quickly as they had come, and Green Creek was once again forgotten. Tragedies occurred everywhere, after all.

We waited.

Six long weeks since Mark had shifted back to a wolf and stayed that way.

Oh, Ox had tried to call him back. Tried to do the same for Carter. But while he could still feel them, while he could still feel *all* of them, they were still Omegas. It was only under extraordinary duress that Mark had been able to shift back when he had, when his mate had been in danger. All his protective instincts had come rushing forward, and he'd *forced* himself to shift back to human.

But that had passed, and even as that long night had ended, he had shifted back and remained that way.

He never left my side. We slept in his bed at the Bennett house. I'd only been back to the garage a couple of times since we'd rescued Chris and Tanner. At first I'd told myself I needed time to heal. That we'd all been through something traumatic and we couldn't be expected to pick up right where we left off. That I didn't want to leave Mark, not while he was stuck as he was.

Chris and Tanner and Rico said they understood. They handled the day-to-day operations of the shop. Well, Chris and Rico did. Tanner tried as best he could, but his arm was in a cast and would be until after Christmas. Robbie still worked the front office and the phones.

They knew, though, what I was doing.

I figured I'd get at least a few more days of feeling sorry for myself. My hand was done.

There was nothing I could do about that.

The stump was fully healed, the skin slightly gnarled where my hand had once been. It felt strange, the skin bumpy and ridged, with barely any loss of sensation. If I pressed down hard enough, I could feel the jut of bone. Whatever Patrice had done had been effective.

But the skin wasn't unmarked.

The sleeves my father had tattooed onto my arms extended to either wrist. I didn't see they had changed until we got back to the Bennett house as the sun rose after the full moon.

The runes were the same. They hadn't moved.

The roses had, though.

The vines now extended down my forearm, twisting around the runes and symbols, the thorns sharp and curved. And covering the stump was a bloom of roses so red, they looked real. Patrice and

Aileen hadn't been able to explain it. Either my place as the witch of the Bennett pack in our territory under siege had caused my magic to expand to compensate for the loss of my hand, or my mate bond with Mark was so strong, I'd called upon it to make a wall of ice filled with roses. Or a combination of the two.

It was beautiful, regardless. It looked like the work of a master.

But my hand was gone.

I wallowed.

Yeah, it wouldn't be long before the guys came to kick my ass.

And Ox, always Ox, knew what was going on in my head.

He'd been busy these past weeks. Maintaining control of a couple dozen Omega wolves would do that to an Alpha. There hadn't been much time for anything other than holding ourselves together as best we could, especially when more Omegas arrived every few days, still drawn by the pull of their Alpha.

But the new moon was tomorrow, and the sky would be dark.

"Shop looks good," Ox said, and I sighed, knowing what was coming. I'd hoped we could avoid all this, but it was probably time to get it over with. "Everything almost looks back to normal. The diner's about to reopen. Lighthouse is on track for March. Main Street repaired from all that storm damage."

I snorted. "Storm damage. Right. I forgot about that."

"I'm sure. But everything is going good with the garage, in case you were wondering."

"Great."

"Since you haven't really been back to town in a few weeks."

I rolled my eyes. "You're not very subtle. You know that, right?"

He shrugged. "Not trying to be. The guys know you'll be back when you're ready."

"Oh?"

"Well. They're giving you until the New Year to be ready."

"Figured."

"I thought you might have. You need to go back."

I refused to look at him. "I'm needed here."

"Why?"

"Mark. He—"

"Mark is fine. I've got him. Try again."

"Jesus Christ."

"Yeah. Sounds about right."

Mark turned to look at me at the uptick of my heart. He cocked his head, and it was *gordo gordo gordo* in a constant hum.

"Thank you," Ox said quietly.

"I'm not going to do this. Not with you."

I felt that big hand of his on the back of my neck, squeezing tightly. "You saved me. Again. You always do that, don't you?"

I stepped out of his reach. The wooden porch creaked underneath us. Mark slowly rose as I glared at Ox. "I'm your witch. It's what I'm supposed to do. You would do the same for me."

"I would."

"So then don't. I don't need your gratitude. I don't need your pity."

"You're hurting, Gordo. You've tried to hide yourself for so long that it's become second nature for you. But you always seem to forget that you can't hide shit from me. I'm your—"

"Alpha," I spat bitterly. "I know. You're always in my head."

"I was going to say friend."

Goddammit. "I—I don't—"

"I'm your friend, Gordo. And your tether. Yes, I am your Alpha, but it's always been more than that between us. Even before . . . all of this. You were there after my daddy left. When it was just Mom and me. When I called you on the phone and told you we needed help. You—you came for me. You always have."

"I'm fine," I told him stubbornly. "You don't have to feel guilty for—"

"You aren't alone."

I swallowed with an audible click.

"You've always been this . . . force," Ox said, not unkindly. "This immovable force. A mountain, I told myself. A constant. Always watching. Over me. And then over Joe and Carter and Kelly. Yeah, maybe it wasn't what you wanted. Maybe it wasn't what you expected it to be. But you were always there, Gordo. For us. It's time you let us be there for you."

"I don't need—"

His eyes flashed. "Don't lie to me. Not about this."

"It's not as easy as you're making it out to be."

"I know. But surely it isn't as hard as you seem to think it is."

"I'm fucking *broken*, Ox," I snapped at him. "Why can't you see that? Why can't *any* of you see that? All of you, you're treating me like—like I'm—"

"A member of the Bennett pack," Ox said. "Just as you've always been."

"That's not fair," I said hoarsely. "You can't just—goddammit."

He stepped forward slowly, like he was approaching a skittish animal. I gave brief thought to jumping down the stairs and heading for the trees. Instead I just sagged when he stood in front of me. He leaned forward, pressing his forehead against mine, and even though I tried to fight it, this was my Alpha, and I needed him here, with me. He hummed a little under his breath, mingling my scent with his.

"You gave part of yourself for me," he whispered, and my eyes stung. I could barely breathe. "You protected me. And I will never forget that. I wish—I wish things could have been different. For all of us. But we are here. And we are together. And I will do everything in my power to make sure it stays that way. Do you believe me?"

Of course I did. I loved him. I nodded, not trusting myself to speak.

"It will work."

I opened my eyes to stare directly into his.

"It will work," he said again. "Because we are pack. We will sing them home, and one day they will be as they once were."

A wolf climbed the steps, and a moment later a cold nose pressed against the roses.

gordo, the wolf whispered. *gordo gordo gordo.*

"A tether is the strength behind the wolf," Abel Bennett told me once. "A feeling or a person or an *idea* that keeps us in touch with our human sides. It's a song that calls us home when we are shifted. It reminds us of where we come from. My tether is my pack. The people who count on me to keep them safe. To protect them from those who would do them harm. Do you understand?"

I hadn't. Not then.

But I did now.

"It won't be the same," Aileen told us. "I need you to understand that right now. It won't be like it was before. Carter and Mark, they . . . won't be Betas, at least not in the traditional sense. They'll still be Omegas. But they will belong to Ox just as they did before, and to a lesser extent, to Joe. This isn't a cure. It's a stopgap. There's nothing we can do to end whatever Robert Livingstone has brought upon them. It's a magic that we have never seen before, this infection. It is corruption on a level that is unprecedented. We don't know how he's managed to achieve this, but we can do our best to contain it. The only way it can be completely broken is if the witch responsible breaks it himself, or . . . or if he's dead. As for the others, they only feel an allegiance to Ox. They will see only him as their Alpha. Some are infected. Others are just feral, either because their pack was taken from them or their tethers lost. I can't make any promises about them. They will not be your pack. Not really. But you will be tied to them because you are tied to Ox.

"It will need to be during the new moon, when the pull is at its weakest. It will require all of you, and all of us. Our combined strength. But I believe it will work. There are doors in the mind. Gordo shattered the door between Ox and the Omegas. We need to close the doors between the wolves and the wild that calls to them. Those infected will affix to Ox. Carter to Kelly. Mark to Gordo. But you must remember that they will scratch on the door. They'll still feel it in their heads. It will not take much for the doors to blow wide open. And I cannot promise you that we can ever close it again should that happen. We need to find him. We need to find Robert Livingstone and end this once and for all. You have the support of the witches. We will do all we can to help you in this war."

She smiled sadly. "Though I know not of what the future brings, this moment will be the greatest test of the strength of your pack. Of the bonds between you all. Only if they are true, and only if they are pure, will this ever have a chance of working. I believe you're all capable of bringing them back. I just hope that you believe it too."

.   .   .

We lay in the bed. The sounds of the pack moved through the house beneath us. In the basement, the Omegas gathered, sleeping on top of each other. Outside, daylight was giving way to night. I could hear Elizabeth singing somewhere in the house at the end of the lane, her voice mixing with Judy Garland's, telling us to have a merry little Christmas. It was blue and blue and blue.

Mark's massive head rested on my chest, rising with every breath

I took. I ran a finger between his eyes. He rumbled his contentment, and I heard him whispering my name.

"You need to come back to me," I whispered as the room darkened. "You need to come back to me, because we've only just begun. I'm sorry. For all the time I've wasted. For all my anger. For everything that's happened between us. And I know I don't deserve it after all we've been through, but I need you. I need you here with me. I can't do this without you. Not anymore. I love you, and I don't ever want to stop."

His eyes flared violet, and for a moment, I felt *GordoPackMate-Love.*

It was dirt and leaves and rain.

I hoped it would be enough.

It was almost time.

A cold November had given way to a mild December. The snow had melted almost entirely, leaving behind a waterlogged earth. The ground squelched beneath our feet as we made our way through the forest.

Ox and Joe led the way, their pack moving behind them. Omegas crawled through the trees, trailing behind their Alpha.

Mark was at my side. Always.

The trees gave way to a clearing.

There, waiting for us, were witches.

Aileen stood as we approached. Patrice stayed sitting where he was, off from all the others, eyes closed and legs crossed. His hands were on his knees as he breathed in and out slowly.

"Alphas Bennett and Matheson," Aileen said, bowing low. It was the most formal I'd seen her since she arrived in Green Creek the night Ox had called the Omegas. "It is a pleasure to see you again."

Ox and Joe bowed in return, eyes flashing in respect. I didn't think we needed to stand on ceremony, but Thomas had drilled it into Joe, and he wouldn't have it any other way. "We are well met in Bennett territory," Joe said, sounding a little stiff. "You and yours are welcome here in the spirit of unity."

Aileen looked as if she was trying to keep a smile from her face.

"Indeed. The spirit of unity. Tell me, Alpha. Will you do what you must for your pack?"

"Yes," Joe said without hesitation.

"I expected as much. Patrice has been meditating since the sun reached its zenith. The land here, this place—it speaks to him. To all of us, I think. I understand why your family chose it. And why others have tried to take it from you."

"They have tried," Elizabeth said coolly. "Again and again. But they haven't succeeded."

There was the smile Aileen had tried to hide. "No, I don't suppose they have. A message has been sent, I think. But I worry it will still be ignored by nonbelievers. This is but one ending. There are other things to come."

"We'll be ready," Kelly said, standing next to his brother. Carter growled in response.

"I know you will. Shall we?"

The witches began to spread out around the edges of the clearing. I recognized a few of them when they nodded in my direction. They were all without a pack. I wondered what Michelle Hughes would think of them being here with us. If she wasn't scared yet, she would be soon enough.

It was similar to how it'd been when we destroyed the door between Ox and the Omegas. Only this seemed bigger somehow, beyond anything that I'd ever been part of. Kelly and I sat in front of Patrice. The ground was wet beneath us, but I ignored it. Without hesitation, Kelly reached over and took my hand.

"All right?" I asked him quietly.

He nodded tightly. "If this doesn't work—"

"It will."

He squeezed my hand. "If it doesn't, I need you to know I don't blame you. For Carter. For Mark. For anything."

"You should."

"No. I shouldn't. You did what you thought was right. And we're all still here. If this doesn't work, there will be another way. We'll find it. I know we will."

"Yeah," I said, looking away. "We will."

"Gordo?"

"Yeah?"

"I'm scared."

"Me too."

He let out a shuddering breath. "But we're strong. All of us. Because there's never been a pack like ours."

"Nevermore," I whispered, and somehow he knew what I was trying to say.

Mark lay next to me, resting his head in my lap. Carter did the same to Kelly. Our pack gathered behind us. Rico's hand was on one shoulder and Tanner's on the other. Chris touched the top of my head, fingers tangling with my hair. Elizabeth stood above her sons, her legs pressed against Kelly's back. Robbie was next to her and, after a moment of hesitation, reached down and touched the side of Kelly's face.

Jessie stood with the timber wolf, who didn't look too happy being away from Carter. We didn't know what would happen with it. If it would shift back or stay as it was. He didn't fit like the others. He'd barely let us remove the silver chain that had been embedded around his neck, and that was only because Carter had been there. Ox couldn't feel him. Not like the others. We didn't know why.

The Alphas stood on either side of Patrice, facing their pack. They placed their hands on his shoulders. The Omegas gathered behind them, yipping and growling as if agitated. They knew. Somehow, they knew something was coming.

In the distance, I felt the first pulse of magic. Witches stood, arms raised, palms flat toward us. Their eyes were closed, and all of them muttered under their breaths. Aileen was closest, and I could hear her quiet murmur. It was almost soothing.

"Dis won't be easy," Patrice said quietly. "Healing what's sick. It's not a flesh wound or a fever. Dis is bone-deep. In da head and heart. You'll need to be strong, Bennett pack. For dose you love. For dose you don't even know. Gordo and Kelly, dey gonna need you. It's easy, I tink, to get lost. Help dem find your packmates and bring dem home."

"We got this," Chris said.

"Damn right we do," Tanner said.

Rico snorted. "I can't believe this is how we spend our Sunday nights. If we're not watching shit blow up, we're in the middle of the woods with strangers chanting around us and feral werewolves getting ready to gnaw on our nuts."

"Oh, please," Jessie said. "Like you'd want to be anywhere else."

"And if you said that you did," Elizabeth told him, "we wouldn't believe you."

"I could be getting *laid* right now, I'll have you know."

"Bambi said you haven't groveled enough yet," Kelly reminded him.

"Oooh," Chris and Tanner said.

"Jesus Christ," Joe muttered.

"Are you all *finished*?" Ox growled. "We're kind of doing something important here."

"Yes," Patrice said, smile widening. "I tink you'll do just fine. Prepare yourselves, Bennett pack. Dis will come quickly."

He reached out and put one hand on my knee and the other on Kelly's. Kelly didn't let me go. It made me feel better. I looked down at Mark. His eyes were violet as he gazed up at me. "I need you to fight as hard as you can," I whispered. "Because I'm coming for you."

There were bursts of light around the clearing, and Patrice's hand felt like it was burning. The roses grew and the raven screamed and I—

I stood in front of my house.

The sun was rising.

The street was quiet.

Somewhere, a dog was barking.

It was the same, but . . .

The shutters hadn't been painted.

Those bushes I'd torn out were still there.

I—

No. No. No.

I knew this.

I knew when this was.

A car pulled up to the curb.

Mark sat inside. He was young. Younger than he'd been in a long time.

"Don't," I begged. "Don't do this. Leave. Drive away."

He didn't hear me. He pushed open the door and climbed out of the car.

I reached for him and—

here he's home i'm home hear his heartbeat resting sleeping home home home

—my hand went right *through* him, my hand that had been taken from me but was here now, in this place.

He walked toward the front door.

It turned violet, and the ground cracked beneath our feet.

From somewhere behind me, I heard the snarl of a feral wolf.

I screamed at him to stop.

I saw the moment it hit him. His nostrils flared. His eyes flashed orange.

His shoulders slumped.

But still he knocked on the door.

I answered eventually, standing there with jeans low on my hips, the marks of another man littering my skin.

"Who?" Mark asked, and now, with everything I'd seen, with all that we'd been through, I could hear the sound of his heart breaking in that single word.

"You don't call, you don't write," the younger version of myself said, as if I didn't have a care in the world. "What's it been? Five months? Six?"

Six months. Fifteen days. Eight hours.

"Who is he?"

The house shook. I was the only one who could see it.

I grinned, and I *hated* how it looked. "Don't know. Got his name, but you know how it goes."

"Who the *fuck* is he?"

I stood up straight. The tattoos glowed briefly, the roses shifting, the raven spreading its wings. "Whoever the fuck he is is no goddamn concern of yours. You think you can show up here? After *months* of radio silence? Fuck off, Mark."

"I didn't have a choice. Thomas—"

"Yeah. Thomas. Tell me, Mark. Just how is our dear Alpha? Because I haven't heard from him in *years*. Tell me. How's the family? Good? Got the kiddos, right? Building a pack all over again."

I took a step up behind Mark. I leaned forward, and even though it wasn't real, it couldn't be real, I *felt* the heat of his skin near mine. "Don't listen to him," I whispered fiercely. "I'm here. I'm here with you."

"It's not like that," Mark snapped.

"The fuck it isn't."

"Things have changed. He's—"

"I don't care."

"You can shit all over me all you want. But you don't get to talk about him like that. Regardless of how angry you are, he's still your Alpha."

"No. No, he's not."

Mark took a step back, and for a moment we *merged* and I felt it all, his anguish, his horror, the devastation each of my words caused when they landed like goddamn *grenades,* blowing apart everything he'd ever hoped for. It hurt to breathe, and I choked as I pulled myself away from him.

"Think about it, Mark. You're here. You can *smell* me. Underneath the spunk and sweat, I'm still dirt and leaves and rain. But that's it. Maybe you're too close, maybe you're overwhelmed by the very sight of me, but I haven't been pack for a long time. Those bonds are broken. I was left here. Because I was human. Because I was a *liability*—"

He said "it's not like that" and "Gordo" and "I promise you, okay? I would never—"

"A little late, Bennett."

He reached for me. He always reached for me.

And I just knocked his hand away as if it were *nothing*.

"You don't understand," and oh my Christ, he was *begging* me.

But I didn't hear it. I didn't *want* to hear it. "There's a world of things I don't understand, I'm sure. But I'm a witch without a pack, and you don't get to tell me shit. Not anymore."

"So—what. Poor you, huh? Poor Gordo, having to stay behind for the good of his pack. Doing what his Alpha told him. Protecting the territory and fucking anything that moves." And even though his words were hot with anger, everything he (I) felt was blue and violet, emptiness and rage.

"You wouldn't touch me. Remember? I kissed you. I touched you. I *begged* for it. I would have let you fuck me, Mark. I would have let you put your mouth on me, but you told me no. You told me I had to *wait*. That things weren't right, that the timing wasn't right. That you couldn't be distracted. You had *responsibilities*. And then you disappeared. For months on end. No calls. No check-ins. No *how you doin', Gordo? How you been? Remember me? Your mate?* I would have let you do so much to me."

"Gordo," he growled, sounding more wolf than man, and I wanted him to tear my skin from my bones. I wanted his teeth in my neck and my blood down his throat.

"You can, you know," I told him quietly. "You can have me. Right now. Here. Choose me. Mark. Choose me. Stay here. Or don't. We can go anywhere you want. We can leave right now. You and me. Fuck everything else. No packs, no Alphas. No *wolves*. Just . . . us."

"You would have me be an Omega?"

"No. Because I can be your tether. You can still be mine. And we can be together. Mark, I'm asking you, for once in your life, to choose me."

He said, "No," even though it was the hardest thing he'd ever had to do.

I saw the moment it hit me.

That single word.

My face stuttered . . . and then hardened. It was over even before it had begun.

He said, "Gordo. I can't—you can't expect me to—it's not *like* that—"

I took a step back.

"Of course you can't," I said, voice hoarse. "What was I thinking?"

I turned and went back into the house, leaving the door wide open.

He didn't follow.

"This isn't how it ends," I told him as he watched the empty doorway, the house filling with shadows as it shook on its foundation. "I know it feels like it, but this isn't our ending. We find our way back to each other. No matter how long it takes, we find our way back again. It's how we always are. It's how we'll always be."

The younger version of myself came back into the doorway, a box in hand.

Mark said, "No."

Mark said, "Gordo."

Mark said, "Just wait. Please just wait."

I said, "You take it. You take it now."

He said, "Please."

I thrust it against his chest. He flinched. "Take it," I snapped at him. He did.

I screamed at him, at myself.

"It doesn't have to be this way."

The door slammed in his face. The violet of the wood pulsed brightly. The house began to split apart.

He stood there for the longest time, listening to the sound of my racing heart on the other side of the door, even as the roof caved in.

Eventually he turned and walked past me, walked *through* me, and I felt him giving in to his wolf, giving in to—

run must run must put paws on ground hurts it hurts it hurrrts and

—the animal that lurked underneath. But this was *different*. It wasn't like it should have been. He was a Beta here, eyes like Halloween, and though he felt himself collapsing, he should have remained that way, should have felt the pull of his pack.

But it wasn't the same.

I could feel the wild call of the feral wolf, and it'd sunk its claws into him, dragging him by the *throat* into—

I turned to follow him and—

I stood on the outskirts of the clearing.

Mark Bennett was on his knees, his clothes having been shredded during his shift. His head was tilted back toward the sky, and he held that little box in his hand as he *howled* at the sun, *sang* for the hidden moon. It was a song of sorrow, an aria of grief that thundered through the trees as if the very sky was cracking right down the middle.

I felt it coming.

I began to run toward him.

But I was too late.

The gnarled hand of a half-shifted wolf burst through the ground beneath him, wrapping around his bare thigh, claws digging into his skin and causing blood to bloom like roses. Then came another, and another, and *another,* the last of which was thickly muscled, an entire *arm* rising from the ground, dirt and grass still stuck to its rotting skin. It reached up and wrapped its hand around his throat where my mark should have been, where the raven should have been from the very beginning.

The hands began to pull him down into the earth.

His eyes were open toward the sky.

They were ice.

Then orange.

Then they flickered violet.

His mouth opened in a silent scream, fangs lengthening as he clutched the box that held his stone wolf, a gift he'd given that I'd taken for granted. That I'd thrown back in his face.

I was halfway to him when I slammed into an invisible barrier, the pain bright and glassy as I fell back. I pushed myself back to my feet, reaching out to find what was keeping me from him, to find what it was that would keep us from each other.

My palm pressed flat against—

Wards.

They were wards.

Unlike any I'd ever felt before.

The magic here was ancient. It was ugly and rotten, and I swore I felt it *squirming* against my skin. I ground my teeth and *pushed* against it, pushed with everything I had even though my hand was long gone and—

It pushed *back*.

And I knew it then.

Though I hadn't felt it in years.

I knew it.

Magic, it—it has a signature. A fingerprint. Specific to a witch. But amongst family, it'll be similar. Not the same, but familiar. If my father did this, if this is his magic breaking the tethers of the Omegas, his magic is in them.

And they're recognizing him in me.

It was him.

Robert Livingstone.

The proof I needed.

And he was stronger than I was.

I couldn't break through.

Oh, but how I screamed for the wolf. How I banged my hands against the wards until my bones splintered. How I tried everything to get to him.

He was up to his chest now. In the earth, those feral wolves pulling him down.

But nothing I did was enough.

Until—

Magic comes from the earth. From the ground. From the trees. The flowers and the soil. This place, it's . . . old. Far older than you could possibly imagine. It's like . . . a beacon. It calls to us. It thrums through our blood. The wolves hear it too, but not like us. It sings to them. They are . . . animals. We aren't like them. We are more. They bond with the earth. The Alpha more so than anyone else. But we use it. We bend it to our whim. They are enslaved by it, by the moon overhead when it rises full and white. We control it. Don't ever forget that.

My father had taught me that.

I stepped back from his poison.

I breathed in the scents of the territory around me.

It smelled of dirt and leaves and rain.

I sank to my knees and dug my fingers into the earth.

Once, the moon had loved the sun.

Once, there was a boy.

Once, there was a wolf.

He had sat with his back against a tree.

His bare feet were in the grass.

The boy leaned forward and kissed the wolf.

And knew then that nothing would ever be the same.

An unkindness of ravens swirled around me, feathers rustling.

The air was redolent of roses.

And I gave everything I could. For him.

For my wolf.

"Gordo."

I opened my eyes.

Mark Bennett stood before me, on the other side of my father's wards. Not as he'd been before, but as he was now. We could never be who we once were.

He smiled his secret smile. His eyes were blue.

He said "hey" and "hi" and "hello" and "you came for me, you really came for me."

I said, "I did," and "I had to," and "You need to fight this, you need to fight this. For your pack. For me. Please do it for me."

He nodded slowly before glancing over his shoulder.

Behind him, the younger version of himself was fighting against the wolf-hands.

And I thought maybe he was winning.

Mark turned back toward me. "He has to stay here, doesn't he?"

"Yeah," I said miserably. "We can't—*I* can't fix this. Not on my own. But we can contain it. We can close this door and keep it locked until we're ready. I'll help you. It'll be you and me, okay? It'll be you and me, and I will keep you safe."

"Why?"

"I would do anything for you."

He reached up and touched the raven on his throat. "Because you're my mate?"

I laughed wetly. "Yeah. Because I'm your mate."

Oh, how that pleased him. How he *smiled,* the corners of his eyes crinkling, and I was consumed by the sight of him.

And then beside him, against the wards, was a door.

"Will this work?" he asked as we walked toward it.

"Yes."

"How do you know?"

"Because we're the goddamn Bennett pack. Nothing will stop us. Not anymore."

"It's gonna be rough."

"We've survived worse."

The smile faded slightly. "We have, haven't we?"

"And we're still standing."

He said, "Okay," because it was that easy for him. To have faith in me.

"You push. You hear me? You push as hard as you can. And when you're through, we close the door—"

A loud roar came from behind him.

The other Mark, the Omega, had burst out of the ground, the hands that had been trying to drag him down sinking into the earth.

He was caught in his shift, back rippling as the wolf came forward, face elongating, spittle dripping into the grass beneath him. His body shook as hair sprouted along bare skin, as his fangs sank into his lips, causing blood to spill.

He looked up at us.

His eyes glowed violet.

He roared again.

And began to run.

"*The door!*" I screamed. "*Get through the door!*"

I pulled on the doorknob, the metal burning into my hand as I pulled with all my strength. Mark threw himself against it from the other side, and I could hear the feral wolf getting closer and closer and—

The door flew open, knocking me to the side.

Mark burst through, sliding in the grass.

The Omega howled in triumph.

I kicked out against the door, and it slammed shut just as the feral wolf crashed into it. The wards pulsed as the door seemed to bend, and a nauseous feeling bowled through me, like I could *feel* the infection my father had caused.

But the door held.

Even as the feral wolf charged at it again and again and again, it held.

Mark collapsed beside me, both of us on our backs, breathing heavily.

I took his hand in mine.

Or I tried to.

It didn't work.

Because I didn't have a hand anymore.

He gripped my forearm instead, turning his head toward me.

He said—

.   .   .

"*Gordo.*"

I opened my eyes.

I was in the clearing.

The air was cold.

The sky was bright with stars.

"Gordo."

I blinked.

Three faces appeared above me, foreheads wrinkled.

"You think he's all right?" one asked.

"His brains aren't leaking out his ears," another said. "So I think he'll be okay."

"I don't think that's physically possible," the third said.

"Of course it is. I saw it on the internet."

"Oh, because you saw it on the *internet*—"

"Jesus Christ," I groaned. "What the hell are you *talking* about?"

Rico, Tanner, and Chris smiled. "Yeah," Chris said. "He's all right."

And then I remembered.

Mark.

I sat up quickly. "Did it work? *Did it work?* Where is he? Oh god, please tell me where he—"

"Gordo."

I turned my head.

Mark Bennett was sitting a few feet away, Jessie crouched in front of him.

My breath hitched.

He was here.

He was really here.

I was moving even before I gave it much thought. I needed to be as close to him as I could. He wrapped his arms around me as I crashed into him, and his breath was warm in my ear when he said, "I've got you. I've got you. I've got you," and I heard the wolfsong and the ravensong rising through us, etching themselves into our skin.

. . .

It took longer than I thought it would before I let him go. Every time I decided to pull away, I couldn't bring myself to do it. He didn't seem too bothered, so I didn't worry.

Over his shoulder I could see Kelly. His shoulders were shaking as he sobbed against Carter's chest. Elizabeth held them both, and she kissed each of them in turn over and over again. Robbie stood above them, arms across his chest, as if he was guarding them.

Carter must have felt me staring and gave me a small smile. Whatever Kelly had seen, whatever he'd done to bring Carter back, seemed to have worked.

For the most part. The timber wolf lay a few feet away, eyes on Carter. Whatever we'd done hadn't been enough to force his shift.

Beyond them was a group of strangers, people I'd never seen. They huddled together, shivering in the night air. Ox and Joe stood side by side in front of them.

"I know you're scared," Ox said, and Mark held me tighter. "And I know you're confused. But there is nothing here for you to fear. You are safe now. My name is Ox. This is my mate, Joe. We are the Alphas of the Bennett pack. And we're going to help you find your way home."

EPILOGUE

Their eyes were still violet.
All of them.
They were Omegas.
Mark and Carter too.
Even with the bonds between us.
My father's magic was strong.
But the doors had been shut.
Robert Livingstone had hurt us.
But he should have killed us.
Because now we were pissed.
And there was nothing he could do to stop us.

.   .   .

I stared at the computer as I sat in my office. Robbie had updated our software yet again, and I couldn't figure it out. Every key I hit on the computer made the goddamn thing chime, and I was a few seconds away from grabbing him by the scruff of his neck and rubbing his face in it.

Out in the garage, the radio was tuned to some sort of butt rock, most likely Tanner's doing. I could hear them laughing and shouting at each other as they worked. It should have been irritating, but it was soothing in ways I couldn't explain. It was normal. It was years and years of our shared history. It was the sound of survival. Two months later, and they could laugh.

I sighed and sat back in my ancient chair, tilting my face toward the ceiling. There was a small water stain in the corner that I'd never gotten around to doing anything about. I stared at it for a while until someone cleared their throat in the doorway.

"I'm fine," I said, because they were nothing if not predictable.

"Okay," Ox said easily.

I looked at him, the chair creaking underneath me. "I'm fine."

He shrugged, rubbing oil from his hands with an old rag. "That's good. I'm just happy to see you back here."

"I needed time."

"I know. We all did."

"Robbie updated the software again."

"Yeah. He does that. Thinks it'll help."

"It doesn't."

"He's making a website. For the garage."

"Goddammit," I muttered.

Ox grinned. "Couldn't hurt."

"You don't know that."

"Don't you have somewhere to be?"

I rolled my eyes. "They're doing fine without me."

"Oh, I know they are. I just thought you'd want to be there. You're very . . . particular about how things are set up in your house."

My eye twitched.

"Mark has a lot of stuff." I stood up, the chair rolling into the wall.

"Yeah," Ox said. "Had to rent one of those twenty-footers."

"I have to go," I said, fumbling for my keys.

Ox laughed and stepped aside as I walked past him through the doorway. Without thinking too much about it, I reached out and grabbed his hand, squeezing it just once before letting it go.

"You too, Gordo," my Alpha told me. "You too. We'll see you tonight."

Oh, he would. We had a message to deliver.

Tanner and Chris were bent over a 2009 Toyota Camry with a transmission problem. They looked up at me as I headed toward the front of the garage.

"Uh-oh," Tanner said. "He's got that look."

"Someone is either going to get murdered or laid," Chris said. Then he frowned. "I wish I didn't know that much about him."

"I'm taking the rest of the day off," I told them, trying desperately to ignore the knowing grins on their faces. "I want the parts ordered for the Buick before you leave. And don't forget to call Mr. Simmons and tell him that there is absolutely *nothing* rattling around that we could hear. For the sixth time."

"Sure, boss," Tanner said easily. "Glad to have you back."

"Go kill or have sex or whatever," Chris said. He grimaced. "Holy fuck, do we need better boundaries."

That was the first thing they'd said that I agreed with in weeks.

Rico was in the break room, feeding Bambi grapes by hand as she sat in his lap.

I didn't understand straight people.

"Gordo," Rico said, sighing dreamily, "Bambi has decided to do me the honor of forgiving me for the whole secret society of were-wolves thing! Isn't that amazing?"

"You can still get out of this," I told her. "No one would blame you."

"Eh," she said. "The so-called anonymous donation I received to help rebuild the Lighthouse went a long way to putting him back in my good graces. That and the fact there was enough for me to buy it outright."

"*I* wasn't the one who blew up the bar," Rico said, sounding out-raged. "If you're gonna be pissed at *anyone,* it should be Gordo. He's the one that—"

"Sacrificed a hand?" she asked, arching an eyebrow.

Rico gaped at her. "But—but I got *shot.* I have a *scar.*"

"Bambi, nice to see you again," I said. "Rico, back on the clock in five or you're fired."

"Bullshit!" he cried after me. "Like you would *ever* let me go, *brujo.*"

Robbie was squinting over some invoices, pen scratching in the logbook. His glasses were perched low on his nose. He looked up at me when I went to grab my coat. "Heading out already?" He waggled his eyebrows. "Maybe a little afternoon de—and by the look on your face, I should not finish that sentence."

"You're not as stupid as you sound. Good to know. And do you mind telling me why I can't get anything on my computer to work? *Again?*"

He rolled his eyes. "Because for some reason you seem to think it's 1997 and that the internet still comes from free AOL discs you get at a place called Blockbuster." He pushed his glasses back on his nose. "Whatever *that* is."

I pointed my finger at him. "I want it working by the time I come in tomorrow. If it's not, I will take your glasses and shove them up your ass." I turned for the door.

"You know, with all the things you've threatened to shove in me, it's a wonder Mark doesn't get more jealous."

I turned slowly back to look at him.

He blanched. "Um. I didn't say anything. Ignore me. Go about your business." The phone rang. "Thank you, Jesus." He picked up the phone. "Gordo's, this is Robbie speaking, how can I help you?"

The air was cool when I stepped outside the garage. It made my lungs burn when I took a deep breath. I wanted a cigarette. I reached in my pocket and pulled out a pack of nicotine gum. I tore a piece from the wrapper and crunched it between my teeth. It wasn't the same.

The blacktop on Main Street was still shiny from where it'd been repaved. The banner on the diner advertising their reopening was faded and flapping in the breeze. People waved at me from the other side of the street as I walked to the truck. I wanted to ignore them, but we couldn't do that anymore. Not with what the townsfolk now knew. I forced a smile on my face and waved back. It must not have been very convincing, because they quickly walked away.

It was fine.

I wasn't a people person anyway.

.   .   .

It was a twenty-footer, just as Ox had said.

It blocked the driveway, the ramp crossing the sidewalk.

Kelly stuck his head out the back as I turned the truck off. He waved.

I glared at him.

He rolled his eyes.

"You're not fooling anyone," he said as I approached the back of the U-Haul. "I can hear your heartbeat. You're excited."

"Shut up." I looked inside. It was still half-full, and Kelly was reaching for a box marked KITCHEN in a familiar scrawl. "There's no fucking way all of this is fitting inside my house."

"We had to get rid of some of the crap," Carter said, coming out of the house.

"The crap," I repeated.

"You know. The junk. The stuff in your house that should have been thrown away a long time ago."

"I don't *own* junk."

"Uh-huh," Carter said, walking up the ramp. "Of course not. I accidentally broke your coffee table into a bunch of tiny pieces, so it's a good thing that Mark had another one in storage that's much nicer than yours was."

"*Accidentally*?"

Carter shrugged. "Yeah, it was this whole thing. The wolf tried to follow me into the living room, I told it to stay where it was, and then I accidentally broke the coffee table."

"Those two things don't have *anything to do with each other*."

Carter took the box from his brother. "Weird how that happens, right?"

"And why is that *thing* in my house?"

"Wherever I go, it goes. You know that." Carter sounded particularly aggrieved, which made me feel a little better. "I still don't know why. Although it seemed very interested in how your house smelled. It pissed on the floor in the kitchen. I forgot to clean it up. So, just . . . you know. Keep that in mind."

"I am going to kill *all* of you," I growled.

Carter reached out and patted the side of my face as he went down the ramp. "Sure, Gordo. Okay. Still totally believe your threats after I've seen you make heart eyes at my uncle."

Kelly laughed in the truck.

I stalked after Carter inside the house.

Sure enough, all my junk was gone. The old couch. The coffee table. For some reason I now had *bookcases* in the living room and a TV that didn't have a dial on the front. There were speakers set up on either side of it, and everything looked bright and shiny in this old house, like it was something new. A beginning.

The timber wolf rose from behind the couch and moved to follow Carter into the kitchen. Before it did, it glanced at me, nostrils flaring. It cocked its head, but then it turned away.

"Mark!" I bellowed. "When I said you could move in, I meant *you*." I paused, considering. "Maybe some clothes."

I heard him laugh down the hallway.

I followed the sound. I was helpless to do anything but.

He was in my—*our*—bedroom, boxes stacked on either side of the closet. There were picture frames stacked on the floor near my side of the bed, piles of books in the far corner, clothes on hangers lying on the bed.

Some of the boxes had been torn open, their contents shuffled. He was bent over one on the trunk at the end of the bed, brow furrowed, muttering under his breath.

I leaned against the doorway, watching him.

We were here. We were alive. We were together. There were good days. Oh, were there good days, days in which I'd wake up and feel him curled around me, his breath warm on my neck. Days when I'd feel him wake up, his lips trailing along my skin, and he'd *hum* as he stretched his sleep-slack muscles, hands tightening on my waist. His voice would be a rumble when he'd say *hey* and *hi* and *good morning*.

Those were the good days.

But there were other days too.

Days when the scratching at the door in his head was loud. Days when his shoulders were stiff and his eyes flickered violet. Days when he and Carter would disappear into the woods for hours on end, running themselves ragged until they collapsed and slept away the sound of claws against wood.

And there were days where I wasn't any better.

I still wasn't okay. I was getting there, and maybe it'd take a little longer, but I knew about those bad days. I'd be reaching for something, or scratching an itch, only to be violently reminded that my right hand was gone, that it'd been taken from me while I protected my Alpha. I would do it again. Of course I would. Anything to keep Ox safe. Always. But I had an underlying bitterness that sometimes wrapped around me, and it took a while for it to let me go.

Mark would run, and I'd be there waiting for him when he got back.

I'd lose myself in my head, and he'd be there to pull me close.

Rarely did our bad days coincide. But when they did, it felt chaotic. Wild. Both of us were dangerously close to being feral.

But those days were few and far between.

They were worth it, though. Everything about him was worth it. And even though I was putting up a fight, it was half-assed, the sight of him filling up my space making me feel more at ease than I'd been in a long time. I never thought we'd get to this point. I never thought we'd belong to each other.

"You just gonna stand there and stare at my ass?" he asked without looking up at me.

"It's a nice ass."

He laughed. If only Marty could see what had happened in his old house. I thought he'd be okay with it. "That so?"

I pushed off the doorway. "I could show you, if you wanted."

He arched an eyebrow as he looked up at me. "You could . . . show me my ass?"

"How nice it is. What can be done with it, if one was so inclined."

"We can *hear* you!" Carter shouted down the hallway. "What the fuck. No one should ever have to hear their witch trying to have sexy talk with their uncle. Are you *trying* to traumatize us further? Jesus, Gordo. Haven't we all been through enough?"

The timber wolf growled in agreement.

"How much longer until we can make them leave?" I muttered, pressing myself against Mark's back. I reached up and closed my hand over the raven on his throat. He tilted his head back on my shoulder.

"Depends on what's left in the truck." His beard scraped against my cheek as he rubbed his face on mine. Fucking wolves. Always with the scenting. "Have to have it back by the end of the day."

"I like it," I admitted.

"What?"

"Having you here. With me."

I felt his laugh underneath my hand. "Don't worry. I won't tell anyone you're getting soft."

I had to ask one last time. "You're sure about this? Being here. With me. It's not—I know it's not the pack house, but—"

"Wherever you are, that's where my home is."

Jesus fucking Christ. I couldn't—"And you say *I'm* getting soft." It was a deflection. He knew it, but he let me have it. I didn't do well when he said things that burned me from the inside out.

"You are. I can feel you blushing."

I bit the side of his neck in retaliation but stepped away. I wanted more, but apparently two virginish prudes and a feral wolf wouldn't take the hint and leave.

He went back to digging in the box. The lines on his forehead appeared again.

"Everything okay today?"

"Yeah," he said. "You?"

"Yeah." It was something we asked each other. Kept us honest. "Felt good. Being back in the shop."

"Told you it would."

I rolled my eyes. "Yeah, yeah." I sat on the bed next to the box he was digging in. "Elizabeth and Jessie see that girl off okay?"

"She got picked up this morning," Mark said. One of the Omegas. Not like him or Carter. Not infected. A regular girl bitten by a rogue Alpha last year who had turned Omega after being abandoned. She'd been placed with a pack up in Washington. She was the twelfth we'd sent to another pack. There were only a few noninfected Omegas left. There wasn't any rush. They could stay here if they wanted, or we would find them a home.

The infected ones, they needed to stay as close to Ox as possible. At least until we could find my father. They needed the Alpha most of all. Carter and Mark were better off. Their bonds with the pack were stronger, even if they did have violet eyes. The threads between us were tenuous, but they were holding and becoming more fibrous every day. It would be enough until Robert Livingstone showed himself.

And he would. That much we knew.

Mark growled in frustration, and his eyes flashed. He dropped something back inside the box. It sounded like it broke.

"Hey," I said, reaching out to grab his arm. "It's okay. Take a breath. What are you looking for? I can help you find it."

He scrubbed a hand over his face. I saw a hint of claw and fang. "It's not . . . I know it's here. I *know* it. I just can't remember where I put it."

I tugged him toward me. He resisted, but only just. He stood between my legs, breathing in through his nose and out his mouth. I waited, rubbing my thumb over the back of his hand, thinking.

He settled eventually.

We'd caught it early enough this time.

"Sorry," he muttered, obviously frustrated.

I shrugged. "It's okay. It happens. You do the same for me."

"It's not—"

"It is," I said fiercely. "It is the same, and don't you try and tell me otherwise. Remember what you told me? What we would be for each other?"

He softened, and it felt green. "I'll be your hands."

"And I'll be your sanity."

He leaned forward then. He kissed me. In our room, as cool winter sunlight filtered in through the window. It was sweet and warm, and I'd never wanted anything more.

"Sap," he muttered, kissing me once, twice, three times.

"Just as long as you don't tell anyone."

"Secret's safe with me, Livingstone."

"Damn right it is, Bennett."

We grinned at each other like fools.

But that was okay too. We'd earned it. Earned this.

Then his eyes widened. "I know where—" He stepped away from me, turning toward the stack of boxes near the closet. He set aside two of them, reaching for the one on the bottom. I waited, wondering what the hell could be so important that it'd caused him to almost lose himself to his wolf.

He sliced the tape with a single claw and opened the box, rifling through it until—"I knew. I *knew* it was here."

I had no idea what he was on about. "What are you—" And then I couldn't speak.

He turned toward me.

In his hand was a little box.

I knew that box.

The last time I'd held it, our hearts were breaking.

He took a step toward me, watching me like I was something revered. Something beautiful. Something he couldn't believe he got to call his own. I felt the faint pulse in the scar on my neck, a perfect indentation of the teeth of a wolf.

"I just—" He coughed, shaking his head before trying again. "I know it's dumb. It's—you're already my mate. I know that. I can feel it. Between us. Okay? I can. I know it's not how it should be, but I know it will be one day. But even if it never gets better than it is right now, then that's okay. Because I get to have you. I get to love you. I get to be loved *by* you."

"I swear to god," I said roughly, "if you bring me dead rabbits or a basket of mini muffins, I'm going to skin you myself."

"Duly noted," he said dryly. Then, "Can I give this to you? Please? Gordo. I just—can you take this? From me?"

He opened the box.

Inside, lying on a blue cloth, was a stone wolf.

It looked just as I remembered.

I gently took it out of the box. It was heavy and ornately carved. The tail was long and thin, and the head was cocked, the wolf's lips curved as if it was smiling secretly.

"Yeah," I told him, because he needed to hear it said out loud. "I'll take it."

He tackled me onto the bed.

Outside, I could hear Carter and Kelly shouting in joy.

And in the distance, the howling of wolves.

.   .   .

We gathered in the office at the house at the end of the lane.

All of us.

Ox sat in the chair behind the desk where Abel and Thomas had once been.

Joe stood at his side, hand on his shoulder.

Carter leaned near the doorway, the timber wolf lying at his feet.

Kelly sat on the arm of the sofa against the wall. Robbie was next to him, biting his bottom lip nervously, gaze focused on the tablet in his hand.

Elizabeth sat next to her son, eyes closed as she waited.

Rico and Tanner sat on the edge of the desk.

Jessie and Chris were against a bookcase, arms crossed over their chests.

Mark and I stood near the window.

Ox said, "Robbie. It's time."

Robbie nodded as he sighed. Kelly reached up and squeezed his arm. Robbie looked surprised at this, but pleased.

He tapped on the screen of the tablet.

The monitor on the wall lit up.

There was a beep. And then another. And then another.

And then—

Michelle Hughes appeared on the screen.

Her face was blank.

"Alphas Bennett and Matheson," she said, voice cool.

"Alpha Hughes," Joe said.

"I must admit I expected to hear from you sooner." She took in the room. "And the entire pack, no less. This must be important. Robbie, how are you?"

Robbie's eyes narrowed. "Do you even care?"

"I wouldn't ask if I didn't."

"I'm fine. I'm with my pack, where I belong."

"So I see. You've been busy, Bennett pack."

"We have," Joe said. "Which is why we've requested this meeting."

"A curious thing, that," she said. "A request. After all that you've done. The good people you've killed."

I snorted. "Lady, you've seriously got a fucked-up ideology if you think there was anything good about the hunters. Especially Elijah. You knew her history with this pack."

"The witches," she snapped. "The witches those—those *things* slaughtered."

"Casualties of the war you've brought upon yourself. If anyone is to blame, it's you."

And *that* caught her attention. "War. Dale said—"

"Dale," I said, a nasty smile on my face. "Is he there? Can he hear me?"

It only lasted a split second, but her eyes flickered away from the camera before looking back at us. "I don't see what my witch has to do with—"

"He ran before we could get to him," I said, and Mark growled beside me. "He should know there's nowhere he can go that I won't find him. And I will find him."

"Are you threatening my witch, Livingstone?"

"You're goddamn right I am."

She glared at me before looking at the Alphas. "I demand that you—"

"See, that's where you should stop," Ox said, and we felt his great anger rolling through us. "Because you don't have the right to demand anything of us."

"You are out of *line,* Alpha Matheson. I suggest—"

"It's time for you to step down," Ox said, and I saw the moment the words hit her, landing like a punch to her gut. She inhaled sharply. Her eyes looked as if they were filling with blood. "Your time as the Alpha of all has come to an end. My mate, Joe Bennett, is ready to claim what is rightfully his."

"It's far too late for that," Michelle Hughes said, claws digging into the desktop. "The Bennett pack has proven itself to be the enemy. You have allowed the Omegas into your territory. Into your *home*. Two of your pack remain infected. I don't know how you have slowed the process, but it doesn't matter. They will become feral, and if you don't kill them first, they will slaughter all of you."

"Like you sent the hunters to do to my family?" Elizabeth asked.

"Elizabeth, I don't know what they've told you—"

"The truth," she said easily. "Obviously more than I'd ever expect from the likes of you. That you sit in the position once occupied by my husband is one of the greatest farces to ever befall the wolves. You have to know this will not end well for you. For your people. You were entrusted with the power of the Alpha of all. But it was always meant to be temporary. It belongs to my son."

Hughes slammed her hand on the desk. "It will *never* go to him. You are one pack filled with ferals and humans and abominations. You can't win this."

Ox rose slowly. "That's where you're wrong."

And I saw it then. On her face.

Fear.

Michelle Hughes was scared.

"I will give you," Oxnard Matheson said, "one last chance. Step down. Now."

"I will not be intimidated by the likes of you. You are *nothing*. Your pack is *nothing*—"

"Then you should remember," Ox said, eyes flashing red and violet, and *oh*, she hadn't expected that. "That in the end, I gave you a chance. To end this peacefully. But that moment is now over. You should prepare yourself, Alpha Hughes. Because we're coming for you. We're coming for all of you."

The screen went dark.

Ox turned toward us, eyes blazing. "You are my family. You are my pack. You have helped make me who I am. I will do everything I can to keep you safe. But we knew this day would come. It's time. It's time for us to bring the fight to them."

The roses bloomed.

The raven took flight.

The wolves howled.
Their humans cried along with them.
And I did the only thing I could.
I tilted my head back and sang a song of war.

SOMEWHERE
IN
MAINE

OTHER

The screen went black.

Michelle Hughes sat back in her chair, claws gouging the wood on her desk.

"That didn't go very well," Dale said mildly.

She gave serious consideration to tearing out his throat.

Somehow, she stopped herself. "All of them," she said. "All of them have lost their minds. It's . . . a tragedy, to be sure. Such a fall from grace." She thought quickly. "And that's how it will be spun. That's what we'll tell the others. The . . . infection. It has spread through the pack bonds. It's contaminated the others. There were already rumors about Matheson. But now we have definitive proof. You saw his eyes. He is becoming one of them. And he's the mate of Bennett. Which means Joe won't be long to follow."

Dale nodded slowly. "That could work, but . . ."

"But *what*?" she snapped.

"It's just . . . Ox."

"What about him?"

"There's never been anything like him."

"He's a *fluke*," she snarled. "A freak. Whatever he is, whatever Thomas Bennett did to him, it doesn't matter. He can't be trusted. And if those goddamn hunters could have actually done what they were sent to do, we wouldn't even be *having* this conversation. The humans are useless." She couldn't admit out loud she'd been stunned into inaction in the weeks that followed the destruction of the hunters. It'd been over so *quickly*. She never should have trusted Meredith King. Humans were weak. The Bennetts were stronger than she expected.

She wouldn't underestimate them again.

"You haven't stood before him," Dale said quietly. "Not like I have. He exudes power. Unlike anything I've ever seen. Be it the territory or something else, it's . . . intoxicating."

Michelle shook her head. "It doesn't matter. He bleeds. Which means he can die."

"And what of the packs that have helped them? The ones who have taken in Omegas?"

"We'll deal with them later. They won't dare stand with him. Not if it means the eradication of their entire pack."

"I think you shouldn't underestimate his reach," Dale said. "He's already proven himself formidable. They all—"

Shouts and snarls. From out in the compound.

Michelle rose behind her desk.

Dale went to the door and slammed it shut. He pressed his palm flat against it, muttering under his breath. There was a pulse of light underneath his hand as he warded the door.

It didn't help.

The door exploded, knocking him back. He slammed against the far wall, slid down, and slumped against the floor. Blood trickled from his nose. He groaned, looking dazed.

A man walked in through the ruined doorway.

He was older, his skin wrinkled, his hair in thin white wisps around his head. He was dressed for the Maine winter, heavy trousers and a thick black coat.

But every step he took was measured and fluid. He moved with purpose.

And she knew who this was.

She'd just seen a version of his face glaring angrily at her moments ago on a connection to the other side of the country.

She should have seen this coming.

"Alpha," Robert Livingstone said, a small smile on his face. "I thought it time we meet."

"You can't be here."

He arched an eyebrow. "Oh, I think you'll find I can be wherever I wish. We need to have a chat, you and I. It would seem that you're no better than Richard Collins at handling a meager threat. Hunters, Michelle. Honestly. What could you have possibly been thinking? Even with my assistance at the wards, you still failed. The level of incompetence I seem to find myself surrounded by is astounding."

"Assistance? What assist—"

"Though you did do me a favor," he said, as if she hadn't spoken. "I'd been tracking Meredith King for months once I discovered she was in possession of something that belonged to me."

"You come into *my* territory uninvited," Michelle said, her shift starting to come over her. "You are not *welcome* here, witch."

He laughed. "Oh, I don't need an invitation. Sit down."

Her claws popped and her fangs lengthened.

"I said sit. *Down.*"

And she did. She couldn't stop herself. Her legs folded, and she sat in her chair.

"Good girl," Robert said. "Now, I'm going to talk, and you're going to listen. Do you understand me?"

She nodded, though she tried to fight it.

He tapped his boot against Dale's thigh. Dale groaned but otherwise didn't move. "I have little use for wolves. You're animals, the lot of you. Enslaved to the moon. I've always found lycanthropy not unlike a virus." He sighed. "Which is why I attempted to make it one. The results have been varied, but there is always a trial-and-error phase with any experiment. One must learn from their mistakes in order to push the boundaries further. And I planned to push them until they broke. But I find myself at an impasse. There are . . . wolves that I did not account for. Variables I didn't expect. Richard Collins was a failure. Your attempt with the hunters was a failure. Because of these *variables.*"

"The Bennett pack," Michelle managed to say.

Robert sighed. "Yes. Them. Still. Even with the fall of Thomas Bennett, even with a separation, even *with* nothing but a human to guide them, they managed to survive." He shook his head. "And now . . . well. They've become something more, haven't they? Somehow they've been able to contain my magic in the Omegas. And they have my son."

"Gordo?" Michelle asked. "But he's always been—"

"No," Robert Livingstone said as he came to stand in front of her desk. "Not Gordo. Gordo is lost to me. I'm talking about my second son. His brother."

There was a sharp buzzing in her ears. "I don't understand," she said weakly. "There isn't any other Livingstone. We would have—"

"Do you know what it feels like to lose your tether?" he asked, leaning forward, hands flat on the desk. "What it feels like to have it ripped from you when you least expect it? Because I do. My wife, she . . . didn't understand. She quite lost her mind, in the end. And she took my tether from me. Murdered her in cold blood, even though she was an innocent in all of this. When she became pregnant, Abel Bennett made me send her away. Made her give up the child. She returned, but she wasn't the same, after. And then my wife . . ." His hands tightened into fists. "I promised myself when my magic was being ripped from me that I would return. That I would bring my children back into the fold. That I would see the end of the wolves. But Gordo . . . I knew that no matter what I said, he wouldn't understand. And my other son . . . somehow he'd been *bitten*. He'd been *changed*. I could heal him, if only I could find him. And then came news he was the pet of that hunter, and I—I did everything I could to get to him." His voice grew cold. "Instead he finds himself with the Bennett pack and his brother, feral and stuck as a wolf. That will not do. I have come to you with an offer. Help me break them apart. Give me back my son. And you will be allowed to remain as the Alpha of all. I no longer care about the fates of wolves. I only want what's mine."

"How?" she asked. He lied, she knew, even though his heartbeat didn't stutter. But she also knew that she would agree.

He leaned closer. "Even after all they've done to you, there's still one who you're fond of, isn't there? A wolf in their pack who used to be yours. Someone who I can turn against them. Someone who I can use to take back my son."

Her eyes widened. "Robbie," she whispered.

And he smiled.

You may also enjoy . . .

by TJ Klune

THE HOUSE IN THE CERULEAN SEA

An enchanting story, masterfully told, *The House in the Cerulean Sea* is about the profound experience of discovering an unlikely family in an unexpected place—and realizing that family could be yours.

Linus Baker leads a quiet life. At forty, he has a tiny house with a devious cat and his beloved records for company. And at the Department in Charge of Magical Youth, he's spent many dull years monitoring their orphanages.

Then one day, Linus is summoned by Extremely Upper Management and given a highly classified assignment. He must travel to an orphanage where six dangerous children reside, including the Antichrist. There, Linus must somehow determine if they could bring on the end of days. But their guardian, charming and enigmatic Arthur Parnassus, will do anything to protect his wards. As Arthur and Linus grow ever closer, Linus must choose between duty and his dreams.

Out now

You may also enjoy . . .

by TJ Klune

UNDER THE WHISPERING DOOR

Witty, haunting and kind, *Under the Whispering Door*
is a gift for troubled times. TJ Klune brings us a warm hug
of a story about a man who spent his life at the office—
and his afterlife building a home.

When a reaper comes to collect Wallace from his own sparsely
attended funeral, Wallace is outraged. But he begins to suspect
she's right, and he is in fact dead. Then when Hugo, owner of
a most peculiar tea shop, promises to help him cross over,
Wallace reluctantly accepts the truth.

Yet even in death, he refuses to abandon his life—even though
Wallace spent all of it working, correcting colleagues and
hectoring employees. He'd had no time for frivolities like fun
and friends. But as Wallace drinks tea with Hugo and talks to
his customers, he wonders if he was missing something.

The feeling grows as he shares jokes with the resident ghost,
manifests embarrassing footwear and notices the stars. So when
he's given one week to pass through the door to the other side,
Wallace sets about living a lifetime in just seven days.

Out now